Praise for Lee Child's Jack Reacher Novels

DIE TRYING

"It takes a brave man to move into the macho territory of suspense writer Stephen Hunter, but Lee Child is making his move with [*Die Trying*]."

—*Chicago Tribune*

"A literate scenario-cum-thriller."

—*The Philadelphia Inquirer*

"Lee Child's knowledge of the modern military and its combat tactics amazed me. A chilling and all-too-realistic story, and a damn good book."

—Steve Thayer

"[A] redoubtable yet romantic hero . . . [a] fast-paced misadventure . . . Cunning and explosive, it's a thumping good read."

—*Time Out*

"Furiously suspenseful."

—*Kirkus Reviews*

THE KILLING FLOOR

A *People* Magazine Page-Turner

"This is such a brilliantly written first novel that [Child] must be channeling Dashiell Hammett . . . Reacher handles the maze of clues and the criminal unfortunates with a flair that would make Sam Spade proud."

—*Playboy*

"A tough, compelling thriller with characters who jump off the page."

—*Houston Chronicle*

"Combines high suspense with almost nonstop action. From its jolting opening scene to its fiery final confrontation, *Killing Floor* is irresistible."

—*People*

continued . . .

TRIPWIRE

"A stylish thriller as complex and disturbing as its hero."
—Stephen White

"Not only bang-on suspense but an insightful look into how humans work." —*Houston Chronicle*

"A sort of millennial reshaping of John D. MacDonald's Travis McGee character." —*The Dallas Morning News*

RUNNING BLIND

"Swift and brutal." —*The New York Times*

"A masterpiece." —*Booklist*

"Spectacular . . . muscular, energetic prose and pell-mell pacing." —*The Seattle Times*

WITHOUT FAIL

"If *Without Fail* doesn't hook you on Lee Child, I give up." —*The New York Times*

"Child's plot is ingenious, his characters are first-rate, and his writing is fine indeed. I don't often shed tears over fictional folk, but he makes the unexpected death of one character genuinely moving. This is a superior series."
—*The Washigton Post Book World*

ECHO BURNING

"Constantly escalating tension and a host of sinister villains . . . a Texas version of *Deliverance*. Child is a vigorous storyteller, gradually building the suspense to almost unbearable levels." —*St. Louis Post-Dispatch*

"Sizzling. As sweltering as the El Paso sun. Bottom line: Jalapeno-hot suspense." —*People*

Titles by Lee Child

WITHOUT FAIL
ECHO BURNING
RUNNING BLIND
TRIPWIRE
DIE TRYING
KILLING FLOOR

DIE TRYING

LEE CHILD

BERKLEY BOOKS, NEW YORK

THE BERKLEY PUBLISHING GROUP
Published by the Penguin Group
Penguin Group (USA) Inc.
375 Hudson Street, New York, New York 10014, USA
Penguin Group (Canada), 10 Alcorn Avenue, Toronto, Ontario M4V 3B2, Canada
(a division of Pearson Penguin Canada Inc.)
Penguin Books Ltd., 80 Strand, London WC2R 0RL, England
Penguin Group Ireland, 25 St. Stephen's Green, Dublin 2, Ireland (a division of Penguin Books Ltd.)
Penguin Group (Australia), 250 Camberwell Road, Camberwell, Victoria 3124, Australia
(a division of Pearson Australia Group Pty. Ltd.)
Penguin Books India Pvt. Ltd., 11 Community Centre, Panchsheel Park, New Delhi—110 017, India
Penguin Group (NZ), Cnr. Airborne and Rosedale Roads, Albany, Auckland 1310, New Zealand
(a division of Pearson New Zealand Ltd.)
Penguin Books (South Africa) (Pty.) Ltd., 24 Sturdee Avenue, Rosebank, Johannesburg 2196,
South Africa

Penguin Books Ltd., Registered Offices: 80 Strand, London WC2R 0RL, England

PRINTING HISTORY
G. P. Putnam's Sons hardcover edition / July 1998
Jove mass market edition / May 1999
Berkley trade edition / May 2005

Berkley trade paperback ISBN: 0-425-20621-1

The Library of Congress catalogues the G. P. Putnam's Sons hardcover edition as follows:

Child, Lee.
Die trying / by Lee Child
    p. cm.
ISBN 0-399-14379-3 (alk. paper)
I. Title
PS3553.H4838D54   1998   97-39763 CIP
813'.54—dc21

PRINTED IN THE UNITED STATES OF AMERICA

10 9 8 7 6 5 4 3

If I listed all the ways she helps me,
this dedication would be longer
than the book itself.
So I'll just say:

To my wife, Jane, with thanks

DIE TRYING

1

NATHAN RUBIN DIED because he got brave. Not the sustained kind of thing that wins you a medal in a war, but the split-second kind of blurting outrage that gets you killed on the street.

He left home early, as he always did, six days a week, fifty weeks a year. A cautious breakfast, appropriate to a short round man aiming to stay in shape through his forties. A long walk down the carpeted corridors of a lakeside house appropriate to a man who earned a thousand dollars on each of those three hundred days he worked. A thumb on the button of the garage-door opener and a twist of the wrist to start the silent engine of his expensive imported sedan. A CD into the player, a backward sweep into his gravel driveway, a dab on the brake, a snick of the selector, a nudge on the gas, and the last short drive of his life was under way. Six forty-nine in the morning, Monday.

The only light on his route to work was green, which was the proximate cause of his death. It meant that as he pulled into his secluded slot behind his professional building the prelude ahead of Bach's B Minor Fugue still had thirty-eight seconds left to run. He sat and heard it out until the last organ blast echoed to silence, which meant that as he got out of his car the three men were near enough for him to interpret some kind of intention in their approach. So he glanced at them. They looked away and altered course, three men in step, like dancers or soldiers. He turned toward his building. Started walking. But then he stopped. And looked back. The three men were at his car. Trying the doors.

"Hey!" he called.

It was the short universal sound of surprise, anger, challenge. The sort of instinctive sound an earnest, naive citizen makes when something should not be happening. The sort of instinctive sound which gets an earnest, naive citizen killed. He found himself heading straight back to his car. He was outnumbered three to one, but he was in the right, which swelled him up and gave him confidence. He strode back and felt outraged and fit and commanding.

But those were illusory feelings. A soft suburban guy like him was never going to be in command of a situation like that. His fitness was just health club tone. It counted for nothing. His tight abdominals ruptured under the first savage blow. His face jerked forward and down and hard knuckles pulped his lips and smashed his teeth. He was caught by rough hands and knotted arms and held upright like he weighed nothing at all. His keys were snatched from his grasp and he was hit a crashing blow on the ear. His mouth filled with blood. He was dropped onto the blacktop and heavy boots smashed into his back. Then his gut. Then his head. He blacked out like a television set in a thunderstorm. The world just disappeared in front of him. It collapsed into a thin hot line and sputtered away to nothing.

So he died, because for a split second he got brave. But not then. He died much later, after the split second of bravery had faded into long hours of wretched gasping fear, and after the long hours of fear had exploded into long minutes of insane screaming panic.

JACK REACHER STAYED alive, because he got cautious. He got cautious because he heard an echo from his past. He had a lot of past, and the echo was from the worst part of it.

He had served thirteen years in the Army, and the only time he was wounded it wasn't with a bullet. It was with a fragment of a Marine sergeant's jawbone. Reacher had been stationed in Beirut, in the U.S. compound out by the airport. The compound was truck-bombed. Reacher was standing at the gate. The Marine sergeant was standing a hundred yards nearer the explosion. The jawbone fragment was the only piece left of the guy. It hit Reacher a hundred yards away and went tumbling through his gut like a bullet. The Army surgeon who patched Reacher up told him afterward he was lucky. He told him a real bullet in the gut would have felt much worse. That was the echo Reacher was hearing. And he was paying a whole lot of attention to it, because thirteen years later he was standing there with a handgun pointing straight at his stomach. From a range of about an inch and a half.

The handgun was a nine-millimeter automatic. It was brand-new. It was oiled. It was held low, lined up right on his old scar. The guy holding it looked more or less like he knew what he was doing. The safety mechanism was released. There was no visible tremor in the muzzle. No tension. The trigger finger was ready to go to work. Reacher could see that. He was concentrating hard on that trigger finger.

He was standing next to a woman. He was holding her arm. He had never seen her before. She was staring at an identical nine-millimeter pointed at her own gut. Her guy was more tensed up than his. Her guy looked uneasy. He looked worried. His gun was trembling with tension. His fingernails were chewed. A nervous, jumpy guy. The four of them were standing there on the street, three of them still like statues and the fourth hopping slightly from foot to foot.

They were in Chicago. Center of the city, a busy sidewalk, a Monday, last day of June. Broad daylight, bright summer sunshine. The whole situation had materialized in a split second. It had happened in a way that couldn't have been choreographed in a million years. Reacher had been walking down the street, going nowhere, not fast, not slow. He had been about to pass the exit door of a storefront dry cleaner. The door had opened up in his face and an old metal walking cane had clattered out on the sidewalk right in front of him. He'd glanced up to see a woman in the doorway. She was about to drop an armful of nine dry-cleaning bags. She was some way short of thirty, expensively dressed, dark, attractive, self-assured. She had some kind of a bad leg. Some kind of an injury. Reacher could see from her awkward posture it was causing her pain. She'd thrown him a would-you-mind look and he'd thrown her a no-problem look and scooped up the metal cane. He'd taken the nine bags from her with one hand and given her the cane with the other. He'd flicked the bags up over his shoulder and felt the nine wire hangers bite into his finger. She had planted the cane on the sidewalk and eased her forearm into the curved metal clip. He had offered his hand. She had paused. Then she had nodded in an embarrassed fashion and he had taken her arm and waited a beat, feeling helpful but awkward. Then they had turned together to move away. Reacher had figured he would maybe stroll a few steps with her until she was steady on her feet. Then he would let her arm go and hand back her garments. But he'd turned straight into the two men with the nine-millimeter automatics.

The four of them stood there, face-to-face in pairs. Like four people eating together in a tight booth in a diner. The two guys with the guns were white, well fed, vaguely military, vaguely alike. Medium height, short brown hair. Big hands, muscular. Big, obvious faces, bland pink features. Tense expressions, hard eyes. The nervous guy was smaller, like he burned up his energy worrying. They both wore checked shirts and poplin windbreakers. They stood there, pressed together. Reacher was a lot taller than the other three. He could see all around them, over their heads. He stood there, surprised, with the woman's dry cleaning slung over his shoulder. The woman was leaning on her crutch, just staring, silent. The two men were pointing the guns. Close in. Reacher felt they'd all been standing like that for a long time. But he knew that feeling was deceptive. It probably hadn't been more than a second and a half.

The guy opposite Reacher seemed to be the leader. The bigger one. The calmer one. He looked between Reacher and the woman and jerked his automatic's barrel toward the curb.

"In the car, bitch," the guy said. "And you, asshole."

He spoke urgently, but quietly. With authority. Not much of an accent. Maybe from California, Reacher thought. There was a sedan at the curb. It had been waiting there for them. A big car, black, expensive. The driver was leaning across and behind the front passenger seat. He was stretching over to pop the rear door. The guy opposite Reacher motioned with the gun again. Reacher didn't move. He glanced left and right. He figured he had about another second and a half to make some kind of an assessment. The two guys with the nine-millimeter automatics didn't worry him too much. He was one-handed, because of the dry cleaning, but he figured the two guys would go down without too much of a problem. The problems lay beside him and behind him. He stared up into the dry cleaner's window and used it like a mirror. Twenty yards behind him was a solid mass of hurrying people at a crosswalk. A couple of stray bullets would find a couple of targets. No doubt about that. No doubt at all. That was the problem behind him. The problem beside him was the unknown woman. Her capabilities were an unknown quantity. She had some kind of a bad leg. She would be slow to react. Slow to move. He wasn't prepared to go into combat. Not in that environment, and not with that partner.

The guy with the California accent reached up and grabbed Reacher's wrist where it was pinned against his collar by the weight of the nine clean garments hanging down his back. He used it to pull him toward the car. His trigger finger still looked ready to go to work. Reacher was watching it, corner of his eye. He let the woman's arm go. Stepped over to the car. Threw the bags into the rear seat and climbed in after them. The woman was pushed in behind him. Then the jumpy guy crowded in on them and slammed the door. The leader got in front on the right. Slammed the door. The driver nudged the selector and the car moved smoothly and quietly away down the street.

THE WOMAN WAS gasping in pain and Reacher figured she had the jumpy guy's gun jammed in her ribs. The leader was twisted around in the front seat with his gun hand resting against the thick leather headrest. The gun was pointed straight at Reacher's chest. It was a Glock 17. Reacher knew all about that weapon. He had evaluated the prototype for his unit. That had been his assignment during his light-duty convalescence after the Beirut wound. The Glock was a tough little weapon. Seven and a half inches long from firing pin to muzzle tip. Long enough to make it accurate. Reacher had hit thumbtack heads at seventy-five feet with it. And it fired a decent projectile. It delivered quarter-ounce bullets at nearly eight hundred miles an hour. Seventeen rounds to a magazine, hence the name. And it was light. For all its power, it weighed under two pounds. The important parts were steel. The rest of it was plastic. Black polycarbonate, like an expensive camera. A fine piece of craftsmanship.

But he hadn't liked it much. Not for the specialized requirements of his unit. He'd recommended rejection. He'd supported the Beretta 92F instead. The Beretta was also a nine-millimeter, a half-pound heavier, an inch longer, two fewer rounds in the magazine. But it had about ten percent more stopping power than the Glock. That was important to him. And it wasn't plastic. The Beretta had been Reacher's choice. His unit commander had agreed. He had circulated Reacher's paper and the Army as a whole had backed his recommendation. The same week they promoted him and pinned on his Silver Star and his Purple Heart, they ordered Berettas even though the Beretta was more expensive and NATO was crazy for the Glock and Reacher had been just about a lone voice and was not long out of West Point. Then he had been assigned elsewhere and served all around the world and hadn't really seen a Glock 17 since. Until now. Twelve years later, he was getting a pretty damn good second look at one.

He switched his attention away from the gun and took a second look at the guy holding it. He had a decent tan which whitened near his hairline. A recent haircut. The driver had a big shiny brow, thinning hair swept back, pink and vivid features, the smirk that pig-ugly guys use when they think they're handsome. Same cheap chain store shirt, same windbreaker. Same corn-fed bulk. Same in-charge confidence, edged around with a slight breathlessness. Three guys, all of them maybe thirty or thirty-five, one leader, one solid follower, one jumpy follower. All of them tense but rehearsed, racing through some kind of a mission. A puzzle. Reacher glanced past the steady Glock into the leader's eyes. But the guy shook his head.

"No talking, asshole," he said. "Start talking, I'll shoot

you. That's a damn promise. Keep quiet, you could be OK.''

Reacher believed him. The guy's eyes were hard and his mouth was a tight line. So he said nothing. Then the car slowed and pulled onto a lumpy concrete forecourt. It headed around behind an abandoned industrial building. They had driven south. Reacher figured they were now maybe five miles south of the Loop. The driver eased the big sedan to a stop with the rear door lined up with the back of a small panel truck. The truck was standing alone on the empty lot. It was a Ford Econoline, dirty white, not old, but well used. There had been some kind of writing on the side. It had been painted over with fresh white paint which didn't exactly match the bodywork. Reacher scanned around. The lot was full of trash. He saw a paint can discarded near the truck. A brush. There was nobody in sight. The place was deserted. If he was going to make some kind of a move, this was the right time to make it, and the right location. But the guy in front smiled a thin smile and leaned right over into the back of the car. Caught Reacher's collar with his left hand and ground the tip of the Glock's muzzle into Reacher's ear with his right.

''Sit still, asshole,'' the guy said.

The driver got out of the car and skipped around the hood. Pulled a new set of keys from his pocket and opened up the rear doors of the truck. Reacher sat still. Jamming a gun into a person's ear is not necessarily a smart move. If the person suddenly jerks his head around toward it, the gun comes out. It rolls around the person's forehead. Then even a quick trigger finger won't do much damage. It might blow a hole in the person's ear, just the outside flap, and it's sure to shatter the person's eardrum. But those are not fatal wounds. Reacher spent a second weighing those odds. Then the jumpy guy dragged the woman out of the car and hustled her straight into the back of the truck. She hopped and limped across the short distance. Straight out of one door and in through the other. Reacher watched her, corner of his eye. Her guy took her pocketbook from her and tossed it back into the car. It fell at Reacher's feet. It thumped heavily on the thick carpet. A big pocketbook, expensive leather, something heavy in it. Something metal. Only one metal thing women carry could make a heavy thump like that. He glanced across at her, suddenly interested.

She was sprawled in the back of the truck. Impeded by her leg. Then the leader in the front pulled Reacher along the leather seat and passed him on to the jumpy guy. As soon as one Glock was out of his ear, the other was jammed into his side. He was dragged over the rough ground. Across to the rear of the truck. He was pushed inside with the woman. The jumpy guy covered them both with the trembling Glock while the leader reached into the car and pulled out the woman's metal crutch. He walked over and tossed it into the truck. It clanged and boomed on the metal siding. He left her dry cleaning in the back of the sedan with her handbag. Then he pulled a set of handcuffs from the pocket of his jacket. He caught the woman's right wrist and cuffed it with half the handcuff. Pulled her roughly sideways and caught Reacher's left wrist. Snapped the other half of the cuff onto it. Shook the cuff to check it was secure. Slammed the truck's left rear door. Reacher saw the driver emptying plastic bottles into the sedan. He caught the pale color and the strong smell of gasoline. One bottle into the back seat, one into the front. Then the leader swung the truck's right rear door shut. Last thing Reacher saw before darkness enveloped him was the driver, pulling a matchbook from his pocket.

2

ONE THOUSAND SEVEN hundred and two miles from Chicago by road, guest quarters were being prepared. They took the form of a single room. The room was following an unconventional design, specified by a thorough man after a great deal of careful thought. The design called for several unusual features.

The quarters were designed for a specific purpose, and for a specific guest. The nature of the purpose and the identity of the guest had dictated the unusual features. The construction was concentrated on the second floor of an existing building. A corner room had been selected. It had a series of large windows on the two outside walls. They faced south and east. The glass had been smashed out and was replaced by heavy plywood sheeting nailed to the remaining window frames. The plywood was painted white on the outside, to match the building's siding. On the inside, the plywood was left unfinished.

The corner room's ceiling was torn out. It was an old building, and the ceiling had been made of heavy plaster. It had been pulled down in a shower of choking dust. The room was now open to the rafters. The interior walling was torn off. The walls had been paneled in old pine, worn smooth with age and polish. That was all gone. The framing of the building and the heavy old tar paper behind the exterior siding was exposed. The floorboards were pulled up. The dusty ceiling of the room below was visible under the heavy joists. The room was just a shell.

The old plaster from the ceiling and the boards from the walls and the floor had been thrown out through the windows before they were covered over with the plywood. The two men who had done the demolition work had shoveled all that debris into a large pile, and they had backed their truck up to the pile ready to cart the trash away. They were very anxious to leave the place looking neat and tidy. This was the first time they had worked for this particular employer, and there had been hints of more work to come. And looking around, they could see that there was plenty more needed doing. All in all, an optimistic situation. New contracts were hard to find, and this particular employer had shown no concern over price. The two men felt that to make a good first impression was very much in their long-term interest. They were hard at work loading their truck with every last plaster fragment when the employer himself stopped by.

"All done?" he asked.

The employer was a huge guy, freakishly bloated, with a high voice and two nickel-sized red spots burning on his pale cheeks. He moved lightly and quietly, like a guy a quarter his size. The overall effect was a guy people looked away from and answered quickly.

"Just clearing up," the first guy said to him. "Where do we dump this stuff?"

"I'll show you," the employer said. "You'll need to make two trips. Bring those boards separately, right?"

The second guy nodded. The floorboards were eighteen inches wide, from back when lumbermen had the pick of any tree they wanted. No way would they fit into the flatbed with the rest of the junk. They finished loading the plaster and their employer squeezed into their truck with them. He was such a big guy, it made for a tight fit. He pointed beyond the old building.

"Drive north," he said. "About a mile."

The road led them straight out of town and then wound upward through some steep bends. The employer pointed to a place.

"In there," he said. "All the way in back, OK?"

He strolled quietly away and the two guys unloaded their truck. Drove it back south and heaved the old pine boards in. Followed the winding bends again and unloaded. They carried the boards inside and stacked them neatly. All the way in back of the dark space. Then the employer stepped out of the shadows. He had been waiting for them. He had something in his hand.

"We're all done," the first guy said.

The employer nodded.

"You sure are," he said.

His hand came up. He was holding a gun. A dull black automatic. He shot the first guy in the head. The crash of the bullet was deafening. Blood and bone and brain sprayed everywhere. The second guy froze in terror. Then he ran. He launched himself sideways in a desperate sprint for cover. The employer smiled. He liked it when they ran. He dropped his huge arm to a shallow angle. Fired and put a bullet through the back of the guy's knee. Smiled again. Now it was better. He liked it when they ran, but he liked it better when they were squirming on the floor. He stood and listened to the guy's yelping for a long moment. Then he strolled quietly over and took careful aim. Put a bullet through the other knee. He watched for a while, then he tired of the game. Shrugged and put a final bullet through the guy's head. Then he laid the gun on the ground and rolled the two bodies over and over until they were stacked neatly in line with the old floorboards.

3

THEY HAD BEEN on the road an hour and thirty-three minutes. Some urban crawling, then an acceleration to a steady cruise. Maybe sixty miles covered. But in the noisy darkness inside the panel truck Reacher had no idea which direction those sixty miles were taking him.

He was handcuffed to the young woman with the bad leg and within the first few minutes of their forced acquaintance they had worked out how to get as comfortable as they were ever going to get. They had crabbed around inside the truck until they were sitting sideways on the floor, legs straight out, propped against the big wheel well on the right, braced against the motion. The woman sat against the rear side and Reacher sat on the forward side. Their cuffed wrists lay together on the flat top of the metal bulge like they were lovers idling their time away in a café.

At first, they hadn't spoken. They just sat for a long time in stunned silence. The immediate problem was the heat. It was the middle of the last day of June in the Midwest. They were shut into an enclosed metal space. There was no ventilation. Reacher figured the rush of air over the outside of the truck's body must be cooling it to an extent, but nowhere near enough.

He just sat there in the gloom and used the hot dead time thinking and planning like he was trained to do. Staying calm, staying relaxed, staying ready, not burning his energy away

with useless speculation. Assessing and evaluating. The three
guys had shown a measure of efficiency. No great talent, no
real finesse, but no significant mistakes. The jumpy guy with
the second Glock was the weakest component of the team,
but the leader had covered for him pretty well. An efficient
threesome. Not at all the worst he'd ever seen. But at that
point, he wasn't worrying. He'd been in worse situations and
survived them. Much worse situations, and more than once.
So he wasn't worrying yet.

Then he noticed something. He noticed that the woman
was not worrying yet, either. She was calm, too. She was just
sitting there, swaying, cuffed to his wrist, thinking and planning like maybe she was trained to do, as well. He glanced
across at her in the gloom and saw her looking steadily at
him. A quizzical stare, calm, in control, faintly superior,
faintly disapproving. The confidence of youth. She met his
gaze. Held it for a long moment. Then she stuck out her
cuffed right hand, which jarred his left wrist, but it was an
encouraging gesture. He reached around and shook her hand
and they smiled brief ironic smiles together at their mutual
formality.

"Holly Johnson," she said.

She was assessing him carefully. He could see her eyes
traveling around his face. Then they flicked down to his
clothing, and back up to his face. She smiled again, briefly,
like she had decided he merited some kind of courtesy.

"Nice to meet you," she said.

He looked back at her. Looked at her face. She was a very
good-looking woman. Maybe twenty-six, twenty-seven. He
looked at her clothes. A line from an old song ran through
his head: hundred-dollar dresses, that I ain't paid for yet. He
waited for the next line, but it didn't come. So he smiled
back at her and nodded.

"Jack Reacher," he said. "Pleasure's all mine, Holly, believe me."

It was difficult to speak, because the truck was cruising
noisily. The sound of the engine was fighting with the roar
from the road. Reacher would have been happy to sit quiet
for a time, but Holly wasn't.

"I need to get rid of you," she said.

A confident woman, well in control of herself. He made no reply. Just glanced at her and glanced away. The next line was: cold, cold-blooded woman. A dying fall, a sad poignant line. An old Memphis Slim song. But the line was not right for her. Not right at all. This was not a cold-blooded woman. He glanced over again and shrugged at her. She was staring at him. Impatient with his silence.

"You understand exactly what's happening?" she asked him.

He watched her face. Watched her eyes. She was staring straight at him. Astonishment on her face. She thought she was stuck in there with an idiot. She thought he didn't understand exactly what was happening.

"It's pretty clear, right?" he said. "From the evidence?"

"What evidence?" she said. "It was all over in a split second."

"Exactly," he said. "That's all the evidence I need, right? Tells me more or less what I need to know."

He stopped talking and started resting again. Next opportunity to get away would be the next time the truck stopped. Could be some hours away. He felt he could be in for a long day. Felt he should be prepared to conserve his resources.

"So what do you need to know?" the woman said.

Her eyes were steady on his.

"You've been kidnapped," he said. "I'm here by accident."

She was still looking at him. Still confident. Still thinking. Still not sure whether or not she was cuffed to an idiot.

"It's pretty clear, right?" he said again. "It wasn't me they were after."

She made no reply. Just arched a fine eyebrow.

"Nobody knew I was going to be there," he said. "I didn't even know I was going to be there. Until I got there. But it was a well-planned operation. Must have taken time to set up. Based on surveillance, right? Three guys, one in the car, two on the street. The car was parked exactly level. They had no idea where I was going to be. But obviously they knew for sure where you were going to be. So don't be looking at me like I'm the idiot here. You're the one made the big mistake."

"Mistake?" the woman said.

"You're too regular in your habits," Reacher said. "They studied your movements, maybe two or three weeks, and you walked right into their arms. They weren't expecting anybody else to be there. That's clear, right? They only brought one set of handcuffs."

He raised his wrist, which raised hers too, to make his point. The woman went quiet for a long moment. She was revising her opinion of him. Reacher rocked with the motion of the vehicle and smiled.

"And you should know better," he said. "You're a government agent of some sort, right? DEA, CIA, FBI, something like that, maybe a Chicago PD detective? New in the job, still fairly dedicated. And fairly wealthy. So somebody is either looking for a ransom, or you've already become a potential problem to somebody, even though you're new, and either way you should have taken more care of yourself."

She looked across at him. Nodded, eyes wide in the gloom. Impressed.

"Evidence?" she asked.

He smiled at her again.

"Couple of things," he said. "Your dry cleaning? My guess is every Monday lunch break you take last week's clothes in to get them cleaned, and you pick up this week's clothes to wear. That means you must have about fifteen or twenty outfits. Looking at that thing you got on, you're not a cheap dresser. Call it four hundred bucks an outfit, you've got maybe eight grand tied up in things to wear. That's what I call moderately wealthy, and that's what I call too regular in your habits."

She nodded slowly.

"OK," she said. "Why am I a government agent?"

"Easy enough," he said. "You had a Glock 17 shoved at you, you were bundled into a car, you were thrown in a truck, handcuffed to a complete stranger and you've got no idea where the hell they're taking you, or why. Any normal person would be falling apart over all that, screaming the place down. But not you. You're sitting there quite calmly, which suggests some kind of training, maybe some kind of familiarity with upsetting or dangerous situations. And maybe some kind of sure knowledge there'll be a bunch of people looking to get you back soon as they can."

He stopped and she nodded for him to continue.

"Also, you had a gun in your bag," he said. "Something fairly heavy, maybe a thirty-eight, long barrel. If it was a private weapon, a dresser like you would choose something dainty, like a snub twenty-two. But it was a big revolver, so you were issued with it. So you're some kind of an agent, maybe a cop."

The woman nodded again, slowly.

"Why am I new in the job?" she asked.

"Your age," Reacher said. "What are you? Twenty-six?"

"Twenty-seven," she said.

"That's young for a detective," he said. "College, a few years in uniform? Young for the FBI, DEA, CIA, too. So whatever you are, you're new at it."

She shrugged.

"OK," she said. "Why am I fairly dedicated?"

Reacher pointed, left-handed, rattling their shared handcuff.

. "Your injury," he said. "You're back to work after some kind of an accident, before you're really recovered. You're still using that crutch for your bad leg. Most people in your position would be staying home and drawing sick pay."

She smiled.

"I could be handicapped," she said. "Could have been born this way."

Reacher shook his head in the gloom.

"That's a hospital crutch," he said. "They loaned it to you, short-term, until you're over your injury. If it was a permanent thing, you'd have bought your own crutch. Probably you'd have bought a dozen. Sprayed them all different to match all your expensive outfits."

She laughed. It was a pleasant sound above the drone and boom of the truck's engine and the roar of the road.

"Pretty good, Jack Reacher," she said. "I'm an FBI Special Agent. Since last fall. I just ripped up my cruciate ligaments playing soccer."

"You play soccer?" Reacher said. "Good for you, Holly Johnson. What kind of an FBI agent since last fall?"

She was quiet for a beat.

"Just an agent," she said. "One of many at the Chicago office."

Reacher shook his head.

"Not just an agent," he said. "An agent who's doing something to somebody who maybe wants to retaliate. So who are you doing something to?"

She shook her head back at him.

"I can't discuss that," she said. "Not with civilians."

He nodded. He was comfortable with that.

"OK," he said.

"Any agent makes enemies," she said.

"Naturally," he replied.

"Me as much as anybody," she said.

He glanced across at her. It was a curious remark. Defensive. The remark of a woman trained and eager and ready to go, but chained to a desk since last fall.

"Financial section?" he guessed.

She shook her head.

"I can't discuss it," she said again.

"But you already made enemies," he said.

She gave him a half-smile which died fast. Then she went quiet. She looked calm, but Reacher could feel in her wrist that she was worried for the first time. But she was hanging in there. And she was wrong.

"They're not out to kill you," he said. "They could have killed you in that vacant lot. Why haul you away in this damn truck? And there's your crutch, too."

"What about my crutch?" she said.

"Doesn't make any sense," he said. "Why would they toss your crutch in here if they're going to kill you? You're a hostage, Holly, that's what you are. You sure you don't know these guys? Never saw them before?"

"Never," she said. "I don't know who the hell they are, or what the hell they want from me."

He stared at her. She sounded way too definite. She knew more than she was telling him. They went quiet in the noise. Rocked and bounced with the movement of the truck. Reacher stared into the gloom. He could feel Holly making decisions, next to him. She turned sideways again.

"I need to get you out of here," she said again.

He glanced at her. Glanced away and grinned.

"Suits me, Holly," he said. "Sooner the better."

"When will somebody miss you?" she asked.

That was a question he would have preferred not to answer. But she was looking hard at him, waiting. So he thought about it, and he told her the truth.

"Never," he said.

"Why not?" she asked. "Who are you, Reacher?"

He looked across at her and shrugged.

"Nobody," he said.

She kept on looking at him, quizzically. Maybe irritated.

"OK, what kind of nobody?" she asked.

He heard Memphis Slim in his head: got me working in a steel mill.

"I'm a doorman," he said. "At a club in Chicago."

"Which club?" she asked.

"A blues place on the South Side," he said. "You probably don't know it."

She looked at him and shook her head.

"A doorman?" she said. "You're playing this pretty cool for a doorman."

"Doormen deal with a lot of weird situations," he said.

She looked like she wasn't convinced and he put his face down near his wristwatch to check the time. Two-thirty in the afternoon.

"And how long before somebody misses you?" he asked.

She looked at her own watch and made a face.

"Quite a while," she said. "I've got a case conference starting at five o'clock this afternoon. Nothing before then. Two and a half hours before anybody even knows I'm gone."

4

RIGHT INSIDE THE shell of the second-floor room, a second shell was taking shape. It was being built from brand-new softwood two-by-fours, nailed together in the conventional way, looking like a new room growing right there inside the old room. But the new room was going to be about a foot smaller in every dimension than the old room had been. A foot shorter in length, a foot narrower in width, and a foot shorter in height.

The new floor joists were going to be raised a foot off the old joists with twelve-inch lengths of the new softwood. The new lengths looked like a forest of short stilts, ready to hold the new floor up. More short lengths were ready to hold the new framing a foot away from the old framing all the way around the sides and the ends. The new framing had the bright yellowness of new wood. It gleamed against the smoky honey color of the old framing. The old framing looked like an ancient skeleton which was suddenly growing a new skeleton inside itself.

Three men were building the new shell. They were stepping from joist to joist with practiced skill. They looked like men who had built things before. And they were working fast. Their contract demanded they finish on time. The employer had been explicit about it. Some kind of a rush job. The three carpenters were not complaining about that. The employer had accepted their first bid. It had been an inflated bid, with a large horse-trading margin built in. But the guy had not eaten into that margin. He had not negotiated at all. He had just nodded and told them to start work as soon as the wrecking crew had finished. Work was hard to find, and employers who accepted your first price were even harder to find. So the three men were happy to work hard, and work fast, and work late. They were anxious to make a good first impression. Looking around, they could see the potential for plenty more employment.

So they were giving it their best shot. They ran up and down the stairs with tools and fresh lumber. They worked by eye, marking cut-lines in the wood with their thumbnails, using their nail guns and their saws until they ran hot. But they paused frequently to measure the gap between the old framing and the new. The employer had made it clear that dimension was critical. The old framing was six inches deep. The new framing was four. The gap was twelve inches.

"Six and four and twelve," one guy said. "Twenty-two inches total."

"OK?" the second guy asked the crew chief.

"Ideal," the crew chief said. "Exactly what he told us."

5

HOLLY JOHNSON'S FIVE o'clock case conference was allocated to the Chicago FBI office's third-floor meeting room. This was a large room, better than forty feet by twenty, and it was more or less filled by a long polished table flanked by thirty chairs, fifteen on each side. The chairs were substantial and leather, and the table was made of fine hardwood, but any tendency for the place to look like a corporate boardroom was defused by the scruffy government wall covering and the cheap carpet. There were ninety square yards of carpet on the floor, and the whole ninety together had probably cost less than just one of the chairs.

Five o'clock in the summer, the afternoon sun streamed in through the wall of windows and gave the people arriving in the room a choice. If they sat facing the windows, they got the sun in their eyes and squinted through the meeting and ended up with a blinding headache. And the sun overpowered the air conditioning, so if they sat backs to the window, they got heated up to a point where it got uncomfortable and they started worrying about whether their deodorant was still OK at five o'clock in the afternoon. A tough choice, but the top option was to avoid the headache and take the risk of heating up. So the early attendees took the seats on the window side.

First into the room was the FBI lawyer with special responsibility for financial crime. He stood for a moment and made a judgment about the likely duration of the meeting.

Maybe forty-five minutes, he thought, knowing Holly, so he turned and tried to assess which seat might get the benefit of the shade from the slim pillar splitting the wall of windows into two. The bar of shadow was lying to the left of the third chair in the row, and he knew it would inch toward the head of the table as time passed. So he spilled his pile of folders onto the table in front of the second chair and shrugged his jacket off and claimed the place by dropping it onto the chair. Then he turned again and strolled to the credenza at the end of the room for a cup of coffee from the filter machine.

Next in were two agents working on cases that might be tied into the mess that Holly Johnson was dealing with. They nodded to the lawyer and saw the place he'd claimed. They knew there was no point in choosing between the other four-teen chairs by the window. They were all going to get equally hot. So they just dumped their portfolios at the nearest two places and lined up for coffee.

"She not here yet?" one of them said to the lawyer.

"Haven't seen her all day," the lawyer said.

"Your loss, right?" the other guy said.

Holly Johnson was a new agent, but talented, and that was making her popular. In the past, the Bureau would have taken no pleasure at all in busting the sort of businessmen that Holly was employed to chase down, but times had changed, and the Chicago office had gotten quite a taste for it. The businessmen now looked like scumbags, not solid citizens, and the agents were sick and tired of looking at them as they rode the commuter trains home. The agents would be getting off the train miles before the bankers and the stockbrokers were anywhere near their expensive suburbs. They would be thinking about second mortgages and even second jobs, and they'd be thinking about the years of private detective work they were going to have to put in to boost up the mean gov-ernment pension. And the executives would be sitting there with smug smiles. So when one or two of them started to take a fall, the Bureau was happy enough about it. When the ones and twos turned into tens and twenties, and then hun-dreds, it became a blood sport.

The only drawback was that it was hard work. Probably more difficult to nail than anything else. That was where

Holly Johnson's arrival had made things easier. She had the talent. She could look at a balance sheet and just know if anything was wrong with it. It was like she could smell it. She'd sit at her desk and look at the papers, and cock her head slightly to one side, and think. Sometimes, she'd think for hours, but when she stopped thinking, she'd know what the hell was going on. Then she'd explain it all in the case conference. She'd make it all sound easy and logical, like there was no way anybody could be in any kind of doubt about it. She was a woman who made progress. She was a woman who made her fellow agents feel better on those commuter trains at night. That's what was making her popular.

Fourth person into the third-floor meeting room was the agent assigned to help Holly out with the fetching and carrying until she recovered from her soccer injury. His name was Milosevic. A slight frame, a slight West Coast accent. Less than forty, casually dressed in expensive designer khaki, gold at his neck and on his wrist. He was also a new arrival, recently transferred in to the Chicago office, because that was where the Bureau found it needed its financial people. He joined the line for coffee and looked around the room.

"She's late?" he said.

The lawyer shrugged at him and Milosevic shrugged back. He liked Holly Johnson. He had worked with her five weeks, since the accident on the soccer field, and he had enjoyed every minute of it.

"She's not usually late for anything," he said.

Fifth person in was Brogan, Holly's section head. Irish, from Boston via California. The young side of middle age. Dark hair, red Irish face. A tough guy, handsomely dressed in an expensive silk jacket, ambitious. He'd come to Chicago the same time as Milosevic, and he was pissed it wasn't New York. He was looking for the advancement he was sure he deserved. There was a theory that Holly's arrival in his section was enhancing his chances of getting it.

"She not here yet?" he said.

The other four shrugged at him.

"I'll kick her ass," Brogan said.

Holly had been a stock analyst on Wall Street before applying to join the FBI. Nobody was clear why she'd made the change. She had some kind of exalted connections, and some kind of an illustrious father, and the easy guess was she wanted to impress him somehow. Nobody knew for sure whether the old guy was impressed or not, but the feeling was he damn well ought to be. Holly had been one of ten thousand applicants in her year, and she'd passed in right at the top of the four hundred who made it. She'd creamed the recruitment criteria. The Bureau had been looking for college graduates in law or accountancy, or else graduates in flimsier disciplines who'd then worked somewhere for three years at least. Holly had qualified in every way. She had an accountancy degree from Yale, and a master's from Harvard, and three years on Wall Street on top of all that. She'd blitzed the intelligence tests and the aptitude assessments. She'd charmed the three serving agents who'd grilled her at her main interview.

She'd sailed through the background checks, which was understandable on account of her connections, and she'd been sent to the FBI Academy at Quantico. Then she'd really started to get serious. She was fit and strong, she learned to shoot, she murdered the leadership reaction course, she scored outstanding in the simulated shoot-outs in Hogan's Alley. But her major success was her attitude. She did two things at once. First, she bought into the whole Bureau ethic in the biggest way possible. It was totally clear to everybody that here was a woman who was going to live and die for the FBI. But second, she did it in a way which avoided the slightest trace of bullshit. She tinged her attitude with a gentle mocking humor which saved people from hating her. It made them love her instead. There was no doubt the Bureau had signed a major new asset. They sent her to Chicago and sat back to reap the benefits.

LAST INTO THE third-floor conference room was a bunch of men who came in together. Thirteen agents and the Agent-in-Charge, McGrath. The thirteen agents were clustered around their boss, who was conducting a sort of rolling policy review as he walked. The thirteen agents were hanging on to every word. McGrath had every advantage in the book. He was a man who'd been to the top, and then come back down

again into the field. He'd spent three years in the Hoover
Building as an Assistant Director of the FBI, and then he'd
applied for a demotion and a pay cut to take him back to a
Field Office. The decision had cost him ten thousand dollars
a year in income, but it had bought him back his sanity, and
it had bought him undying respect and blind affection from
the agents he worked with.

An Agent-in-Charge in a Field Office like Chicago is like
the captain on a great warship. Theoretically, there are people
above him, but they're all a couple of thousand miles away
in Washington. They're theoretical. The Agent-in-Charge is
real. He runs his command like the hand of God. That's how
the Chicago office looked at McGrath. He did nothing to
undermine the feeling. He was remote, but he was approach-
able. He was private, but he made his people feel he'd do
anything at all for them. He was a short, stocky man, burning
with energy, the sort of tireless guy who radiates total confidence. The sort of guy who makes a crew better just by
leading it. His first name was Paul, but he was always called
Mack, like the truck.

He let his thirteen agents sit down, ten of them backs to
the window and three of them with the sun in their eyes.
Then he hauled a chair around and stuck it at the head of the
table ready for Holly. He walked down to the other end and
hauled another chair around for himself. Sat sideways on to
the sun. Started getting worried.

"Where is she?" he said. "Brogan?"

The section head shrugged, palms up.

"She should be here, far as I know," he said.

"She leave a message with anybody?" McGrath asked.
"Milosevic?"

Milosevic and the other fifteen agents and the Bureau lawyer all shrugged and shook their heads. McGrath started worrying more. People have a pattern, a rhythm, like a behavioral
fingerprint. Holly was only a minute or two late, but that was
so far from normal that it was setting the bells ringing. In
eight months, he had never known her to be late. It had never
happened. Other people could be five minutes late into the
meeting room and it would seem normal. Because of their
pattern. But not Holly. At three minutes past five in the af-

ternoon, McGrath stared at her empty chair and knew there was a problem. He stood up again in the quiet room and walked to the credenza on the opposite wall. There was a phone next to the coffee machine. He picked it up and dialed his office.

"Holly Johnson call in?" he asked his secretary.

"No, Mack," she said.

So he dabbed the cradle and dialed the reception counter, two floors below.

"Any messages from Holly Johnson?" he asked the agent at the door.

"No, chief," the agent said. "Haven't seen her."

He hit the button again and called the main switchboard.

"Holly Johnson call in?" he asked.

"No, sir," the switchboard operator said.

He held the phone and gestured for pen and paper. Then he spoke to the switchboard again.

"Give me her pager number," he said. "And her cell phone, will you?"

The earpiece crackled and he scrawled down the numbers. Cut the switchboard off and dialed Holly's pager. Just got a long low tone telling him the pager was switched off. Then he tried the cell phone number. He got an electronic bleep and a recorded message of a woman telling him the phone he was dialing was unreachable. He hung up and looked around the room. It was ten after five, Monday afternoon.

6

Six-thirty on Reacher's watch, the motion inside the truck changed. Six hours and four minutes they'd cruised steadily, maybe fifty-five or sixty miles an hour, while the heat peaked and fell away. He'd sat, hot and rocking and bouncing in the dark with the wheel well between him and Holly Johnson, ticking off the distance against a map inside his head. He figured they'd been taken maybe three hundred and ninety miles. But he didn't know which direction they were headed. If they were going east, they would be right through Indiana and just about out of Ohio by now, maybe just entering Pennsylvania or West Virginia. South, they would be out of Illinois, into Missouri or Kentucky, maybe even into Tennessee if he'd underestimated their speed. West, they'd be hauling their way across Iowa. They might have looped around the bottom of the lake and headed north up through Michigan. Or straight out northwest, in which case they could be up near Minneapolis.

But they'd gotten somewhere, because the truck was slowing. Then there was a lurch to the right, like a pull off a highway. There was gear noise and thumping over broken pavement. Cornering forces slammed them around. Holly's crutch slid and rattled side to side across the ridged metal floor. The truck whined up grades and down slopes, paused at invisible road junctions, accelerated, braked hard, turned a tight left, and then drove slowly down a straight lumpy surface for a quarter hour.

"Farming country somewhere," Reacher said.

"Obviously," Holly said. "But where?"

Reacher just shrugged at her in the gloom. The truck slowed almost to a stop and turned a tight right. The road surface got worse. The truck bounced forward maybe a hundred and fifty yards and stopped. There was the sound of the passenger door opening up in front. The engine was still running. The passenger door slammed shut. Reacher heard a big door opening and the truck moved slowly forward. The engine noise boomed against metal walls. Reacher heard the door noise again and the engine noise echoed louder. Then it shut down and died away into stillness.

"We're in some sort of a barn," Reacher said. "With the door closed."

Holly nodded impatiently.

"I know that," she said. "A cow barn. I can smell it."

Reacher could hear muffled conversation outside the truck. Footsteps walking around to the rear doors. A key going into the lock. The handle turning. A blinding flood of light as the door opened. Reacher blinked against the sudden electric brightness and stared out across Holly at three men, two Glocks and a shotgun.

"Out," the leader said.

They struggled out, handcuffed together. Not easy. They were stiff and sore and cramped from bracing themselves against the wheel well for six solid hours. Holly's knee had gone altogether. Reacher started back for her crutch.

"Leave it there, asshole," the leader said.

The guy sounded tired and irritable. Reacher gave him a steady look and shrugged. Holly stiffened and tried her weight on her leg. Gasped in pain and gave it up. Glanced impersonally at Reacher like he was some kind of a tree and stretched around with her free left hand to hold on tight around his neck. It was the only way she could stay upright.

"Excuse me, please," she muttered.

The leader gestured with his Glock over to his left. They were in a large cow barn. No cows, but they hadn't been long absent, judging by the odor. The truck was parked in a wide central aisle. Either side were cow stalls, roomy, made up from galvanized steel piping efficiently welded together. Reacher twisted and held Holly's waist and the two of them hopped and staggered over to the stall the guy with the Glock was pointing at. Holly seized a railing and held on, embarrassed.

"Excuse me," she muttered again.

Reacher nodded and waited. The driver with the shotgun covered them and the leader walked away. He heaved the big door open and stepped through. Reacher caught a glimpse of darkening sky. Cloudy. No clue at all to their location.

The leader was gone five minutes. There was silence in the barn. The other two guys stood still, weapons out and ready. The jumpy guy with the Glock was staring at Reacher's face. The driver with the shotgun was staring at Holly's breasts. Smiling a half-smile. Nobody spoke. Then the leader stepped back in. He was carrying a second pair of handcuffs and two lengths of heavy chain.

"You're making a big mistake here," Holly said to him. "I'm an FBI agent."

"I know that, bitch," the guy said. "Now be quiet."

"You're committing a serious crime," Holly said.

"I know that, bitch," the guy said again. "And I told you to be quiet. Another word out of you, I'll shoot this guy in the head. Then you can spend the night with a corpse chained to your wrist, OK?"

He waited until she nodded silently. Then the driver with the shotgun took up position behind them and the leader unlocked their cuff and freed their wrists. He looped one of the chains around the stall railing and locked the ends into the spare half of the cuff dangling from Reacher's left arm. Pulled it and rattled it to check it was secure. Then he dragged Holly two stalls away and used the new cuffs and the second length of chain to lock her to the railing, twenty feet from Reacher. Her knee gave way and she fell heavily with a gasp of pain onto the dirty straw. The leader ignored her. Just walked back to where Reacher was chained up. Stood right in front of him.

"So who the hell are you, asshole?" he said.

Reacher didn't reply. He knew the keys to both cuffs were

in this guy's pocket. He knew it would take him about a second and a half to snap his neck with the loop of chain hanging off his wrist. But the other two guys were out of reach. One Glock, one shotgun, too far away to grab before he'd unlocked himself, too near to get a chance to do that. He was dealing with a reasonably efficient set of opponents. So he just shrugged and looked at the straw at his feet. It was clogged with dung.

"I asked you a damn question," the guy said.

Reacher looked at him. In the corner of his eye, he saw the jumpy guy ratchet his Glock upward a degree or two.

"I asked you a question, asshole," the leader said again, quietly.

The jumpy guy's Glock was jutting forward. Then it was straight out, shoulder-high. Aimed right at Reacher's head. The muzzle was trembling through a small jerky circle, but probably not trembling enough to make the guy miss. Not from that sort of a close distance. Reacher looked from one guy to the other. The guy with the shotgun tore his attention away from Holly's breasts. He raised the weapon to his hip. Pointed it in Reacher's direction. It was an Ithaca 37. Twelve-bore. The five-shot version with the pistol grip and no shoulder stock. The guy racked a round into the chamber. The crunch-crunch of the mechanism was loud in the barn. It echoed off the metal walls. Died into silence. Reacher saw the trigger move through the first eighth-inch of its short travel.

"Name?" the leader asked.

The shotgun trigger tightened another eighth. If it fired on that trajectory, Reacher was going to lose both his legs and most of his stomach.

"Name?" the leader asked for the second time.

It was a twelve-bore, wouldn't kill him outright, but he'd bleed to death in the dirty straw. Femoral artery gone, about a minute, maybe a minute and a half. In those circumstances, no real reason to make a big deal out of giving this guy a name.

"Jack Reacher," he said.

The leader nodded in satisfaction, like he'd achieved a victory.

"You know this bitch?" he asked.

Reacher glanced across at Holly.

"Better than I know some people," he said. "I just spent six hours handcuffed to her."

"You some kind of a wise guy, asshole?" the leader asked.

Reacher shook his head.

"Innocent passerby," he said. "I never saw her before."

"You with the Bureau?" the guy asked.

Reacher shook his head again.

"I'm a doorman," he said. "Club back in Chicago."

"You sure, asshole?" the guy said.

Reacher nodded.

"I'm sure," he said. "I'm a wise enough guy that I can recall what I do for a living, one day to the next."

There was silence for a long moment. Tension. Then the jumpy guy with the Glock came out of his shooting stance. The driver with the shotgun swung his weapon down toward the straw on the floor. He turned his head and went back to staring at Holly's breasts. The leader nodded at Reacher.

"OK, asshole," he said. "You behave yourself, you stay alive for now. Same for the bitch. Nothing's going to happen to anybody. Not just yet."

The three men regrouped in the center aisle and walked out of the barn. Before they locked the door, Reacher saw the sky again, briefly. Darker. Still cloudy. No stars. No clues. He tested the chain. It was securely fastened to the handcuff at one end and the railing at the other. Maybe seven feet long. He could hear Holly doing the same experiment. Tightening her chain and scoping out the radius it gave her to move through.

"Would you mind looking away?" she called across.

"Why?" he called back.

There was a short silence. Then a sigh. Part embarrassed, part exasperated.

"Do you really need to ask?" she called. "We were in that truck six hours, and it didn't have a bathroom, did it?"

"You going in the next stall?" he asked.

"Obviously," she said.

"OK," he said. "You go right and I'll go left. I won't look if you won't."

THE THREE MEN came back to the barn within an hour with food. Some kind of a beef stew in a metal messtin, one for each of them. Mostly rare steak chunks and a lot of hard carrots. Whoever these guys were, cooking was not their major talent. Reacher was clear on that. They handed out an enamel mug of weak coffee, one for each of them. Then they got in the truck. Started it up and backed it out of the barn. Turned the bright lights off. Reacher caught a glimpse of dim emptiness outside. Then they pulled the big door shut and locked it. Left their prisoners in the dark and the quiet.

"Gas station," Holly called from twenty feet away. "They're filling up for the rest of the ride. Can't do it with us inside. They figure we'd be banging on the side and shouting out for help."

Reacher nodded and finished his coffee. Sucked the fork from the stew clean. Bent one of the prongs right out and put a little kink into the end with pressure from his thumbnail. It made a little hook. He used it to pick the lock on his handcuff. Took him eighteen seconds, beginning to end. He dropped the cuff and the chain in the straw and walked over to Holly. Bent down and unlocked her wrist. Twelve seconds. Helped her to her feet.

"Doorman, right?" she said.

"Right," he said. "Let's take a look around."

"I can't walk," she said. "My crutch is in the damn truck."

Reacher nodded. She stayed in her stall, clinging to the railing. He scouted around the big empty barn. It was a sturdy metal structure, built throughout with the same flecked galvanized metal as the stall railings. The big door was locked from the outside. Probably a steel bar padlocked into place. No problem if he could get at the padlock, but he was inside and the padlock was outside.

The walls met the floor with a right-angle flange bolted firmly into the concrete. The walls themselves were horizontal metal panels maybe thirty feet long, maybe four feet tall. They were joined together with more right-angle flanges bolted together. Each flange gave a lip about six inches deep. Like a giant stepladder, with the treads four feet apart.

He climbed the wall, hauling himself quickly upward, flange to flange, four feet at a time. The way out of the barn was right there at the top of the wall, seven sections up, twenty-eight feet off the ground. There was a ventilation slot between the top of the wall and the overhanging slope of the metal roof. About eighteen inches high. A person could roll horizontally through the gap like an old-fashioned high jumper, hang down outside and drop twenty feet to the ground below.

He could do that, but Holly Johnson couldn't. She couldn't even walk over to the wall. She couldn't climb it and she sure as hell couldn't hang down outside and drop twenty feet onto a set of wrecked cruciate ligaments.

"Get going," she called up to him. "Get out of here, right now."

He ignored her and peered out through the slot into the darkness. The overhanging eaves gave him a low horizon. Empty country as far as the eye could see. He climbed down and went up the other three walls in turn. The second side gave out onto country just as empty as the first. The third had a view of a farmhouse. White shingles. Lights in two windows. The fourth side of the barn looked straight up the farm track. About a hundred and fifty yards to a featureless road. Emptiness beyond. In the far distance, a single set of headlight beams. Flicking and bouncing. Widely spaced. Growing larger. Getting nearer. The truck, coming back.

"Can you see where we are?" Holly called up to him.

"No idea," Reacher called back. "Farming country somewhere. Could be anywhere. Where do they have cows like this? And fields and stuff?"

"Is it hilly out there?" Holly called. "Or flat?"

"Can't tell," Reacher said. "Too dark. Maybe a little hilly."

"Could be Pennsylvania," Holly said. "They have hills and cows there."

Reacher climbed down the fourth wall and walked back to her stall.

"Get out of here, for Christ's sake," she said to him. "Raise the alarm."

He shook his head. He heard the diesel slowing to turn into the track.

"That may not be the best option," he said.

She stared at him.

"Who the hell gave you an option?" she said. "I'm ordering you. You're a civilian and I'm FBI and I'm ordering you to get yourself to safety right now."

Reacher just shrugged and stood there.

"I'm ordering you, OK?" Holly said again. "You going to obey me?"

Reacher shook his head again.

"No," he said.

She glared at him. Then the truck was back. They heard the roar of the diesel and the groan of the springs on the rough track outside. Reacher locked Holly's cuff and ran back to his stall. They heard the truck door slam and footsteps on the concrete. Reacher chained his wrist to the railing and bent the fork back into shape. When the barn door opened and the light came on, he was sitting quietly on the straw.

7

THE MATERIAL USED to pack the twenty-two-inch cavity between the outside of the old walls and the inside of the new walls was hauled over from its storage shed in an open pickup truck. There was a ton of it, and it took four trips. Each consignment was carefully unloaded by a team of eight volunteers. They worked together like an old-fashioned bucket brigade attending a fire. They passed each box along, hand to hand, into the building, up the stairs to the second floor. The boxes were stacked in the hallway outside the modified corner room. The three builders opened each box in turn and carried the material into the room. Then they stacked it carefully into the wide spaces behind the new soft-wood framing. The unloaders generally paused for a moment and watched them, grateful for a moment of rest.

The process lasted most of the afternoon, because of the amount of material and the care they took in moving it. When the last of the four loads was stacked upstairs, the eight volunteers dispersed. Seven of them headed for the mess hall. The eighth stretched in the last of the afternoon sun and strolled off. It was his habit. Four or five times a week, he would take a long walk on his own, especially after a period of heavy work. It was assumed to be his way of relaxing.

He strolled in the forest. There was a beaten path running west through the silence. He followed it for a half-mile. Then he paused and stretched again. He used the weary twisting

motion of a tired man easing a sore back to glance around a
complete circle. Then he stepped sideways off the path.
Stopped strolling. Started an urgent walk. He dodged trees
and followed a wide looping course west, then north. He went
straight for a particular tree. There was a large flat rock bed-
ded in needles at its base. He stood still and waited. Listened
hard. Then he ducked down and heaved the rock to one side.
Underneath was a rectangular shape wrapped in oilcloth. He
unfolded the cloth and took out a small hand-held radio.
Pulled the stubby antenna and hit a button and waited. Then
he whispered a long and excited message.

WHEN THE OLD building was quiet again, the employer
stopped by with some strange new instructions. The three
builders asked no questions. Just listened carefully. The guy
was entitled to get what he wanted. The new instructions
meant a certain amount of work would have to be redone. In
the circumstances, not a problem. Even less of a problem
when the employer offered a cash bonus on top of the bid
price.

The three builders worked fast and it took them less time
than it might have. But it was already evening by the time
they finished. The junior man stayed behind to pack tools and
coil cables. The crew chief and the other guy drove north in
the dark and parked exactly where the employer had told
them to. Got out of their truck and waited in the silence.

"In here," a voice called. The employer. "All the way in
back."

They went in. The place was dark. The guy was waiting
for them, somewhere in the shadows.

"These boards any use to you?" the employer asked.

There was a stack of old pine boards, way in back.

"They're good lumber," the employer said. "Maybe you
can use them. Like recycling, you know?"

There was something else on the ground beside the stack
of boards. Something strange. The two carpenters stared.
Strange humped shapes. The two carpenters stared at the
strange humped shapes, then they stared at each other. Then
they turned around. The employer smiled at them and raised
a dull black automatic.

• • •

THE RESIDENT AGENT at the FBI's remote satellite station was a smart enough guy to realize it was going to be important. He didn't know exactly how or why it was going to be important, but an undercover informant doesn't risk a radio message from a concealed location for no reason. So he copied the details into the FBI computer system. His report flashed across the computer network and lodged in the massive mainframe on the first floor of the FBI's Hoover Building in Washington, D.C. The Hoover Building database handles more new reports in a day than there are seconds, so it took a long moment for the FBI software to scan through and pick out the key words. Once it had done so, it lodged the bulletin high in its memory and waited.

At exactly the same time, the system was logging a message from the FBI Field Office in Chicago. The bureau chief up there, Agent-in-Charge McGrath, was reporting that he'd lost one of his people. Special Agent Holly Johnson was missing, last seen twelve o'clock Chicago time, whereabouts currently unknown, contact attempted but not achieved. And because Holly Johnson was a pretty special case, the message carried an eyes-only code which kept it off every terminal in the building except the one all the way upstairs in the Director's office.

THE DIRECTOR OF the FBI got out of a budget review meeting just before seven-thirty in the evening. He walked back to his office suite and checked his messages. His name was Harland Webster and he had been with the Bureau thirty-six years. He had one more year to run on his term as Director, and then he'd be gone. So he wasn't looking for trouble, but he found it glowing on the monitor of his desktop terminal. He clicked on the report and read it through twice. He sighed at the screen.

"Shit," he said. "Shit, shit, shit."

The report in from McGrath in Chicago was not the worst news Webster had ever had in thirty-six years, but it came pretty damn close. He buzzed the intercom on his desk and his secretary answered.

"Get me McGrath in Chicago," he said.

"He's on line one," his secretary told him. "He's been waiting for you."

Webster grunted and hit the button for line one. Put the call on the speakerphone and leaned back in his chair.

"Mack?" he said. "So what's the story?"

McGrath's voice came in clear from Chicago.

"Hello, chief," he said. "There is no story. Not yet. Maybe we're worrying too early, but I got a bad feeling when she didn't show. You know how it is."

"Sure, Mack," Webster said. "You want to confuse me with some facts?"

"We don't have any facts," McGrath said. "She didn't show for a five o'clock case conference. That struck me as unusual. There were no messages from her anywhere. Her pager and her cell phone are out of commission. I asked around and the last anybody saw of her was about twelve o'clock."

"She was in the office this morning?" Webster asked.

"All morning," McGrath said.

"Any appointments before this five o'clock thing?" Webster said.

"Nothing in her diary," McGrath said. "I don't know what she was doing or where she was doing it."

"Christ, Mack," Webster said. "You were supposed to take care of her. You were supposed to keep her off the damn streets, right?"

"It was her lunchbreak," McGrath said. "What the hell could I do?"

There was a silence in the Director's suite, broken only by the faint hum on the speakerphone. Webster drummed his fingers on his desk.

"What was she working on?" he asked.

"Forget it," McGrath said. "We can assume this is not interference by a Bureau suspect, right? Doesn't make any kind of sense in her case."

Webster nodded to himself.

"In her case, I agree, I guess," he said. "So what else are we looking at?"

"She was injured," McGrath said. "Tore up her knee playing ball. We figure maybe she fell, made it worse, maybe ended up in the ER. We're checking the hospitals now.''

Webster grunted.

"Or else there's a boyfriend we don't know about,''
McGrath said. "Maybe they're in a motel room somewhere,
getting laid.''

"For six hours?'' Webster said. "I should be so lucky.''

There was silence again. Then Webster sat forward.

"OK, Mack,'' he said. "You know what to do. And you
know what not to do, case like hers, right? Keep in touch.
I've got to go to the Pentagon. I'll be back in an hour. Call
me then if you need me.''

Webster broke the connection and buzzed his secretary to
call his car. Then he walked out to his private elevator and
rode down to the underground parking lot. His driver met
him there and they walked together over to the Director's
bulletproof limousine.

"Pentagon,'' Webster said to his driver.

TRAFFIC WASN'T BAD, seven-thirty on a June Monday evening. Took about eleven minutes to do the two and a half
miles. Webster spent the time making urgent calls on his
mobile. Calls to various locations within such a tight geo-
graphical radius that he could probably have reached them
all by shouting. Then the big car came up to the Pentagon
River Entrance and the Marine sentry stepped over. Webster
clicked off his phone and buzzed his window down for the
identification ritual.

"The Director of the FBI,'' he said. "To see the Chairman
of the Joint Chiefs of Staff.''

The sentry snapped a salute and waved the limousine
through. Webster buzzed the window back up and waited for
the driver to stop. Then he got out and ducked in through the
personnel door. Walked through to the Chairman's suite. The
Chairman's secretary was waiting for him.

"Go right through, sir,'' she said. "The General will be
along in a moment.''

Webster walked into the Chairman's office and stood waiting. He looked out through the window. The view was magnificent, but it had a strange metallic tint. The window was
made of one-way bulletproof Mylar. It was a great view, but

the window was on the outside of the building, right next to the River Entrance, so it had to be protected. Webster could see his car, with his driver waiting beside it. Beyond the car was a view of the Capitol, across the Potomac. Webster could see sailboats in the Tidal Basin, with the last of the evening sun glinting low on the water. Not a bad office, Webster thought. Better than mine, he thought.

Meeting with the Chairman of the Joint Chiefs of Staff was a problem for the Director of the FBI. It was one of those Beltway oddities, a meeting where there was no cast-iron ranking. Who was superior? Both were presidential appointees. Both reported to the President through just one intermediary, the Defense Secretary or the Attorney General. The Chairman of the Joint Chiefs of Staff was the highest-ranking military post that the nation had to offer. The Director of the FBI was the highest-ranking law enforcement post. Both men were at the absolute top of their respective greasy poles. But which greasy pole was taller? It was a problem for Webster. In the end, it was a problem for him because the truth was his pole was shorter. He controlled a budget of two billion dollars and about twenty-five thousand people. The Chairman oversaw a budget of two hundred billion and about a million people. Two million, if you added in the National Guard and the Reserves. The Chairman was in the Oval Office about once a week. Webster got there twice a year, if he was lucky. No wonder this guy's office was better.

The Chairman himself was impressive, too. He was a four-star general whose rise had been spectacular. He had come from nowhere and blitzed upward through the Army just about faster than his tailor could sew the ribbons on his uniform. The guy had ended up lopsided with medals. Then he had been hijacked by Washington and moved in and made the place his own, like it was some military objective. Webster heard his arrival in the anteroom and turned to greet him as he came into the office.

"Hello, General," he said.

The Chairman sketched a busy wave and grinned.

"You want to buy some missiles?" he said.

Webster was surprised.

"You're selling them?" he said. "What missiles?"

The Chairman shook his head and smiled.

"Just kidding," he said. "Arms limitation. Russians have gotten rid of a bomber base in Siberia, so now we've got to get rid of the missiles we assigned against it. Treaty compliance, right? Got to play fair. The big stuff, we're selling to Israel. But we've still got about a couple hundred little ones, you know, Stingers, shoulder-launch surface-to-air things. All surplus. Sometimes I think we should sell them to the dope dealers. God knows they've got everything else they want. Better weapons than we've got, most of them."

The Chairman talked his way around to his chair and sat down. Webster nodded. He'd seen Presidents do a similar thing, tell a joke, tell a lighthearted story, man to man, get the ice broken, make the meeting work. The Chairman leaned back and smiled.

"So what can I do for you, Director?" he asked.

"We got a report in from Chicago," Webster said. "Your daughter is missing."

8

By MIDNIGHT IN Chicago, the third-floor conference room was set up as a command center. FBI technicians had swarmed all evening, running phone lines into the room and installing computer terminals in a line down the center of the hardwood table. Now at midnight it was dark and cool and quiet. Shiny blackness outside the wall of glass. No scramble to decide which side of the table was better.

Nobody had gone home. There were seventeen agents sprawled in the leather chairs. Even the Bureau lawyer was still there. No real reason for that, but the guy was feeling the same triple-layered response they all were. The Bureau looks after its own. That was layer number one. The Chicago Field Office looks after Holly Johnson. That was layer number two. Not just because of her connections. That had nothing to do with it. Holly was Holly. And if layer number three was what McGrath wanted, McGrath got. If McGrath was worried about Holly, then they all were worried, and they all were going to stay worried until she was found, safe and sound. So they were all still there. Quiet, and worried. Until McGrath came loudly and cheerfully into the room, making a big entrance, smoking like his life depended on it.

"Good news, people, listen up, listen up," he called out.

He dodged his way through to the head of the table. Murmuring died into sudden silence. Eighteen pairs of eyes followed him.

"We found her," he called out. "We found her, OK? She's safe and well. Panic's over, folks. We can all relax now."

Eighteen voices started talking all at once. All asking the same urgent questions. McGrath held his hands up for quiet, like a nominee at a rally.

"She's in the hospital," he said. "What happened is her surgeon got a window for this afternoon he wasn't expecting. He called her, she went right over, they took her straight to the OR. She's fine, she's convalescing, and she's embarrassed as all hell for the fuss she's caused."

The eighteen voices started up again, and McGrath let them rumble on for a moment. Then he held his hands up again.

"So, panic over, right?" he called out again, smiling.

The rumbling got lighter in tone as relief fueled the voices.

"So, people, home to bed," McGrath said. "Full working day tomorrow, right? But thanks for being here. From me, and from Holly. Means a lot to her. Brogan and Milosevic, you stay awhile, share out her workload for the rest of the week. The rest of you, goodnight, sleep well, and thanks again, gentlemen."

Fifteen agents and the lawyer smiled and yawned and stood up. Jostled cheerfully and noisily out of the room. McGrath and Brogan and Milosevic were left scattered in random seats, far from each other. McGrath walked over in the sudden silence to the door. Closed it quietly. Turned back and faced the other two.

"That was all bullshit," he said. "As I'm sure you both guessed."

Brogan and Milosevic just stared at him.

"Webster called me," McGrath said. "And I'm sure you can both guess why. Major, major D.C. involvement. They're going apeshit down there. VIP kidnap, right? Webster's been given personal responsibility. He wants total secrecy and minimum numbers. He wants everybody up here off this case right now except me plus a team of two. My choice. I picked the two of you, because you know her best. So it's the three of us. We deal direct with Webster, and we don't talk to anybody else at all, OK?"

Brogan stared at him and nodded. Milosevic nodded in turn. They knew they were the obvious choices for the job. But to be chosen by McGrath for any reason was an honor. They knew it, and they knew McGrath knew they knew it. So they nodded again, more firmly. Then there was silence for a long moment. McGrath's cigarette smoke mingled with the silence up near the ceiling. The clock on the wall ticked around toward half past midnight.

"OK," Brogan said finally. "So what now?"

"We work all night, is what," McGrath said. "All day, all night, every day, every night, until we find her."

He glanced at the two of them. Reviewed his choices. An adequate team, he thought. A good mixture. Brogan was older, drier, a pessimist. A compact man with a tidy, ordered approach, laced with enough imagination to make him useful. An untidy private life, with a girlfriend and a couple of ex-wives somewhere, all costing him big bucks and worry, but it never interfered with his work. Milosevic was younger, less intuitive, flashier, but solid. A permanent sidekick, which was not necessarily a fault. A weakness for big expensive four-wheel-drives, but everybody needs some kind of a hobby. Both of them were medium-term Bureau veterans, with mileage on their clocks and scalps on their belts. Both of them were focused, and neither of them ever bitched about the work or the hours. Or the salary, which made them just about unique. An adequate team. They were new to Chicago, but this investigation was not going to stay in Chicago. McGrath was just about sure of that.

"Milo, you figure out her movements," he said. "Every step, every minute from twelve noon."

Milosevic nodded vaguely, like he was already lost in doing that.

"Brogan, background checks," McGrath said. "We need to find some reason here."

Brogan nodded dourly, like he knew the reason was going to be the beginning and the end of the whole thing.

"I start with the old guy?" he asked.

"Obviously," McGrath said. "That's what I would do."

"OK, which one?" Brogan asked.

"Whichever one," McGrath replied. "Your choice."

• • •

SEVENTEEN HUNDRED AND two miles away, another executive decision had been taken. A decision about the third carpenter. The employer drove back to the white building in the crew chief's pickup. The third carpenter had finished up stacking the tools and he took a step forward when he saw the vehicle approaching. Then he stopped in puzzlement when he saw the huge figure at the wheel. He stood, uncertain, while the employer pulled up at the curb and heaved himself out.

"OK?" the employer said to him.

"Where are the guys?" the carpenter asked.

"Something came up," the employer said.

"Problem?" the guy asked.

He went quiet, because he was thinking about his share of the price. A minority share, for sure, because he was the junior guy, but a minority share of that price was still more cash than he'd seen in a long time.

"You got a saw there?" the employer asked.

The guy just looked at him.

"Dumb question, right?" the employer said. "You're a carpenter and I'm asking you if you got a saw? Just show me your best saw."

The guy stood still for a moment, then he ducked down and pulled a power saw from the stack of tools. A big thing in dull metal, wicked circular blade, fresh sawdust caked all around it.

"Crosscut?" the employer asked. "Good for ripping through real tough stuff?"

The guy nodded.

"It does the job," he said, cautiously.

"OK, here's the deal," the employer said. "We need a demonstration."

"Of the saw?" the guy asked.

"Of the room," the employer said.

"The room?" the guy repeated.

"Supposed to be nobody can get out of it," the employer said. "That's the idea behind it, right?"

"You designed it," the guy said.

"But did you build it right?" the employer said. "That's

what I'm asking here. We need a trial run. A demonstration to prove it serves its purpose."

"OK, how?" the guy asked.

"You go in there," the employer said. "See if you can get out by morning. You built it, right? So you know all the weak spots. If anybody can get out, you can, that's for damn sure, right?"

The guy was quiet for a long moment. Trying to understand.

"And if I can?" he asked.

The employer shrugged.

"Then you don't get paid," he said. "Because you didn't build it right."

The guy went quiet again. Wondering if the employer was joking.

"You spot the flaw in my logic?" the employer asked. "The way you're figuring it right now, it's in your interest just to sit there on your ass all night, then tomorrow you say to me no sir, I couldn't get out of there, no sir, not at all."

The carpenter laughed a short nervous laugh.

"That's how I was thinking," he said.

"So what you need is an incentive," the employer said. "Understand? To make sure you try real hard to get out."

The carpenter glanced up at the blanked-off second-story corner. When he glanced back down, there was a dull black automatic in the employer's hand.

"There's a sack in the truck," the employer said. "Go get it, OK?"

The carpenter just looked around, astonished. The employer pointed the gun at his head.

"Get the sack," he said quietly.

There was nothing in the pickup bed. There was a burlap sack on the passenger seat. Wrapped into a package maybe a foot and a half long. It was heavy. Felt like reaching into a freezer at the market and pulling out a side of pig.

"Open it up," the employer called. "Take a look."

The carpenter peeled back the burlap. First thing he saw was a finger. Icy white, because the blood had drained. Yellow workman's calluses standing out, big and obvious.

"I'm going to put you in the room now," the employer called to him. "You don't get out by morning, I'm going to do that to you, OK? With your own damn saw, because mine went dull doing those."

9

REACHER LAY QUIETLY on the dirty straw in his stall in the cow barn. Not asleep, but his body was shut down to the point where he might as well have been. Every muscle was relaxed and his breathing was slow and even. His eyes were closed because the barn was dark and there was nothing to see. But his mind was wide awake. Not racing, but just powering steadily along with that special nighttime intensity you get in the absence of any other distractions.

He was doing two things at once. First, he was keeping track of time. It was nearly two hours since he had last looked at his watch, but he knew what time it was to within about twenty seconds. It was an old skill, born of many long wakeful nights on active service. When you're waiting for something to happen, you close your body down like a beach house in winter and you let your mind lock onto the steady pace of the passing seconds. It's like suspended animation. It saves energy and it lifts the responsibility for your heartbeat away from your unconscious brain and passes it on to some kind of a hidden clock. Makes a huge black space for thinking in. But it keeps you just awake enough to be ready for whatever you need to be ready for. And it means you always know what time it is.

The second simultaneous thing Reacher was doing was playing around with a little mental arithmetic. He was multiplying big numbers in his head. He was thirty-seven years and eight months old, just about to the day. Thirty-seven multiplied by three hundred and sixty-five was thirteen thousand five hundred and five. Plus twelve days for twelve leap years was thirteen thousand five hundred and seventeen. Eight months counting from his birthday in October forward to this date in June was two hundred and forty-three days. Total of thirteen thousand seven hundred and sixty days since he was born. Thirteen thousand seven hundred and sixty days, thirteen thousand seven hundred and sixty nights. He was trying to place this particular night somewhere on that endless scale. In terms of how bad it was.

Truth was, it wasn't the best night he had ever passed, but it was a long way from being the worst. A very long way. The first four or so years of his life, he couldn't remember anything at all, which left about twelve thousand three hundred nights to account for. Probability was, this particular night was up there in the top third. Without even trying hard, he could have reeled off thousands of nights worse than this one. Tonight, he was warm, comfortable, uninjured, not under any immediate threat, and he'd been fed. Not well, but he felt that came from a lack of skill rather than from active malice. So physically he had no complaints.

Mentally, it was a different story. He was suspended in a vacuum just as impenetrable as the darkness inside the cow barn. The problem was the total lack of information. He was not a guy who necessarily felt uncomfortable with some lack of information. He was the son of a Marine officer and he had lived the military life literally all the way since birth. Therefore confusion and unpredictability were what he was accustomed to. But tonight, there was just too much missing.

He didn't know where he was. Whether by accident or by design, the three kidnappers had given him absolutely no clue at all where they were headed. It made him feel adrift. His particular problem was, living the military life from birth, out of those thirteen thousand seven hundred and sixty days of his life, he'd spent probably much less than a fifth of them actually inside the United States. He was as American as the President, but he'd lived and served all over the world most of his life. Outside the United States. It had left him knowing his own country about as well as the average seven-year-old knows it. So he couldn't decode the subtle rhythms and feel and smells of America as well as he wanted to. It was possible that somebody else could interpret the unseen contours of the invisible landscape or the feel of the air or the temperature of the night and say yes, I'm in this state now or that state now. It was possible people could do that. But Reacher couldn't. It gave him a problem.

Added to that he had no idea who the kidnappers were. Or what their business was. Or what their intentions were. He'd studied them closely, every opportunity he'd had. Conclusions were difficult. The evidence was all contradictory. Three of them, youngish, maybe somewhere between thirty and thirty-five, fit, trained to act together with a measure of efficiency. They were almost military, but not quite. They were organized, but not official. Their appearance shrieked: amateurs.

Because they were so neat. They all had new clothes, plain chain store cottons and poplins, fresh haircuts. Their weapons were fresh out of the box. The Glocks were brand-new. The shotgun was brand-new, packing grease still visible. Those factors meant they weren't any kind of professionals. Because professionals do this stuff every day. Whoever they are, Special Forces, CIA, FBI, detectives, it's their job. They wear working clothes. They use weapons they signed out last year, the year before, tried and trusted weapons, chipped weapons, scratched weapons, working tools. Put three professionals together on any one day, and you'll see last night's pizza on one guy's shirt, another guy won't have shaved, the third guy will be wearing the awful old pants his buddies make jokes about behind his back. It's possible you'll see a new jacket once in a while, or a fresh gun, or new shoes, but the chances of seeing everything new all at once on three working professionals on the same day are so slim as to be absurd.

And their attitude betrayed them. Competent, but jumpy, uptight, hostile, rude, tense. Trained to some degree, but not practiced. Not experienced. They'd rehearsed the theory, and they were smart enough to avoid any gross errors, but they didn't have the habituation of professionals. Therefore these three were some kind of amateurs. And they had kidnapped a brand-new FBI agent. Why? What the hell could a brand-new FBI agent have done to anybody? Reacher had no idea. And the brand-new FBI agent in question wasn't saying. Just another component he couldn't begin to figure. But not the biggest component. The biggest component he couldn't begin to figure was why the hell he was still there.

He had no problem with how he had gotten grabbed up in the first place. Just a freak of chance had put him alongside Holly Johnson at the exact time the snatch was going down. He was comfortable with that. He understood freak chances. Life was built out of freak chances, however much people would like to pretend otherwise. And he never wasted time speculating about how things might have been different, if this and if that. Obviously if he'd been strolling on that particular Chicago street a minute earlier or a minute later, he'd have been right past that dry cleaner and never known a damn thing about all this. But he hadn't been strolling a minute earlier or a minute later, and the freak chance had happened, and he wasn't about to waste his time wondering where he would be now if it hadn't.

But what he did need to pin down was why he was still there, just over fourteen hours later, according to the clock inside his head. He'd had two marginal chances and one cast-iron certainty of getting out. Right away, on the street, he could have made it. Probably. The possibility of collateral damage had stopped him. Then in the abandoned lot, getting into the white truck, he might have made it. Probably. Three against one, both times, but they were three amateurs against Jack Reacher, and he felt comfortable enough about those odds.

The cast-iron certainty was he could have been out of the cow barn, say an hour after the three guys returned from the gas station with the truck. He could have slipped the cuff again, climbed the wall and dropped down into the barnyard and been away. Just jogged over to the road and walked away and disappeared. Why hadn't he done that?

He lay there in the huge inky blackness of relaxation and realized it was Holly that was keeping him there. He hadn't bailed out because he couldn't take the risk. The three guys could have panicked and wasted her and run. Reacher didn't want that to happen. Holly was a smart, spirited woman.

Sharp, impatient, confident, tough as hell. Attractive, in a shy, unforced sort of a way. Dark, slim, a lot of intelligence and energy. Great eyes. Eyes were Reacher's thing. He was lost in a pair of pretty eyes.

But it wasn't her eyes that were doing it to him. Not her looks. Or her intelligence or her personality. It was her knee. That's what was doing it to him. Her guts and her dignity. The sight of a good-looking spirited woman cheerfully fighting an unaccustomed disability seemed like a brave and noble thing to Reacher. It made her his type of person. She was coping with it. She was doing it well. She wasn't complaining. She wasn't asking for his help. And because she wasn't asking for it, she was going to get it.

10

FIVE-THIRTY TUESDAY MORNING FBI Special Agent Brogan was alone in the third-floor meeting room, using one of
the newly installed phone lines for an early call to his girlfriend. Five-thirty in the morning is not the best time to deliver an apology for a broken date from the night before, but
Brogan had been very busy, and he anticipated being busier
still. So he made the call. He woke her and told her he had
been tied up, and probably would be for the rest of the week.
She was sleepy and annoyed, and made him repeat it all
twice. Then she chose to interpret the message as a cowardly
prelude to some kind of a brush-off. Brogan got annoyed in
turn. He told her the Bureau had to come first. Surely she
understood that? It was not the best point to be making to a
sleepy annoyed woman at five-thirty in the morning. They
had a short row and Brogan hung up, depressed.

His partner Milosevic was alone in his own office cubicle.
Slumped in his chair, also depressed. His problem was a lack
of imagination. It was his biggest weakness. McGrath had
told him to trace Holly Johnson's every move from noon
yesterday. But he hadn't come up with anything. He had seen
her leaving the FBI building. Stepping out of the door, onto
the street, forearm jammed into the curved metal clip of her
hospital cane. He had seen her getting that far. But then the
picture just went blank. He'd thought hard all night, and told
McGrath nothing.

Five-forty, he went to the bathroom and got more coffee. Still miserable. He walked back to his desk. Sat down, lost in thought for a long time. Then he glanced at the heavy gold watch on his wrist. Checked the time. Smiled. Felt better. Thought some more. Checked his watch again. He nodded to himself. Now he could tell McGrath where Holly Johnson had gone at twelve o'clock yesterday.

SEVENTEEN HUNDRED AND two miles away, panic had set in. Numb shock had carried the carpenter through the first hours. It had made him weak and acquiescent. He had let the employer hustle him up the stairs and into the room. Then numb shock had made him waste his first hours, just sitting and staring. Then he had started up with a crazy optimism that this whole thing was some kind of bad Halloween joke. That made him waste his next hours convinced nothing was going to happen. But then, like prisoners everywhere locked up alone in the cold small hours of the night, all his defenses had stripped away and left him shaking and desperate with panic.

With half his time gone, he burst into frantic action. But he knew it was hopeless. The irony was crushing him. They had worked hard on this room. They had built it right. Dollar signs had danced in front of their eyes. They had cut no corners. They had left out all their usual shoddy carpenter's tricks. Every single board was straight and tight. Every single nail was punched way down below the grain. There were no windows. The door was solid. It was hopeless. He spent an hour running around the room like a madman. He ran his rough palms over every square inch of every surface. Floor, ceiling, walls. It was the best job they had ever done. He ended up crouched in a corner, staring at his hands, crying.

THE DRY CLEANER'S," McGrath said. "That's where she went."

He was in the third-floor conference room. Head of the table, seven o'clock, Tuesday morning. Opening a fresh pack of cigarettes.

"She did?" Brogan said. "The dry cleaner's?"

McGrath nodded.

"Tell him, Milo," he said.

Milosevic smiled.

"I just remembered," he said. "I've worked with her five weeks, right? Since she busted up her knee? Every Monday lunchtime, she takes in her cleaning. Picks up last week's stuff. No reason for it to be any different yesterday."

"OK," Brogan said. "Which cleaner's?"

Milosevic shook his head.

"Don't know," he said. "She always went on her own. I always offered to do it for her, but she said no, every time, five straight Mondays. OK if I helped her out on Bureau business, but she wasn't about to have me running around after her cleaning. She's a very independent type of a woman."

"But she walked there, right?" McGrath said.

"Right," Milosevic said. "She always walked. With maybe eight or nine things on hangers. So we're safe to conclude the place she used is fairly near here."

Brogan nodded. Smiled. They had some kind of a lead. He pulled the Yellow Pages over and opened it up to D.

"What sort of a radius are we giving it?" he said.

McGrath shrugged.

"Twenty minutes there, twenty minutes back," he said. "That would be about the max, right? With that crutch, I can't see her doing more than a quarter-mile in twenty-minutes. Limping like that? Call it a square, a half-mile on a side, this building in the center. What does that give us?"

Brogan used the AAA street map. He made a crude compass with his thumb and forefinger. Adjusted it to a half-mile according to the scale in the margin. Drew a square across the thicket of streets. Then he flipped back and forth between the map and the Yellow Pages. Ticked off names with his pencil. Counted them up.

"Twenty-one establishments," he said.

McGrath stared at him.

"Twenty-one?" he said. "Are you sure?"

Brogan nodded. Slid the phone book across the shiny hardwood.

"Twenty-one," he said. "Obviously people in this town like to keep their clothes real clean."

"OK," McGrath said. "Twenty-one places. Hit the road, guys."

Brogan took ten addresses and Milosevic took eleven. McGrath issued them both with large color blowups of Holly Johnson's file photograph. Then he nodded them out and waited in his chair at the head of the conference room table, next to the telephones, slumped, staring into space, smoking, drumming a worried little rhythm with the blunt end of his pencil.

HE HEARD FAINT sounds much earlier than he thought he should. He had no watch and no windows, but he was certain it was not yet morning. He was certain he had another hour. Maybe two. But he could hear noise. People moving in the street outside. He held his breath and listened. Maybe three or four people. He quartered the room again. Frozen with indecision. He should be pounding and kicking at the new pine boards. He knew that. But he wasn't. Because he knew it was hopeless, and because he felt in his gut he must be silent. He had become sure of that. Convinced. If he was silent, they might leave him alone. They might forget he was in there.

MILOSEVIC FOUND THE right place, the seventh of the eleven establishments on his list. It was just opening up for business, seven-forty in the morning. Just a store-front place, but elegant, not really aimed at the typical commuter's cheap worsteds. It advertised all kinds of specialized processes and custom treatments. There was a Korean woman in charge of the store. Milosevic showed her his FBI shield and placed Holly's file picture flat on the counter in front of her.

"You ever see this person?" he asked her.

The Korean woman looked at the picture, politely, with concentration, her hands clasped together behind her back.

"Sure," she said. "That's Miss Johnson, comes in every Monday."

Milosevic stepped closer to the counter. He leaned up close to the woman.

"She come in yesterday?" Milosevic asked her.

The woman thought about it and nodded.

"Sure," she said. "Like I told you, she comes in every Monday."

"What kind of time?" he asked.

"Lunch hour," the woman said. "Always lunch hour."

"About twelve?" he said. "Twelve-thirty, something like that?"

"Sure," the woman said. "Always lunch hour on a Monday."

"OK, yesterday," Milosevic said. "What happened?"

The woman shrugged.

"Nothing happened," she said. "She came in, she took her garments, she paid, she left some garments to be cleaned."

"Anybody with her?" he asked.

"Nobody with her," the woman said. "Nobody ever with her."

"Which direction was she headed?" Milosevic asked.

The woman pointed back toward the Federal Building.

"She came from that direction," she said.

"I didn't ask you where she came from," Milosevic said. "Where did she head when she left?"

The woman paused.

"I didn't see," she said. "I took her garments through to the back. I heard the door open, but I couldn't see where she went. I was in back."

"You just grabbed her stuff?" Milosevic said. "Rushed through to the back before she was out of here?"

The woman faltered, like she was being accused of an impoliteness.

"Not rushed," she said. "Miss Johnson was walking slow. Bad leg, right? I felt I shouldn't stare at her. I felt she was embarrassed. I walked her clothes through to the back so she wouldn't feel I was watching her."

Milosevic nodded and tilted his head back and sighed up at the ceiling. Saw a video camera mounted high above the counter.

"What's that?" he said.

The Korean woman twisted and followed his gaze.

"Security," she said. "Insurance company says we got to have it."

"Does it work?" he asked.

"Sure it works," the woman said. "Insurance company says it's got to."

"Does it run all the time?" Milosevic asked.

The woman nodded and giggled.

"Sure it does," she said. "It's running right now. You'll be on the tape."

Milosevic checked his watch.

"I need yesterday's tape," he said. "Immediately."

The woman faltered again. Milosevic pulled his shield for the second time.

"This is an FBI investigation," he said. "Official federal business. I need that tape, right now, OK?"

The woman nodded and held up her hand to make him wait. Stepped through a door to the rear of the establishment. Came back out after a long moment with a blast of chemical smell and a videocassette in her hand.

"You let me have it back, OK?" she said. "Insurance company says we got to keep them for a month."

MILOSEVIC TOOK IT straight in, and by eight-thirty the Bureau technicians were swarming all over the third-floor conference room again, hooking up a standard VHS player to the bank of monitors piled down the middle of the long table. There was a problem with a fuse, and then the right wire proved too short, so a computer had to be moved to allow the video player to get nearer to the center of the table. Then the head tech handed McGrath the remote and nodded.

"All yours, chief," he said.

McGrath sent him out of the room and the three agents crowded around the screens, waiting for the picture to roll. The screens faced the wall of windows, so they all three had their backs to the glass. But at that time of day, there was no danger of anybody getting uncomfortable, because right then the bright morning sun was blasting the other side of the building.

THAT SAME SUN rolled on seventeen hundred and two miles from Chicago and made it bright morning outside the white building. He knew it had come. He could hear the quiet ticking as the old wood frame warmed through. He could hear muffled voices outside, below him, down at street level. The sound of people starting a new day.

His fingernails were gone. He had found a gap where two boards were not hard together. He had forced his fingertips down and levered with all his strength. His nails had torn off, one after the other. The board had not moved. He had scuttled backward into a corner and curled up on the floor. He had sucked his bloodied fingers and now his mouth was smeared all around with blood, like a child's with cake.

He heard footsteps on the staircase. A big man, moving lightly. The sound halted outside the door. The lock clicked back. The door opened. The employer looked in at him. Bloated face, two nickel-sized red spots burning high on his cheeks.

"You're still here," he said.

The carpenter was paralyzed. Couldn't move, couldn't speak.

"You failed," the employer said.

There was silence in the room. The only sound was the slow ticking of the wood frame as the morning sun slid over the roof.

"So what shall we do now?" the employer asked.

The carpenter just stared blankly at him. Didn't move. Then the employer smiled a relaxed, friendly smile. Like he was suddenly surprised about something.

"You think I meant it?" he said, gently.

The carpenter blinked. Shook his head, slightly, hopefully.

"You hear anything?" the employer asked him.

The carpenter listened hard. He could hear the quiet ticking of the wood, the song of the forest birds, the silent sound of sunny morning air.

"You were just kidding around?" he asked.

His voice was a dry croak. Relief and hope and dread were jamming his tongue into the roof of his mouth.

"Listen," the employer said.

The carpenter listened. The frame ticked, the birds sang, the warm air sighed. He heard nothing else. Silence. Then he heard a click. Then he heard a whine. It started slow and quiet and stabilized up at a familiar loud pitch. It was a sound he knew. It was the sound of a big power saw being run up to speed.

"Now do you think I meant it?" the employer screamed.

11

Holly JOHNSON HAD been mildly disappointed by Reacher's assessment of the cash value of her wardrobe. Reacher had said he figured she had maybe fifteen or twenty outfits, four hundred bucks an outfit, maybe eight grand in total. Truth was she had thirty-four business suits in her closet. She'd worked three years on Wall Street. She had eight grand tied up in the shoes alone. Four hundred bucks was what she had spent on a blouse, and that was when she felt driven by native common sense to be a little economical.

She liked Armani. She had thirteen of his spring suits. Spring clothes from Milan were just about right for most of the Chicago summer. Maybe in the really fierce heat of August she'd break out her Moschino shifts, but June and July, September too if she was lucky, her Armanis were the thing. Her favorites were the dark peach shades she'd bought in her last year in the brokerage house. Some mysterious Italian blend of silks. Cut and tailored by people whose ancestors had been fingering fine materials for hundreds of years. They look at it and consider it and cut it and it just falls into marvelous soft shapes. Then they market it and a Wall Street broker buys it and loves it and is still wearing it two years into the future when she's a new FBI agent and she gets snatched off a Chicago street. She's still wearing it eighteen hours later after a sleepless night on the filthy straw in a cow barn. By that point, the thing is no longer something that Armani would recognize.

The three kidnappers had returned with the truck and backed it into the cow barn's central concrete aisle. Then they had locked the barn door and disappeared. Holly guessed they had spent the night in the farmhouse. Reacher had slept quietly in his stall, chained to the railing, while she tossed and turned in the straw, sleepless, thinking urgently about him.

His safety was her responsibility. He was an innocent passerby, caught up in her business. Whatever else lay ahead for her, she had to take care of him. That was her duty. He was her burden. And he was lying. Holly was absolutely certain he was not a blues club doorman. And she was pretty certain what he was. The Johnson family was a military family. Because of her father, Holly had lived on Army bases her whole life, right up to Yale. She knew the Army. She knew the soldiers. She knew the types and she knew Reacher was one. To her practiced eye, he looked like one. Acted like one. Reacted like one. It was possible a doorman could pick locks and climb walls like an ape, but if a doorman did go ahead and do that, he would do it with an air of unfamiliarity and daring and breathlessness which would be quite distinctive. He wouldn't do it like it came as naturally as blinking. Reacher was a quiet, contained man, relaxed, fit, clearly trained to the point of some kind of superhuman calm. He was probably ten years older than she was, but somewhere less than forty, about six feet five, huge, maybe two-twenty, blue eyes, thinning fair hair. Big enough to be a doorman, and old enough to have been around, that was for sure, but he was a soldier. A soldier, claiming to be a doorman. But why?

Holly had no idea. She just lay there, uncomfortable, listening to his quiet breathing, twenty feet away. Doorman or soldier, ten years older or not, it was her responsibility to get him to safety. She didn't sleep. Too busy thinking, and her knee was too painful. At eight-thirty on her watch, she heard him wake up. Just a subtle change in the rhythm of his breathing.

"Good morning, Reacher," she called out.

"Morning, Holly," he said. "They're coming back."

It was silent, but after a long moment she heard footsteps outside. Climbs like an ape, hears like a bat, she thought. Some doorman.

"You OK?" Reacher called to her.

She didn't answer. His welfare was her responsibility, not the other way around. She heard a rattle as the barn door was unlocked. It rolled open and daylight flooded in. She caught a glimpse of empty green country. Pennsylvania, maybe, she thought. The three kidnappers walked in and the door was pulled shut.

"Get up, bitch," the leader said to her.

She didn't move. She was seized by an overpowering desire not to be put back inside the truck. Too dark, too uncomfortable, too tedious. She didn't know if she could take another day in there, swaying, jolting, above all totally unaware of where the hell she was being taken, or why, or by who. Instinctively, she grabbed the metal railing and held on, arm tensed, like she was going to put up a struggle. The leader stood still and pulled out his Glock. Looked down at her.

"Two ways of doing this," he said. "The easy way, or the hard way."

She didn't reply. Just sat there in the straw and held on tight to the railing. The ugly driver took three steps nearer and started smiling, staring at her breasts again. She felt naked and revolted under his gaze.

"Your choice, bitch," the leader said.

She heard Reacher moving in his stall.

"No, it's your choice," she heard him call to the guy. "We need to be a little mutual here. Cooperative, right? You want us to get back in your truck, you need to make it worth our while."

His voice was calm and low. Holly stared across at him. Saw him sitting there, chained up, unarmed, facing a loaded automatic weapon, totally powerless by any reasonable definition of the word, three hostile men staring down at him.

"We need some breakfast," Reacher said. "Toast, with grape jelly. And coffee, but make it a lot stronger than last night's crap, OK? Good coffee is very important to me. You need to understand that. Then put a couple of mattresses in the truck. One queen-size, one twin. Make us a sofa in there. Then we'll get in.''

There was total silence. Holly glanced between the two men. Reacher was fixing the leader with a calm, level gaze from the floor. His blue eyes never blinked. The leader was staring down at him. Tension visible in the air. The driver had torn his gaze away from her body and was looking at Reacher. Anger in his eyes. Then the leader snapped around and nodded the other two out of the barn with him. Holly heard the door locking behind them.

''You eat toast?'' Reacher said to her.

She was too breathless to answer.

''When they bring it, send it back,'' he said. ''Make them do it over. Say it's too pale or too burnt or something.''

''What the hell do you think you're doing?'' she asked.

''Psychology,'' Reacher said. ''We need to start getting some dominance here. Situation like this, it's very important.''

She stared at him.

''Just do it, OK?'' he said, calmly.

SHE DID IT. The jumpy guy brought the toast. It was just about perfect, but she rejected it. She looked at it with the disdain she'd use on a sloppy balance sheet and said it was too well-done. She was standing with all her weight on one foot, looking like a mess, dung all over her peach Armani, but she managed enough haughty contempt to intimidate the guy. He went back to the farmhouse kitchen and made more.

It came with a pot of strong coffee and Holly and Reacher ate their separate breakfasts, chains clanking, twenty feet apart, while the other two guys hauled mattresses into the barn. One queen, one twin. They pulled them up into the back of the truck and laid the queen out on the floor and stood the twin at right angles to it, up against the back of the cab bulkhead. Holly watched them do it and felt a whole lot better about the day. Then she suddenly realized exactly where Reacher's psychology had been aimed. Not just at the three kidnappers. At her, too. He didn't want her to get into a fight. Because she'd lose. He'd risked doing what he'd done to defuse a hopeless confrontation. She was amazed. Totally amazed. She thought blankly: for Christ's sake, this guy's got it ass backward. He's trying to take care of me.

"You want to tell us your names?" Reacher asked, calmly. "We're spending some time together, we can be a little civilized about it, right?"

Holly saw the leader just looking at him. The guy made no reply.

"We've seen your faces," Reacher said. "Telling us your names isn't going to do you any harm. And we might as well try to get along."

The guy thought about it and nodded.

"Loder," he said.

The little jumpy guy shifted feet.

"Stevie," he said.

Reacher nodded. Then the ugly driver realized all four were looking at him. He ducked his head.

"I'm not telling you my name," he said. "Hell should I?"

"And let's be real clear," the guy called Loder said. "Civilized is not the same thing as friendly, right?"

Holly saw him aim his Glock at Reacher's head and hold it there for a long moment. Nothing in his face. Not the same thing as friendly. Reacher nodded. A small cautious movement. They left their toast plates and their coffee mugs lying on the straw and the guy called Loder unlocked their chains. They met in the central aisle. Two Glocks and a shotgun aimed at them. The ugly driver leering. Reacher looked him in the eye and ducked down and picked Holly up like she weighed nothing at all. Carried her the ten paces to the truck. Put her down gently inside. They crawled forward together to the improvised sofa. Got themselves comfortable.

The truck's rear doors slammed and locked. Holly heard the big barn door open up. The truck's engine turned over and caught. They drove out of the barn and bounced a hundred and fifty yards over the rough track. Turned an invisible right angle and cruised straight and slow down a road for fifteen minutes.

"We aren't in Pennsylvania," Holly said. "Roads are too straight. Too flat."

Reacher just shrugged at her in the dark.

"We aren't in handcuffs anymore, either," he said. "Psychology."

12

"HELL IS THIS?" Agent-in-Charge McGrath said.

He thumbed the remote and rewound the tape. Then he pressed play and watched it again. But what he saw meant nothing at all. The video screens were filled with jerky speeding images and shashy white snow.

"Hell is going on here?" he asked again.

Brogan crowded in and shook his head. Milosevic pushed closer to look. He'd brought the tape in, so he felt personally responsible for it. McGrath hit rewind again and tried once more. Same result. Just a blur of disjointed flashing pictures.

"Get the damn tech guy back in here," he shouted.

Milosevic used the phone on the credenza next to the coffeepot. Called upstairs to tech services. The head tech was in the room within a minute. The tone of Milosevic's voice had told him to hurry more effectively than any words could have.

"Damn tape won't run properly," McGrath told him.

The technician took the remote in his hand with that blend of familiarity and unfamiliarity that tech guys use the world over. They're all at home with complex equipment, but each individual piece has its own peculiarities. He peered at the buttons and pressed rewind, firmly, with a chewed thumb. The tape whirred back and he pressed play and watched the disjointed stream of flashing images and video snow.

"Can you fix that?" McGrath asked him.

The tech stopped the tape and hit rewind again. Shook his head.

"It's not broken," he said. "That's how it's supposed to be. Typical cheap surveillance video. What it does is record a freeze-frame, probably every ten seconds or so. Just one frame, every ten seconds. Like a sequence of snapshots."

"Why?" McGrath asked him.

"Cheap and easy," the guy said. "You can get a whole day on one tape that way. Low-cost, and you don't have to remember to change the cassette every three hours. You just change it in the morning. And assuming a stickup takes longer than ten seconds to complete, you've got the perp's face right there on tape, at least once."

"OK," McGrath said impatiently. "So how do we use it?"

The tech used two fingers together. Pressed play and freeze at the same time. Up on the screen came a perfect black-and-white still picture of an empty store. In the bottom left corner was Monday's date and the time, seven thirty-five in the morning. The tech held the remote out to McGrath and pointed to a small button.

"See this?" he said. "Frame-advance button. Press this and the tape rolls on to the next still. Usually for sports, right? Hockey? You can see the puck go right in the net. Or for porn. You can see whatever you need to see. But on this type of a system, it jumps you ahead ten seconds. Like on to the next snapshot, right?"

McGrath calmed down and nodded.

"Why's it in black and white?" he said.

"Cheap camera," the tech guy said. "The whole thing is a cheap system. They only put them in because the insurance companies tell them they got to."

He handed the remote to McGrath and headed back for the door.

"You want anything else, you let me know, OK?" he called.

He got no reply because everybody was staring at the screen as McGrath started inching his way through the tape. Every time he hit the frame-advance button, a broad band of white snow scrolled down the screen and unveiled a new picture, same aspect, same angle, same dim monochrome gray, but with the time code at the bottom jumped ahead ten seconds. The third frame showed a woman behind the counter. Milosevic touched the screen with his finger.

"That's the woman I spoke to," he said.

McGrath nodded.

"Wide field of view," he said. "You can see all the way from behind the counter right out into the street."

"Wide-angle lens on the camera," Brogan said. "Like a fisheye sort of thing. The owner can see everything. He can see the customers coming in and out, and he can see if the help is fiddling the register."

McGrath nodded again and trawled through Monday morning, ten seconds at a time. Customers jumped in and out of shot. The woman behind the counter jumped from side to side, fetching and carrying and ringing up the payments. Outside, cars flashed in and out of view.

"Fast-forward to twelve o'clock," Milosevic said. "This is taking way too long."

McGrath nodded and fiddled with the remote. The tape whirred forward. He pressed stop and play and freeze and came up with four o'clock in the afternoon.

"Shit," he said.

He wound back and forward a couple of times and came up with eleven forty-three and fifty seconds.

"Close as we're going to get," he said.

He kept his finger hard on the frame-advance button and the white snow scrolled continuously down the screen. One hundred and fifty-seven frames later, he stopped.

"There she is," he said.

Milosevic and Brogan shouldered together for a closer look. The still frame showed Holly Johnson on the far right of the picture. She was outside, on the sidewalk, crutch in one hand, clothes on hangers in the other. She was hauling the door open with a spare finger. The time in the bottom left of the frame was stopped at ten minutes and ten seconds past twelve noon.

"OK," McGrath said quietly. "So let's see."

He hit the button and Holly jumped halfway over to the counter. Even frozen on the misty monochrome screen, her awkward posture was plain to see. McGrath hit the button again and the snow rolled over and Holly was at the counter. Ten seconds later the Korean woman was there with her. Ten seconds after that, Holly had folded back a hem on one of her suits and was showing the woman something. Probably the position of a particular stain. The two women stayed like that for a couple of minutes, heads together for twelve frames, jumping slightly from one shot to the next. Then the Korean woman was gone and the clothes were off the counter and Holly was standing alone for five frames. Fifty seconds. Behind her on the left, a car nosed into shot on the second frame and stayed there for the next three, parked at the curb.

Then the woman was back with an armful of clean clothes in bags. She was frozen in the act of laying them flat on the counter. Ten seconds later she had torn five tags off the hangers. Ten seconds after that, she had another four lined up next to the register.

"Nine outfits," McGrath said.

"That's about right," Milosevic said. "Five for work, Monday to Friday, and I guess four for evening wear, right?"

"What about the weekend?" Brogan said. "Maybe it's five for work, two for evening wear and two at the weekend?"

"Probably wears jeans at the weekend," Milosevic said. "Jeans and a shirt. Just throws them in the machine, maybe."

"God's sake, does it matter?" McGrath said.

He pressed the button and the Korean woman's fingers were caught dancing over the register keys. The next two stills showed Holly paying in cash and accepting a couple of dollars change.

"How much is all that costing her?" Brogan asked out loud.

"Nine garments?" Milosevic said. "Best part of fifty bucks a week, that's for damn sure. I saw the price list in there. Specialized processes and gentle chemicals and all."

The next frame showed Holly starting toward the exit door on the left of the picture. The top of the Korean woman's head was visible, on her way through to the back of the store. The time was showing at twelve fifteen exactly. McGrath hitched his chair closer and stuck his face a foot from the glowing monochrome screen.

"OK," he said. "So where did you go now, Holly?"

She had the nine cleaned garments in her left hand. She was holding them up, awkwardly, so they wouldn't drag on the floor. Her right elbow was jammed into the curved metal clip of her crutch, but her hand wasn't gripping the handle. The next frame showed it reaching out to push the door open. McGrath hit the button again.

"Christ," he shouted.

Milosevic gasped out loud and Brogan looked stunned. There was no doubt about what they were seeing. The next frame showed an unknown man attacking Holly Johnson. He was tall and heavy. He was seizing her crutch with one hand and her cleaning with the other. No doubt about it. Both his arms were extended and he was taking her crutch and her cleaning away from her. He was caught in a perfect snapshot through the glass door. The three agents stared at him. There was total silence in the conference room. Then McGrath hit the button again. The time code jumped ahead ten seconds. There was another gasp as they caught their breath simultaneously.

Holly Johnson was suddenly surrounded by a triangle of three men. The tall guy who had attacked her had been joined by two more. The tall guy had Holly's cleaning slung up over his shoulder and he had seized Holly's arm. He was staring straight up into the store window like he knew a camera was in there. The other two guys were facing Holly head-on.

"They pulled guns on her," McGrath shouted. "Son of a bitch, look at that."

He thumbed the button again until the bar of snow cleared away from the bottom of the frame and the whole picture stabilized into perfect sharpness. The two new guys had their right arms bent at ninety degrees, and there was tension showing in their shoulder muscles.

"The car," Milosevic said. "They're going to put her in the car."

Beyond Holly and the triangle of men was the car which had parked up fourteen frames ago. It was just sitting there at the curb. McGrath hit the button again. The bar of white snow scrolled down. The small knot of people on the screen jumped sideways ten feet. The tall guy who had attacked Holly was leading the way into the back of the car. Holly was being pushed in after him by one of the new guys. The other new guy was opening the front passenger door. Inside the car, a fourth man was plainly visible through the side glass, sitting at the wheel.

McGrath hit the button again. The bar of snow scrolled down. The street was empty. The car was gone. Like it had never been there at all.

13

"WE NEED TO talk," Holly said.

"So talk," Reacher replied.

They were sprawled out on the mattresses in the gloom inside the truck, rocking and bouncing, but not much. It was pretty clear they were heading down a highway. After fifteen minutes of a slow straight road, there had been a deceleration, a momentary stop, and a left turn followed by steady acceleration up a ramp. Then a slight sway as the truck nudged left onto the pavement. Then a steady droning cruise, maybe sixty miles an hour, which had continued ever since and was feeling like it would continue forever.

The temperature inside the dark space had slowly climbed higher. Now it was pretty warm. Reacher had taken his shirt off. But the truck had started to cool, from the night in the cow barn, and Reacher felt as long as it kept moving through the air, it was going to be tolerable. The problem would come if they stopped for any length of time. Then the truck would heat up like a pizza oven and it would get as bad as it had gotten the day before.

The twin-sized mattress had been standing upright on its long edge, up against the forward bulkhead, and the queen-size had been flat on the floor, jammed up against it, making a crude sofa. But the ninety-degree angle between the seat and the back had made the whole thing uncomfortable. So Reacher had slid the queen-size backward, with Holly riding on it like a sled, and laid the twin flat next to it. Now they had an eight-foot by six-six flat padded area. They were lying down on their backs, heads together so they could talk, bodies apart in a decorous V shape, rocking gently with the motion of the ride.

"You should do what I tell you," Holly said. "You should have gotten out."

He made no reply.

"You're a burden to me," she said. "You understand that? I've got enough on my hands here without having to worry about you."

He didn't reply. They lay rocking in silence. He could smell yesterday morning's shampoo in her hair.

"So you've got to do what I tell you from now on," she said. "Are you listening to me? I just can't afford to be worrying about you."

He turned his head to look at her, close up. She was worrying about him. It came as a big surprise, out of nowhere. A shock. Like being on a train, stopped next to another train in a busy railroad station. Your train begins to move. It picks up speed. And then all of a sudden it's not your train moving. It's the other train. Your train was stationary all the time. Your frame of reference was wrong. He thought his train was moving. She thought hers was.

"I don't need your help," she said. "I've already got all the help I need. You know how the Bureau works? You know what the biggest crime in the world is? Not bombing, not terrorism, not racketeering. The biggest crime in the world is messing with Bureau personnel. The Bureau looks after its own."

Reacher stayed quiet for a spell. Then he smiled.

"So then we're both OK," he said. "We just lay back here, and pretty soon a bunch of agents is going to come bursting in to rescue us."

"I trust my people," Holly said to him.

There was silence again. The truck droned on for a couple of minutes. Reacher ticked off the distance in his head. About four hundred fifty miles from Chicago, maybe. East, west, north, or south. Holly gasped and used both hands to shift her leg.

"Hurting?" Reacher said.

"When it gets out of line," she said. "When it's straight, it's OK."

"Which direction are we headed?" he asked.

"Are you going to do what I tell you?" she asked.

"Is it getting hotter or colder?" he said. "Or staying the same?"

She shrugged.

"Can't tell," she said. "Why?"

"North or south, it should be getting hotter or colder," he said. "East or west, it should be staying more or less the same."

"Feels the same to me," she said. "But inside here, you can't really tell."

"Highway feels fairly empty," Reacher said. "We're not pulling out to pass people. We're not getting slowed down by anybody. We're just cruising."

"So?" Holly said.

"Might mean we're not going east," he said. "There's a kind of barrier, right? Cleveland to Pittsburgh to Baltimore. Like a frontier. Gets much busier. We'd be hitting more traffic. What is it, Tuesday? About eleven o'clock in the morning? Roads feel too empty for the East."

Holly nodded.

"So we're going north or west or south," she said.

"In a stolen truck," he said. "Vulnerable."

"Stolen?" she said. "How do you know that?"

"Because the car was stolen too," he said.

"How do you know that?" she repeated.

"Because they burned it," he said.

Holly rolled her head and looked straight at him.

"Think about it," he said. "Think about their plan. They came to Chicago in their own vehicle. Maybe some time ago. Could have taken them a couple of weeks to stake you out. Maybe three."

"Three weeks?" she said. "You think they were watching me three weeks?"

"Probably three," he said. "You went to the cleaners every Monday, right? Once a week? Must have taken them a while to confirm that pattern. But they couldn't grab you in their own vehicle. Too easy to trace, and it probably had windows and all, not suitable for long-distance transport of a kidnap victim. So I figure they stole this truck, in Chicago, probably yesterday morning. Painted over whatever writing was on the side. You notice the patch of white paint? Fresh, didn't match the rest? They disguised it, maybe changed the plates. But it was still a hot truck, right? And it was their getaway vehicle. So they didn't want to risk it on the street. And people getting into the back of a truck looks weird. A car is better. So they stole the black sedan and used that instead. Switched vehicles in that vacant lot, burned the black car, and they're away."

Holly shrugged. Made a face.

"Doesn't prove they stole anything," she said.

"Yes it does," Reacher said. "Who buys a new car with leather seats, knowing they're going to burn it? They'd have bought some old clunker instead."

She nodded, reluctantly.

"Who are these people?" she said, more to herself than to Reacher.

"Amateurs," Reacher said. "They're making one mistake after another."

"Like what?" she said.

"Burning is dumb," he said. "Attracts attention. They think they've been smart, but they haven't. Probability is they burned their original car, as well. I bet they burned it right near where they stole the black sedan."

"Sounds smart enough to me," Holly said.

"Cops notice burning cars," Reacher said. "They'll find the black sedan, they'll find out where it was stolen from, they'll go up there and find their original vehicle, probably still smoldering. They're leaving a trail, Holly. They should have parked both cars in the long-term lot at O'Hare. They would have been there a year before anybody noticed. Or just left them both down on the South Side somewhere, doors open, keys in. Two minutes later, two residents down there got themselves a new motor each. Those cars would never have been seen again. That's how to cover your tracks. Burning feels good, feels like it's real final, but it's dumb as hell."

Holly turned her face back and stared up at the hot metal roof. She was asking herself: Just who the hell is this guy?

14

THIS TIME, MCGRATH did not make the tech chief come down to the third floor. He led the charge himself up to his lab on the sixth, with the videocassette in his hand. He burst in through the door and cleared a space on the nearest table. Laid the cassette in the space like it was made of solid gold. The guy hurried over and looked at it.

"I need photographs made," McGrath told him.

The guy picked up the cassette and took it across to a bank of video machines in the corner. Flicked a couple of switches. Three screens lit up with white snow.

"You tell absolutely nobody what you're seeing, OK?" McGrath said.

"OK," the guy said. "What am I looking for?"

"The last five frames," McGrath said. "That should just about cover it."

The tech chief didn't use a remote. He stabbed at buttons on the machine's own control panel. The tape rolled backward and the story of Holly Johnson's kidnap unfolded in reverse.

"Christ," he said.

He stopped on the frame showing Holly turning away from the counter. Then he inched the tape forward. He jumped Holly to the door, then face-to-face with the tall guy, then into the muzzles of the guns, then to the car. He rolled back and did it for a second time. Then a third.

"Christ," he said again.

"Don't wear the damn tape out," McGrath said. "I want big photographs of those five frames. Lots of copies."

The tech chief nodded slowly.

"I can give you laser prints right now," he said.

He punched a couple of buttons and flicked a couple of switches. Then he ducked away and booted up a computer on a desk across the room. The monitor came up with Holly leaving the dry cleaner's counter. He clicked on a couple of menus.

"OK," he said. "I'm copying it to the hard disk. As a graphics file."

He darted back to the video bank and nudged the tape forward one frame. Came back to the desk and the computer captured the image of Holly making to push open the exit door. He repeated the process three more times. Then he printed all five graphics files on the fastest laser he had. McGrath stood and caught each sheet as it flopped into the output bin.

"Not bad," he said. "I like paper better than video. Like it really exists."

The tech chief gave him a look and peered over his shoulder.

"Definition's OK," he said.

"I want blowups," McGrath told him.

"No problem, now it's in the computer," the tech said. "That's why the computer is better than paper."

He sat down and opened the fourth file. The picture of Holly and the three kidnappers in a tight knot on the sidewalk scrolled onto the screen. He clicked the mouse and pulled a tight square around the heads. Clicked again. The monitor redrew into a large blowup. The tall guy was staring straight out of the screen. The two new guys were caught at an angle, staring at Holly.

The tech hit the print button and then he opened the fifth file. He zoomed in with the mouse and put a tight rectangle around the driver, inside the car. He printed that out, too. McGrath picked up the new sheets of paper.

"Good," he said. "Good as we're going to get, anyway.

Shame your damn computer can't make them all look right at the camera.''

"It can," the tech chief said.

"It can?" McGrath said. "How?"

"In a manner of speaking," the guy said. He touched the blowup of Holly's face with his finger. "Suppose we wanted a face-front picture of her, right? We'd ask her to move around right in front of the camera and look right up at it. But suppose for some reason she can't move at all. What would we do? We could move the camera, right? Suppose you climbed up on the counter and unbolted the camera off the wall and moved it down and around a certain distance until it was right in front of her. Then you'd be seeing a face-front picture, correct?''

"OK," McGrath said.

"So what we do is we calculate," the tech said. "We calculate that if we did hypothetically move that camera right in front of her, we'd have to move it what? Say six feet downward, say ten feet to the left, and turn it through about forty degrees, and then it would be plumb face-on to her. So we get those numbers and we enter them into the program and the computer will do a kind of backward simulation, and draw us a picture, just the same as if we'd really moved the actual camera right around in front of her.''

"You can do that?" McGrath said. "Does it work?"

"Within its limitations," the tech chief said. He touched the image of the nearer gunman. "This guy, for instance, he's pretty much side-on. The computer will give us a full-face picture, no problem at all, but it's going to be just guessing what the other side of his face looks like, right? It's programmed to assume the other side looks pretty much like the side it can see, with a little bit of asymmetry built in. But if the guy's got one ear missing or something, or a big scar, it can't tell us that.''

"OK," McGrath said. "So what do you need?"

The chief tech picked up the wide shot of the group. Pointed here and there on it with a stubby forefinger.

"Measurements," he said. "Make them as exact as possible. I need to know the camera position relative to the doorway and the sidewalk level. I need to know the focal length of the camera lens. I need Holly's file photograph for calibration. We know exactly what she looks like, right? I can use her for a test run. I'll get it set up so she comes out right, then the other guys will come out right as well, assuming they've all got two ears and so on, like I said. And bring me a square of tile off the store's floor and one of those smocks the counter woman was wearing.''

"What for?" McGrath said.

"So I can use them to decode the grays in the video," the tech said. "Then I can give you your mug shots in color."

THE COMMANDER SELECTED six women from that morning's punishment detail. He used the ones with the most demerits, because the task was going to be hard and unpleasant. He stood them at attention and drew his huge bulk up to its full height in front of them. He waited to see which of them would be the first to glance away from his face. When he was satisfied none of them dared to, he explained their duties. The blood had sprayed all over the room, hurled around by the savage centrifugal force of the blade. Chips of bone had spattered everywhere. He told them to heat water in the cookhouse and carry it over in buckets. He told them to draw scrubbing brushes and rags and disinfectant from the stores. He told them they had two hours to get the room looking pristine again. Any longer than that, they would earn more demerits.

IT TOOK TWO hours to get the data. Milosevic and Brogan went out to the dry-cleaning establishment. They closed the place down and swarmed all over it like surveyors. They drew a plan with measurements accurate to the nearest quarter-inch. They took the camera off the wall and brought it back with them. They tore up the floor and took the tiles. They took two smocks from the woman and two posters off the wall, because they thought they might help with the colorizing process. Back on the sixth floor of the Federal Building, the chief tech took another two hours to input the data. Then he ran the test, using Holly Johnson to calibrate the program.

"What do you think?" he asked McGrath.

McGrath looked hard at the full-face picture of Holly. Then he passed it around. Milosevic got it last and stared at it hardest. Covered some parts with his hand and frowned.

"Makes her look too thin," he said. "I think the bottom right quarter is wrong. Not enough width there, somehow."

"I agree," McGrath said. "Makes her jaw look weird."

The chief tech exited to a menu screen and adjusted a couple of numbers. Ran the test again. The laser printer whirred. The sheet of stiff paper came out.

"That's better," McGrath said. "Just about on the nose."

"Color OK?" the tech asked.

"Should be a darker peach," Milosevic said. "On her dress. I know that dress. Some kind of an Italian thing."

The tech exited to a color palette.

"Show me," he said.

Milosevic pointed to a particular shade.

"More like that," he said.

They ran the test again. The hard disk chattered and the laser printer whirred.

"That's better," Milosevic said. "Dress is right. Hair color is better as well."

"OK," the tech said. He saved all the parameters to disk. "Let's go to work here."

The FBI never uses latest-generation equipment. The feeling is it's better to use stuff that has been proven in the field. So the tech chief's computer was actually a little slower than the computers in the rich kids' bedrooms up and down the North Shore. But not much slower. It gave McGrath five prints within forty minutes. Four mug shots of the four kidnappers, and a close-up side view of the front half of their car. All in glowing color, all with the grain enhanced and smoothed away. McGrath thought they were the best damn pictures he had ever seen.

"Thanks, chief," he said. "These are brilliant. Best work anybody has done around here for a long time. But don't say a word. Big secret, right?"

He clapped the tech on the shoulder and left him feeling like the most important guy in the whole building.

• • •

THE SIX WOMEN worked hard and finished just before their two hours were up. The tiny cracks between the boards were their biggest problem. The cracks were tight, but not tight enough to stop the blood seeping in. But they were too tight to get a brush down in there. They had to sluice them out with water and rag them dry. The boards were turning a wet brown color. The women were praying they wouldn't warp as they dried. Two of them were throwing up. It was adding to their workload. But they finished in time for the commander's inspection. They stood rigidly at attention on the damp floor and waited. He checked everywhere, with the wet boards creaking under his bulk. But he was satisfied with their work and gave them another two hours to clean the smears off the corridor and the staircase, where the body had been dragged away.

THE CAR WAS easy. It was quickly identified as a Lexus. Four-door. Late-model. The pattern of the alloy wheel dated it exactly. Color was either black or dark gray. Impossible to be certain. The computer process was good, but not good enough to be definitive about dark automotive paint standing in bright sunshine.

"Stolen?" Milosevic said.

McGrath nodded.

"Almost certainly," he said. "You do the checking, OK?"

Fluctuations in the value of the yen had put the list price of a new Lexus four-door somewhere up there with Milosevic's annual salary, so he knew which jurisdictions were worth checking with and which weren't. He didn't bother with anywhere south of the Loop. He put in calls to the Chicago cops, and then all the departments on the North Shore right up to Lake Forest.

He got a hit just before noon. Not exactly what he was looking for. Not a stolen Lexus. But a missing Lexus. The police department in Wilmette came back to him and said a dentist up there had driven his brand-new Lexus to work, before seven on Monday morning, and parked it in the lot behind his professional building. A chiropractor from the next office suite had seen him turn into the lot. But the dentist had never made it into the building. His nurse had called his home and his wife had called the Wilmette PD. The cops had taken the report and sat on it. It wasn't the first case of a husband disappearing they'd ever heard of. They told Milosevic the guy's name was Rubin and the car was the new shade of black, mica flecks in the paint to make it sparkle, and it had vanity plates reading: ORTHO 1.

Milosevic put the phone down on that call and it rang again straightaway with a report from the Chicago Fire Department. A unit had attended an automobile fire which was putting up a cloud of oily smoke into the land-side flight path into Meigs Field Airport. The fire truck had arrived in an abandoned industrial lot just before one o'clock Monday and found a black Lexus burning fiercely. They had figured it was burned to the metal anyway, not much more smoke to come, so they had saved their foam and just left it to burn out. Milosevic copied the location and hung up. Ducked into McGrath's office for instructions.

"Check it out," McGrath told him.

Milosevic nodded. He was always happy with road work. It gave him the chance to drive his own brand-new Ford Explorer, which he liked to use in preference to one of the Bureau's clunky sedans. And the Bureau liked to let him do exactly that, because he never bothered to claim for his personal gas. So he drove the big shiny four-wheel-drive five miles south and found the wreck of the Lexus, no trouble at all. It was parked at an angle on a lumpy concrete area behind an abandoned industrial building. The tires had burned away and it was settled on the rims. The plates were still readable: ORTHO 1. He poked through the drifts of ash inside, still slightly warm, and then he pulled the shaft of the burned key from the ignition and popped the trunk. Then he staggered four steps away and threw up on the concrete. He retched and spat and sweated. He pulled his cellular phone from his pocket and fired it up. Got straight through to McGrath in the Federal Building.

"I found the dentist," he said.

"Where?" McGrath asked.

"In the damn trunk," Milosevic said. "Slow-roasted. Looks like he was alive when the fire started."

"Christ," McGrath said. "Is it connected?"

"No doubt about that," he said.

"You sure?" McGrath asked him.

"No doubt about it," Milosevic said again. "I found other stuff. Burned, but it's all pretty clear. There's a thirty-eight right in the middle of what looks like a metal hinge, could be from a woman's pocketbook, right? Coins, and a lipstick tube, and the metal parts from a mobile phone and a pager. And there are nine wire hangers on the floor. Like you get from a dry cleaner?"

"Christ," McGrath said again. "Conclusions?"

"They stole the Lexus up in Wilmette," Milosevic said. "Maybe the dentist guy disturbed them in the act. So he went for them and they overpowered him and put him in the trunk. Burned him along with the rest of the evidence."

"Shit," McGrath said. "But where's Holly? Conclusions on that?"

"They took her to Meigs Field," Milosevic said. "It's about a half-mile away. They put her in a private plane and dumped the car right here. That's what they did, Mack. They flew her out somewhere. Four guys, capable of burning another guy up while he was still alive, they've got her alone somewhere, could be a million miles away from here by now."

15

THE WHITE TRUCK droned on, steadily, another hour, maybe sixty more miles. The clock inside Reacher's head ticked around from eleven to twelve noon. The first faint stirrings of worry were building inside him. They had been gone a day. Nearly a full twenty-four hours. Out of the first phase, into the middle phase. No progress. And he was uncomfortable. The air inside the vehicle was about as hot as air could get. They were still lying flat on their backs on the hot mattress, heads together. The horsehair padding was overheating them. Holly's dark hair was damp and spread out. On her left, it was curled against Reacher's bare shoulder.

"Is it because I'm a woman?" she asked. Tense. "Or because I'm younger than you? Or both?"

"Is what because?" he asked back. Wary.

"You think you've got to take care of me," she said. "You're worrying about me, because I'm young and a woman, right? You think I need some older man's help."

Reacher stirred. He didn't really want to move. He wasn't comfortable, but he guessed he was happy enough where he was. In particular, he was happy with the feel of Holly's hair against his shoulder. His life was like that. Whatever happened, there were always some little compensations available.

"Well?" she asked.

"It's not a gender thing, Holly," he said. "Or an age thing. But you do need help, right?"

"And I'm a younger woman and you're an older man,"
she said. "Therefore obviously you're the one qualified to
give it. Couldn't be the other way around, right?"

Reacher shook his head, lying down.

"It's not a gender thing," he said again. "Or an age thing.
I'm qualified because I'm qualified, is all. I'm just trying to
help you out."

"You're taking stupid risks," she said. "Pushing them and
antagonizing them is not the way to do this, for God's sake.
You'll get us both killed."

"Bullshit," Reacher said. "They need to see us as people,
not cargo."

"Says who?" Holly snapped. "Who suddenly made you
the big expert?"

He shrugged at her.

"Let me ask you a question," he said. "If the boot was
on the other foot, would you have left me alone in that
barn?"

She thought about it.

"Of course I would have," she said.

He smiled. She was probably telling the truth. He liked her
for it.

"OK," he said. "Next time you tell me, I'm gone. No
argument."

She was quiet for a long moment.

"Good," she said. "You really want to help me out, you
do exactly that."

He shrugged. Moved a half-inch closer to her.

"Risky for you," he said. "I get away, they might figure
on just wasting you and disappearing."

"I'll take the risk," she said. "That's what I'm paid for."

"So who are they?" he asked her. "And what do they
want?"

"No idea," she said.

She said it too quickly. He knew she knew.

"They want you, right?" he said. "Either because they
want you personally, or because they want any old FBI agent
and you were right there on the spot. How many FBI agents
are there?"

"Bureau has twenty-five thousand employees," she said. "Of which ten thousand are agents."

"OK," he said. "So they want you in particular. One out of ten thousand is too big a coincidence. This is not random."

She looked away. He glanced at her.

"Why, Holly?" he asked.

She shrugged and shook her head.

"I don't know," she said.

Too quickly. He glanced at her again. She sounded sure, but there was some big defensive edge there in her reply.

"I don't know," she said again. "All I can figure is maybe they mistook me for somebody else from the office."

Reacher laughed and turned his head toward her. His face touched her hair.

"You're joking, Holly Johnson," he said. "You're not the type of woman gets confused with somebody else. And they watched you three weeks. Long enough to get familiar."

She smiled away from him, up at the metal roof, ironically.

"Once seen, never forgotten, right?" she said. "I wish."

"You in any doubt about that?" Reacher said. "You're the best-looking person I saw this week."

"Thanks, Reacher," she said. "It's Tuesday. You first saw me Monday. Big compliment, right?"

"But you get my drift," he said.

She sat up, straight from the waist like a gymnast, and used both hands to flip her leg sideways. Propped herself on one elbow on the mattress. Hooked her hair behind her ear and looked down at him.

"I don't get anything about you," she said.

He looked back up at her. Shrugged.

"You got questions, you ask them," he said. "I'm all in favor of freedom of information."

"OK," she said. "Here's the first question: who the hell are you?"

He shrugged again and smiled.

"Jack Reacher," he said. "No middle name, thirty-seven years and eight months old, unmarried, club doorman in Chicago."

"Bullshit," she said.

"Bullshit?" he repeated. "Which part? My name, my age, my marital status, or my occupation?"

"Your occupation," she said. "You're not a club doorman."

"I'm not?" he said. "So what am I?"

"You're a soldier," she said. "You're in the Army."

"I am?" he said.

"It's pretty obvious," she said. "My dad is Army. I've lived on bases all my life. Everybody I ever saw was in the Army, right up until I was eighteen years old. I know what soldiers look like. I know how they act. I was pretty sure you were one. Then you took your shirt off, and I knew for definite."

Reacher grinned.

"Why?" he said. "Is that a really uncouth, soldierly kind of a thing to do?"

Holly grinned back at him. Shook her head. Her hair came loose. She swept it back behind her ear, one finger bent like a small pale hook.

"That scar on your stomach," she said. "Those awful stitches. That's a MASH job for sure. Some field hospital somewhere, took them about a minute and a half. Any civilian surgeon did stitches like that, he'd get sued for malpractice so fast he'd get dizzy."

Reacher ran his finger over the lumpy skin. The stitches looked like a plan of the ties at a railroad yard.

"The guy was busy," he said. "I thought he did pretty well, considering the circumstances. It was in Beirut. I was a long way down the priority list. I was only bleeding to death slowly."

"So I'm right?" Holly said. "You're a soldier?"

Reacher smiled up at her again and shook his head.

"I'm a doorman," he said. "Like I told you. Blues joint on the South Side. You should try it. Much better than the tourist places."

She glanced between his huge scar and his face. Clamped her lips and slowly shook her head. Reacher nodded at her, like he was conceding the point.

"I used to be a soldier," he said. "I got out, fourteen months ago."

"What unit?" she asked.

"Military police," he said.

She screwed her face up in a mock grimace.

"The baddest of the bad," she said. "Nobody likes you guys."

"Tell me about it," Reacher said.

"Explains a lot of things," she said. "You guys get a lot of special training. So I guess you really are qualified. You should have told me, damn it. Now I guess I have to apologize for what I said."

He made no reply to that.

"Where were you stationed?" she asked.

"All over the world," he said. "Europe, Far East, Middle East. Got so I didn't know which way was up."

"Rank?" she asked.

"Major," he said.

"Medals?" she asked.

He shrugged.

"Dozens of the damn things," he said. "You know how it is. Theater medals, of course, plus a Silver Star, two Bronzes, Purple Heart from Beirut, campaign things from Panama and Grenada and Desert Shield and Desert Storm."

"A Silver Star?" she asked. "What for?"

"Beirut," he said. "Pulled some guys out of the bunker."

"And you got wounded doing that?" she said. "That's how you got the scar and the Purple Heart?"

"I was already wounded," he said. "Got wounded before I went in. I think that was what impressed them."

"Hero, right?" she said.

He smiled and shook his head.

"No way," he said. "I wasn't feeling anything. Wasn't thinking. Too shocked. I didn't even know I was hit until afterward. If I'd known, I'd have fallen down in a dead faint. My intestine was hanging out. Looked really awful. It was bright pink. Sort of squashy."

Holly was quiet for a second. The truck droned on. Another twenty miles covered. North or south or west. Probably.

"How long were you in the service?" she asked.

"All my life," he said. "My old man was a Marine officer, served all over. He married a Frenchwoman in Korea. I was born in Berlin. Never even saw the States until I was nine years old. Five minutes later we were in the Philippines. Round and round the world we went. Longest I was ever anywhere was four years at West Point. Then I joined up and it started all over again. Round and round the world.''

"Where's your family now?'' she asked.

"Dead,'' he said. "The old man died, what? Ten years ago, I guess. My mother died two years later. I buried the Silver Star with her. She won it for me, really. Do what you're supposed to do, she used to tell me. About a million times a day, in a thick French accent.''

"Brothers and sisters?'' she said.

"I had a brother,'' he said. "He died last year. I'm the last Reacher on earth, far as I know.''

"When did you muster out?'' she said.

"April last year,'' he said. "Fourteen months ago.''

"Why?'' she asked.

Reacher shrugged.

"Just lost interest, I guess,'' he said. "The defense cuts were happening. Made the Army seem unnecessary, somehow. Like if they didn't need the biggest and the best, they didn't need me. Didn't want to be part of something small and second-rate. So I left. Arrogant, or what?''

She laughed.

"So you became a doorman?'' she said. "From a decorated Major to a doorman? Isn't that kind of second-rate?''

"Wasn't like that,'' he said. "I didn't set out to be a doorman, like it was a new career move or anything. It's only temporary. I only got to Chicago on Friday. I was planning to move on, maybe Wednesday. I was thinking about going up to Wisconsin. Supposed to be a nice place, this time of year.''

"Friday to Wednesday?'' Holly said. "You got a problem with commitment or something?''

"I guess,'' he said. "Thirty-six years I was always where somebody else told me to be. Very structured sort of a life. I suppose I'm reacting against it. I love moving around when I feel like it. It's like a drug. Longest I've ever stayed anywhere was ten consecutive days. Last fall, in Georgia. Ten days, out of fourteen months. Apart from that, I've been on the road, more or less all the time.''

"Making a living by working the door at clubs?'' she asked.

"That was unusual,'' he said. "Mostly I don't work at all, just live off my savings. But I came up to Chicago with a singer, one thing led to another, I got asked to work the door at the club the guy was headed for.''

"So what do you do if you don't work?'' she asked.

"I look at things,'' he said. "You got to remember, I'm a thirty-seven-year-old American, but I've never really been in America much. You been up the Empire State Building?''

"Of course,'' she said.

"I hadn't,'' he said. "Not before last year. You been to the Washington museums?''

"Sure,'' she said.

"I hadn't,'' he said again. "Not before last year. All that kind of stuff. Boston, New York, Washington, Chicago, New Orleans, Mount Rushmore, the Golden Gate, Niagara. I'm like a tourist. Like I'm catching up, right?''

"I'm the other way around,'' Holly said. "I like to travel overseas.''

Reacher shrugged.

"I've seen overseas,'' he said. "Six continents. I'm going to stay here now.''

"I've seen the States,'' she said. "My dad traveled all the time, but we stayed here, apart from two tours to Germany.''

Reacher nodded. Thought back to the time he'd spent in Germany, man and boy. Many years, in total.

"You picked up on the soccer in Europe?'' he asked.

"Right,'' Holly said. "Really big deal there. We were stationed one time near Munich, right? I was just a kid, eleven maybe. They gave my father tickets to some big game in Rotterdam, Holland. European Cup, the Bayern Munich team against some English team, Aston Villa, you ever heard of them?''

Reacher nodded.

"From Birmingham, England,'' he said. "I was stationed near a place called Oxford at one point. About an hour away.''

"I hated the Germans," Holly said. "So arrogant, so over-powering. They were so sure they were going to cream these Brits. I didn't want to go and watch it happen. But I had to, right? NATO protocol sort of a thing, would have been a big scandal if I'd refused. So we went. And the Brits creamed the Germans. The Germans were so furious. I loved it. And the Aston Villa guys were so cute. I was in love with soccer from that night on. Still am."

Reacher nodded. He enjoyed watching soccer, to an extent. But you had to be exposed early and gradually. It looked very free-form, but it was a very technical game. Full of hidden attractions. But he could see how a young girl could be seduced by it, long ago in Europe. A frantic night under floodlights in Rotterdam. Resentful and unwilling at first, then hypnotized by the patterns made by the white ball on the green turf. Ending up in love with the game afterward. But something was ringing a warning bell. If the eleven-year-old daughter of an American serviceman had refused to go, it would have caused some kind of an embarrassment within NATO? Was that what she had said?

"Who was your father?" he asked her. "Sounds like he must have been an important sort of a guy."

She turned her head away. Wouldn't answer. Reacher stared at her. Another warning bell was ringing.

"Holly, who the hell is your father?" he asked urgently.

The defensive tone that had been in her voice spread to her face. No answer.

"Who, Holly?" Reacher asked again.

She looked away from him. Spoke to the metal siding of the truck. Her voice was almost lost in the road noise. Defensive as hell.

"General Johnson," she said quietly. "At that time, he was C-in-C Europe. Do you know him?"

Reacher stared up at her. General Johnson. Holly Johnson. Father and daughter.

"I've met him," he said. "But that's not the point, is it?"

She glared at him. Furious.

"Why?" she said. "What exactly is the damn point?"

"That's the reason," he said. "Your father is the most important military man in America, right? That's why you've been kidnapped, Holly, for God's sake. These guys don't want Holly Johnson, FBI agent. The whole FBI thing is incidental. These guys want General Johnson's daughter.''

She looked down at him like he had just slapped her hard in the face.

"Why?" she said. "Why the hell does everybody assume everything that ever happens to me is because of who my damn father is?''

16

MCGRATH BROUGHT BROGAN with him and met Milosevic at Meigs Field Airport in Chicago. He brought the four
computer-aided mug shots and the test picture of Holly Johnson. He came expecting total cooperation from the airport
staff. And he got it. Three hyped-up FBI agents in the grip
of fear about a colleague are a difficult proposition to handle
with anything other than total cooperation.

Meigs Field was a small commercial operation, right out
in the lake, water on three sides, just below the 12th Street
beach, trying to make a living in the gigantic shadow of
O'Hare. Their recordkeeping was immaculate and their efficiency was first-class. Not so they could be ready to handle
FBI inquiries on the spur of the moment, but so they could
keep on operating and keep on getting paid right under the
nose of the world's toughest competitor. But their records
and their efficiency helped McGrath. Helped him realize
within about thirty seconds that he was heading up a blind
alley.

The Meigs Field staff were certain they had never seen
Holly Johnson or any of the four kidnappers at any time.
Certainly not on Monday, certainly not around one o'clock.
They were adamant about it. They weren't overdoing it. They
were just sure about it, with the quiet certainty of people who
spend their working days being quietly sure about things, like

sending small planes up into the busiest air lanes on the planet.

And there were no suspicious takeoffs from Meigs Field, nowhere between noon and, say, three o'clock. That was clear. The paperwork was explicit on the subject. The three agents were out of there as briskly as they had entered. The tower staff nodded to themselves and forgot all about them before they were even back in their cars in the small parking lot.

"OK, square one," McGrath said. "You guys go check out this dentist situation up in Wilmette. I've got things to do. And I've got to put in a call to Webster. They must be climbing the walls down there in D.C."

SEVENTEEN HUNDRED AND two miles from Meigs Field the young man in the woods wanted instructions. He was a good agent, well trained, but as far as undercover work was concerned he was new and relatively inexperienced. Demand for undercover operators was always increasing. The Bureau was hard put to fill all the slots. So people like him got assigned. Inexperienced people. He knew as long as he always remembered he didn't have all the answers, he'd be OK. He had no ego problem with it. He was always willing to ask for guidance. He was careful. And he was realistic. Realistic enough to know he was now in over his head. Things were turning bad in a way which made him sure they were about to explode into something much worse. How, he didn't know. It was just a feeling. But he trusted his feelings. Trusted them enough to stop and turn around before he reached his special tree. He breathed hard and changed his mind and set off strolling back the way he had come.

WEBSTER HAD BEEN waiting for McGrath's call. That was clear. McGrath got him straightaway, like he'd been sitting there in his big office suite just waiting for the phone to ring.

"Progress, Mack?" Webster asked.

"Some," McGrath said. "We know exactly what happened. We got it all on a security video in a dry cleaner's store. She went in there at twelve-ten. Came out at twelve-fifteen. There were four guys. Three on the street, one in a car. They grabbed her.''

''Then what?'' Webster asked.

''They were in a stolen sedan,'' McGrath said. ''Looks like they killed the owner to get it. Drove her five miles south, torched the sedan. Along with the owner in the trunk. They burned him alive. He was a dentist, name of Rubin. What they did with Holly, we don't know yet.''

In Washington, Harland Webster was silent for a long time.

''Is it worth searching the area?'' he asked, eventually.

McGrath's turn to be quiet for a second. Unsure of the implications. Did Webster mean search for a hideout, or search for another body?

''My gut says no,'' he said. ''They must know we could search the area. My feeling is they moved her somewhere else. Maybe far away.''

There was silence on the line again. McGrath could hear Webster thinking.

''I agree with you, I guess,'' Webster said. ''They moved her out. But how, exactly? By road? By air?''

''Not air,'' McGrath said. ''We covered commercial flights yesterday. We just hit a private field. Nothing doing.''

''What about a helicopter?'' Webster said. ''In and out, secretly?''

''Not in Chicago, chief,'' McGrath said. ''Not right next door to O'Hare. More radar here than the Air Force has got. Any unauthorized choppers in and out of here, we'd know about it.''

''OK,'' Webster said. ''But we need to get this under control. Abduction and homicide, Mack, it's not giving me a good feeling. You figure a second stolen vehicle? Rendezvoused with the stolen sedan?''

''Probably,'' McGrath said. ''We're checking now.''

''Any ideas who they were?'' Webster said.

''No,'' McGrath told him. ''We got pretty good pictures off the video. Computer enhancements. We'll download them to you right away. Four guys, white, somewhere between thirty and forty, three of them kind of alike, ordinary, neat, short hair. The fourth guy is real tall, computer says he's maybe six five. I figure him for the ringleader. He was the one got to her first.''

"You got any feeling for a motive yet?'' Webster asked.

"No idea at all,'' McGrath said.

There was silence on the line again.

"OK,'' Webster said. "You keeping it real tight up there?''

"Tight as I can,'' McGrath said. "Just three of us.''

"Who are you using?'' Webster asked.

"Brogan and Milosevic,'' McGrath said.

"They any good?'' Webster asked.

McGrath grunted. Like he would choose them if they weren't?

"They know Holly pretty well,'' he said. "They're good enough.''

"Moaners and groaners?'' Webster asked. "Or solid, like people used to be?''

"Never heard them complain,'' McGrath said. "About anything. They do the work, they do the hours. They don't even bitch about the pay.''

Webster laughed.

"Can we clone them?'' he said.

The levity peaked and died within a couple of seconds. But McGrath appreciated the attempt at morale.

"So how you doing down there?'' he asked.

"In what respect, Mack?'' Webster said, serious again.

"The old man,'' McGrath said. "He giving you any trouble?''

"Which one, Mack?'' Webster asked.

"The General?'' McGrath said.

"Not yet,'' Webster said. "He called this morning, but he was polite. That's how it goes. Parents are usually pretty calm, the first day or two. They get worked up later. General Johnson won't be any different. He may be a big shot, but people are all the same underneath, right?''

"Right,'' McGrath said. "Have him call me, if he wants firsthand reports. Might help his situation.''

"OK, Mack, thanks,'' Webster said. "But I think we should keep this dentist thing away from everybody, just for the moment. Makes the whole deal look worse. Meantime, send me your stuff. I'll get our people working on it. And don't worry. We'll get her back. Bureau looks after its own, right? Never fails."

The two Bureau chiefs let the lie die into silence and hung up their phones together.

THE YOUNG MAN strolled out of the forest and came face-to-face with the commander. He was smart enough to throw a big salute and look nervous, but he kept it down to the sort of nervousness any grunt showed around the commander. Nothing more, nothing suspicious. He stood and waited to be spoken to.

"Job for you," the commander said. "You're young, right? Good with all this technical shit?"

The man nodded cautiously.

"I can usually puzzle stuff out, sir," he said.

The commander nodded back.

"We got a new toy," he said. "Scanner, for radio frequencies. I want a watch kept."

The young man's blood froze hard.

"Why, sir?" he asked. "You think somebody's using a radio transmitter?"

"Possibly," the commander said. "I trust nobody and I suspect everybody. I can't be too careful. Not right now. Got to look after the details. You know what they say? Genius is in the details, right?"

The young man swallowed and nodded.

"So get it set up," the commander said. "Make a duty rota. Two shifts, sixteen hours a day, OK? Constant vigilance is what we need right now."

The commander turned away. The young man nodded and breathed out. Glanced instinctively back in the direction of his special tree and blessed his feelings.

MILOSEVIC DROVE BROGAN north in his new truck. They detoured via the Wilmette post office so Brogan could mail his twin alimony checks. Then they went looking for the dead dentist's building. There was a local uniform waiting for them in the parking lot in back. He was unapologetic about sitting on the report from the dentist's wife. Milosevic started giving him a hard time about that, like it made the guy personally responsible for Holly Johnson's abduction.

"Lots of husbands disappear," the guy said. "Happens all the time. This is Wilmette, right? Men are the same here as anywhere, only here they got the money to make it all happen. What can I say?"

Milosevic was unsympathetic. The cop had made two other errors. First, he had assumed that it was the murder of the dentist that had brought the FBI out into his jurisdiction. Second, he was more uptight about covering his own ass on the issue than he was about four killers snatching Holly Johnson right off the street. Milosevic was out of patience with the guy. But then the guy redeemed himself.

"What is it with people?" he said. "Burning automobiles? Some asshole burned a car out by the lake. We got to get it moved. Residents are giving us noise."

"Where exactly?" Milosevic asked him.

The cop shrugged. He was anxious to be very precise.

"That turnout on the shore," he said. "On Sheridan Road, just this side of Washington Park. Never saw such a thing before, not in Wilmette."

Milosevic and Brogan went to check it out. They followed the cop in his shiny cruiser. He led them to the place. It wasn't a car. It was a pickup, a ten-year-old Dodge. No license plates. Doused with gasoline and pretty much totally burned out.

"Happened yesterday," the cop said. "Spotted about seven-thirty in the morning. Commuters were calling it in, on their way to work, one after the other."

He circled around and looked over the wreck, carefully.

"Not local," he said. "That's my guess."

"Why not?" Milosevic asked him.

"This is ten years old, right?" the guy said. "Around here, there are a few pickups, but they're toys, you know? Big V-8s, lots of chrome? An old thing like this, nobody would give it room on their driveway."

"What about gardeners?" Brogan asked. "Pool boys, something like that?"

"Why would they burn it?" the cop said. "They needed

to change it, they'd chop it in against a new one, right? Nobody burns a business asset, right?''

Milosevic thought about it and nodded.

"OK," he said. "This is ours. Federal investigation. We'll send a flatbed for it soon as we can. Meanwhile, you guard it, OK? And do it properly, for God's sake. Don't let anybody near it.''

"Why?" the cop asked.

Milosevic looked at him like he was a moron.

"This is their truck," he said. "They dumped it here and stole the Lexus for the actual heist.''

The Wilmette cop looked at Milosevic's agitated face and then he looked across at the burned truck. He wondered for a moment how four guys could fit across the Dodge's bench seat. But he didn't say anything. He didn't want to risk more ridicule. He just nodded.

17

HOLLY WAS SITTING up on the mattress, one knee under her chin, the injured leg straight out. Reacher was sitting up beside her, hunched forward, worried, one hand fighting the bounce of the truck and the other hand plunged into his hair.

"What about your mother?" he asked.

"Was your father famous?" Holly asked him back.

Reacher shook his head.

"Hardly," he said. "Guys in his unit knew who he was, I guess."

"So you don't know what it's like," she said. "Every damn thing you do, it happens because of your father. I got straight A's in school, I went to Yale and Harvard, went to Wall Street, but it wasn't me doing it, it was this weird other person called General Johnson's daughter doing it. It's been just the same with the Bureau. Everybody assumes I made it because of my father, and ever since I got there half the people are still treating me especially nice, and the other half are still treating me especially tough just to prove how much they're not impressed."

Reacher nodded. Thought about it. He was a guy who had done better than his father. Forged ahead, in the traditional way. Left the old man behind. But he'd known guys with famous parents. The sons of great soldiers. Even the grandsons. However bright they burned, their light was always lost in the glow.

"OK, so it's tough," he said. "And the rest of your life you can try to ignore it, but right now it needs dealing with. It opens up a whole new can of worms."

She nodded. Blew an exasperated sigh. Reacher glanced at her in the gloom.

"How long ago did you figure it out?" he asked.

"Immediately, I guess," she said. "Like I told you, it's a habit. Everybody assumes everything happens because of my father. Me too."

"Well, thanks for telling me so soon," Reacher said.

She didn't reply to that. They lapsed into silence. The air was stifling and the heat was somehow mixing with the relentless drone of the noise. The dark and the temperature and the sound were like a thick soup inside the truck. Reacher felt like he was drowning in it. But it was the uncertainty that was doing it to him. Many times he'd traveled thirty hours at a stretch in transport planes, worse conditions than these. It was the huge new dimension of uncertainty that was unsettling him.

"So what about your mother?" he asked her again.

She shook her head.

"She died," she said. "I was twenty, in school. Some weird cancer."

"I'm sorry," he said. Paused, nervously. "Brothers and sisters?"

She shook her head again.

"Just me," she said.

He nodded, reluctantly.

"I was afraid of that," he said. "I was kind of hoping this could be about something else, you know, maybe your mother was a judge or you had a brother or a sister who was a congressman or something."

"Forget it," she said. "There's just me. Me and Dad. This is about Dad."

"But what about him?" he said. "What the hell is this supposed to achieve? Ransom? Forget about it. Your old man's a big deal, but he's just a soldier, been clawing his way up the Army pay scales all his life. Faster than most guys, I agree, but I know those pay scales. I was on those scales thirteen years. Didn't make me rich and they won't have made him rich. Not rich enough for anybody to be thinking about a ransom. Somebody wanted a ransom out of kidnapping somebody's daughter, there are a million people ahead of you in Chicago alone.''

Holly nodded.

"This is about influence,'' she said. ''He's responsible for two million people and two hundred billion dollars a year. Scope for influence there, right?''

Reacher shook his head.

"No,'' he said. ''That's the problem. I can't see what this is liable to achieve.''

He got to his knees and crawled forward along the mattresses.

"Hell are you doing?'' Holly asked him.

"We got to talk to them,'' he said. ''Before we get where we're going.''

He lifted his big fist and started pounding on the bulkhead. Hard as he could. Right behind where he figured the driver's head must be. He kept on pounding until he got what he wanted. Took a while. Several minutes. His fist got sore. But the truck lurched off the pavement and started slowing. He felt the front wheels washing into gravel. The brakes bit in. He was pressed up against the bulkhead by the momentum. Holly rolled a couple of feet along the mattress. Gasped in pain as her knee twisted against the motion.

"Pulled off the highway,'' Reacher said. ''Middle of nowhere.''

"This is a big mistake, Reacher,'' Holly said.

He shrugged and took her hand and helped her into a sitting position, back against the bulkhead. Then he slid forward and put himself between her and the rear doors. He heard the three guys getting out of the cab. Doors slammed. He heard their footsteps crunching over the gravel. Two coming down the right flank, one down the left. He heard the key sliding into the lock. The handle turned.

The left-hand rear door opened two inches. First thing into the truck was the muzzle of the shotgun. Beyond it, Reacher saw a meaningless sliver of sky. Bright blue, small white clouds. Could have been anywhere in the hemisphere. Second thing into the truck was a Glock 17. Then a wrist. The cuff of a cotton shirt. The Glock was rock-steady. Loder.

"This better be good, bitch," he called.

Hostile. A lot of tension in the voice.

"We need to talk," Reacher called back.

The second Glock appeared in the narrow gap. Shaking slightly.

"Talk about what, asshole?" Loder called.

Reacher listened to the stress in the guy's voice and watched the second Glock trembling through its random zigzags.

"This isn't going to work, guys," he said. "Whoever told you to do this, he isn't thinking straight. Maybe it felt like some kind of a smart move, but it's all wrong. It isn't going to achieve anything. It's just going to get you guys in a shitload of trouble."

There was silence at the rear of the truck. Just for a second. But long enough to tell Reacher that Holly was right. Long enough to know he'd made a bad mistake. The steady Glock snapped back out of sight. The shotgun jerked, like it had just changed ownership. Reacher flung himself forward and smashed Holly down flat on the mattress. The shotgun barrel tipped upward. Reacher heard the small click of the trigger a tiny fraction before an enormous explosion. The shotgun fired into the roof. A huge blast. A hundred tiny holes appeared in the metal. A hundred tiny points of blue light. Spent shot rattled and bounced down and ricocheted around the truck like hail. Then the sound of the gun faded into the hum of temporary deafness.

Reacher felt the slam of the door. The sliver of daylight cut off. He felt the rock of the vehicle as the three men climbed back into the cab. He felt the shake as the rough diesel caught. Then a forward lurch and a yaw to the left as the truck pulled back onto the highway.

FIRST THING REACHER heard as his hearing came back was a quiet keening as the air whistled out through the hundred pellet holes in the roof. It grew louder as the miles rolled by. A hundred high-pitched whistles, all grouped together a couple of semitones apart, fighting and warbling like some kind of demented birdsong.

"Insane, right?" Holly said.

"Me or them?" he said.

He nodded an apology. She nodded back and struggled up to a sitting position. Used both hands to straighten her knee. The holes in the roof were letting light through. Enough light that Reacher could see her face clearly. He could interpret her expression. He could see the flicker of pain. Like a blind coming down in her eyes, then snapping back up. He knelt and swept the spent pellets off the mattress. They rattled across the metal floor.

"Now you've got to get out," she said. "You'll get yourself killed soon."

The highlights in her hair flashed under the random bright illumination.

"I mean it," she said. "Qualified or not, I can't let you stay."

"I know you can't," he said.

He used his discarded shirt to sweep the pellets into a pile near the doors. Then he straightened the mattresses and lay back down. Rocked gently with the motion. Stared at the holes in the sheet metal above him. They were like a map of some distant galaxy.

"My father would do what it takes to get me back," Holly said.

Talking was harder than it had been before. The drone of the motor and the rumble of the road were complicated by the high-pitched whistle from the roof. A full spectrum of noise. Holly lay down next to Reacher. She put her head next to his. Her hair fanned out and brushed his cheek and fell to his neck. She squirmed her hips and straightened her leg. There was still space between their bodies. The decorous V shape was still there. But the angle was a little tighter than it had been before.

"But what can he do?" Reacher said. "Talk me through it."

"They're going to make some kind of demand," she said. "You know, do this or do that, or we hurt your girl."

She spoke slowly and there was a tremor in her voice. Reacher let his hand drop into the space between them and found hers. He took it and squeezed gently.

"Doesn't make any sense," he said. "Think about it. What does your father do? He implements long-term policy, and he's responsible for short-term readiness. Congress and the President and the Defense Secretary thrash out the long-term policy, right? So if the Joint Chairman tried to stand in their way, they'd just replace him. Especially if they know he's under this kind of pressure, right?"

"What about short-term readiness?" she said.

"Same sort of a thing," Reacher said. "He's only chairman of a committee. The individual Chiefs of Staff are in there, too. Army, Navy, Air Force, Marines. If they're all singing a different song from what your father is reporting upward, that's not going to stay a secret for long, is it? They'll just replace him. Take him out of the equation altogether."

Holly turned her head. Looked straight at him.

"Are you sure?" she said. "Suppose these guys are working for Iraq or something? Suppose Saddam wants Kuwait again. But he doesn't want another Desert Storm. So he has me kidnapped, and my father says sorry, can't be done, for all kinds of invented reasons?"

Reacher shrugged.

"The answer's right there in the words you used," he said. "The reasons would be invented. Fact is, we could do Desert Storm again, if we had to. No problem. Everybody knows that. So if your father started denying it, everybody would know he was bullshitting, and everybody would know why. They'd just sideline him. The military is a tough place, Holly, no room for sentiment. If that's the strategy these guys are pursuing, they're wasting their time. It can't work."

She was quiet for a long moment.

"Then maybe this is about revenge," she said slowly. "Maybe somebody is punishing him for something in the past. Maybe I'm going to Iraq. Maybe they want to make him apologize for Desert Storm. Or Panama, or Grenada, or lots of things."

Reacher lay on his back and rocked with the motion. He could feel slight breaths of air stirring, because of the holes in the roof. He realized the truck was now a lot cooler, because of the new ventilation. Or because of his new mood.

"Too arcane," he said. "You'd have to be a pretty acute analyst to blame the Joint Chairman for all that stuff. There's a string of more obvious targets. Higher-profile people, right? The President, the Defense Secretary, Foreign Service people, field generals. If Baghdad was looking for a public humiliation, they'd pick somebody their people could identify, not some paper shuffler from the Pentagon."

"So what the hell is this about?" Holly said.

Reacher shrugged again.

"Ultimately, nothing," he said. "They haven't thought it through properly. That's what makes them so dangerous. They're competent, but they're stupid."

THE TRUCK DRONED on another six hours. Another three hundred and fifty miles, according to Reacher's guess. The inside temperature had cooled, but Reacher wasn't trying to estimate their direction by the temperature anymore. The pellet holes in the roof had upset that calculation. He was relying on dead reckoning instead. A total of eight hundred miles from Chicago, he figured, and not in an easterly direction. That left a big spread of possibilities. He trawled clockwise around the map in his head. Could be in Georgia, Alabama, Mississippi, Louisiana. Could be in Texas, Oklahoma, the southwest corner of Kansas. Probably no farther west than that. Reacher's mental map had brown shading there, showing the eastern slopes of the mountains, and the truck wasn't laboring up any grades. Could be in Nebraska or South Dakota. Maybe he was going to pass right by Mount Rushmore, second time in his life. Could have kept on past Minneapolis, into North Dakota. Eight hundred miles from Chicago, anywhere along a giant arc drawn across the continent.

THE LIGHT COMING in through the pellet holes had been gone for hours when the truck slowed and steered right. Up a ramp. Holly stirred and turned her head. Looked straight at Reacher. Questions in her eyes. Reacher shrugged back and waited. The truck paused and swung a right. Cruised down a straight road, then hung a left, a right, and continued on straight, slower. Reacher sat up and found his shirt. Shrugged himself into it. Holly sat up.

"Another hideout," she said. "This is a well-planned operation, Reacher."

This time it was a horse farm. The truck bumped down a long track and turned. Backed up. Reacher heard one of the guys getting out. His door slammed. The truck lurched backward into another building. Reacher heard the exhaust noise beat against the walls. Holly smelled horse smell. The engine died. The other two guys got out. Reacher heard the three of them grouping at the rear of the truck. Their key slid into the lock. The door cracked open. The shotgun poked in through the gap. This time, not pointing upward. Pointing level.

"Out," Loder called. "The bitch first. On its own."

Holly froze. Then she shrugged at Reacher and slid across the mattresses. The door snapped wide open and two pairs of hands seized her and dragged her out. The driver moved into view, aiming the shotgun straight in at Reacher. His finger was tight on the trigger.

"Do something, asshole," he said. "Please, just give me a damn excuse."

Reacher stared at him. Waited five long minutes. Then the shotgun jabbed forward. A Glock appeared next to it. Loder gestured. Reacher moved slowly forward toward the two muzzles. Loder leaned in and snapped a handcuff onto his wrist. Looped the chain into the free half and locked it. Used the chain to drag him out of the truck by the arm. They were in a horse barn. It was a wooden structure. Much smaller than the cow barn at their previous location. Much older. It came from a different generation of agriculture. There were two rows of stalls flanking an aisle. The floor was some kind of cobbled stone. Green with moss.

The central aisle was wide enough for horses, but not wide enough for the truck. It was backed just inside the door. Reacher saw a frame of sky around the rear of the vehicle. A big, dark sky. Could have been anywhere. He was led like a horse down the cobbled aisle. Loder was holding the chain. Stevie was walking sideways next to Reacher. His Glock was jammed high up against Reacher's temple. The driver was following, with the shotgun pressed hard into Reacher's kidney. It bumped with every step. They stopped at the end stall, farthest from the door. Holly was chained up in the space opposite. She was wearing a handcuff, right wrist, chain looped through the spare half into an iron ring bolted into the back wall of the stall.

The two guys with the guns fanned out in a loose arc and Loder shoved Reacher into his stall. Opened the cuff with the key. Looped the chain through the iron ring bolted into the timber on the back wall, looped it again, twice, and re-locked it into the cuff. He pulled at it and shook it to confirm it was secure.

"Mattresses," Reacher said. "Bring us the mattresses out of the truck."

Loder shook his head, but the driver smiled and nodded.

"OK," he said. "Good idea, asshole."

He stepped up inside and dragged the queen-size out. Struggled with it all the way down the aisle and flopped it into Holly's stall. Kicked it straight.

"The bitch gets one," he said. "You don't."

He started laughing and the other two joined in. They strolled away down the aisle. The driver pulled the truck forward out of the barn and the heavy doors creaked shut behind it. Reacher heard a heavy crossbeam slamming down into its retaining brackets on the outside and the rattle of another chain and a padlock. He glanced across at Holly. Then he looked down at the damp stone floor.

Reacher was squatted down, jammed into the far angle of the stall's wooden walls. He was waiting for the three guys to come back with dinner. They arrived after an hour. With one Glock and the shotgun. And one metal messtin. Stevie walked in with it. The driver took it from him and handed it to Holly. He stood there leering at her for a second and then turned to face Reacher. Pointed the shotgun at him.

"Bitch eats," he said. "You don't."

Reacher didn't get up. He just shrugged through the gloom.

"That's a loss I can just about survive," he said.

Nobody replied to that. They just strolled back out. Pushed the heavy wooden doors shut. Dropped the crossbeam into place and chained it up. Reacher listened to their footsteps fade away and turned to Holly.

"What is it?" he asked.

She shrugged across the distance at him.

"Some sort of a thin stew," she said. "Or a thick soup, I guess. One or the other. You want some?"

"They give you a fork?" he asked.

"No, a spoon," she said.

"Shit," he said. "Can't do anything with a damn spoon."

"You want some?" she asked again.

"Can you reach?" he said.

She spent some time eating, then she stretched out. One arm tight against the chain, the other pushing the messtin across the floor. Then she swiveled and used her good foot to slide the tin farther across the stone. Reacher slid forward, feet first, as far as his chain would let him go. He figured if he could stretch far enough, he could hook his foot around the tin and drag it in toward him. But it was hopeless. He was six five, and his arms were about the longest the Army tailors had ever seen, but even so he came up four feet short. He and Holly were stretched out in a perfect straight line, as near together as their chains would let them get, but the messtin was still way out of his reach.

"Forget it," he said. "Get it back while you can."

She hooked her own foot around the tin and pulled it back.

"Sorry," she said. "You're going to be hungry."

"I'll survive," he said. "Probably awful, anyway."

"Right," she said. "It's shit. Tastes like dog food."

Reacher stared through the dark at her. He was suddenly worried.

HOLLY LAY DOWN apologetically on her mattress and calmly went to sleep, but Reacher stayed awake. Not because of the stone floor. It was cold and damp, and hard. The cobblestones were wickedly lumpy. But that was not the reason. He was waiting for something. He was ticking off the minutes in his head, and he was waiting. His guess was it would be about three hours, maybe four. Way into the small hours, when resistance is low and patience runs out.

A long wait. The thirteen-thousand-seven-hundred-and-sixty-first night of his life, way down there in the bottom third of the scale, lying awake and waiting for something to happen. Something bad. Something he maybe had no chance of preventing. It was coming. He was certain of that. He'd seen the signs. He lay and waited for it, ticking off the minutes. Three hours, maybe four.

IT HAPPENED AFTER three hours and thirty-four minutes. The nameless driver came back into the barn. Wide awake and alone. Reacher heard his soft footsteps on the track outside. He heard the rattle of the padlock and the chain. He heard him lift the heavy crossbar out of its brackets. The barn door opened. A bar of bright moonlight fell across the floor. The driver stepped through it. Reacher saw a flash of his pink pig's face. The guy hurried down the aisle. No weapon in his hand.

"I'm watching you," Reacher said, quietly. "You back off, or you're a dead man."

The guy stopped opposite. He wasn't a complete moron. He stayed well out of range. His bright eyes traveled up from the handcuff on Reacher's wrist, along the chain, and rested on the iron ring in the wall. Then he smiled.

"You watch if you want to," he said. "I don't mind an audience. And you might learn something."

Holly stirred and woke up. Raised her head and glanced around, blinking in the dark.

"What's going on?" she said.

The driver turned to her. Reacher couldn't see his face. It was turned away. But he could see Holly's.

"We're going to have us a little fun, bitch," the driver said. "Just you and me, with your asshole friend here, watching and learning."

He put his hands down to his waist and unbuckled his belt. Holly stared at him. Started to sit up.

"Got to be joking," she said. "You come near me, I'll kill you."

"You wouldn't do that," the driver said. "Now would you? After I gave you a mattress and all? Just so we could be comfortable while we're doing it?"

Reacher stood up in his stall. His chain clanked loudly in the silent night.

"I'll kill you," he called. "You touch her, you're a dead man."

He said it once, and then he said it again. But it was like the guy wasn't hearing him. Like he was deaf. Reacher was hit with a clang of fear. If the guy wasn't going to listen to him, there was nothing he could do. He shook his chain. It rattled loudly through the silence of the night. It had no effect. The guy was just ignoring him.

"You come near me, I'll kill you," Holly said again.

Her leg was slowing her down. She was trapped in an awkward struggle to stand up. The driver darted into her stall. Raised his foot and stamped it down on her knee. She screamed in agony and collapsed and curled into a ball.

"You do what I tell you, bitch," the driver said. "Exactly what I tell you, or you'll never walk again."

Holly's scream died into a sob. The driver pulled his foot back and carefully kicked her knee like he was aiming for a field goal right at the end of the last quarter. She screamed again.

"You're a dead man," Reacher yelled.

The driver turned around and faced him. Smiled a wide smile.

"You keep your mouth tight shut," he said. "One more squeak out of you, it'll be harder on the bitch, OK?"

The ends of his belt were hanging down. He balled his fists and propped them on his hips. His big vivid face was glowing. His hair was bushed up like he'd just washed it and combed it back. He turned his head and spoke to Holly over his shoulder.

"You wearing anything under that suit?" he asked her.

Holly didn't speak. Silence in the barn. The guy turned to face her. Reacher saw her tracking his movements.

"I asked you a question, bitch," he said. "You want another kick?"

She didn't reply. She was breathing hard. Fighting the pain. The driver unzipped his pants. The sound of the zip was loud. It fought with the rasping of three people breathing hard.

"You see this?" he asked. "You know what this is?"

"Sort of," Holly muttered. "It looks a little like a penis, only smaller."

He stared at her, blankly. Then he bellowed in rage and

rushed into her stall, swinging his foot. Holly dodged away. His short wide leg swung and connected with nothing. He staggered off balance. Holly's eyes narrowed in a gleam of triumph. She dodged back and smashed her elbow into his stomach. She did it right. Used his own momentum against him, used all her weight like she wanted to punch his spine right out through his back. Caught him with a solid blow. The guy gasped and spun away.

Reacher whooped in admiration. And relief. He thought: couldn't have done it better myself, kid. The guy was heaving. Reacher saw his face, crumpled in pain. Holly was snarling in triumph. She scrambled on one knee after him. Going for his groin. Reacher willed her on. She launched herself at him. The guy turned and took it on the thigh. Holly had planned for that. It left his throat open to her elbow. Reacher saw it. Holly saw it. She lined it up. The killing blow. A vicious arcing curve. It was going to rip his head off. She swung it in. Then her chain snapped tight and stopped her short. It clanked hard against the iron ring and jerked her backward.

Reacher's grin froze on his face. The guy staggered out of range. Stooped and panted and caught his breath. Then he straightened up and hitched his belt higher. Holly faced him, one-handed. Her chain was tight against the wall, vibrating with the tension she had on it.

"I like a fighter," the guy gasped. "Makes it more interesting for me. But make sure you save yourself some energy for later. I don't want you just lying there."

Holly glared at him, breathing hard. Crackling with aggression. But she was one-handed. The guy stepped in again and she swung a stinging punch. Fast and low. He crowded left and blocked it. She couldn't deliver the follow-up. Her other arm was pinned back. He raised his foot and kicked for her stomach. She arched around it. He kicked out again and stumbled straight into an elbow, hard against his ear. It was the wrong elbow, with no force behind it because of her impossible position. A poor blow. It left her off balance. The driver stepped close and kicked her in the gut. She went down. He kicked out again and caught her knee. Reacher heard it crunch. She screamed in agony. Collapsed on the mattress. The driver breathed fast and stood there.

"I asked you a damn question," he said.

Holly was deathly white and trembling. She was writhing around on the mattress, one arm pinned behind her, gasping with the pain. Reacher saw her face, flashing through the bar of bright moonlight.

"I'm waiting, bitch," the guy said.

Reacher saw her face again. Saw she was beaten. The fight was out of her.

"Want another kicking?" the driver said.

There was silence in the barn again.

"I'm waiting for an answer," the guy said.

Reacher stared over, waiting. There was still silence. Just the rasping of three people breathing hard in the quiet. Then Holly spoke.

"What was the question?" she said quietly.

The guy smiled down at her.

"You wearing anything under that suit?" he said.

Holly nodded. Didn't speak.

"OK, what?" the guy said to her.

"Underwear," she said, quietly.

The guy cupped a hand behind his ear.

"Can't hear you, bitch," he said.

"I'm wearing, underwear, you bastard," she said, louder.

The guy shook his head.

"Bad name," he said. "I'm going to need an apology for that."

"Screw you," Holly said.

"I'll kick you again," the guy said. "In the knee. I do that, you'll never walk without a stick, the whole rest of your life, you bitch."

Holly looked away.

"Your choice, bitch," the guy said.

He raised his foot. Holly stared down at her mattress.

"OK, I apologize," she said. "I'm sorry."

The guy nodded, happily.

"Describe your underwear to me," he said. "Lots of detail."

She shrugged. Turned her face away and spoke to the wooden wall.

"Bra and pants," she said. "Victoria's Secret. Dark peach."

"Skimpy?" the driver asked.

She shrugged again, miserably, like she knew for sure what the next question was going to be.

"I guess," she said.

"Want to show it to me?" the guy said.

"No," she said.

The driver took a step closer.

"So you do want another kicking?" he said.

She didn't speak. The guy cupped his hand behind his ear again.

"Can't hear you, bitch," he said.

"What was the question?" Holly muttered.

"You want another kicking?" the guy said.

Holly shook her head.

"No," she said again.

"OK," he said. "Show me your underwear, and you won't get one."

He raised his foot. Holly raised her hand. It went to the top button on her suit. Reacher watched her. There were five buttons down the front of the suit. Reacher willed her to undo each of them slowly and rhythmically. He needed her to do that. It was vital. Slowly and rhythmically, Holly, he pleaded silently. He gripped his chain with both hands. Four feet from where it looped into the iron ring on the back wall. He tightened his hands around it.

She undid the top button. Reacher counted: one. The driver leered down. Her hand slid to the next button. Reacher tightened his grip again. She undid the second button. Reacher counted: two. Her hand slid down to the third button. Reacher turned square-on to face the rear wall of his stall and took a deep breath. Turned his head and watched over his shoulder. Holly undid the third button. Her breasts swelled out. Dark peach brassiere. Skimpy and lacy. The driver shuffled from foot to foot. Reacher counted: three. He exhaled right from the bottom of his lungs. Holly's hand slid down to the fourth button. Reacher took a deep breath, the deepest breath of his life. He tightened his hold on the chain until his knuckles shone white. Holly undid the fourth button. Reacher counted: four. Her hand slid down. Paused a beat. Waited. Undid the

fifth button. Her suit fell open. The driver leered down and
made a small sound. Reacher jerked back and smashed his
foot into the wall. Right under the iron ring. He smashed his
weight backward against the chain, two hundred and twenty
pounds of coiled fury exploding against the force of his kick.
Splinters of damp wood burst out of the wall. The old planks
shattered. The bolts tore right out of the timber. Reacher was
hurled backward. He swarmed up to his feet, his chain whipping and flailing angrily behind him.

"Five!" he screamed.

He seized the driver by the arm and hurled him into his
stall. Threw him against the back wall. The guy smashed into
it and hung like a broken doll. He staggered forward and
Reacher kicked him in the stomach. The guy jackknifed in
the air, feet right off the ground, and smashed flat on his face
on the cobblestones. Reacher doubled his chain and swung it
through the air. Aimed the lethal length at the guy's head
like a giant metal whip. The iron ring centrifuged out like an
old medieval weapon. But at the last second Reacher changed
his mind. Wrenched the chain out of its trajectory and let it
smash and spark into the stones on the floor. He grabbed the
driver, one hand on his collar and one hand in his hair. Lifted
him bodily across the aisle to Holly's mattress. Jammed his
ugly face down into the softness and leaned on him until he
suffocated. The guy bucked and thrashed, but Reacher just
planted a giant hand flat on the back of his skull and waited
patiently until he died.

HOLLY WAS STARING at the corpse and Reacher was sitting
next to her, panting. He was spent and limp from the explosive force of tearing the iron ring out of the wall. It felt like
a lifetime of physical effort had gone into one split second.
A lifetime supply of adrenaline was boiling through him. The
clock inside his head had stopped. He had no idea how long
they had been sitting there. He shook himself and staggered
to his feet. Dragged the body away and left it in the aisle, up
near the open door. Then he wandered back and squatted next
to Holly. His fingers were bruised from his desperate grip on
the chain, but he forced them to be delicate. He did up all
her buttons, one by one, right to the top. She was taking quick

short breaths. Then she flung her arms round his neck and held on tight. Her breathing sucked and blew against his shirt.

They held each other for a long moment. He felt the fury drain out of her. They let each other go and sat side by side on the mattress, staring into the gloom. She turned to him and put her small hand lightly on top of his.

"Now I guess I owe you," she said.

"My pleasure," Reacher said. "Hey, believe me."

"I needed help," she said quietly. "I've been fooling myself."

He flipped his hand over and closed it around hers.

"Bullshit, Holly," he said, gently. "Time to time, we all need help. Don't feel bad about it. If you were fit, you'd have slaughtered him. I could see that. One arm and one leg, you were nearly there. It's just your knee. Pain like that, you've got no chance. Believe me, I know what it's like. After the Beirut thing, I couldn't have taken candy from a baby, best part of a year."

She smiled a slight smile and squeezed his hand. The clock inside his head started up again. Getting close to dawn.

18

SEVEN-TWENTY WEDNESDAY MORNING East Coast time, General Johnson left the Pentagon. He was out of uniform, dressed in a lightweight business suit, and he walked. It was his preferred method of getting around. It was a hot morning in Washington, and already humid, but he stepped out at a steady speed, arms swinging loosely through a small arc, head up, breathing hard.

He walked north through the dust on the shoulder of George Washington Boulevard, along the edge of the great cemetery on his left, through Lady Bird Johnson Park, and across the Arlington Memorial Bridge. Then he walked clockwise around the Lincoln Memorial, past the Vietnam Wall, and turned right along Constitution Avenue, the reflecting pool on his right, the Washington Monument up ahead. He walked past the National Museum of American History, past the National Museum of Natural History, and turned left onto 9th Street. Exactly three and a half miles, on a glorious morning, an hour's brisk walk through one of the world's great capital cities, past landmarks the world's tourists flock to photograph, and he saw absolutely nothing at all except the dull mist of worry hanging just in front of his eyes.

He crossed Pennsylvania Avenue and entered the Hoover Building through the main doors. Laid his hands palms down on the reception counter.

"The Chairman of the Joint Chiefs of Staff," he said. "To see the Director."

His hands left two palm-shaped patches of dampness on the laminate. The agent who came down to show him upstairs noticed them. Johnson was silent in the elevator. Harland Webster was waiting for him at the door to his private suite. Johnson nodded to him. Didn't speak. Webster stood aside and gestured him into the inner office. It was dark. There was a lot of mahogany paneling, and the blinds were closed. Johnson sat down in a leather chair and Webster walked around him to his desk.

"I don't want to get in your way," Johnson said.

He looked at Webster. Webster worked for a moment, decoding that sentence. Then he nodded, cautiously.

"You spoke with the President?" he asked.

Johnson nodded.

"You understand it's appropriate for me to do so?" he asked.

"Naturally," Webster said. "Situation like this, nobody should worry about protocol. You call him or go see him?"

"I went to see him," Johnson said. "Several times. I had several long conversations with him."

Webster thought: face-to-face. Several long conversations. Worse than I thought, but understandable.

"And?" he asked.

Johnson shrugged.

"He told me he'd placed you in personal command," he said.

Webster nodded.

"Kidnapping," he said. "It's Bureau territory, whoever the victim is."

Johnson nodded, slowly.

"I accept that," he said. "For now."

"But you're anxious," Webster said. "Believe me, General, we're all anxious."

Johnson nodded again. And then he asked the question he'd walked three and a half miles to ask.

"Any progress?" he said.

Webster shrugged.

"We're into the second full day," he said. "I don't like that at all."

He lapsed into silence. The second full day of a kidnap is a kind of threshold. Any early chance of a resolution is gone. The situation starts to harden up. It starts to become a long, intractable set-piece. The danger to the victim increases. The best time to clear up a kidnap is the first day. The second day, the process gets tougher. The chances get smaller.

"Any progress?" Johnson asked again.

Webster looked away. The second day is when the kidnappers start to communicate. That had always been the Bureau's experience. The second day, sick and frustrated about missing your first and best chance, you sit around, hoping desperately the guys will call. If they don't call on the second day, chances are they aren't going to call at all.

"Anything I can do?" Johnson asked.

Webster nodded.

"You can give me a reason," he said. "Who would threaten you like this?"

Johnson shook his head. He had been asking himself the same question since Monday night.

"Nobody," he said.

"You should tell me," Webster said. "Anything secret, anything hidden, better you tell me right now. It's important, for Holly's sake."

"I know that," Johnson said. "But there's nothing. Nothing at all."

Webster nodded. He believed him, because he knew it was true. He had reviewed the whole of Johnson's Bureau file. It was a weighty document. It started on page one with brief biographies of his maternal great-grandparents. They had come from a small European principality which no longer existed.

"Will Holly be OK?" Johnson asked quietly.

The recent file pages recounted the death of Johnson's wife. A surprise, a vicious cancer, no more than six weeks, beginning to end. Covert psychiatric opinion commissioned by the Bureau had predicted the old guy would hold up because of his daughter. It had proven to be a correct diagnosis. But if he lost her too, you didn't need to be a psychiatrist to know he wouldn't handle it well. Webster nodded again and put some conviction into his voice.

"She'll be fine," he said.

"So what have we got so far?" Johnson asked.

"Four guys," Webster said. "We've got their pickup truck. They abandoned it prior to the snatch. Burned it and left it. We found it north of Chicago. It's being airlifted down here to Quantico, right now. Our people will go over it."

"For clues?" Johnson said. "Even though it burned?"

Webster shrugged.

"Burning is pretty dumb," he said. "It doesn't really obscure much. Not from our people, anyway. We'll use that pickup to find them."

"And then what?" Johnson asked.

Webster shrugged again.

"Then we'll go get your daughter back," he said. "Our Hostage Rescue Team is standing by. Fifty guys, the best in the world at this kind of thing. Waiting right by their choppers. We'll go get her, and we'll tidy up the guys who grabbed her."

There was a short silence in the dark quiet room.

"Tidy them up?" Johnson said. "What does that mean?"

Webster glanced around his own office and lowered his voice. Thirty-six years of habit.

"Policy," he said. "A major D.C. case like this? No publicity. No media access. We can't allow it. This sort of thing gets on TV, every nut in the country is going to be trying it. So we go in quietly. Some weapons will get discharged. Inevitable in a situation like this. A little collateral damage here and there."

Johnson nodded slowly.

"You're going to execute them?" he asked, vaguely.

Webster just looked at him, neutrally. Bureau psychiatrists had suggested to him the anticipation of deadly revenge could help sustain self-control, especially with people accustomed to direct action, like other agents, or soldiers.

"Policy," he said again. "My policy. And like the man says, I've got personal command."

• • •

THE CHARRED PICKUP was lifted onto an aluminum platform and secured with nylon ropes. An Air Force Chinook hammered over from the military compound at O'Hare and hovered above it, its downdraft whipping the lake into a frenzy. It winched its chain down and eased the pickup into the air. Swung around over the lake and dipped its nose and roared back west to O'Hare. Set its load down right in front of the open nose of a Galaxy transport. Air Force ground crew winched the platform inside. The cargo door closed on it and four minutes later the Galaxy was taxiing. Four minutes later again it was in the air, groaning east toward Washington. Four hours after that, it was roaring over the capital, heading for Andrews Air Force Base. As it landed, another borrowed Chinook took off and waited in midair. The Galaxy taxied to its apron and the pickup was winched out. The Chinook swooped down and swung it into the air. Flew it south, following I-95 into Virginia, forty miles, all the way to Quantico.

The Chinook set it down gently on the tarmac right outside the vehicle lab. Bureau techs ran out, white coats flapping in the fierce downdraft, and dragged the platform in through the roller door. They winched the wreck off the platform and pulled it into the center of the large shed. They rolled arc lights into a rough circle around it and lit them up. Then they stood there for a second, looking exactly like a team of pathologists getting ready to go to work on a corpse.

GENERAL JOHNSON RETRACED his steps exactly. He made it down 9th Street, past Natural History, past American History, his mouth forced into a tense rigid oval, breathing hard. He walked the length of the reflecting pool with his throat clamping and gagging. He swung left onto Constitution Avenue and made it as far as the Vietnam Wall. Then he stopped. There was a fair crowd, stunned and quiet, as always. He looked at them. He looked at himself in the black granite. He didn't stand out. He was in a lightweight gray suit. It was OK. So he let his vision blur with his tears and he moved forward and turned and sat against the base of the wall, sobbing and crying with his back pressed against the golden names of boys who had died thirty years ago.

19

REACHER BALLED HIS loose chain into his hand and slipped out of the barn into the predawn twilight. He walked twenty paces and stopped. Freedom. The night air was soft and infinite around him. He was unconfined. But he had no idea where he was. The barn stood alone, isolated fifty yards from a clutch of farm buildings of similar old vintage. There was a house, and a couple of small sheds, and an open structure with a new pickup parked in it. Next to the pickup was a tractor. Next to the tractor, ghostly white in the moonlight, was the truck. Reacher walked over the rocky track toward it. The front doors were locked. The rear doors were locked. He ran back to the horse barn and searched through the dead driver's pockets. Nothing except the padlock key from the barn door. No keys to the truck.

He ran back, squeezing the mass of chain to keep it from making a sound, past the motor barn, and looked at the house. Walked right around it. The front door was locked tight. The back door was locked tight. And there was a dog behind it. Reacher heard it move in its sleep. He heard a low, sleepy growl. He walked away.

He stood on the track, halfway back to the horse barn, and looked around. He trained his eyes on the indistinct horizon and turned a full circle in the dark. Some kind of a huge, empty landscape. Flat, endless, no discernible features. The damp night smell of a million acres of something growing.

A pale streak of dawn in the east. He shrugged and ducked back inside. Holly raised herself on one elbow and looked a question at him.

"Problems," he said. "The handcuff keys are in the house. So are the truck keys. I can't go in for them because there's a dog in there. It's going to bark and wake everybody up. There's more than the two others in there. This is some kind of a working farm. There's a pickup and a tractor. Could be four or five armed men in there. When that damn dog barks, I've had it. And it's nearly daylight."

"Problems," Holly said.

"Right," he said. "We can't get at a vehicle, and we can't just walk away, because you're chained up and you can't walk and we're about a million miles from anywhere, anyway."

"Where are we?" she asked.

He shrugged.

"No idea," he said.

"I want to see," she said. "I want to see outside. I'm sick of being closed in. Can't you get this chain off?"

Reacher ducked behind her and looked at the iron ring in her wall. The timber looked a little better than his had been. Closer-grained. He shook the ring and he knew it was hopeless. She nodded, reluctantly.

"We wait," she said. "We wait for a better chance."

He hurried back to the middle stalls and checked the walls, low down, where it was dampest and the siding was made from the longest boards. He tapped and kicked at them. Chose one particular place and pressed hard with his foot. The board gave slightly and opened a gap against its rusty nail. He worked the gap and sprung the next board, and the next, until he had a flap which would open tall enough to crawl through. Then he ducked back into the center aisle and piled the loose end of his chain onto the dead driver's stomach. Fished in the trouser pocket and pulled out the padlock key. Held it in his teeth. Bent down and picked up the body and the chain together. Carried it out through the open door.

He carried it about twenty-five yards. Away from the house. Then he rested the body on its feet, supporting it by the shoulders, like he was dancing with a drunken partner.

Ducked forward and jacked it up onto his shoulder. Caught the chain with one hand and walked away down the track.

He walked fast for twenty minutes. More than a mile. Along the track to a road. Turned left down the road and out into the empty countryside. It was horse country. Railed paddocks ran left and right beside the road. Endless flat grassland, cool and damp in the last of the night. Occasional trees looming through the dark. A narrow, straight, lumpy road surface.

He walked down the center of the road. Then he ducked onto the grassy shoulder and found a ditch. It ran along the base of the paddock rail. He turned a complete circle, with the dead driver windmilling on his shoulder. He could see nothing. He was more than a mile from the farm and he could have been more than a hundred from the next one. He bent over and dropped the body into the ditch. It flopped down through the long grass and landed facedown in mud. Reacher turned and ran the mile back to the farm. The streak of dawn was lightening the sky.

He turned into the rough track. There were lights in the windows of the farmhouse. He sprinted for the barn. Pushed the heavy wooden doors closed from the outside. Lifted the crossbeam into its supports and locked it in place with the padlock key. Ran back to the track and hurled the key far into the field. Wednesday was flaming up over the horizon. He sprinted for the far side of the barn and found the gap he'd sprung in the siding. Pushed his chain in ahead of him. Squeezed his shoulders through and forced his way back inside. Pulled the boards back flush with the old timbers, best as he could. Then he came back into the aisle and stood bent over, breathing hard.

"All done," he said. "They'll never find him."

He scooped up the metal messtin with the cold remains of the soup in it. Scratched around in his stall for the fallen bolts. He gathered as many wood splinters as he could find. Slopped them around in the cold soup and forced them back into the ragged bolt holes. He walked over to Holly's stall and put the tin back on the ground. Kept the spoon. He assembled the bolts through the holes in the base of the iron ring, hanging there off his length of chain. Forced them home among the sticky splinters. Used the back of the spoon to press them firmly in. He ran the chain through the loop until it was hanging straight down and resting on the stone floor. Minimum stress on the fragile assembly.

He tossed the spoon back to Holly. She caught it one-handed and put it back in the tin. Then he ducked down and listened through the boards. The dog was outside. He could hear it snuffling. Then he heard people. Footsteps on the track. They ran to the doors of the barn. They shook and rattled the crossbeam. Retreated. There was shouting. They were calling a name, over and over again. The crack around the barn door was lighting up with morning. The timbers of the barn were creaking as the sun flooded over the horizon and warmed them through.

The footsteps ran back to the barn. The padlock rattled and the chain came off. The crossbeam thumped to the ground. The door groaned open. Loder stepped inside. He had the Glock in his hand and strain showing in his face. He stood just inside the door. His eyes were flicking back and forth between Reacher and Holly. The strain in his face was edged by anger. Some kind of a cold light in his eyes. Then the jumpy guy stepped in behind him. Stevie. He was carrying the driver's shotgun. And smiling. He crowded past Loder and ran down the central cobbled aisle. Raised the shotgun and pointed it straight at Reacher. Loder started after him. Stevie crunched a round into the chamber. Reacher shifted a foot to his left, so the iron ring was hidden from view behind him.

"What's the problem?" he asked.

"You are, asshole," Loder said. "Situation has changed. We're a man short. So you just became one person too many."

Reacher was on his way to the floor as Stevie pulled the trigger. He landed flat on the hard cobbles and hurled himself forward as the shotgun boomed and the stall blew apart. The air was instantly thick with splinters of damp wood and the stink of gunpowder. The plank holding the iron ring fell out of the shattered wall and the chain clattered to the floor. Reacher rolled over and glanced up. Stevie lifted the shotgun vertical and crunched another round into the chamber. Swung the barrel down and aimed again.

"Wait!" Holly screamed.

Stevie glanced at her. Impossible not to.

"Don't be a damn fool," she yelled. "Hell are you doing? You don't have the time for this."

Loder turned to face her.

"He's run, right?" she said. "Your driver? Is that what happened? He bailed out and ran for it, right? So you need to get going. You don't have time for this."

Loder stared at her.

"Right now you're ahead of the game," Holly said urgently. "But you shoot this guy, you got the local cops a half hour behind you. You need to get going."

Reacher gasped up at her from the floor. She was magnificent. She was sucking all their attention her way. She was saving his life.

"Two of you, two of us," she said urgently. "You can handle it, right?"

There was silence. Dust and powder drifted in the air. Then Loder stepped back, covering them both with his automatic. Reacher watched the disappointment on Stevie's face. He stood slowly and pulled the chain clear of the wreckage. The iron ring fell out of the smashed wood and clanked on the stones.

"Bitch is right," Loder said. "We can handle it."

He nodded to Stevie. Stevie ran for the door and Loder turned and pulled his key and unlocked Holly's wrist. Dropped her cuff on her mattress. The weight of the chain pulled it back toward the wall. It pulled off the edge of the mattress and slid onto the cobblestones with a loud metallic sound.

"OK, asshole, real quick," Loder said. "Before I change my mind."

Reacher looped his chain into his hand. Ducked down and picked Holly up, under her knees and shoulders. They heard the truck start up. It slewed backward into the entrance. Jammed to a stop. Reacher ran Holly to the truck. Laid her down inside. Climbed in after her. Loder slammed the doors and shut them into darkness.

• • •

Now I GUESS I owe you," Reacher said quietly.

Holly just waved it away. An embarrassed little gesture. Reacher stared at her. He liked her. Liked her face. He gazed at it. Recalled it white and disgusted as the driver taunted her. Saw the smooth swell of her breasts under his filthy drooling gaze. Then the picture changed to Stevie smiling and shooting at him, chained to the wall. Then he heard Loder say: the situation has changed.

Everything had changed. He had changed. He lay and felt the old anger inside him grinding like gears. Cold, implacable anger. Uncontrollable. They had made a mistake. They had changed him from a spectator into an enemy. A bad mistake to make. They had pushed open the forbidden door, not knowing what would come bursting back out at them. He lay there and felt like a ticking bomb they were carrying deep into the heart of their territory. He felt the flood of anger, and thrilled with it, and savored it, and stored it up.

Now THERE WAS only one mattress inside the truck. It was only three feet wide. And Stevie was a very erratic driver. Reacher and Holly were lying down, pressed tight together. Reacher's left wrist still had the cuff and the chain locked onto it. His right arm was around Holly's shoulders. He was holding her tight. Tighter than he really needed to.

"How much farther?" she asked.

"We'll be there before nightfall," he said, quietly. "They didn't bring your chain. No more overnight stops."

She was silent for a moment.

"I don't know if I'm glad or not," she said. "I hate this truck, but I don't know if I want to actually arrive anywhere."

Reacher nodded.

"It reduces our chances," he said. "Rule of thumb is escape while you're on the move. It gets much harder after that."

The motion of the truck indicated they were on a highway. But either the terrain was different, or Stevie couldn't handle the truck, or both, because they were swaying violently. The guy was swinging late into turns and jamming the vehicle

from side to side, like he was having a struggle staying between the lane markers. Holly was getting thrown against
Reacher's side. He pulled her closer and held her tighter. She
snuggled in close, instinctively. He felt her hesitate, like she
realized she'd acted without thinking, then he felt her decide
not to pull away again.

"You feel OK?" she asked him. "You killed a man."

He was quiet for a long moment.

"He wasn't the first," he said. "And I just decided he
won't be the last."

She turned her head to speak at the same time he did. The
truck swayed violently to the left. Their lips were an inch
apart. The truck swayed again. They kissed. At first it was
light and tentative. Reacher felt the new soft lips on his, and
the unfamiliar new taste and smell and feel. Then they kissed
harder. Then the truck started hammering through a series of
sharp curves, and they forgot all about kissing and just held
on tight, trying not to be thrown right off the mattress onto
the ridged metal floor.

20

Brogan was the guy who made the breakthrough in Chicago. He was the third guy that morning to walk past the can of white paint out there on the abandoned industrial lot, but he was the first to realize its significance.

"The truck they stole was white," Brogan said. "Some kind of ID on the side. They painted over it. Got to be that way. The can was right there, with a brush, about ten feet from the Lexus. Stands to reason they would park the Lexus right next to the truck, right? Therefore the paint can was next to where the truck had been."

"What sort of paint?" McGrath asked.

"Ordinary household paint," Brogan said. "A quart can. Two-inch brush. Price tag still on it, from a hardware store. And there are fingerprints in the splashes on the handle."

McGrath nodded and smiled.

"OK," he said. "Go to work."

Brogan took the computer-aided mug shots with him to the hardware store named on the paintbrush handle. It was a cramped, family-owned place, two hundred yards from the abandoned lot. The counter was attended by a stout old woman with a mind like a steel trap. Straightaway she identified the picture of the guy the video had caught at the wheel of the Lexus. She said the paint and the brush had been purchased by him about ten o'clock Monday morning. To prove it, she rattled open an ancient drawer and pulled out Monday's register roll. Seven-ninety-eight for the paint, five-ninety-eight for the brush, plus tax, right there on the roll.

"He paid cash," she said.

"You got a video system in here?" Brogan asked her.

"No," she said.

"Doesn't your insurance company say you got to?" he asked.

The stout old woman just smiled.

"We're not insured," she said.

Then she leaned under the counter and came up with a shotgun.

"Not by no insurance company, anyway," she said.

Brogan looked at the weapon. He was pretty sure the barrel was way too short for the piece to be legal. But he wasn't about to start worrying over such a thing. Not right then.

"OK," he said. "You take care now."

MORE THAN SEVEN million people in the Chicago area, something like ten million road vehicles, but only one white truck had been reported stolen in the twenty-four-hour period between Sunday and Monday. It was a white Ford Econoline. Owned and operated by a South Side electrician. His insurance company made him empty the truck at night, and store his stock and tools inside his shop. Anything left inside the truck was not covered. That was the rule. It was an irksome rule, but on Monday morning when the guy came out to load up and the truck was gone, it started to look like a rule which made a whole lot of sense. He had reported the theft to the insurance broker and the police, and he was not expecting to hear much more about it. So he was duly impressed when two FBI agents turned up, forty-eight hours later, asking all kinds of urgent questions.

OK," MCGRATH SAID. "We know what we're looking for. White Econoline, new paint on the sides. We've got the plates. Now we need to know where to look. Ideas?"

"Coming up on forty-eight hours," Brogan said. "Assume an average speed of fifty-five? That would make the max range somewhere more than twenty-six hundred miles. That's effectively anywhere on the North American continent, for God's sake.''

"Too pessimistic," Milosevic said. "They probably stopped nights. Call it six hours' driving time on Monday, maybe ten on Tuesday, maybe four so far today, total of twenty hours, that's a maximum range of eleven hundred miles."

"Needle in a haystack," Brogan said.

McGrath shrugged.

"So let's find the haystack," he said. "Then we'll go look for the needle. Call it fifteen hundred maximum. What does that look like?"

Brogan pulled a road atlas from the stack of reference material on the table. He opened it up to the early section where the whole country was shown all at once, all the states splattered over one page in a colorful mosaic. He checked the scale and traced his fingernail in a circle.

"That's anywhere shy of California," he said. "Half of Washington State, half of Oregon, none of California and absolutely all of everywhere else. Somewhere around a zillion square miles."

There was a depressed silence in the room.

"Mountains between here and Washington State, right?" McGrath said. "So let's assume they're not in Washington State yet. Or Oregon. Or California. Or Alaska or Hawaii. So we've cut it down already. Only forty-five states to call, right? Let's go to work."

"They might have gone to Canada," Brogan said. "Or Mexico, or a boat or a plane."

Milosevic shrugged and took the atlas from him.

"You're too pessimistic," he said again.

"Needle in a damn haystack," Brogan said back.

THREE FLOORS ABOVE them, the Bureau fingerprint technicians were looking at the paintbrush Brogan had brought in. It had been used once only, by a fairly clumsy guy. The paint was matted up in the bristles, and had run onto the mild steel ferrule which bound the bristles into the wooden handle. The guy had used an action which had put his thumb on the back of the ferrule, and his first two fingers on the front. It was suggestive of a medium-height guy reaching up and brushing paint onto a flat surface, level with his head, maybe a little higher, the paintbrush handle pointing downward. A Ford Econoline was just a fraction less than eighty-one inches tall. Any sign writing would be about seventy inches off the ground. The computer could not calculate this guy's height, because it had only seen him sitting down inside the Lexus, but the way the brush had been used, he must have been five eight, five nine, reaching up and brushing just a little above his eye level. Brushing hard, with some lateral force. There wasn't going to be a lot of finesse in the finished job.

Wet paint is a pretty good medium for trapping fingerprints, and the techs knew they weren't going to have a lot of trouble. But for the sake of completeness, they ran every process they had, from fluoroscopy down to the traditional gray powder. They ended up with three and a half good prints, clearly the thumb and the first two fingers of the right hand, with the extra bonus of a lateral half of the little finger. They enhanced the focus in the computer and sent the prints down the digital line to the Hoover Building in Washington. They added a code instructing the big database down there to search with maximum speed.

IN THE LABS at Quantico, the hunters were divided into two packs. The burned pickup had been torn apart, and half the staff was examining the minute physical traces unique to that particular vehicle. The other half was chasing through the fragmented records held by the manufacturers, listening out for the faint echoes of its construction and subsequent sales history.

It was a Dodge, ten years old, built in Detroit. The chassis number and the code stamped into the iron of the engine block were both original. The numbers enabled the manufacturer to identify the original shipment. The pickup had rolled out of the factory gate one April and had been loaded onto a railroad wagon and hauled to California. Then it had been driven to a dealership in Mojave. The dealer had paid the invoice in May, and beyond that, the manufacturer had no further knowledge of the vehicle.

The dealership in Mojave had gone belly-up two years

later. New owners had bought the franchise. Current records were in their computer. Ancient history from before the change in ownership was all in storage. Not every day that a small automotive dealership on the edge of the desert gets a call from the FBI Academy at Quantico, so there was a promise of rapid action. The sales manager himself undertook to get the information and call right back.

The vehicle itself was pretty much burned out. All the soft clues were gone. There were no plates. There was nothing significant in the interior. There were no bridge tokens, no tunnel tokens. The windshield stickers were gone. All that was left was the mud. The vehicle technicians had cut away both of the rear wheel wells, the full hoop of sheet metal right above the driven tires, and carried them carefully across to the Materials Analysis Unit. Any vehicle writes its own itinerary in the layers of mud it throws up underneath. Bureau geologists were peeling back the layers and looking at where the pickup had been, and where it had come from.

The mud was baked solid by the burning tires. Some of the softer crystals had vitrified into glass. But the layers were clear. The outer layers were thin. The geologists concluded they had been deposited during a long journey across the country. Then there was a couple of years' worth of mixed rock particles. The particular mixture was interesting. There was such a combination of sands there that identifying their exact origin should be easy enough. Under that mixture was a thick base layer of desert dust. Straightaway, the geologists agreed that the truck had started its life out near the Mojave Desert.

EVERY SINGLE LAW enforcement agency in forty-five states had the description and the plate number of the stolen white Econoline. Every single officer on duty in the whole nation had been briefed to look for it, parked or mobile, burned or hidden or abandoned. For a short time that Wednesday, that white Econoline was the most hunted vehicle on the planet.

McGrath was sitting at the head of the table in the quiet conference room, smoking, waiting. He was not optimistic. If the truck was parked and hidden, it would most likely never be found. The task was too huge. Any closed garage

g or barn could hide it forever. If it was still some-
the road, the chances were better. So the biggest
f his life was: after forty-eight hours, had they gotten
ey were going, or were they still on their way?

Two hours after starting the patient search, the fingerprint
database brought back a name: Peter Wayne Bell. There was
a perfect match, right hand, thumb and first two fingers. The
computer rated the match on the partial from the little finger
as very probable.

"Thirty-one years old," Brogan said. "From Mojave, California. Two convictions for sex offenses. Charged with a
double rape, three years ago, didn't go down. Victims were
three months in the hospital. This guy Bell had an alibi from
three of his friends. Victims couldn't make the ID, too shaken
up by the beatings."

"Nice guy," McGrath said.

Milosevic nodded.

"And he's got Holly," he said. "Right there in the back
of his truck."

McGrath said nothing in reply to that. Then the phone
rang. He picked it up. Listened to a short barked sentence.
He sat there and Brogan and Milosevic saw his face light up
like a guy who sees his teams all win the pennant on the
same day, baseball and football and basketball and hockey,
all on the same day that his son graduates summa cum laude
from Harvard and his gold stocks go through the roof.

"Arizona," he shouted. "It's in Arizona, heading north on
U.S. 60."

An old hand in an Arizona State Police cruiser had spotted
a white panel truck making bad lane changes round the sharp
curves on U.S. 60 as it winds away from the town of Globe,
seventy miles east of Phoenix. He had pulled closer and read
the plate. He saw the blue oval and the Econoline script on
the back. He had thumbed his mike and called it in. Then the
world had gone crazy. He was told to stick with the truck,
no matter what. He was told that helicopters would be coming
in from Phoenix and Flagstaff, and from Albuquerque way
over in New Mexico. Every available mobile unit would be

coming in behind him from the south. Up ahead, the National Guard would be assembling a roadblock. Within twenty minutes, he was told, you'll have more backup than you've ever dreamed of. Until then, he was told, you're the most important lawman in America.

THE SALES MANAGER from the Dodge dealership in Mojave, California, called Quantico back within an hour. He'd been over to the storage room and dug out the records for the sales made ten years ago by the previous franchise owners. The pickup in question had been sold to a citrus farmer down in Kendall, fifty miles south of Mojave, in May of that year. The guy had been back for servicing and emissions testing for the first four years, and after that, they'd never seen him again. He had bought on a four-year time payment plan and his name was Dutch Borken.

A HALF-HOUR LATER, the stolen white Econoline was twenty-eight miles farther north on U.S. 60 in Arizona and it was the tip of a long teardrop shape of fifty vehicles cruising behind it. Above it, five helicopters were hammering through the air. In front of it, ten miles to the north, the highway was closed and another forty vehicles were stationary on the pavement, parked up in a neat arrowhead formation. The whole operation was being coordinated by the Agent-in-Charge from the FBI's Phoenix office. He was in the lead helicopter, staring down through the clear desert air at the roof of the truck. He was wearing a headset with a throat mike, and he was talking continuously.

"OK, people," he said. "Let's go for it, right now. Go go go!"

His lead chopper swooped upward out of the way and two others arrowed down. They hovered just in front of the truck, low down, one on each side, keeping pace. The police cars behind fanned out across the whole width of the highway and they all hit their lights and sirens together. A third chopper swung down and flew backward, right in front of the truck, eight feet off the ground, strobes flashing, rotors beating the air. The copilot started a sequence of clear gestures, hands wide, palms out, like he was personally slowing the truck.

Then the sirens all stopped and the enormous bullhorn on the front of the helicopter fired up. The copilot's voice boomed out, amplified grotesquely beyond the point of distortion, clearly audible even over the thrashing and hammering of the rotor blades.

"Federal agents," his voice screamed. "You are commanded to stop at once. I repeat, you are commanded to stop your vehicle at once."

The truck kept on going. The helicopter right in front of it swung and wobbled in the air. Then it settled again, even closer to the windshield, flying backward, not more than ten feet away.

"You are surrounded," the copilot shouted through the huge bullhorn. "There are a hundred police officers behind you. The road is closed ahead. You have no option. You must slow your vehicle and come to a complete stop. You must do that right now."

The cruisers all lit up their sirens again and two of them pulled alongside. The truck was locked into a solid raft of hostile traffic. It sped on for a long moment, then it slowed. Behind it, the frantic convoy braked and swerved. The helicopters rose up and kept pace. The truck slowed more. Police cruisers pulled alongside, two deep, door to door, bumper to bumper. The truck coasted to a halt. The helicopters held station overhead. The lead cars swerved around in front and jammed to a stop, inches from the truck's hood. All around, officers jumped out. The highway was thick with police. Even over the beating of the helicopter rotors, the crunching of shotgun mechanisms and the clicking of a hundred revolver hammers were clearly audible.

IN CHICAGO, MCGRATH did not hear the shotguns and the revolvers, but he could hear the Phoenix Agent-in-Charge shouting over the radio. The output from the throat mike in his helicopter was patched through Washington and was crackling out through a speaker on the long hardwood table. The guy was talking continuously, excited, half in a stream of instructions to his team, half as a running commentary on the sight he was seeing on the road below. McGrath was sitting there, hands cold and wet, staring at the noisy speaker like if he stared at it hard enough, it would change into a crystal ball and let him see what was going down.

"He's stopping, he's stopping," the guy in the helicopter was saying. "He's stationary now, he's stopped on the road, he's surrounded. Hold your fire, wait for my word, they're not coming out, open the doors, open the damn doors and drag them out, OK, we got two guys in the front, two guys, one driver, one passenger, they're coming out, they're out, secure them, put them in a car, get the keys, open up the back, but watch out, there are two more in there with her. Ok, we're going to the back, we're going around to the rear, the doors are locked back there, we're trying the key. You know what? There's still writing on the side of this truck. The writing is still there. It says Bright Spark Electrics. I thought it was supposed to be blanked out, right? Painted over or something?"

In Chicago, a deathly hush fell over the third-floor conference room. McGrath went white. Milosevic looked at him. Brogan stared calmly out of the window.

"And why is it heading north?" McGrath asked. "Back toward Chicago?"

The crackling from the speaker was still there. They turned back toward it. Listened hard. They could hear the thump of the rotor blades behind the urgent voice.

"The rear doors are open," the voice said. "The doors are open, they're open, we're going in, people are coming out, here they come, what the hell is this? There are dozens of people in there. There are maybe twenty people in there. They're all coming out. They're still coming out. There are twenty or thirty people in there. What the hell is going on here?"

The guy broke off. Evidently he was listening to a report radioed up from the ground. McGrath and Brogan and Milosevic stared at the hissing speaker. It stayed quiet for a long time. Nothing coming through at all except the guy's loud breathing and the hammering of the blades and the waterfall of static. Then the voice came back.

"Shit," it said. "Shit, Washington, you there? You listening to this? You know what we just did? You know what you sent us to do? We just busted a load of wetbacks. About thirty illegals from Mexico. Just got picked up from the border. They're on their way up to Chicago. They say they all got jobs promised up there."

21

THE WHITE ECONOLINE droned on. It was moving faster than it had been before. But it was out of the curves. It had lurched around the last of the tight bends, and it had settled to a fast, straight cruise. Noisier than before, because of the extra speed and the whine of the slipstream through the hundred random holes in the roof.

Reacher and Holly were tight together on the three-foot mattress. They were lying on their backs, staring up at the holes. Each hole was a bright point of light. Not blue, just a point of light so bright it had no color at all. Just a bright point in the dark. Like a mathematical proposition. Total light against the total dark of the surrounding sheet metal. Light, the opposite of dark. Dark, the absence of light. Positive and negative. Both propositions were contrasted vividly up there on the metal roof.

"I want to see the sky," Holly said.

It was warm in the truck. Not hot, like it had been the first day and a half. The whistling slipstream had solved that problem. The rush of air was keeping it comfortable. But it was warm enough that Reacher had taken his shirt off. He had balled it up and crammed it under his head.

"I want to see the whole sky," Holly said. "Not just little bits of it."

Reacher said nothing in reply. He was counting the holes.

"What time is it?" Holly asked him.

"Hundred and thirteen," Reacher said.

Holly turned her head to him.

"What?" she said.

"Hundred and thirteen holes in the roof," he said.

"Great," she said. "What time is it?"

"Three-thirty, Central," he said.

She snuggled closer. She moved her weight onto her side. Her head was resting on his right shoulder. Her leg was resting on his. His thigh was jammed between hers.

"Wednesday, right?" she said.

"Wednesday," he said.

She was physically closer to him than many women had allowed themselves to get. She felt lithe and athletic. Firm, but soft. Young. Scented. He was drifting away and enjoying the sensation. He was slightly breathless. But he wasn't kidding himself about her motivation. She was relaxed about it, but she was doing it to rest her painful knee, and to keep herself from rolling off the mattress onto the floor.

"Fifty-one hours," she said. "Fifty-one hours, and I haven't seen the sky."

One hundred and thirteen was a prime number. You couldn't make it by multiplying any other numbers together. Hundred and twelve, you could make by multiplying fifty-six by two, or twenty-eight by four, or fourteen by eight. Hundred and fourteen, you could make by multiplying fifty-seven by two or nineteen by six, or thirty-eight by three. But one hundred and thirteen was prime. No factors. The only way to make a hundred and thirteen was by multiplying a hundred and thirteen by one. Or by firing a shotgun into a truck in a rage.

"Reacher, I'm getting worried," Holly said.

Fifty-one hours. Fifty-one was not a prime number. You could make fifty-one by multiplying seventeen by three. Three tens are thirty, three sevens are twenty-one, thirty and twenty-one make fifty-one. Not a prime number. Fifty-one had factors. He dragged the weight of the chain up with his left wrist and held her tight, both arms around her.

"You'll be OK," he said to her. "They're not going to hurt you. They want to trade you for something. They'll keep you fit and well."

He felt her shake her head against his shoulder. Just one small shake, but it was very definite.

"I'm not worried about me," she said. "I'm worried about you. Who the hell's going to trade something for you?"

He said nothing. Nothing he could say to that. She snuggled closer. He could feel the scratch of her eyelashes against the skin on the side of his chest as she blinked. The truck roared on, faster than it wanted to go. He could feel the driver pushing it against its natural cruising speed.

"So I'm getting a little worried," she said.

"You look out for me," he said. "And I'll look out for you."

"I'm not asking you to do that," she said.

"I know you're not," he said.

"Well, I can't let you do that," she said.

"You can't stop me," he said. "This is about me now, too. They made it that way. They were going to shoot me down. I've got a rule, Holly: people mess with me at their own risk. I try to be patient about it. I had a teacher once, grade school somewhere. Philippines, I think, because she always wore a big white hat. So it was somewhere hot. I was always twice the size of the other kids, and she used to say to me: count to ten before you get mad, Reacher. And I've counted way past ten on this one. Way past. So you may as well face it, win or lose, now we do it together."

They went quiet. The truck roared on.

"Reacher?" Holly said.

"What?" he said.

"Hold me," she said.

"I am holding you," he said.

He squeezed her gently, both arms, to make his point. She pressed closer.

"Reacher?" she said again.

"Yes?" he said.

"You want to kiss me again?" she said. "Makes me feel better."

He turned his head and smiled at her in the dark.

"Doesn't do me a whole lot of harm, either," he said.

•   •   •

Eight hours at maybe sixty-five or seventy miles an hour. Somewhere between five hundred and five hundred and fifty miles. That's what they'd done. That was Reacher's estimation. And it was beginning to give him a clue about where they were.

"We're somewhere where they abolished the speed limit," he said.

Holly stirred and yawned.

"What?" she said.

"We've been going fast," he said. "Up to seventy miles an hour, probably, for hours. Loder is pretty thorough. He wouldn't let Stevie drive this fast if there was any danger of getting pulled over for it. So we're somewhere where they raised the limit, or abolished it altogether. Which states did that?"

She shrugged.

"I'm not sure," she said. "Mainly the western states, I think."

Reacher nodded. Traced an arc on the map in his head.

"We didn't go east," he said. "We figured that already. So I figure we're in Texas, New Mexico, Colorado, Wyoming, or Montana. Maybe as far as Idaho, Utah, Nevada, or Arizona. Not in California yet."

The truck slowed slightly, and they heard the engine note harden up. Then they heard the crunch as the driver came down out of fifth gear into fourth.

"Mountains," Holly said.

It was more than a hill. More than an upgrade. It was a smooth, relentless climb. A highway through the mountains. Clearly engineered to help out the laboring traffic, but they were adding hundreds of feet, every mile they drove. Reacher felt the lurch as the truck pulled out to pass slower vehicles. Not many, but a few. It stayed in fourth gear, the guy's foot hard down, hammering uphill, then relaxing, changing up to fifth, then down again, charging upward.

"We could run out of gas," Holly said.

"It's diesel, not gas," Reacher said. "We used these things in the Army. Thirty-five-gallon tank. Diesel will do maybe twenty-five to the gallon, highway mileage. Best part of nine hundred miles, before they run out."

"That could get us all the way out of the States," she said.

• • •

THEY CRUISED ON. The truck roared through the mountains for hours, then it left the highway. Night had fallen. The bright holes in the roof had dimmed. Then they had disappeared. They had turned darker than the roof itself. Positive and negative. They felt the lurch as the truck pulled to the right, off the highway, and they felt the tires grabbing at the pavement as the truck hauled around a tight right. Then there was a confusing blur of turns and stops and starts. Bumpy downhill bends and tight uphill turns with the truck grinding in a low gear. Periods of cruising down gently winding roads, bad surfaces, good surfaces, gradients, gravel under the wheels, potholes in the road. Reacher could imagine the headlight beams flicking left and right and bouncing up and down.

The truck slowed almost to a stop. Turned a tight right. Pattered over some kind of a wooden bridge. Then it yawed and bumped its way along a rutted track. It was moving slowly, shuddering from side to side. It felt like they were driving up a dry riverbed. Some kind of a stony narrow track. It felt like this was the very last leg of the journey. It felt like they were very close to their destination. The urgency had gone out of the guy's driving. It felt like the truck was nearly home.

But the final leg took a long time. The speed was low and the road was bad. Stones and small rocks were popping under the tires. The tires were squirming sideways across the loose surface. The truck ground on for forty minutes. Fifty minutes. Reacher got cold. He sat up and shook out his shirt. Put it on. An hour on the bumpy track. At this speed, maybe fifteen miles, maybe twenty.

Then they were there. The truck lurched up over a final heave and leveled out. Rolled forward another few yards and stopped. The engine noise died. It was replaced by an awesome silence. Reacher could hear nothing at all except a vast emptiness and the ticking of the muffler as it cooled. He could hear the two guys in front, sitting quiet and exhausted. Then they got out. He heard their doors open, and their seat springs bounce. He heard their feet on gravel. Their doors slammed, enormously loud metallic clangs in the stillness.

He heard them crunch around to the rear. He could hear the sound of the keys swinging gently in the driver's hand.

The key slid into the lock. The lock clicked back. The handle turned. The door swung open. Loder propped it back with the metal stay. Then he opened the other door. Propped it back. Gestured them out with the Glock. Reacher helped Holly along the ridged floor. He stepped down. The chain on his wrist clattered to the earth. He lifted Holly down beside him. They stood together, leaning back against the edge of the truck's ridged metal floor. Looking out and around.

Holly had wanted to see the sky. She was standing there under the vastest sky Reacher had ever seen. It was a dark inky blue, almost black, and it was huge. It stretched up to an infinite height. It was as big as a planet. It was peppered with a hundred billion bright stars. They were far away, but they were unnaturally vivid. They dusted back to the far cold reaches of the universe. It was a gigantic night sky and it stretched on forever.

They were in a forest clearing. Reacher could smell a heavy scent of pines. It was a strong smell. Clean and fresh. There was a black mass of trees all around. They covered the jagged slopes of mountains. They were in a forest clearing, surrounded by mountainous wooded slopes. It was a big clearing, infinitely dark, silent. Reacher could see the faint black outlines of buildings off to his right. They were long, low huts. Some kind of wooden structures, crouching in the dark.

There were people on the edge of the clearing. Standing among the nearest trees. Reacher could see their vague shapes. Maybe fifty or sixty people. Just standing there, silent. They were in dark clothing. They had darkened faces. Their faces were smudged with night camouflage. He could see their eyes, white against the black trees. They were holding weapons. He could see rifles and machine guns. Slung casually over the shoulders of the silent, staring people. They had dogs. Several big dogs, on thick leather leashes.

There were children among the people. Reacher could make them out. Children, standing together in groups, silent, staring, big sleepy eyes. They were clustered behind the adults, still, their shoulders facing diagonally away in fear and perplexity. Sleepy children, woken up in the middle of the night to witness something.

Loder turned himself around in a slow circle and waved the silent staring people nearer. He moved his arm in a wide inclusive gesture, like a ringmaster in a circus.

"We got her," he yelled into the silence. "The federal bitch is here."

His voice boomed back off the distant mountains.

"Where the hell are we?" Holly asked him.

Loder turned back and smiled at her.

"Our place, bitch," he said, quietly. "A place where your federal buddies can't come get you."

"Why not?" Holly asked him. "Where the hell are we?"

"That could be hard for you to understand," Loder said.

"Why?" Holly said. "We're somewhere, right? Somewhere in the States?"

Loder shook his head.

"No," he said.

Holly looked blank.

"Canada?" she said.

The guy shook his head again.

"Not Canada, bitch," he said.

Holly glanced around at the trees and the mountains. Glanced up at the vast night sky. Shuddered in the sudden chill.

"Well, this isn't Mexico," she said.

The guy raised both arms in a descriptive little gesture.

"This is a brand-new country," he said.

22

THE ATMOSPHERE IN the Chicago Field Office Wednesday evening was like a funeral, and in a way it was a funeral, because any realistic hope of getting Holly back had died. McGrath knew his best chance had been an early chance. The early chance was gone. If Holly was still alive, she was a prisoner somewhere on the North American continent, and he would not get even the chance to find out where until her kidnappers chose to call. And so far, approaching sixty hours after the snatch, they had not called.

He was at the head of the long table in the third-floor conference room. Smoking. The room was quiet. Milosevic was sitting to one side, back to the windows. The afternoon sun had inched its way around to evening and fallen away into darkness. The temperature in the room had risen and fallen with it, down to a balmy summer dusk. But the two men in there were chilled with anticlimax. They barely looked up as Brogan came in to join them. He was holding a sheaf of computer printouts. He wasn't smiling, but he looked reasonably close to it.

"You got something?" McGrath asked him.

Brogan nodded purposefully and sat down. Sorted the printouts into four separate handfuls and held them up, each one in turn.

"Quantico," he said. "They've got something. And the

crime database in D.C. They've got three somethings. And I had an idea.''

He spread his papers out and looked up.

"Listen to this," he said. "Graphic granite, interlocking crystals, cherts, gneisses, schists, shale, foliated meta-morphics, quartzites, quartz crystals, red-bed sandstones, Triassic red sand, acidic volcanics, pink feldspar, green chlorite, ironstone, grit, sand, and silt. You know what all that stuff is?"

McGrath and Milosevic shrugged and shook their heads.

"Geology," Brogan said. "The people down in Quantico looked at the pickup. Geologists, from the Materials Analysis Unit. They looked at the shit thrown up under the wheel arches. They figured out what the stuff is, and they figured out where that pickup has been. Little tiny pieces of rock and sediment stuck to the metal. Like a sort of a geological fingerprint.''

"OK, so where has it been?" McGrath asked.

"Started out in California," Brogan said. "Citrus grower called Dutch Borken bought it, ten years ago, in Mojave. The manufacturer traced that for us. That part is nothing to do with geology. Then the scientists say it was in Montana for a couple of years. Then they drove it over here, northern route, through North Dakota, Minnesota, and Wisconsin.''

"They sure about this?" McGrath said.

"Like a trucker's logbook," Brogan said. "Except written with shit on the underneath, not with a pen on paper.''

"So who is this Dutch Borken?" McGrath asked. "Is he involved?''

Brogan shook his head.

"No," he said. "Dutch Borken is dead.''

"When?" McGrath asked.

"Couple of years ago," Brogan said. "He borrowed money, farming went all to hell, the bank foreclosed, he stuck a twelve-bore in his mouth and blew the top of his head all over California.''

"So?" McGrath said.

"His son stole the pickup," Brogan said. "Technically, it was the bank's property, right? The son took off in it, never been seen again. The bank reported it, and the local cops

looked for it, couldn't find it. It's not licensed. DMV knows
nothing about it. Cops gave up on it, because who cares about
a ratty old pickup? But my guess is this Borken boy stole it
and moved to Montana. The pickup was definitely in Montana two years, scientists are dead sure about that."

"We got anything on this Borken boy?" McGrath asked
him.

Brogan nodded. Held up another sheaf of paper.

"We got a shitload on him," he said. "He's all over our
database like ants at a picnic. His name is Beau Borken.
Thirty-five years old, six feet in height and four hundred
pounds in weight. Big guy, right? Extreme right-winger, par-
anoid tendencies. Now a militia leader. Balls-out fanatic.
Links to other militias all over the damn place. Prime suspect
in a robbery up in the north of California. Armored car carrying twenty million in bearer bonds was hit. The driver was
killed. They figured militia involvement, because the bad
guys were wearing bits and pieces of military uniforms. Borken's outfit looked good for it. But they couldn't make it
stick. Files are unclear as to why not. And also, what's good
for us is before all that, Beau Borken was one of the alibis
Peter Wayne Bell used to get off the rape bust. So he's a
documented associate of somebody we can place on the
scene."

Milosevic looked up.

"And he's based in Montana?" he said.

Brogan nodded.

"We can pinpoint the exact region, more or less," he said.
"The scientific guys at Quantico are pretty hot for a couple
of particular valleys, northwest corner of Montana."

"They can be that specific?" Milosevic said.

Brogan nodded again.

"I called them," he said. "They said this sediment in the
wheel arches was local to a particular type of a place. Something to do with very old rock getting scraped up by glaciers
about a million years ago, lying there nearer the surface than
it should be, all mixed up with the regular rock which is still
pretty old, but newer than the old rock, you know what I
mean? A particular type of a mixture? I asked them, how can
you be so sure? They said they just recognize it, like I would

recognize my mother fifty feet away on the sidewalk. They said it was from one of a couple of north-south glacial valleys, northwest corner of Montana, where the big old glaciers were rolling down from Canada. And there was some sort of crushed sandstone in there, very different, but it's what the Forest Service use on the forest tracks up there.''

"OK," McGrath said. "So our guys were in Montana for a couple of years. But have they necessarily gone back there?"

Brogan held up the third of his four piles of paper. Unfolded a map. And smiled for the first time since Monday.

"You bet your ass they have," he said. "Look at the map. Direct route between Chicago and the far corner of Montana takes you through North Dakota, right? Some farmer up there was walking around this morning. And guess what he found in a ditch?"

"What?" McGrath asked.

"A dead guy," Brogan said. "In a ditch, horse country, miles from anywhere. So naturally the farmer calls the cops, the cops print the corpse, the computer comes back with a name.''

"What name?" McGrath asked.

"Peter Wayne Bell," Brogan said. "The guy who drove away with Holly."

"He's dead?" McGrath said. "How?"

"Don't know how," Brogan said. "Maybe some kind of a falling out? This guy Bell kept his brains in his jockey shorts. We know that, right? Maybe he went after Holly, maybe Holly aced him. But put a ruler on the map and take a look. They were all on their way back to Montana. That's for damn sure. Has to be that way."

"In what?" McGrath said. "Not in a white truck."

"Yes in a white truck," Brogan said.

"That Econoline was the only truck missing," McGrath said.

Brogan shook his head. He held up the fourth set of papers.

"My new idea," he said. "I checked if Rubin rented a truck.''

"Who?" McGrath said.

"Rubin is the dead dentist," Brogan said. "I checked if he rented a truck."

McGrath looked at him.

"Why should the damn dentist rent a truck?" he said.

"He didn't," Brogan said. "I figured maybe the guys rented the truck, with the dentist's credit cards, after they captured him. It made a lot of sense. Why risk stealing a vehicle if you can rent one with a stolen wallet full of credit cards and driver's licenses and stuff? So I called around. Sure enough, Chicago-You-Drive, some South Side outfit, they rented an Econoline to a Dr. Rubin, Monday morning, nine o'clock. I ask them, did the photo on the license match the guy? They say they never look. As long as the credit card goes through the machine, they don't care. I ask them, what color was the Econoline? They say all our trucks are white. I ask them, writing on the side? They say sure, Chicago-You-Drive, green letters, head height."

McGrath nodded.

"I'm going to call Harland Webster," he said. "I want to get sent to Montana."

Go to NORTH Dakota first," Webster said.

"Why?" McGrath asked him.

There was a pause on the line.

"One step at a time," Webster said. "We need to check out this Peter Wayne Bell situation. So stop off in North Dakota first, OK?"

"You sure, chief?" McGrath said.

"Patient grunt work," Webster said. "That's what's going to do it for us. Work the clues, right? It's worked so far. Your boy Brogan did some good work. I like the sound of him."

"So let's go with it, chief," McGrath said. "All the way to Montana, right?"

"No good rushing around until we know something," Webster said back. "Like who and where and why. That's what we need to know, Mack."

"We know who and where," he said. "This Beau Borken guy. In Montana. It's clear enough, right?"

There was another pause on the line.

"Maybe," Webster said. "But what about why?"

McGrath jammed the phone into his shoulder and lit up his next cigarette.

"No idea," he said, reluctantly.

"We looked at the mug shots," Webster said. "I sent them over to the Behavioral Science Unit. Shrinks looked them over."

"And?" McGrath asked.

"I don't know," Webster said. "They're a pretty smart bunch of people down there, but how much can you get from gazing at a damn photograph?"

"Any conclusions at all?" McGrath asked.

"Some," Webster said. "They felt three of the guys belonged together, and the big guy was kind of separate. The three looked the same. Did you notice that? Same kind of background, same looks, same genes maybe. They could all three be related. This guy Bell was from California. Mojave, right? Beau Borken, too. The feeling is the three of them are probably all from the same area. All West Coast types. But the big guy is different. Different clothes, different stance, different physically. The anthropologists down there in Quantico think he could be foreign, at least partly, or maybe second-generation. Fair hair and blue eyes, but there's something in his face. They say maybe he's European. And he's big. Not pumped up at the gym, just big, like naturally."

"So?" McGrath asked. "What were their conclusions?"

"Maybe he is European," Webster said. "A big tough guy, maybe from Europe, they're worried he's some kind of a terrorist. Maybe a mercenary. They're checking overseas."

"A terrorist?" McGrath said. "A mercenary? But why?"

"That's the point," Webster said. "The why part is what we need to nail down. If this guy really is a terrorist, what's his purpose? Who recruited who? Who is the motivating force here? Did Borken's militia hire him to help them out, or is it the other way around? Is this his call? Did he hire Borken's militia for local color inside the States?"

"What the hell is going on?" McGrath asked.

"I'm flying up to O'Hare," Webster said. "I'll take over day-to-day from here, Mack. Case this damn big, I've got to, right? The old guy will expect it."

"Which old guy?" McGrath asked sourly.

"Whichever, both," Webster said.

Brogan DROVE OUT to O'Hare, middle of the evening, six hours after the debacle with the Mexicans in the truck in Arizona. McGrath sat beside him in the front seat, Milosevic in the back. Nobody spoke. Brogan parked the Bureau Ford on the military-compound tarmac, inside the wire fence. They sat in the car, waiting for the FBI Lear from Andrews. It landed after twenty minutes. They saw it taxi quickly over toward them. Saw it come to a halt, caught in the glare of the airport floodlights, engines screaming. The door opened and the steps dropped down. Harland Webster appeared in the opening and looked around. He caught sight of them and gestured them over. A sharp, urgent gesture. Repeated twice.

They climbed inside the small plane. The steps folded in and the door sucked shut behind them. Webster led them forward to a group of seats. Two facing two across a small table. They sat, McGrath and Brogan facing Webster, Milosevic next to him. They buckled their belts and the Lear began to taxi again. The plane lurched through its turn onto the runway and waited. It quivered and vibrated and then rolled forward, accelerating down the long concrete strip before suddenly jumping into the air. It tilted northwest and throttled back to a loud cruise.

"OK, try this," Webster said. "The Joint Chairman's daughter's been snatched by some terrorist group, some foreign involvement. They're going to make demands on him. Demands with some kind of a military dimension."

McGrath shook his head.

"That's crap," he said. "How could that possibly work? They'd just replace him. Old soldiers willing to sit on their fat asses in the Pentagon aren't exactly thin on the ground."

Brogan nodded cautiously.

"I agree, chief," he said. "That's a nonviable proposition."

Webster nodded back.

"Exactly," he said. "So what does that leave us with?"

Nobody answered that. Nobody wanted to say the words.

•　　•　　•

THE LEAR CHASED the glow of the setting sun west and landed at Fargo in North Dakota. An agent from the Minneapolis Field Office was up there to meet them with a car. He wasn't impressed by Brogan or Milosevic, and he was too proud to show he was impressed by the Chicago Agent-in-Charge. But he was fairly tense about meeting with Harland Webster. Tense, and determined to show him he meant business.

"We found their hideout, sir," the guy said. "They used it last night and moved on. It's pretty clear. About a mile from where the body was found."

He drove them northwest, two hours of tense darkening silence as the car crawled like an insect through endless gigantic spreads of barley and wheat and beans and oats. Then he swung a right and his headlights opened up a vista of endless grasslands and dark gray sky. The sun was gone in the west. The local guy threaded through the turns and pulled up next to a ranch fence. The fence disappeared onward into the dark, but the headlights caught police tape strung between a couple of trees, and a police cruiser, and a coroner's wagon waiting twenty yards away.

"This is where the body was found," the local guy said.

He had a flashlight. There wasn't much to see. Just a ditch between the blacktop and the fence, overgrown with grass, trampled down over a ten-yard stretch. The body was gone, but the medical examiner had waited with the details.

"Pretty weird," the doctor said. "The guy was suffocated. That's for sure. He was smothered, pushed facedown into something soft. There are petechiae all over the face, and in the eyes. Small pinpoint hemorrhages, which you get with asphyxia."

McGrath shrugged.

"What's weird about that?" he said. "I'd have suffocated the scumbag myself, given half a chance."

"Before and after," the doctor said. "Extreme violence before. Looks to me like the guy was smashed against a wall, maybe the side of a truck. The back of his skull was cracked, and he broke three bones in his back. Then he was kicked in the gut. His insides are a mess. Just slopping around in there. Extreme violence, awesome force. Whoever did that, I wouldn't want him to get mad at me, that's for damn sure."

"What about after?" McGrath said.

"The body was moved," the doctor said. "Hypostasis pattern is all screwed up. Like somebody beat on the guy, suffocated him, left him for an hour, then thought better of it and moved the body out here and dumped it."

Webster and McGrath and Brogan all nodded. Milosevic stared down into the ditch. They regrouped on the shoulder and stood looking at the vast dark landscape for a long moment and then turned together back to the car.

"Thank you, doc," Webster said vaguely. "Good work."

The doctor nodded. The car doors slammed. The local agent started up and continued on down the road, west, toward where the sun had set.

"The big guy is calling the shots," Webster said. "It's clear, right? He hired the three guys to do a job of work for him. Peter Wayne Bell stepped out of line. He started to mess with Holly. A helpless, disabled woman, young and pretty, too much of a temptation for an animal like that, right?"

"Right," Brogan said. "But the big guy is a professional. A mercenary or a terrorist or something. Messing with the prisoner was not in his game plan. So he got mad and offed Bell. Enforcing some kind of discipline on the troops."

Webster nodded.

"Had to be that way," he said. "Only the big guy could do that. Partly because he's the boss, therefore he's got the authority, and partly because he's physically powerful enough to do that kind of serious damage."

"He was protecting her?" McGrath said.

"Protecting his investment," Webster said back, sourly.

"So maybe she's still OK," McGrath said.

Nobody replied to that. The car turned a tight left after a mile and bounced down a track. The headlight beams jumped over a small cluster of wooden buildings.

"This was their stopping place," the local guy said. "It's an old horse farm."

"Inhabited?" McGrath asked.

"It was until yesterday," the guy said. "No sign of anybody today."

He pulled up in front of the barn. The five men got out

into the dark. The barn door stood open. The local guy waited with the car and Webster and McGrath and Brogan and Milosevic stepped inside. Searched with their flashlights. It was dark and damp. Cobbled floor, green with moss. Horse stalls down both sides. They walked in. Down the aisle to the end. The stall on the right had been peppered with a shotgun blast. The back wall had just about disintegrated. Planks had fallen out. Wood splinters lay all around, crumbling with decay.

The end stall on the left had a mattress in it. Laid at an angle on the mossy cobbles. There was a chain looped through an iron ring on the back wall. The ring had been put there a hundred years ago to hold a horse by a rope. But last night it had held a woman, by a chain attached to her wrist. Webster ducked down and came up with the bright chrome handcuff, locked into the ends of the loop of chain. Brogan knelt and picked long dark hairs off the mattress. Then he rejoined Milosevic and searched through the other stalls in turn. McGrath stared at them. Then he walked out of the barn. He turned to face west and stared at the point where the sun had fallen over the horizon. He stood and stared into the infinite dark in that direction like if he stared long enough and hard enough he could focus his eyes five hundred miles away and see Holly.

23

NOBODY COULD SEE Holly because she was alone, locked in the prison room that had been built for her. She had been taken from the forest clearing by four silent women dressed in dull green fatigues, night camouflage smearing their faces, automatic weapons slung at their shoulders, ammunition pouches chinking and rattling on their belts. They had pulled her away from Reacher and dragged her in the dark across the clearing, into the trees, through a gauntlet of hissing, spitting, jeering people. Then a painful mile down a stony path, out of the forest again and over to the large white building. They had not spoken to her. Just marched her in and pushed her up the stairs to the second floor. They had pulled open the stout new door and pushed her up the step into the room. The step was more than a foot high, because the floor inside the room was built up higher than the floor in the hallway outside. She crawled up and in and heard the door slamming and the key turning loudly behind her.

There were no windows. A bulb in the ceiling behind a wire grille lit the room with a vivid hot yellow light. All four walls and the floor and the ceiling were made from new pine boards, unfinished, smelling strongly of fresh lumber. At the far end of the room was a bed. It had a simple iron frame and a thin crushed mattress. Like an Army bed, or a prison cot. On the bed were two sets of clothing. Two pairs of fatigue pants and two shirts. Dull green, like the four silent women had been wearing. She limped over to the bed and touched them. Old and worn, but clean. Pressed. The creases in the pants were like razors.

She turned back and inspected the room, closely. It was not small. Maybe sixteen feet square. But she sensed it was smaller than it should have been. The proportions were odd. She had noticed the raised floor. It was more than a foot higher than it should have been. She guessed the walls and the ceiling were the same. She limped to the wall and tapped the new boarding. There was a dull sound. A cavity behind. Somebody had built this simple timber shell right inside a bigger room. And they had built it well. The new boards were tight and straight. But there was damp in the tiny cracks between them. She stared at the damp and sniffed the air. She shivered. The room smelled of fear.

One corner was walled off. There was a door set in a simple diagonal partition. She limped over to it and pulled it open. A bathroom. A john, a sink. A trash can, with a new plastic liner. And a shower over a tub. Cheap white ceramic, but brand-new. Carefully installed. Neat tiling. Soap and shampoo on a shelf. She leaned on the doorjamb and stared at the shower. She stared at it for a long time. Then she shrugged off her filthy Armani suit. She balled it up and threw it in the trash can. She started the shower running and stepped under the torrent of water. She washed her hair three times. She scrubbed her aching body all over. She stood in the shower for the best part of an hour.

Then she limped back to the bed and selected a set of the old fatigues. They fitted her just about perfectly. She lay down on the bed and stared at the pine ceiling and listened to the silence. For the first time in more than sixty hours, she was alone.

REACHER WAS NOT alone. He was still in the forest clearing. He was twenty feet from the white Econoline, chained to a tree, guarded by six silent men with machine guns. Dogs were padding free through the clearing. Reacher was leaning back on the rough bark, waiting, watching his guards. He was cold. He could feel pine resin sticking to his thin shirt. The guards were cautious. They were standing in a line, six feet away from him, weapons pointed at him, eyes gleaming white out of darkened faces. They were dressed in olive fatigues. There were some kind of semicircular flashes on their shoulders. It was too dark for Reacher to read them.

The six men were all maybe forty years old. They were lean and bearded. Comfortable with their weapons. Alert. Silent. Accustomed to night duty. Reacher could see that. They looked like the survivors of a small infantry platoon. Like they had stepped into the forest on night patrol twenty years ago as young recruits, and had never come back out again.

They snapped to attention at the sound of footsteps approaching behind them. The sounds were grotesquely loud in the still night. Boots smashed into shale and gun stocks slapped into palms. Reacher glanced into the clearing and saw a seventh man approaching. Younger, maybe thirty-five. A tall man, clean-shaven, no camouflage on his face, crisp fatigues, shiny boots. Same semicircular flashes at the shoulder. Some kind of an officer.

The six forty-year-old grunts stood back and saluted and the new guy crunched up face-to-face with Reacher. He took a cigarette pack from his pocket and a cigarette from the pack. Lit it and kept the lighter burning to illuminate Reacher's face. Stared over the wavering flame with an expressionless gaze. Reacher stared back at him. The guy had a small head on wide shoulders, a thin hard face starved into premature lines and crevices. In the harsh shadow of the flame, it looked like he had no lips. Just a slit, where his mouth should be. Cold eyes, burning under the thin skin stretched over his brow. A military buzz cut, maybe a week old, just growing out. He stared at Reacher and let the flame die. Ran a hand across his scalp. Reacher heard the loud rasp of the stubble passing under his palm in the still night air.

"I'm Dell Fowler," the guy said. "I'm chief of staff here."

A quiet voice. West Coast. Reacher looked back at him and nodded, slowly.

"You want to tell me what staff you're chief of?" he said.

"Loder didn't explain?" the guy called Fowler asked.

"Loder didn't explain anything," Reacher said. "He had his hands full just getting us here."

Fowler nodded and smiled a chilly smile.

"Loder's an idiot," he said. "He made five major mistakes. You're one of them. He's in all kinds of deep shit now. And so are you."

He gestured to one of the guards. The guard stepped forward and handed him a key from his pocket. The guard stood with his weapon ready and Fowler unlocked Reacher's chain. It clattered down the tree trunk to the ground. Metal on wood, a loud sound in the forest night. A dog padded near and sniffed. People moved in the trees. Reacher pushed away from the trunk and squeezed some circulation back into his forearm. All six guards took a pace forward. Weapons slapped back to the ready position. Reacher watched the muzzles and Fowler caught his arm and turned him. Cuffed his hands together again, behind his back. Nodded. Two guards melted away into the trees. A third jabbed the muzzle of his gun into Reacher's back. A fourth took up position to the rear. Two walked point out in front. Fowler fell in beside Reacher and caught his elbow. Walked him across toward a small wooden hut on the opposite edge of the clearing. Clear of the trees, the moonlight was brighter. Reacher could make out the writing on Fowler's shoulder flash. It read: Montana Militia.

"This is Montana?" he said. "Loder called it a brand-new country."

Fowler shrugged as he walked.

"He was premature," he said. "Right now, this is still Montana."

They reached the hut. The point men opened the door. Yellow light spilled out into the darkness. The guard with the weapon in Reacher's back used it to push him inside. Loder was standing against the far wall. His hands were cuffed behind him. He was guarded by another lean, bearded man with a machine gun. This guy was a little younger than the other grunts, neater beard. A livid scar running laterally across his forehead.

Fowler walked around and sat behind a plain desk. Pointed to a chair. Reacher sat down, handcuffed, six soldiers behind him. Fowler watched him sit and then transferred his attention across to Loder. Reacher followed his gaze. First time he'd seen Loder on Monday, he'd seen a degree of calm competence, hard eyes, composure. That was all gone. The guy was shaking with fear. His cuffs were rattling behind him. Reacher watched him and thought: this guy is terrified of his leaders.

"So, five mistakes," Fowler said.

His voice was still quiet. And it was confident. Relaxed. The quiet confident voice of a person very secure about his power. Reacher heard the voice die into silence and listened to the creak of boots on wood behind him.

"I did my best," Loder said. "She's here, right?"

His voice was supplicant and miserable. The voice of a man who knows he's in deep shit without really understanding exactly why.

"She's here, right?" he said again.

"By a miracle," Fowler replied. "You caused a lot of stress elsewhere. People had their work cut out covering for your incompetence."

"What did I do wrong?" Loder asked.

He pushed forward off the wall, hands cuffed behind him, and moved into Reacher's view. Glanced desperately at him, like he was asking for a testimonial.

"Five mistakes," Fowler said again. "One, you burned the pickup, and two, you burned the car. Way too visible. Why didn't you just put an ad in the damn paper?"

Loder made no reply. His mouth was working, but no sound was coming out.

"Three, you snarled this guy up," Fowler said.

Loder glanced at Reacher again and shook his head vigorously.

"This guy's a nobody," he said. "No heat coming after him."

"You should still have waited," Fowler said. "And four, you lost Peter. What exactly happened to him?"

Loder shrugged again.

"I don't know," he said.

"He got scared," Fowler said. "You were making so many mistakes, he got scared and he ran. That's what happened. You got any other explanation?"

Loder was just staring blankly.

"And five, you killed the damn dentist," Fowler said. "They're not going to overlook that, are they? This was supposed to be a military operation, right? Political? You added an extra factor there."

"What dentist?" Reacher asked.

Fowler glanced at him and smiled a lipless smile, indulgent, like Reacher was an audience he could use to humiliate Loder a little more.

"They stole the car from a dentist," he said. "The guy caught them at it. They should have waited until he was clear."

"He got in the way," Loder said. "We couldn't bring him with us, could we?"

"You brought me," Reacher said to him.

Loder stared at him like he was a moron.

"The guy was a Jew," he said. "This place isn't for Jews."

Reacher glanced around the room. Looked at the shoulder flashes. Montana Militia, Montana Militia, Montana Militia. He nodded slowly. A brand-new country.

"Where have you taken Holly?" he asked Fowler.

Fowler ignored him. He was still dealing with Loder.

"You'll stand trial tomorrow," he told him. "Special tribunal. The commander presiding. The charge is endangering the mission. I'm prosecuting."

"Where's Holly?" Reacher asked him again.

Fowler shrugged. A cool gaze.

"Close by," he said. "Don't you worry about her."

Then he glanced up over Reacher's head and spoke to the guards.

"Put Loder on the floor," he said.

Loder offered no resistance at all. Just let the younger guy with the scar hold hire upright. The nearest guard reversed his rifle and smashed the butt into Loder's stomach. Reacher heard the air punch out of him. The younger guy dropped him and stepped neatly over him. Walked out of the hut, alone, duty done. The door slammed noisily behind him. Then Fowler turned back to Reacher.

"Now let's talk about you," he said.

His voice was still quiet. Quiet, and confident. Secure. But it was not difficult to be secure holed up in the middle of nowhere with six armed subordinates surrounding a hand-cuffed man on a chair. A handcuffed man who has just wit-nessed a naked display of power and brutality. Reacher shrugged at him.

"What about me?" he said. "You know my name. I told Loder. No doubt he told you. He probably got that right. There isn't much more to say on the subject."

There was silence. Fowler thought about it. Nodded.

"This is a decision for the commander," he said.

IT WAS THE shower which convinced her. She based her con-clusions on it. Some good news, some bad. A brand-new bathroom, cheaply but carefully fitted out in the way a pa-thetic house-proud woman down on her luck in a trailer park would choose. That bathroom communicated a lot to Holly.

It meant she was a hostage, to be held long-term, but to be held with a certain measure of respect. Because of her value in some kind of a trade. There were to be no doubts about her day-to-day comfort or safety. Those factors were to be removed from the negotiation. Those factors were to be taken for granted. She was to be a high-status prisoner. Because of her value. Because of who she was.

But not because of who she was. Because of who her father was. Because of the connections she had. She was supposed to sit in this crushing, fear-filled room and be somebody's daughter. Sit and wait while people weighed her value, one way and the other. While people reacted to her plight, feeling a little reassured by the fact that she had a shower all to herself.

She eased herself off the bed. To hell with that, she thought. She was not going to sit there and be negotiated over. The anger rose up inside her. It rose up and she turned it into a steely determination. She limped to the door and tried the handle for the twentieth time. Then she heard foot-steps on the stairs. They clattered down the corridor. Stopped at her door. A key turned the lock. The handle moved against her grip. She stepped back and the door opened.

Reacher was pushed up into the room. A blur of camou-flaged figures behind him. They shoved him up through the door and slammed it shut. She heard it locking and the footsteps tramping away. Reacher was left standing there, gazing around.

"Looks like we have to share," he said.

She looked at him.

"They were only expecting one guest," he added.

She made no reply to that. She just watched his eyes examining the room. They flicked around the walls, the floor, the ceiling. He twisted and glanced into the bathroom. Nodded to himself. Turned back to face her, waiting for her comment. She was pausing, thinking hard about what to say and how to say it.

"It's only a single bed," she said at last.

She tried to make the words count for more. She tried to make them like a long speech. Like a closely reasoned argument. She tried to make them say: OK, in the truck, we were close. OK, we kissed. Twice. The first time, it just happened. The second time, I asked you to, because I was looking for comfort and reassurance. But now we've been apart for an hour or two. Long enough for me to get to feeling a little silly about what we did. She tried to make those five words say all that, while she watched his eyes for his reaction.

"There's somebody else, right?" he said.

She saw that he said it as a joke, as a throwaway line to show her he agreed with her, that he understood, as a way to let them both off the hook without getting all heavy about it. But she didn't smile at him. Instead, she found herself nodding.

"Yes, there is somebody," she said. "What can I say? If there wasn't, maybe I would want to share."

She thought: he looks disappointed.

"In fact, I probably would want to," she added. "But there is somebody, and I'm sorry. It wouldn't be a good idea."

It showed in his face, and she felt she had to say more.

"I'm sorry," she said again. "It's not that I wouldn't want to."

She watched him. He just shrugged at her. She saw he was thinking: it's not the end of the world. And then he was thinking: it just feels like it. She blushed. She was absurdly gratified. But ready to change the subject.

"What's going on here?" she asked. "They tell you anything?"

"Who's the lucky guy?" Reacher asked.

"Just somebody," she said. "What's going on here?"

His eyes were clouded. He looked straight at her.

"Lucky somebody," he said.

"He doesn't even know," she said.

"That you're gone?" he asked.

She shook her head.

"That I feel this way," she said.

He stared at her. Didn't reply. There was a long silence in the room. Then she heard footsteps again. Hurrying, outside the building. Clattering inside. Coming up the stairs. They stopped outside the door. The key slid in. The door opened. Six guards clattered inside. Six machine guns. She took a painful step backward. They ignored her completely.

"The commander is ready for you, Reacher," the point man said.

He signaled him to turn around. He clicked handcuffs on, behind his back. Tightened them hard. Pushed him to the door with the barrel of his gun and out into the corridor. The door slammed and locked behind the gaggle of men.

FOWLER PULLED THE headphones off and stopped the tape recorder.

"Anything?" the commander asked him.

"No," Fowler said. "She said it's only a single bed, and he sounded pissed, like he wants to get in her pants. So she said she's got another boyfriend."

"I didn't know that," the commander said. "Did she say who?"

Fowler shook his head.

"But it works OK?" the commander asked him.

"Clear as a bell," Fowler said.

REACHER WAS PUSHED down the stairs and back out into the night. Back the way he had come, a mile up a stony path. The point man gripped his elbow and hustled him along.

They were hurrying. Almost running. They were using their gun muzzles like cattle prods. They covered the distance in fifteen minutes. They crunched across the clearing to the small wooden hut. Reacher was pushed roughly inside.

Loder was still on the floor. But there was somebody new sitting at the plain wooden desk. The commander. Reacher was clear on that. He was an extraordinary figure. Maybe six feet tall, probably four hundred pounds. Maybe thirty-five years old, thick hair, so blond it was nearly white, cut short at the sides and brushed long across the top like a German schoolboy's. A smooth pink face, bloated tight by his bulk, bright red nickel-sized spots burning high up on the cheeks. Tiny colorless eyes forced into slits between the cheeks and the white eyebrows. Wet red lips pursed above a chin strong enough to hold its shape in the blubber.

He was wearing an enormous black uniform. An immaculate black shirt, military cut, no insignia except a pair of the same shoulder flashes everybody else was wearing. A wide leather belt, gleaming like a mirror. Crisp black riding pants, flared wide at the top, tucked into high black boots which matched the belt for shine.

"Come in and sit down," he said, quietly.

Reacher was pushed over to the chair he had occupied before. He sat, with his hands crushed behind him. The guards stood to rigid attention all around him, not daring to breathe, just staring blankly into space.

"I'm Beau Borken," the big man said. "I'm the commander here."

His voice was high. Reacher stared at the guy and felt some kind of an aura radiating out of him, like a glow. The glow of total authority.

"I have to take a decision," Borken said. "I need you to help me with it."

Reacher realized he was looking away from the guy. Like the glow was overpowering him. He forced himself to turn his head slowly and stare directly into the big white face.

"What decision?" he asked.

"Whether you should live," Borken said. "Or whether you should die."

•   •   •

HOLLY PULLED THE side panel off the bath. She had known plumbers leave trash under the tub, out of sight behind the panel. Offcuts of pipe, scraps of wood, even tools. Used blades, lost wrenches. Stuff that could prove useful. Some apartments she'd had, she'd found all kinds of things. But there was nothing. She lay down and felt right into the back recesses and came up with nothing at all.

And the floor was solid all the way under the fixtures. The plumbing ran down through tight holes. It was an expert job. It was possible she could force a lever down alongside the big pipe running down out of the john. If she had a pry bar she might get a board loose. But there was no pry bar in the room. Nor any substitute. The towel bar was plastic. It would bend and break. There was nothing else. She sat on the floor and felt the disappointment wash over her. Then she heard more footsteps outside her door.

This time, they were quiet. They were muffled, not clattering. Somebody approaching quietly and cautiously. Somebody with no official business. She stood up slowly. Stepped out of the bathroom and pulled the door to hide the dismantled tub. Limped back toward the bed as the lock clicked and the door opened.

A man came into the room. He was a youngish man, dressed in camouflage fatigues, black smears on his face. A vivid red scar running laterally across his forehead. A machine gun slung at his shoulder. He turned and closed the door, quietly. Turned back with his fingers to his lips.

She stared at him. Felt her anger rising. This time, she wasn't chained up. This time, the guy was going to die. She smiled a crazy smile at the logic of it. The bathroom was going to save her. She was a high-status prisoner. Supposed to be held with dignity and respect. Somebody came in to abuse her, and she killed him, they couldn't argue with that, could they?

But the guy with the scar just held his fingers to his lips and nodded toward the bathroom. He crept quietly over and pushed the door. Gestured for her to follow. She limped after him. He glanced down at the side panel on the floor and shook his head. Reached in and started the shower. Set it running hard against the empty tub.

"They've got microphones," the guy said. "They're listening for me."

"Who the hell are you?" she asked.

He squatted down and put the panel back on the bath.

"No good," he said. "There's no way out."

"Got to be," she said.

The guy shook his head.

"They had a trial run," he said. "The commander put one of the guys who built this place in here. Told him if he didn't get out, he'd cut his arms off. So I assume he tried real hard."

"And what happened?" she asked.

The guy shrugged.

"The commander cut his arms off," he said.

"Who the hell are you?" she asked again.

"FBI," the guy said. "Counterterrorism. Undercover. I guess I'm going to have to get you out."

"How?" she asked.

"Tomorrow," he said. "I can get a jeep. We'll have to make a run for it. I can't call in for assistance because they're scanning for my transmitter. We'll just get the jeep and head south and hope for the best."

"What about Reacher?" she asked. "Where have they taken him?"

"Forget him," the guy said. "He'll be dead by morning."

Holly shook her head.

"I'm not going without him," she said.

LODER DISPLEASED ME," Beau Borken said.

Reacher glanced downward. Loder had squirmed up into a sideways sitting position, crammed into the angle between the floor and the wall.

"Did he displease you?" Borken asked.

Reacher made no reply.

"Would you like to kick him?" Borken asked.

Reacher kept quiet. He could see where this game was going. If he said yes, he'd be expected to hurt the guy badly. Which he had no objection to in principle, but he'd prefer to do it on his own terms. If he said no, Borken would call him a coward with no sense of natural justice and no self-respect. An obvious game, with no way to win. So he kept quiet, which was a tactic he'd used a thousand times before: when in doubt, just keep your mouth shut.

"In the face?" Borken asked. "In the balls, maybe?"

Loder was staring up at Reacher. Something in his face. Reacher saw what it was. His eyes widened in surprise. Loder was pleading with him to give him a kicking, so that Borken wouldn't.

"Loder, lie down again," Borken said.

Loder squirmed his hips away from the wall and dropped his shoulders to the floor. Wriggled and pushed until he was lying flat on his back. Borken nodded to the nearest guard.

"In the face," he said.

The guard stepped over and used the sole of his boot to force Loder's head sideways, so his face was presented to the room. Then he stepped back and kicked out. A heavy blow from a heavy boot. Loder's head snapped backward and thumped into the wall. Blood welled from his nose. Borken watched him bleed for a long moment, mildly interested. Then he turned back to Reacher.

"Loder's one of my oldest friends," he said.

Reacher said nothing.

"Begs two questions, doesn't it?" Borken said. "Question one: why am I enforcing such strict discipline, even against my old friends? And question two: if that's how I treat my friends, how the hell do I treat my enemies?"

Reacher said nothing. When in doubt, just keep your mouth shut.

"I treat my enemies a hell of a lot worse than that," Borken said. "So much worse, you really don't want to think about it. You really don't, believe me. And why am I being so strict? Because we're two days away from a unique moment in history. Things are going to happen which will change the world. Plans are made and operations are under way. Therefore I have to bring my natural caution to a new pitch. My old friend Loder has fallen victim to a historical force. So, I'm afraid, have you."

Reacher said nothing. He dropped his gaze and watched Loder. He was unconscious. Breathing raggedly through clotting blood in his nose.

"You got any value to me as a hostage?" Borken asked.

Reacher thought about it. Made no reply. Borken watched his face and smiled. His red lips parted over small white teeth.

"I thought not," he said. "So what should I do with a person who's got no value to me as a hostage? During a moment of great historical tension?"

Reacher stayed silent. Just watching. Easing his weight forward, ready.

"You think you're going to get a kicking?" Borken asked.

Reacher tensed his legs, ready to spring.

"Relax," Borken said. "No kicking for you. When the time comes, it'll be a bullet through the head. From behind. I'm not stupid, you know. I've got eyes, and a brain. What are you, six-five? About two-twenty? Clearly fit and strong. And look at you, tension in your thighs, getting ready to jump up. Clearly trained in some way. But you're not a boxer. Because your nose has never been broken. A heavyweight like you with an unbroken nose would need to be a phenomenal talent, and we'd have seen your picture in the newspapers. So you're just a brawler, probably been in the service, right? So I'll be cautious with you. No kicking, just a bullet."

The guards took their cue. Six rifles came down out of the slope and six fingers hooked around six triggers.

"You got felony convictions?" Borken asked.

Reacher shrugged and spoke for the first time.

"No," he said.

"Upstanding citizen?" Borken asked.

Reacher shrugged again.

"I guess," he said.

Borken nodded.

"So I'll think about it," he said. "Live or die, I'll let you know, first thing in the morning, OK?"

He lifted his bulky arm and snapped his fingers. Five of the six guards moved. Two went to the door and opened it. A third went out between them. The other two waited. Borken stood up with surprising grace for a man of his size and walked out from behind the desk. The wooden floor creaked under his bulk. The four waiting guards fell in behind him and he walked straight out into the night without a backward glance.

HE WALKED ACROSS the clearing and into another hut. Fowler was waiting for him, the headphones in his hand.

"I think somebody went in there," he said.

"You think?" Borken said.

"The shower was running," Fowler said. "Somebody went in there who knows about the microphones. She wouldn't need another shower. She just had one, right? Somebody went in there and ran the shower to mask the talking."

"Who?" Borken asked.

Fowler shook his head.

"I don't know who," he said. "But I can try to find out."

Borken nodded.

"Yes, you can do that," he said. "You can try to find out."

IN THE ACCOMMODATION huts, men and women were working in the gloom, cleaning their rifles. The word about Loder had traveled quickly. They all knew about the tribunal. They all knew the likely outcome. Any six of them could be selected for the firing squad. If there was going to be a firing squad. Most people figured there probably was. An officer like Loder, the commander might limit it to a firing squad. Probably nothing worse. So they cleaned their rifles, and left them locked and loaded next to their beds.

Those of them with enough demerits to be on tomorrow's punishment detail were trying to get some sleep. If he didn't limit it to a firing squad, they could be in for a lot of work. Messy, unpleasant work. And even if Loder got away with it, there was always the other guy. The big guy who had come in with the federal bitch. There wasn't much chance of him surviving past breakfast time. They couldn't remember the last time any stray stranger had lasted longer than that.

HOLLY JOHNSON HAD a rule. It was a rule bred into her, like a family motto. It had been reinforced by her long training at Quantico. It was a rule distilled from thousands of

years of military history and hundreds of years of law enforcement experience. The rule said: hope for the best, but
plan for the worst.

She had no reason to believe she would not be speeding
south in a jeep just as soon as her new ally could arrange it.
He was Bureau-trained, the same as she was. She knew that
if the tables were turned, she would get him out, no problem
at all. So she knew she could just sit tight and wait. But she
wasn't doing that. She was hoping for the best, but she was
planning for the worst.

She had given up on the bathroom. No way out there. Now
she was going over the room itself, inch by inch. The new
pine boarding was nailed tight to the frame, all six surfaces.
It was driving her crazy. Inch-thick pine board, the oldest
possible technology, used for ten thousand years, and there
was no way through it. For a lone woman without any tools,
it might as well have been the side of a battleship.

So she concentrated on finding tools. It was like she was
personally speeding through Darwin's evolutionary process.
Apes came down from the trees and they made tools. She
was concentrating on the bed. The mattress was useless. It
was a thin, crushed thing, no wire springs inside. But the bed
frame was more promising. It was bolted together from iron
tubes and flanges. If she could take it apart, she could put
one of the little right-angle flanges in the end of the longest
tube and make a pry bar seven feet long. But the bolts were
all painted over. She had strong hands, but she couldn't begin
to move them. Her fingers just bruised and slipped on her
sweat.

LODER HAD BEEN dragged away and Reacher was locked up
alone with the last remaining guard from the evening detail.
The guard sat behind the plain desk and propped his weapon
on the wooden surface with the muzzle pointing directly at
him sitting on his chair. His hands were still cuffed behind
him. He had decisions to make. First was no way could he
sit all night like that. He glanced calmly at the guard and
eased himself up and slid his hands underneath. Pressed his
chest down onto his thighs and looped his hands out under

his feet. Then he sat up and leaned back and forced a smile, hands together in his lap.

"Long arms," he said. "Useful."

The guard nodded slowly. He had small piercing eyes, set back in a narrow face. They gleamed out above the big beard, through the camouflage smudges, but the gleam looked innocent enough.

"What's your name?" Reacher asked him.

The guy hesitated. Shuffled in his seat. Reacher could see some kind of natural courtesy was prompting a reply. But there were obvious tactical considerations for the guy. Reacher kept on forcing the smile.

"I'm Reacher," he said. "You know my name. You got a name? We're here all night, we may as well be a little civilized about it, right?"

The guy nodded again, slowly. Then he shrugged.

"Ray," he said.

"Ray?" Reacher said. "That your first name or your last?"

"Last," the guy said. "Joseph Ray."

Reacher nodded.

"OK, Mr. Ray," he said. "Pleased to meet you."

"Call me Joe," Joseph Ray said.

Reacher forced the smile again. The ice was broken. Like conducting an interrogation. Reacher had done it a thousand times. But never from this side of the desk. Never when he was the one wearing the cuffs.

"Joe, you're going to have to help me out a little," he said. "I need some background here. I don't know where I am, or why, or who all you guys are. Can you fill me in on some basic information?"

Ray was looking at him like he was maybe having difficulty knowing where to start. Then he was glancing around the room like maybe he was wondering whether he was allowed to start at all.

"Where exactly are we?" Reacher asked him. "You can tell me that, right?"

"Montana," Ray said.

Reacher nodded.

"OK," he said. "Where in Montana?"

"Near a town called Yorke," Ray said. "An old mining town, just about abandoned."

Reacher nodded again.

"OK," he said. "What are you guys doing here?"

"We're building a bastion," Ray said. "A place of our own."

"What for?" Reacher asked him.

Ray shrugged. An inarticulate guy. At first, he said nothing. Then he sat forward and launched into what seemed to Reacher like a mantra, like something the guy had rehearsed many times. Or like something the guy had been told many times.

"We came up here to escape the tyranny of America," he said. "We have to draw up our borders and say, it's going to be different inside here."

"Different how?" Reacher asked him.

"We have to take America back, piece by piece," Ray said. "We have to build a place where the white man can live free, unmolested, in peace, with proper freedoms and proper laws."

"You think you can do that?" Reacher said.

"It happened before," Ray said. "It happened in 1776. People said enough is enough. They said we want a better country than this. Now we're saying it again. We're saying we want our country back. And we're going to get it back. Because now we're acting together. There were a dozen militias up here. They all wanted the same things. But they were all acting alone. Beau's mission was to put people together. Now we're unified and we're going to take our country back. We're starting here. We're starting now."

Reacher nodded. Glanced to his right and down at the dark stain where Loder's nose had bled onto the floor.

"Like this?" he said. "What about voting and democracy? All that kind of stuff? You should vote people out and vote new people in, right?"

Ray smiled sadly and shook his head.

"We've been voting for two hundred and twenty years," he said. "Gets worse all the time. Government's not interested in how we vote. They've taken all the power away from us. Given our country away. You know where the government of this country really is?''

Reacher shrugged.

''D.C., right?'' he said.

''Wrong,'' Ray said. ''It's in New York. The United Nations building. Ever asked yourself why the UN is so near Wall Street? Because that's the government. The United Nations and the banks. They run the world. America's just a small part of it. The President is just one voice on a damn committee. That's why voting is no damn good. You think the United Nations and the world banks care what we vote?''

''You sure about all this?'' Reacher asked.

Ray nodded, vigorously.

''Sure I'm sure,'' he said. ''I've seen it at work. Why do you think we send billions of dollars to the Russians when we got poverty here in America? You think that's the free choice of an American government? We send it because the world government tells us to send it. You know we got camps here? Hundreds of camps all over the country? Most of them are for United Nations troops. Foreign troops, waiting to move in when we start any trouble. But forty-three of them are concentration camps. That's where they're going to put us when we start speaking out.''

''You sure?'' Reacher said again.

''Sure I'm sure,'' Ray said again. ''Beau's got the documents. We've got the proof. There are things going on you wouldn't believe. You know it's a secret federal law that all babies born in the hospital get a microchip implanted just under their skin? When they take them away, they're not weighing them and cleaning them up. They're implanting a microchip. Pretty soon the whole population is going to be visible to secret satellites. You think the space shuttle gets used for science experiments? You think the world government would authorize expenditure for stuff like that? You got to be kidding. The space shuttle is there to launch surveillance satellites.''

''You're joking, right?'' Reacher said.

Ray shook his head.

''No way,'' he said. ''Beau's got the documents. There's another secret law, guy in Detroit sent Beau the stuff. Every car built in America since 1985 has a secret radio transmitter box in it, so the satellites can see where it's going. You buy a car, the radar screens in the UN building know where you are, every minute of the day and night. They've got foreign forces training in America, right now, ready for the official takeover. You know why we send so much money to Israel? Not because we care what happens to the Israelis. Why should we care? We send the money because that's where the UN is training the secret world army. It's like an experimental place. Why do you think the UN never stops the Israelis from invading people? Because the UN has told them what to do in the first place. Training them for the world takeover. There are three thousand helicopters right now, at airbases round the U.S., all ready for them to use. Helicopters, painted flat black, no markings.''

''You sure?'' Reacher said again. He was keeping his voice somewhere between worried and skeptical. ''I never heard about any of this stuff.''

''That proves it, right?'' Ray said.

''Why?'' Reacher asked.

''Obvious, right?'' Ray said. ''You think the world government is going to allow media access to that stuff? World government controls the media, right? They own it. So it's logical that whatever doesn't appear in the media is what is really happening, right? They tell you the safe stuff, and they keep the secrets away from you. It's all true, believe me. I told you, Beau's got the documents. Did you know every U.S. highway sign has a secret mark on the back? You drive out and take a look. A secret sign, to direct the world troops around the country. They're getting ready to take over. That's why we need a place of our own.''

''You think they're going to attack you?'' Reacher asked.

''No doubt about it,'' Ray said. ''They're going to come right after us.''

''And you figure you can defend yourselves?'' Reacher said. ''A few guys in some little town in Montana?''

Joe Ray shook his head.

''Not a few guys,'' he said. ''There are a hundred of us.''

''A hundred guys?'' Reacher said. ''Against the world government?''

Ray shook his head again.

"We can defend ourselves," he said. "Beau's a smart leader. This territory is good. We're in a valley here. Sixty miles north to south, sixty miles east to west. Canadian border along the northern edge."

He swept his hand through the air, above eye level, left to right like a karate chop, to demonstrate the geography. Reacher nodded. He was familiar with the Canadian border. Ray used his other hand, up and down the left edge of his invisible map.

"Rapid River," he said. "That's our western border. It's a big river, completely wild. No way to cross it."

He moved the Canadian border hand across and rubbed a small circle in the air, like he was cleaning a pane of glass.

"National forest," he said. "You seen it? Fifty miles, east to west. Thick virgin forest, no way through. You want an eastern border, that forest is as good as you're going to get."

"What about the south?" Reacher asked.

Ray chopped his hand sideways at chest level.

"Ravine," he said. "Natural-born tank trap. Believe me, I know tanks. No way through, except one road and one track. Wooden bridge takes the track over the ravine."

Reacher nodded. He remembered the white truck pattering over a wooden structure.

"That bridge gets blown," Ray said. "No way through."

"What about the road?" Reacher asked.

"Same thing," Ray said. "We blow the bridge, and we're safe. Charges are set right now."

Reacher nodded slowly. He was thinking about air attack, artillery, missiles, smart bombs, infiltration of Special Forces, airborne troops, parachutes. He was thinking about Navy SEALs bridging the river or Marines bridging the ravine. He was thinking about NATO units rumbling straight down from Canada.

"What about Holly?" he asked. "What do you want with her?"

Ray smiled. His beard parted and his teeth shone out as bright as his eyes. "Beau's secret weapon," he said. "Think about it. The world government is going to use her old man to lead the attack. That's why they appointed him. You think the President appoints those guys? You got to be joking. Old man Johnson's a world government guy, just waiting for the secret command to move. But when he gets here, what's he going to find?''

"What?" Reacher asked.

"He comes up from the south, right?" Ray said. "First building he sees is that old courthouse, southeast corner of town. You were just there. She's up on the second floor, right? You notice the new construction? Special room, double walls, twenty-two inches apart. The space is packed with dynamite and blasting caps from the old mine stores. The first stray shell will blow old man Johnson's little girl to kingdom come.''

Reacher nodded again, slowly. Ray looked at him.

"We're not asking much," he said. "Sixty miles by sixty miles, what is that? Thirty-six hundred square miles of territory.''

"But why now?" Reacher asked. "What's the big hurry?''

"What's the date?" Ray asked back.

Reacher shrugged.

"July something?" he said.

"July second," Ray said. "Two days to go.''

"To what?" Reacher said.

"Independence Day," Ray said. "July fourth.''

"So?" Reacher asked.

"We're declaring independence," Ray said. "Day after tomorrow. The birth of a brand-new nation. That's when they'll come for us, right? Freedom for the little guys? That's not in their plan.''

24

THE BUREAU LEAR refueled at Fargo and flew straight south-west to California. McGrath had argued again in favor of heading straight for Montana, but Webster had overruled him. One step at a time was Webster's patient way, so they were going to check out the Beau Borken story in California, and then they were going to Peterson Air Force Base in Colorado to meet with General Johnson, McGrath was about the only Bureau guy alive capable of shouting at Webster, and he had, but arguing is not the same thing as winning, so they were all in the air heading first for Mojave, McGrath and Webster and Brogan and Milosevic, all overtired, overanxious and morose in the hot noisy cabin.

"I need all the background I can get," Webster said. "They put me in personal charge and these are not the type of guys I can be vague with, right?"

McGrath glared at him and thought: don't play your stupid Beltway games with Holly's life, Webster. But he said nothing. Just sat tight until the tiny plane started arrowing down toward the airfield on the edge of the desert.

They were on the ground just after two o'clock in the morning, West Coast time. The Mojave Agent-in-Charge met them on the deserted tarmac in his own car. Drove them south through the sleeping town.

"The Borkens were a Kendall family," he said. "Small town, fifty miles from here. Farming place, mostly citrus.

One-man police department. The sheriff is waiting for us down there.''

''He know anything?'' McGrath asked.

The guy at the wheel shrugged.

''Maybe,'' he said. ''Small town, right?''

Fifty miles through the desert night at eighty-five took them just thirty-six minutes. Kendall was a small knot of buildings adrift in a sea of groves. There was a gas station, a general store, a growers' operation and a low cement building with whip antennas spearing upward from the roof. A smart black-and-white was parked up on the apron outside. It was marked: Kendall County Sheriff. There was a single light in the office window behind the car.

The five agents stretched and yawned in the dry night air and trooped single file into the cement building. The Kendall County sheriff was a guy about sixty, solid, gray. He looked reliable. Webster waved him back into his seat and McGrath laid the four glossy mug shots on his desk in front of him.

''You know these guys?'' he asked.

The sheriff slid the photographs nearer and looked at each of them in turn. He picked them up and shuffled them into a new order. Laid them back down on the desk like he was dealing a hand of giant playing cards. Then he nodded and reached down to his desk pedestal. Rolled open a drawer. Lifted out three buff files. He placed the files underneath three of the photographs. Laid a stubby finger on the first face.

''Peter Wayne Bell,'' he said. ''Mojave kid, but he was down here a lot. Not a very nice boy, as I believe you know.''

He nodded across to his monitor screen on a computer cart at the end of the desk. A page from the National Crime Center Database was glowing green. It was the report from the North Dakota cops about the identity of the body they had found in a ditch. The identity, and the history.

The sheriff moved his wrist and laid a finger on the next photograph. It was the gunman who had pushed Holly Johnson into the back of the Lexus.

''Steven Stewart,'' he said. ''Called Stevie, or Little Stevie. Farm boy, a couple of bushels short of a wagonload, know what I mean? Jumpy, jittery sort of a boy.''

"What's in his file?" Webster asked.

The sheriff shrugged.

"Nothing too serious," he said. "The boy was just too plain dumb for his own good. Group of kids would go out and mess around, and guess who'd be the one still stood there when I roll up? Little Stevie, that's who. I locked him up a dozen times, I guess, but he never did much of what you would want to call serious shit."

McGrath nodded and pointed to the photograph of the gunman who had gotten into the front seat of the Lexus.

"This guy?" he asked.

The sheriff moved his finger and laid it on the guy's glossy throat.

"Tony Loder," he said. "This is a fairly bad guy. Smarter than Stevie, dumber than you or me. I'll give you the file. Maybe it won't keep you Bureau guys awake nights, but it sure won't help you sleep any better than you were going to anyhow."

"What about the big guy?" Webster asked.

The sheriff jumped his finger along the row and shook his grizzled head.

"Never saw this guy before," he said. "That's for damn sure. I'd remember him if I had."

"We think maybe he's a foreigner," Webster said. "Maybe European. Maybe had an accent. That ring any bells with you?"

The sheriff just kept on shaking his head.

"Never saw him before," he said again. "I'd remember."

"OK," McGrath said. "Bell, Little Stevie Stewart, Tony Loder and the mystery man. Where do these Borken guys fit in?"

The sheriff shrugged.

"Old Dutch Borken never fit in nowhere," he said. "That was his problem. He was in Nam, infantry grunt, moved out here when he got out of the service. Brought a pretty wife and a little fat ten-year-old boy with him, started growing citrus, did pretty well for a long while. He was a strange guy, a loner, never saw much of him. But he was happy enough, I guess. Then the wife took sick and died, and the boy started acting weird, the market took a couple of hits, profits were down, the growers all started getting into the banks for loans, interest went up, land went down, the collateral was disappearing, irrigation water got expensive, they all started going belly-up one after the other. Borken took it bad and swallowed his shotgun.''

Webster nodded.

"The little fat ten-year-old was Beau Borken?'' he asked.

The sheriff nodded.

"Beau Borken,'' he said. "Very strange boy. Very smart. But obsessed.''

"With what?'' McGrath asked.

"Mexicans started coming up,'' the sheriff said. "Cheap labor. Young Beau was dead set against it. He started hollering about keeping Kendall white. Joined the John Birch types.''

"So he was a racist?'' McGrath said.

"At first,'' the sheriff said. "Then he got into all that conspiracy stuff. Talking about the Jews running the government. Or the United Nations, or both, or some damn thing. The government was all Communists, taking over the world, secret plans for everything. Big conspiracy against everybody, especially him. Banks controlled the government, or was it the government controlled the banks? So the banks were all Communists and they were out to destroy America. He figured the exact reason the bank loaned his father the money was so it could default him later and give the farm to the Mexicans or the blacks or some damn thing. He was raving about it, all the time.''

"So what happened?'' Webster said.

"Well, of course, the bank did end up defaulting him,'' the sheriff said. "The guy wasn't paying the loan, was he? But they didn't give his land to the Mexicans. They sold it on to the same big corporation owns everything else around here, which is owned by the pension funds, which probably means it's owned by you and me, not Communists or Mexicans or anybody else, right?''

"But the boy blamed the conspiracy for his father's death?'' Brogan asked.

"He sure did,'' the sheriff said. "But the truth is it was Beau himself who did for the old man. I figure old Dutch could have faced just about anything, except his only boy had turned out to be a complete lunatic. A cruel, selfish, weird boy. That's why he swallowed the damn shotgun, if you want to know the truth.''

"So where did Beau go?" Webster asked.

"Montana," the sheriff said. "That's what I heard. He was into all those right-wing groups, you know, the militias. Built himself up to leader. Said the white man was going to have to stand and fight.''

"And those other guys went with him?" Brogan asked.

"The three of them for sure," the sheriff said. "This big guy, I never saw before. But Little Stevie and Loder and Peter Bell, they were all in awe of Beau, like little robots. They all went up there together. They had a little cash, and they stripped the Borken place of anything they could carry, and they headed north. Figured to buy some cheap land up there and defend themselves, you know, although against who I can't say, because the way I hear it there ain't nobody up there, and if there is they're all white people anyway.''

"What's in his file?" Webster asked.

The sheriff shook his head.

"Just about nothing," he said. "Beau's way too smart to get caught doing anything bad.''

"But?" McGrath said. "He's doing stuff without getting caught?''

The sheriff nodded.

"That armored car robbery?" he said. "North of the state somewhere? I heard about that. Didn't stick to him, did it? I told you, way too smart.''

"Anything else we should know?" Webster asked.

The sheriff thought for a while and nodded again.

"There was a fifth guy," he said. "Name of Odell Fowler. He'll turn up alongside of Beau, for sure. You can bet on that. Loder and Stevie and Bell get sent out doing mischief, you can be damn sure Borken and Fowler are sitting there in the shadows pulling their strings.''

"Anything else?" Webster said again.

"Originally there was a sixth guy," the sheriff said. "Guy named Packer. Six of them, all thick as thieves. But Packer took up with a Mexican girl. Couldn't help himself, I guess, just plain fell in love with her. Beau told him to stop seeing her. They fell out about it, a lot of tension going on. One day, Packer's not around anymore, and Beau is all smiling and relaxed. We found Packer out in the scrub, nailed to a big wooden cross. Crucified. Dead for a couple of days.''

"And you figure Borken did it?'' Brogan asked.

"Couldn't prove it,'' the sheriff replied. "But I'm sure of it. And I'm sure he talked the others into helping him do it. He's a born leader. He can talk anybody into doing anything, I can promise you that.''

KENDALL BACK TO Mojave was fifty miles by car. Mojave to Peterson Air Force Base in Colorado was another eight hundred and thirty miles by Lear. Three hours of travel, door to door, which put them down at Peterson through the gorgeous mountain dawn. It was the kind of sight people pay money to see, but the four FBI men took no notice at all. Thursday July third, the fourth day of the crisis, and no proper rest and no proper nutrition had left them ragged and focused on nothing except the job in hand.

General Johnson himself was not available to meet them. He was elsewhere on the giant base, on duty glad-handing the returning night patrols. His aide saluted Webster, shook hands with the other three, and walked them all over to a crew room reserved for their use. There was a huge photograph on the table, black-and-white, crisply focused. Some kind of a landscape. It looked like the surface of the moon.

"That's Anadyr, in Siberia,'' the aide said. "Satellite photograph. Last week, there was a big air base there. A nuclear bomber base. The runway was aimed straight at our missile silos in Utah. Arms reduction treaty required it to be blown up. The Russians complied last week.''

The four agents bent for another look. There was no trace of any man-made structure in the picture. Just savage craters.

"Complied?'' McGrath said. "Looks like they did an enthusiastic job of work.''

"So?'' Webster said.

The aide pulled a map from the portfolio. Unfolded it and stepped around so that the agents could share his view. It was a slice of the world, eastern Asia and the western United

States, with the mass of Alaska right in the center and the North Pole right at the top. The aide stretched his thumb and finger apart and spanned the distance from Siberia southeast down to Utah.

"Anadyr was here," he said. "Utah is here. Naturally we knew all about the bomber base, and we had countermeasures in place, which included big missile bases in Alaska, here, and then a chain of four small surface-to-air facilities strung out north to south all the way underneath Anadyr's flight path into Utah, which are here, here, here and here, straddling the line between Montana and the Idaho panhandle."

The agents ignored the red dots in Idaho. But they looked closely at the locations in Montana.

"What sort of bases are these?" Webster asked.

The aide shrugged.

"They were kind of temporary," he said. "Thrown together in the sixties, just sort of survived ever since. Frankly, we didn't expect to have to use them. The Alaska missiles were more than adequate. Nothing would have gotten past them. But you know how it was, right? Couldn't be too ready."

"What sort of weapons?" McGrath asked.

"There was a Patriot battery at each facility," the aide said. "We pulled those out a while back. Sold them to Israel. All that's left is Stingers, you know, shoulder-launch infantry systems."

Webster looked at the guy.

"Stingers?" he said. "You were going to shoot Soviet bombers down with infantry systems?"

The aide nodded. Looked definite about it.

"Why not?" he said. "Don't forget, those bases were basically window dressing. Nothing was supposed to get past Alaska. But the Stingers would have worked. We supplied thousands of them to Afghanistan. They knocked down hundreds of Soviet planes. Mostly helicopters, I guess, but the principle is good. A heat seeker is a heat seeker, right? Makes no difference if it gets launched off a truck or off a GI's shoulder."

"So what happens now?" Webster asked him.

"We're closing the bases down," the guy said. "That's

why the General is here, gentlemen. We're pulling the equipment and the personnel back here to Peterson, and there's going to be some ceremonies, you know, end-of-an-era stuff.''

''Where are these bases?'' McGrath asked. ''The Montana ones? Exactly?''

The aide pulled the map closer and checked the references.

''Southernmost one is hidden on some farmland near Missoula,'' he said. ''Northern one is hidden in a valley, about forty miles south of Canada, near a little place called Yorke. Why? Is there a problem?''

McGrath shrugged.

''We don't know yet,'' he said.

THE AIDE SHOWED them where to get breakfast and left them to wait for the General. Johnson arrived after the eggs but before the toast, so they left the toast uneaten and walked back together to the crew room. Johnson looked a lot different from the glossy guy Webster had met with Monday evening. The early hour and three days' strain made him look twenty pounds thinner and twenty years older. His face was pale and his eyes were red. He looked like a man on the verge of defeat.

''So what do we know?'' he asked.

''We think we know most of it,'' Webster answered. ''Right now our operational assumption is your daughter's been kidnapped by a militia group from Montana. We know their location, more or less. Somewhere in the northwestern valleys.''

Johnson nodded slowly.

''Any communication?'' he asked.

Webster shook his head.

''Not yet,'' he said.

''So what's the reason?'' Johnson asked. ''What do they want?''

Webster shook his head again.

''We don't know that yet,'' he said.

Johnson nodded again, vaguely.

''Who are they?'' he asked.

McGrath opened the envelope he was carrying.

"We've got four names," he said. "Three of the snatch squad, and there's pretty firm evidence about who the militia leader is. A guy named Beau Borken. That name mean anything to you?"

"Borken?" Johnson said. He shook his head. "That name means nothing."

"OK," McGrath said. "What about this guy? His name's Peter Bell."

McGrath passed Johnson the computer print of Bell at the wheel in the Lexus. Johnson took a long look at it and shook his head.

"He's dead," McGrath said. "Didn't make it back to Montana."

"Good," Johnson said.

McGrath passed him another picture.

"Steven Stewart?" he said.

Johnson paid the print some attention, but ended up shaking his head.

"Never saw this guy before," he said.

"Tony Loder?" McGrath asked.

Johnson stared at Loder's face and shook his head.

"No," he said.

"Those three and Borken are all from California," McGrath said. "There may be another guy called Odell Fowler. You heard that name?"

Johnson shook his head.

"And there's this guy," McGrath said. "We don't know who he is."

He passed over the photograph of the big guy. Johnson glanced at it, then glanced away. But then his gaze drifted back.

"You know this one?" McGrath asked him.

Johnson shrugged.

"He's vaguely familiar," he said. "Maybe somebody I once saw?"

"Recently?" McGrath asked.

Johnson shook his head.

"Not recently," he said. "Probably a long time ago."

"Military?" Webster asked.

"Probably," Johnson said again. "Most of the people I see are military."

His aide crowded his shoulder for a look.

"Means nothing to me," he said. "But we should fax this to the Pentagon. If this guy is military, maybe there'll be somebody somewhere who served with him."

Johnson shook his head.

"Fax it to the military police," he said. "This guy's a criminal, right? Chances are he was in trouble before, in the service. Somebody there will remember him."

25

THEY CAME FOR him an hour after dawn. He was dozing
on his hard chair, hands cuffed in his lap, Joseph Ray awake
and alert opposite him. He had spent most of the night thinking about dynamite. Old dynamite, left over from abandoned
mining operations. He imagined hefting a stick in his hand.
Feeling the weight. Figuring the volume of the cavity behind
Holly's walls. Picturing it packed with old dynamite. Old
dynamite, rotting, the nitroglycerin sweating out, going unstable. Maybe a ton of unstable old dynamite packed in all
around her, still not so far gone it would explode with random
movement, but gone bad enough it would explode under the
impact of a stray artillery shell. Or a stray bullet. Or even a
sharp blow with a hammer.

Then there was a rattle of feet on shale as a detachment
of men halted outside the hut. The door flung open and
Reacher turned his head and saw six guards. The point man
clattered inside and hauled him up by the arm. He was
dragged outside into the bright morning sun to face five men,
line abreast, automatic rifles at the slope. Camouflage fatigues, beards. He stood and squinted in the light. The rifle
muzzles jerked him into rough formation and the six men
marched him across the diameter of the clearing to a narrow
path running away from the sun into the forest.

Fifty yards in, there was another clearing. A rough scrubby
rectangle, small in area. Two plywood-and-cedar structures.

Neither had any windows. The guards halted him and the point man used his rifle barrel to indicate the left-hand building.

"Command hut," he said.

Then he pointed to the right.

"Punishment hut," he said. "We try to avoid that one."

The six men laughed with the secure confidence of an elite detachment and the point man knocked on the command hut door. Paused a beat and opened it. Reacher was shoved inside with a rifle muzzle in the small of his back.

The hut was blazing with light. Electric bulbs added to green daylight from mossy skylights set into the roof. There was a plain oak desk and matching chairs, big old round things like Reacher had seen in old movies about newspaper offices or country banks. There was no decor except flags and banners nailed to the walls. There was a huge red swastika behind the desk, and several similar black-and-white motifs on the other walls. There was a detailed map of Montana pinned to a board on the back wall. A tiny portion of the northwest corner of the state was outlined in black. There were bundles of pamphlets and manuals stacked on the bare floor. One was titled: Dry It, You'll Like It. It claimed to show how food could be preserved to withstand a siege. Another claimed to show how guerrillas could derail passenger trains. There was a polished mahogany bookcase, incongruously fine, packed with books. The bar of daylight from the door fell across them and illuminated their cloth spines and gold-blocked titles. They were standard histories of the art of war, translations from German and Japanese. There was a whole shelf with texts about Pearl Harbor. Texts that Reacher himself had studied, elsewhere and a long time ago.

He stood still. Borken was behind the desk. His hair gleamed white in the light. The black uniform showed up gray. Borken was just staring silently at him. Then he waved him to a chair. Motioned the guards to wait outside.

Reacher sat heavily. Fatigue was gnawing at him and adrenaline was burning his stomach. The guards tramped across the floor and stepped outside. They closed the door quietly. Borken moved his arm and rolled open a drawer.

Took out an ancient handgun. Laid it on the desktop with a loud clatter.

"I made my decision," he said. "About whether you live or die."

Then he pointed at the old revolver lying on the desk.

"You know what this is?" he asked.

Reacher glanced at it through the glare and nodded.

"It's a Marshal Colt," he said.

Borken nodded.

"You bet your ass it is," he said. "It's an original 1873 Marshal Colt, just like the U.S. Cavalry were given. It's my personal weapon."

He picked it up, right-handed, and hefted it.

"You know what it fires?" he said.

Reacher nodded again.

"Forty-fives," he said. "Six shots."

"Right first time," Borken said. "Six forty-fives, nine hundred feet per second out of a seven-and-a-half-inch barrel. You know what those bullets could do to you?"

Reacher shrugged.

"Depends if they hit me or not," he said.

Borken looked blank. Then he grinned. His wet mouth curled upward and his tight cheeks nearly forced his eyes shut.

"They'd hit you," he said. "If I'm firing, they'd hit you."

Reacher shrugged again.

"From there, maybe," he said.

"From anywhere," Borken said. "From here, from fifty feet, from fifty yards, if I'm firing, they'd hit you."

"Hold up your right hand," Reacher said.

Borken looked blank again. Then he put the gun down and held up his huge white hand like he was waving to a vague acquaintance or taking an oath.

"Bullshit," Reacher said.

"Bullshit?" Borken repeated.

"For sure," Reacher said. "That gun's reasonably accurate, but it's not the best weapon in the world. To hit a man at fifty yards with it, you'd need to practice like crazy. And you haven't been."

"I haven't?" Borken said.

"No, you haven't," Reacher said. "Look at the damn thing. It was designed in the 1870s, right? You seen old photographs? People were much smaller. Scrappy little guys, just immigrated from Europe, been starving for generations. Small people, small hands. Look at the stock on that thing. Tight curve, way too small for you. You grab that thing, your hand looks like a bunch of bananas around it. And that stock is hundred-and-twenty-year-old walnut. Hard as a rock. The back of the stock and the end of the frame below the hammer would be pounding you with the recoil. You used that gun a lot, you'd have a pad of callus between your thumb and forefinger I could see from here. But you haven't, so don't tell me you've been practicing with it, and don't tell me you can be a marksman without practicing with it."

Borken looked hard at him. Then he smiled again. His wet lips parted and his eyes closed into slits. He rolled open the opposite drawer and lifted out another handgun. It was a Sig-Sauer nine-millimeter. Maybe five years old. Well used, but well maintained. A big boxy grip for a big hand.

"I lied," he said. "This is my personal weapon. And now I know something. I know my decision was the right one."

He paused, so Reacher could ask him about his decision. Reacher stayed silent. Clamped his lips. He wasn't about to ask him about anything, not even if it would be the last sentence he would ever live to say.

"We're serious here, you know," Borken said to him. "Totally serious. We're not playing games. And we're correct about what's going on."

He paused again, so Reacher could ask him what was going on. Reacher said nothing. Just sat and stared into space.

"America has got a despotic government," Borken said. "A dictatorship, controlled from abroad by our enemies. Our current President is a member of a world government which controls our lives in secret. His federal system is a smokescreen for total control. They're planning to disarm us and enslave us. It's started already. Let's be totally clear about that."

He paused. Picked up the old revolver again. Reacher saw him checking the fit of the stock in his hand. Felt the charisma radiating out of him. Felt compelled to listen to the soft, hypnotic voice.

"Two main methods," Borken said. "The first is the attempt to disarm the civilian population. The Second Amendment guarantees our right to bear arms, but they're going to abolish that. The gun laws, all this beefing about crime, homicides, drug wars, it's all aimed at disarming people like us. And when we're disarmed, they can do what they like with us, right? That's why it was in the Constitution in the first place. Those old guys were smart. They knew the only thing that could control a government was the people's willingness and ability to shoot them down."

Borken paused again. Reacher stared up at the swastika behind his head.

"Second method is the squeeze on small business," Borken said. "This is a personal theory of mine. You don't hear it much around the Movement. But I spotted it. It puts me way ahead of the others in my understanding."

Borken waited, but Reacher still stayed silent. Looking away.

"It's obvious, right?" Borken said to him. "World government is basically a communistic type of government. They don't want a strong small-business sector. But that's what America had. Millions of people, all working hard for themselves and making a living. Too many just to murder out of hand, when the time comes. So the numbers have to be reduced in advance. So the federal government was instructed to squeeze the small businessman. They put on all kinds of regulations, all kinds of laws and taxes, they rig the markets, they bring the small guy to his knees, then they order the banks to come sniffing around with attractive loans, and as soon as the ink is dry on the loan papers they jack up the interest, and rig the market some more, until the poor guy defaults. Then they take away his business, and so that's one less for the gas ovens when the time comes."

Reacher glanced at him. Said nothing.

"Believe it," Borken said. "It's like they're solving a corpse-disposal problem in advance. Get rid of the middle class now, they don't need so many concentration camps later."

Reacher was just staring at Borken's eyes. Like looking at a bright light. The fat red lips were smiling an indulgent smile.

"I told you, we're way ahead of the others," he said. "We've seen it coming. What else is the Federal Reserve for? That's the key to this whole thing. America was basically a nation founded on business, right? Control business, you control everything. How do you control business? You control the banks. How do you control the banks? You set up a bullshit Federal Reserve system. You tell the banks what to do. That's the key. The world government controls everything, through the Fed. I've seen it happen."

His eyes were open wide. Shining with no color.

"I saw them do it to my own father," he screamed. "May his poor soul rest in peace. The Fed bankrupted him."

Reacher tore his gaze away. Shrugged at the corner of the room. Said nothing. He started trying to recall the sequence of titles in Borken's fine mahogany bookcase. Warfare from ancient China through Renaissance Italy through Pearl Harbor. He concentrated on naming the titles to himself, left to right, trying to resist the glare of Borken's attention.

"We're serious here," Borken was saying again. "You may look at me and think I'm some kind of a despot, or a cult leader, or whatever the world would want to label me. But I'm not. I'm a good leader, I won't deny that. Even an inspired leader. Call me intelligent and perceptive, I won't argue with you. But I don't need to be. My people don't need any encouraging. They don't need much leading. They need guidance, and they need discipline, but don't let that fool you. I'm not coercing anybody. Don't make the mistake of underestimating their will. Don't ignore their desire for a change for the better."

Reacher was silent. He was still concentrating on the books, skimming in his mind through the events of December 1941, as seen from the Japanese point of view.

"We're not criminals here, you know," Borken was saying. "When a government turns bad, it's the very best people who stand up against it. Or do you think we should all just act like sheep?"

Reacher risked another glance at him. Risked speaking.

"You're pretty selective," he said. "About who's here and who's not."

Borken shrugged.

"Like unto like," he said. "That's nature's way, isn't it? Black people have got the whole of Africa. White people have got this place."

"What about Jewish dentists?" Reacher asked. "What place have they got?"

Borken shrugged again.

"That was an operational error," he said. "Loder should have waited until he was clear. But mistakes happen."

"Should have waited until I was clear, too," Reacher said.

Borken nodded.

"I agree with you," he said. "It would have been better for you that way. But they didn't, and so here you are among us."

"Just because I'm white?" Reacher said.

"Don't knock it," Borken replied. "White people got precious few rights left."

Reacher stared at him. Stared around the bright, hate-filled room. Shuddered.

"I've made a study of tyranny," Borken said. "And how to combat it. The first rule is you make a firm decision, to live free or die, and you mean it. Live free or die. The second rule is you don't act like a sheep. You stand up and you resist them. You study their system and you learn to hate it. And then you act. But how do you act? The brave man fights back. He retaliates, right?"

Reacher shrugged. Said nothing.

"The brave man retaliates," Borken repeated. "But the man who is both brave and clever acts differently. He retaliates first. In advance. He strikes the first blows. He gives them what they don't expect, when and where they don't expect it. That's what we're doing here. We're retaliating first. It's their war, but we're going to strike the first blows. We're going to give them what they don't expect. We're going to upset their plans."

Reacher glanced back at the bookcase. Five thousand classic pages, all saying the same thing: don't do what they expect you to do.

"Go look at the map," Borken said.

Reacher thrust his cuffed hands forward and lifted himself awkwardly out of the chair. Walked over to the map of Montana on the wall. He found Yorke in the top left-hand corner. Well inside the small black outline. He checked the scale and looked at the contour shading and the colors. The river Joseph Ray had talked about lay thirty miles to the west, on the other side of high mountains. It was a thick blue slash running down the map. There were enormous brown heights shown to the north, all the way up to Canada. The only road ran north through Yorke and terminated at some abandoned mine workings. A few haphazard tracks ran through solid forest to the east. To the south, contour lines merged together to show a tremendous east-west ravine.

"Look at that terrain, Reacher," Borken said quietly. "What does it tell you?"

Reacher looked at it. It told him he couldn't get out. Not on foot, not with Holly. There were weeks of rough walking east and north. Natural barriers west and south. The terrain made a better prison than wire fences or minefields could have. He had once been in Siberia, after glasnost, following up on ancient stories about Korean MIAs. The gulags had been completely open. No wire, no barriers. He had asked his hosts: but where are the fences? The Russians had pointed out over the miles of snow and said: there are the fences. Nowhere to run. He looked up at the map again. The terrain was the barrier. To get out was going to require a vehicle. And a lot of luck.

"They can't get in," Borken said. "We're impregnable. We can't be stopped. And we mustn't be stopped. That would be a disaster of truly historic proportions. Suppose the redcoats had stopped the American Revolution in 1776?"

Reacher glanced around the tiny wooden room and shuddered.

"This isn't the American Revolution," he said.

"Isn't it?" Borken asked. "How is it different? They wanted freedom from a tyrannical government. So do we."

"You're murderers," Reacher said.

"So they were in 1776," Borken said. "They killed people. The established system called that murder, too."

"You're racists," Reacher said.

"Same in 1776," Borken said. "Jefferson and his slaves? They knew black people were inferior. Back then, they were exactly the same as we are now. But then they became the new redcoats. Slowly, over the years. It's fallen to us to get back to how it should have stayed. Live free or die, Reacher. It's a noble aim. Always has been, don't you think?"

He was leaning forward with his great bulk pressing tight against the desk. His hands were in the air. His colorless eyes were shining.

"But there were mistakes made in 1776," he said. "I've studied the history. War could have been avoided if both sides had acted sensibly. And war should always be avoided, don't you think?"

Reacher shrugged.

"Not necessarily," he said.

"Well, you're going to help us avoid it," Borken said. "That's my decision. You're going to be my emissary."

"Your what?" Reacher said.

"You're independent," Borken said. "Not one of us. No ax to grind. An American like them, an upstanding citizen, no felony convictions. A clever, perceptive man. You notice things. They'll listen to you."

"What?" Reacher said again.

"We're organized here," Borken said. "We're ready for nationhood. You need to understand that. We have an army, we have a treasury, we have financial reserves, we have a legal system, we have democracy. I'm going to show all that to you today. I'm going to show you a society ready for independence, ready to live free or die, and just a day away from doing so. Then I'm going to send you south to America. You're going to tell them our position is strong and their position is hopeless."

Reacher just stared at him.

"And you can tell them about Holly," Borken said quietly. "In her special little room. You can tell them about my secret weapon. My insurance policy."

"You're crazy," Reacher said.

The hut went silent. Quieter than silent.

"Why?" Borken whispered. "Why am I crazy? Exactly?"

"You're not thinking straight," Reacher said. "Don't you realize that Holly counts for nothing? The President will replace Johnson faster than you can blink an eye. They'll crush you like a bug and Holly will be just another casualty. You should send her back out with me."

Borken was shaking his bloated head, happily, confidently.

"No," he said. "That won't happen. There's more to Holly than who her father is. Hasn't she told you that?"

Reacher stared at him and Borken checked his watch.

"Time to go," he said. "Time for you to see our legal system at work."

HOLLY HEARD THE quiet footsteps outside her door and eased off the bed. The lock clicked back and the young soldier with the scarred forehead stepped up into the room. He had his finger to his lips and Holly nodded. She limped to the bathroom and set the shower running noisily into the empty tub. The young soldier followed her in and closed the door.

"We can only do this once a day," Holly whispered. "They'll get suspicious if they hear the shower too often."

The young guy nodded.

"We'll get out tonight," he said. "Can't do it this morning. We're all on duty at Loder's trial. I'll come by just after dusk, with a jeep. We'll make a run for it in the dark. Head south. Risky, but we'll make it."

"Not without Reacher," Holly said.

The young guy shook his head.

"Can't promise that," he said. "He's in with Borken now. God knows what's going to happen to him."

"I go, he goes," Holly said.

The young guy looked at her nervously.

"OK," he said, "I'll try."

He opened the bathroom door and crept out. Holly watched him go and turned the shower off. Stared after him.

HE LOOPED NORTH and west and took a long route back through the woods, same way as he had come. The sentry Fowler had hidden in the trees fifteen feet off the main path never saw him. But the one he had hidden in the backwoods did. He caught a glimpse of a camouflage uniform hustling through the undergrowth. Spun around fast, but was too late to make the face. He shrugged and thought hard. Figured he'd keep it to himself. Better to ignore it than report he'd failed to make the actual ID.

So the young man with the scar hurried all the way and was back in his hut two minutes before he was due to escort his commander down to the tribunal hearing.

IN THE DAYLIGHT, the courthouse on the southeast corner of the abandoned town of Yorke looked pretty much the same as a hundred others Reacher had seen all over rural America. Built early in the century. Big, white, pillared, ornate. Enough square solidity to communicate its serious purpose, but enough lightness in its details to make it a handsome structure. He saw a fine cupola floating off the top of the building, with a fine clock in it, probably paid for by a public subscription held long ago among a long-forgotten generation. More or less the same as a hundred others, but the roof was steeper-pitched than some, and heavier built. He guessed it had to be that way in the north of Montana. That roof could be carrying a hundred tons of snow all winter long.

But this was the third morning of July, and there was no snow on the roof. Reacher was warm after walking a mile in the pale northern sun. Borken had gone ahead separately and Reacher had been marched down through the forest by the same six elite guards. Still in handcuffs. They marched him straight up the front steps and inside. The first-floor interior was one large space, interrupted by pillars holding up the second floor, paneled in broad smooth planks sawed from huge pines. The wood was dark from age and polish, and the panels were stern and simple in their design.

Every seat was taken. Every bench was full. The room was a sea of camouflage green. Men and women. Sitting rigidly upright, rifles exactly vertical between their knees. Waiting expectantly. Some children, silent and confused. Reacher was led in front of the crowd, over to a table in the well of the court. Fowler was waiting there. Stevie next to him. He nodded to a chair. Reacher sat. The guards stood behind him. A minute later, the double doors opened and Beau Borken walked over to the judge's bench. The old floor creaked beneath his bulk. Every person in the room except Reacher stood up. Stood to attention and saluted, as if they were hearing an inaudible cue. Borken was still in his black uniform, with belt and boots. He had added a large holster to hold his Sig-Sauer. He held a slim leatherbound book. He came in with six armed men in a loose formation. They took up station in front of the bench and stood at rigid attention, gazing forward, looking blank.

The people sat down again. Reacher glanced up at the ceiling and quartered it with his eyes. Worked out which was the southeast corner. The doors opened again and the crowd drew breath. Loder was pushed into the room. He was surrounded by six guards. They pushed him to the table opposite Fowler's. The accused's table. The guards stood behind him and forced him into the chair with their hands on both his shoulders. His face was white with fear and crusted with blood. His nose was broken and his lips were split. Borken stared across at him. Sat down heavily in the judge's chair and placed his big hands, palms down, on the bench. Looked around the quiet room and spoke.

"We all know why we're here," he said.

Holly COULD SENSE there was a big crowd in the room below her. She could feel the faint rumble of a body of people holding themselves still and quiet. But she didn't stop working. No reason to believe her Bureau contact would fail, but she was still going to spend the day preparing. Just in case.

Her search for a tool had led her to the one she had brought in with her. Her metal crutch. It was a one-inch aluminum tube, with an elbow clip and a handle. The tube was too wide and the metal was too soft to act as a pry bar. But she realized that maybe if she pulled the rubber foot off, the open end of the tube could be molded into a makeshift wrench. She could maybe crush the tube around the shape of the bolts holding the bed together. Then she could bend the tube at a right angle, and maybe use the whole thing like a flimsy tire iron.

But first she had to scrape away the thick paint on the bolts. It was smooth and slick, and it welded the bolts to the frame. She used the edge of the elbow clip to flake the top layers. Then she scraped at the seams until she saw bright metal. Now her idea was to limp back and forth from the bathroom with a towel soaked in hot water. She would press the towel hard on the bolts and let the heat from the water expand the metal and crack its grip. Then the soft aluminum of the crutch might just prove strong enough to do the job.

RECKLESS ENDANGERMENT OF the mission,'' Beau Borken said.

His voice was low and hypnotic. The room was quiet. The guards in front of the judge's bench stared forward. The guard at the end was staring at Reacher. He was the younger guy with the trimmed beard and the scar on his forehead Reacher had seen guarding Loder the previous night. He was staring at Reacher with curiosity.

Borken held up the slim leatherbound volume and swung it slowly, left to right, like it was a searchlight and he wanted to bathe the whole of the room with its bright beam.

"The Constitution of the United States," he said. "Sadly abused, but the greatest political tract ever devised by man. The model for our own constitution."

He turned the pages of the book. The rustle of stiff paper was loud in the quiet room. He started reading.

"The Bill of Rights," he said. "The Fifth Amendment specifies no person shall be held to answer for a capital crime without a grand jury indictment except in cases arising in the militia in times of public danger. It says no person shall be deprived of life or liberty without due process of law. The Sixth Amendment specifies the accused shall have the right to a speedy public trial in front of a local jury. It says the accused has the right to assistance of counsel."

Borken stopped again. Looked around the room. Held up the book.

"This book tells us what to do," he said. "So we need a jury. Doesn't say how many. I figure three men will do. Volunteers?"

There was a flurry of hands. Borken pointed randomly here and there and three men walked across the pine floor. They stacked their rifles and filed into the jury box. Borken turned in his seat and spoke to them.

"Gentlemen," he said. "This is a militia matter and this is a time of public danger. Are we agreed on that?"

The new jurymen all nodded and Borken turned and looked down from the bench toward Loder, alone at his table.

"You had counsel?" he said.

"You offering me a lawyer now?" Loder asked.

His voice was thick and nasal. Borken shook his head.

"There are no lawyers here," he said. "Lawyers are what went wrong with the rest of America. We're not going to have lawyers here. We don't want them. The Bill of Rights doesn't say anything about lawyers. It says counsel. Counsel means advice. That's what my dictionary says. You had advice? You want any?"

"You got any?" Loder said.

Borken nodded and smiled a cold smile.

"Plead guilty," he said.

Loder just shook his head and dropped his eyes.

"OK," Borken said. "You've had counsel, but you're pleading not guilty?"

Loder nodded. Borken looked down at his book again. Turned back to the beginning.

"The Declaration of Independence," he said. "It is the right of the people to alter or to abolish the old government and to institute new government in such form as to them shall seem most likely to effect their safety and happiness."

He stopped and scanned the crowd.

"You all understand what that means?" he said. "The old laws are gone. Now we have new laws. New ways of doing things. We're putting right two hundred years of mistakes. We're going back to where we should have been all along. This is the first trial under a brand-new system. A better system. A system with a far stronger claim to legitimacy. We have the right to do it, and what we are doing is right."

There was a slight murmur from the crowd. Reacher detected no disapproval in the sound. They were all hypnotized. Basking in Borken's bright glow like reptiles in a hot noontime sun. Borken nodded to Fowler. Fowler stood up next to Reacher and turned to the jury box.

"The facts are these," Fowler said. "The commander sent Loder out on a mission of great importance to all our futures. Loder performed badly. He was gone for just five days, but he made five serious mistakes. Mistakes which could have wrecked the whole venture. Specifically, he left a trail by burning two vehicles. Then he mistimed two operations and thereby snarled up two civilians. And finally he allowed Peter Bell to desert. Five serious mistakes."

Fowler stood there. Reacher stared at him, urgently.

"I'm calling a witness," Fowler said. "Stevie Stewart."

Little Stevie stood up fast and Fowler nodded him across to the old witness box, alongside and below the judge's bench. Borken leaned down and handed him a black book. Reacher couldn't see what book it was, but it wasn't a Bible. Not unless they had started making Bibles with swastikas on the cover.

"You swear to tell the truth here?" Borken asked.

Stevie nodded.

"I do, sir," he said.

He put the book down and turned to Fowler, ready for the first question.

"The five mistakes I mentioned?" Fowler said. "You see Loder make them?"

Stevie nodded again.

"He made them," he said.

"He take responsibility for them?" Fowler asked.

"Sure did," Stevie said. "He played the big boss the whole time we were away."

Fowler nodded Stevie back to the table. The courtroom was silent. Borken smiled knowingly at the jurymen and glanced down at Loder.

"Anything to say in your defense?" he asked quietly.

The way he said it, he made it seem absurd that anybody could possibly dream up any kind of defense to those kinds of charges. The courtroom stayed silent. Still. Borken was watching the crowd. Every pair of eyes was locked onto the back of Loder's head.

"Anything to say?" Borken asked him again.

Loder stared forward. Made no reply. Borken turned toward the jury box and looked at the three men sitting on the old worn benches. Looked a question at them. The three men huddled for a second and whispered. Then the guy on the left stood up.

"Guilty, sir," he said. "Definitely guilty."

Borken nodded in satisfaction.

"Thank you, gentlemen," he said.

The crowd set up a buzz. He turned to quell it with a look.

"I am required to pass sentence," he said. "As many of you know, Loder is an old acquaintance of mine. We go back a long way. We were childhood friends. And friendship means a great deal to me."

He paused and looked down at Loder.

"But other things mean more," he said. "Performance of my duties means more. My responsibility to this emerging nation means more. Sometimes, statesmanship must be put above every other value a man holds dear."

The crowd was silent. Holding its breath. Borken sat for a long moment. Then he glanced over Loder's head at the guards behind him and made a small, delicate motion with his head. The guards grabbed Loder's elbows and hauled him to his feet. They formed up and hustled him out of the room. Borken stood and looked at the crowd. Then he turned and walked to the doors and was gone. The people in the public benches shuffled to their feet and hurried out after him.

Reacher saw the guards walking Loder to a flagpole on the patch of lawn outside the courthouse. Borken was striding after them. The guards reached the flagpole and shoved Loder hard up against it, facing it. They held his wrists and pulled, so he was pressed up against the pole, hugging it, face tight against the dull white paint. Borken came up behind him. Pulled the Sig-Sauer from its holster. Clicked the safety catch. Cocked a round into the chamber. Jammed the muzzle into the back of Loder's neck and fired. There was an explosion of pink blood and the roar of the shot cannoned back off the mountains.

26

HIS NAME IS Jack Reacher," Webster said.

"Good call, General," McGrath said. "I guess they remembered him."

Johnson nodded.

"Military police keeps good records," he said.

They were still in the commandeered crew room inside Peterson Air Force Base. Ten o'clock in the morning, Thursday July third. The fax machine was rolling out a long reply to their inquiry. The face in the photograph had been identified immediately. The subject's service record had been pulled straight off the Pentagon computer and faxed along with the name.

"You recall this guy now?" Brogan asked.

"Reacher?" Johnson repeated vaguely. "I don't know. What did he do?"

Webster and the General's aide were crowding the machine, reading the report as the paper spooled out. They twisted it right side up and walked slowly away to keep it up off the floor.

"What did he do?" McGrath asked them urgently.

"Nothing," Webster said.

"Nothing?" McGrath repeated. "Why would they have a record on him if he didn't do anything?"

"He was one of them," Webster said. "Major Jack Reacher, military police."

The aide was racing through the length of paper.

"Silver Star," he said. "Two Bronzes, Purple Heart. This is a hell of a record, sir. This guy was a hero, for God's sake."

McGrath opened up his envelope and pulled out the original video pictures of the kidnap, black-and-white, unenlarged, grainy. He selected the first picture of Reacher's involvement. The one catching him in the act of seizing Holly's crutch and pulling the dry cleaning from her grasp. He slid the photograph across the table.

"Big hero," he said.

Johnson bent to study the picture. McGrath slid over the next. The one showing Reacher gripping Holly's arm, keeping her inside the tight crush of attackers. Johnson picked it up and stared at it. McGrath wasn't sure whether he was staring at Reacher, or at his daughter.

"He's thirty-seven," the General's aide read aloud. "Mustered out fourteen months ago. West Point, thirteen years' service, big heroics in Beirut right at the start. Sir, you pinned a Bronze on him, ten years ago. This is an absolutely outstanding record throughout. He's the only non-Marine in history to win the Wimbledon."

Webster looked up.

"Tennis?" he said.

The aide smiled briefly.

"Not Wimbledon," he said. "The Wimbledon. Marine Sniper School runs a competition, the Wimbledon Cup. For snipers. Open to anybody, but a Marine always wins it, except one year Reacher won it."

"So why didn't he serve as a sniper?" McGrath asked.

The aide shrugged.

"Beats me," he said. "Lots of puzzles in this record. Like why did he leave the service at all? Guy like this should have made it all the way to the top."

Johnson had a picture in each hand and he was staring closely at them.

"So why did he leave?" Brogan asked. "Any trouble?"

The aide shook his head. Scanned the paper.

"Nothing in the record," he said. "No reason given. We were shedding numbers at the time, but the idea was to cull the no-hopers. A guy like this shouldn't have been shaken out."

Johnson switched the photographs into the opposite hands, like he was looking for a fresh perspective.

"Anybody know him real well?" Milosevic asked. "Anybody we can talk to?"

"We can dig up his old commander, I guess," the aide said. "Might take us a day to get hold of him."

"Do it," Webster said. "We need information. Anything at all will help."

Johnson put the photographs down and slid them back to McGrath.

"He must have turned bad," he said. "Sometimes happens. Good men can turn bad. I've seen it myself, time to time. It can be a hell of a problem."

McGrath reversed the photographs on the shiny table and stared at them.

"You're not kidding," he said.

Johnson looked back at him.

"Can I keep that picture?" he said. "The first one?"

McGrath shook his head.

"No," he said. "You want a picture, I'll take one myself. You and your daughter standing together in front of a headstone, this asshole's name on it."

27

FOUR MEN WERE dragging Loder's body away and the crowd was dispersing quietly. Reacher was left standing on the courthouse steps with his six guards and Fowler. Fowler had finally unlocked the handcuffs. Reacher was rolling his shoulders and stretching. He had been cuffed all night and all morning and he was stiff and sore. His wrists were marked with red weals where the hard metal had bitten down.

"Cigarette?" Fowler asked.

He was holding his pack out. A friendly gesture. Reacher shook his head.

"I want to see Holly," he said.

Fowler was about to refuse, but then he thought some more and nodded.

"OK," he said. "Good idea. Take her out for some exercise. Talk to her. Ask her how we're treating her. That's something you're sure to be asked later. It'll be very important to them. We don't want you giving them any false impressions."

Reacher waited at the bottom of the steps. The sun had gone pale and watery. Wisps of mist were gathering in the north. But some of the sky was still blue and clear. After five minutes, Fowler brought Holly down. She was walking slowly, with a little staccato rhythm as her good leg alternated with the thump of her crutch. She walked through the door and stood at the top of the steps.

"Question for you, Reacher," Fowler called down. "How far can you run in a half hour with a hundred and twenty pounds on your back?"

Reacher shrugged.

"Not far enough, I guess," he said.

Fowler nodded.

"Right," he said. "Not far enough. If she's not standing right here in thirty minutes, we'll come looking for you. We'll give it a two-mile radius."

Reacher thought about it and nodded. A half hour with a hundred and twenty pounds on his back might get him more than two miles. Two miles was probably pessimistic. But he thought back to the map on Borken's wall. Thought about the savage terrain. Where the hell would he run? He made a show of checking his watch. Fowler walked away, up behind the ruined office building. The guards slung their weapons over their shoulders and stood easy. Holly smoothed her hair back. Stood face up to the pale sun.

"Can you walk for a while?" Reacher asked her.

"Slowly," she said.

She set off north along the middle of the deserted street. Reacher strolled beside her. They waited until they were out of sight. They glanced at each other. Then they turned and flung themselves together. Her crutch toppled to the ground and he lifted her a foot in the air. She wrapped her arms around him and buried her face in his neck.

"I'm going crazy in there," she said.

"I've got bad news," he said.

"What?" she said.

"They had a helper in Chicago," he said.

She stared up at him.

"They were only gone five days," he said. "That's what Fowler said at the trial. He said Loder had been gone just five days."

"So?" she said.

"So they didn't have time for surveillance," he said. "They hadn't been watching you. Somebody told them where you were going to be, and when. They had help, Holly."

The color in her face drained away. It was replaced by shock.

"Five days?" she said. "You sure?"

Reacher nodded. Holly went quiet. She was thinking hard.

"So who knew?" he asked her. "Who knew where you'd be, twelve o'clock Monday? A roommate? A friend?"

Her eyes were darting left and right. She was racing through the possibilities.

"Nobody knew," she said.

"Were you ever tailed?" he asked.

She shrugged helplessly. Reacher could see she desperately wanted to say yes, I was tailed. Because he knew to say no was too awful for her to contemplate.

"Were you?" he asked again.

"No," she said quietly. "By a bozo like one of these? Forget it. I'd have spotted them. And they'd have had to hang around all day outside the Federal Building, just waiting. We'd have picked them up in a heartbeat."

"So?" he asked.

"My lunch break was flexible," she said. "It varied, sometimes by a couple of hours either way. It was never regular."

"So?" he asked again.

She stared at him.

"So it was inside help," she said. "Inside the Bureau. Had to be. Think about it, no other possibility. Somebody in the office saw me leave and dropped a dime."

He said nothing. Just watched the dismay on her face.

"A mole inside Chicago," she said. A statement, not a question. "Inside the Bureau. No other possibility. Shit, I don't believe it."

Then she smiled. A brief, bitter smile.

"And we've got a mole inside here," she said. "Ironic, right? He identified himself to me. Young guy, big scar on his forehead. He's undercover for the Bureau. He says we've got people in a lot of these groups. Deep undercover, in case of emergency. He called it in when they put the dynamite in my walls."

He stared back at her.

"You know about the dynamite?" he said.

She grimaced and nodded.

"No wonder you're going crazy in there," he said.

Then he stared at her in a new panic.

"Who does this undercover guy call in to?" he asked urgently.

"Our office in Butte," Holly said. "It's just a satellite office. One resident agent. He communicates by radio. He's got a transmitter hidden out in the woods. But he's not using it now. He says they're scanning the frequencies."

He shuddered.

"So how long before the Chicago mole blows his cover?" he said.

Holly went paler.

"Soon, I guess," she said. "Soon as somebody figures we were headed out in this direction. Chicago will be dialing up the computers and trawling for any reports coming out of Montana. His stuff will be top of the damn pile. Christ, Reacher, you've got to get to him first. You've got to warn him. His name is Jackson."

They turned back. Started hurrying south through the ghost town.

"He says he can break me out," Holly said. "Tonight, by jeep."

Reacher nodded grimly.

"Go with him," he said.

"Not without you," she said.

"They're sending me anyway," he said. "I'm supposed to be an emissary. I'm supposed to tell your people it's hopeless."

"Are you going to go?" she asked.

He shook his head.

"Not if I can help it," he said. "Not without you."

"You should go," she said. "Don't worry about me."

He shook his head again.

"I am worrying about you," he said.

"Just go," she said. "Forget me and get out."

He shrugged. Said nothing.

"Get out if you get the chance, Reacher," she said. "I mean it."

She looked like she meant it. She was glaring at him.

"Only if you're gone first," he said finally. "I'm sticking around until you're out of here. I'm definitely not leaving you with these maniacs."

"But you can't stick around," she said. "If I'm gone, they'll go apeshit. It'll change everything."

He looked at her. Heard Borken say: she's more than his daughter.

"Why, Holly?" he said. "Why will it change everything? Who the hell are you?"

She didn't answer. Glanced away. Fowler strolled into view, coming north, smoking. He walked up to them. Stopped right in front of them. Pulled his pack.

"Cigarette?" he asked.

Holly looked at the ground. Reacher shook his head.

"She tell you?" Fowler asked. "All the comforts of home?"

The guards were standing to attention. They were in a sort of honor guard on the courthouse steps. Fowler walked Holly to them. A guard took her inside. At the door, she glanced back at Reacher. He nodded to her. Tried to make it say: see you later, OK? Then she was gone.

Now for the grand tour," Fowler said. "You stick close to me. Beau's orders. But you can ask any questions you want, OK?"

Reacher glanced vaguely at him and nodded. Glanced at the six guards behind him. He walked down the steps and paused. Looked over at the flagpole. It was set dead center in the remains of a fine square of lawn in front of the building. He walked across to it and stood in Loder's blood and looked around.

The town of Yorke was pretty much dead. Looked like it had died some time ago. And it looked like it had never been much of a place to begin with. The road came through north to south, and there had been four developed blocks flanking it, two on the east side and two on the west. The courthouse took up the whole of the southeastern block and it faced what might have been some kind of a county office on the southwestern block. The western side of the street was higher. The ground sloped way up. The foundation of the county office building was about level with the second floor of the court-house. It had started out the same type of structure, but it had fallen into ruin, maybe thirty years before. The paint was peeled and the siding showed through iron-gray. There was no glass in any window. The sloping knoll surrounding it had returned to mountain scrub. There had been an ornamental tree dead center. It had died a long time ago, and it was now just a stump, maybe seven feet high, like an execution post.

The northern blocks were rows of faded, boarded-up stores. There had once been tall ornate frontages concealing simple square buildings, but the decay of the years had left the frontages the same dull brown as the boxy wooden struc-tures behind. The signs above the doors had faded to nothing. There were no people on the sidewalks. No vehicle noise, no activity, no nothing. The place was a ghost. It looked like an abandoned cowboy town from the Old West.

"This was a mining town," Fowler said. "Lead, mostly, but some copper, and a couple of seams of good silver for a while. There was a lot of money made here, that's for damn sure."

"So what happened?" Reacher asked.

Fowler shrugged.

"What happens to any mining place?" he said. "It gets worked out, is what. Fifty years ago, people were registering claims in that old county office like there was no tomorrow, and they were disputing them in that old courthouse, and there were saloons and banks and stores up and down the street. Then they started coming up with dirt instead of metal, and they moved on, and this is what got left behind."

Fowler was looking around at the dismal view and Reacher was following his gaze. Then he transferred his eyes upward a couple of degrees and took in the giant mountains rearing on the horizon. They were massive and indifferent, still streaked with snow on the third of July. Mist hung in the passes and floated through the dense conifers. Fowler moved and Reacher followed him up a track launching steeply north-west behind the ruined county office. The guards followed in single file behind. He realized this was the track he'd stum-bled along twice in the dark the night before. After a hundred yards, they were in the trees. The track wound uphill through the forest. Progress was easier in the filtered green daylight. After a mile of walking they had made maybe a half mile of straight-line progress and they came out in the clearing the white truck had driven into the previous night. There was a small sentry squad, armed and immaculate, standing at attention in the center of the space. But there was no sign of the white truck. It had been driven away.

"We call this the Bastion," Fowler said. "These were the very first acres we bought."

In the clear daylight, the place looked different. The Bastion was a big tidy clearing in the brush, nestled in a mountain bowl three hundred feet above the town itself. There was no man-made perimeter. The perimeter had been supplied a million years ago by the great glaciers grinding down from the Pole. The north and west sides were mountainous, rearing straight up to the high peaks. Reacher saw snow again, packed by the wind into the high north-facing gullies. If it was there in July, it had to be there twelve months of the year.

To the southeast, the town was just visible below them through the gaps in the trees where the track had been carved out. Reacher could see the ruined county building and the white courthouse set below it like models. Directly south, the mountain slopes fell away into the thick forest. Where there were no trees, there were savage ravines. Reacher gazed at them, quietly. Fowler pointed.

"Hundred feet deep, some of those," he said. "Full of elk and bighorn sheep. And we got black bears roaming. A few of the folk have seen mountain lions on the prowl. You can hear them in the night, when it gets real quiet."

Reacher nodded and listened to the stunning silence. Tried to figure out how much quieter the nights could be. Fowler turned and pointed here and there.

"This is what we built," he said. "So far."

Reacher nodded again. The clearing held ten buildings. They were all large utilitarian wooden structures, built from plywood sheet and cedar, resting on solid concrete piles. There was an electricity supply into each building from a loop of heavy cable running between them.

"Power comes up from the town," Fowler said. "A mile

of cable. Running water, too, piped down from a pure mountain lake through plastic tubing, installed by militia labor.''

Reacher saw the hut he'd been locked into most of the night. It was smaller than the others.

"Administration hut," Fowler said.

One of the huts had a whip antenna on the roof, maybe sixty feet high. Shortwave radio. And Reacher could see a thinner cable, strapped to the heavy power line. It snaked into the same hut, and didn't come out again.

"You guys are on the phone?" he asked. "Unlisted, right?"

He pointed and Fowler followed his gaze.

"The phone line?" he said. "Runs up from Yorke with the power cable. But there's no telephone. World government would tap our calls."

He gestured for Reacher to follow him over to the hut with the antenna, where the line terminated. They pushed in together through the narrow door. Fowler spread his hands in a proud little gesture.

"The communications hut," he said.

The hut was dark and maybe twenty feet by twelve. Two men inside, one crouched over a tape recorder, listening to something on headphones, the other slowly turning the dial of a radio scanner. Both long sides of the hut had crude wooden desks built into the walls. Reacher glanced up at the gable and saw the telephone wire running in through a hole drilled in the wall. It coiled down and fed a modem. The modem was wired into a pair of glowing desktop computers.

"The National Militia Internet," Fowler said.

A second wire bypassed the desktops and fed a fax machine. It was whirring away to itself and slowly rolling a curl of paper out.

"The Patriotic Fax Network," Fowler said.

Reacher nodded and walked closer. The fax machine sat on the counter next to another computer and a large shortwave radio.

"This is the shadow media," Fowler said. "We depend on all this equipment for the truth about what's going on in America. You can't get the truth any other way."

Reacher took a last look around and shrugged.

"I'm hungry," he said. "That's the truth about me. No dinner and no breakfast. You got someplace with coffee?"

Fowler looked at him and grinned.

"Sure," he said. "Mess hall serves all day. What do you think we are? A bunch of savages?"

He dismissed the six guards and gestured again for Reacher to follow him. The mess hall was next to the communications hut. It was about four times the size, twice as long and twice as wide. Outside, it had a sturdy chimney on the roof, fabricated from bright galvanized metal. Inside, it was full of rough trestle tables in neat lines, simple benches pushed carefully underneath. It smelled of old food and the dusty smell that large communal spaces always have.

There were three women working in there. They were cleaning the tables. They were dressed in olive fatigues, and they all had long, clean hair and plain, unadorned faces, red hands and no jewelry. They paused when Fowler and Reacher walked in. They stopped working and stood together, watching. Reacher recognized one of them from the courtroom. She gave him a cautious nod of greeting. Fowler stepped forward.

"Our guest missed breakfast," he said.

The cautious woman nodded again.

"Sure," she said. "What can I get you?"

"Anything," Reacher said. "As long as it's got coffee with it."

"Five minutes," the woman said.

She led the other two away through a door where the kitchen was bumped out in back. Fowler sat down at a table and Reacher took the bench opposite.

"Three times a day, this place gets used for meals," Fowler said. "The rest of the time, afternoons and evenings mainly, it gets used as the central meeting place for the community. Beau gets up on the table and tells the folk what needs doing."

"Where is Beau right now?" Reacher asked.

"You'll see him before you go," Fowler said. "Count on it."

Reacher nodded slowly and focused through the small window toward the mountains. The new angle gave him a glimpse of a farther range, maybe fifty miles distant, hanging there in the clear air between the earth and the sky. The silence was still awesome.

"Where is everybody?" he asked.

"Working," Fowler said. "Working, and training."

"Working?" Reacher said. "Working at what?"

"Building up the southern perimeter," Fowler said. "The ravines are shallow in a couple of places. Tanks could get through. You know what an abatis is?"

Reacher looked blank. He knew what an abatis was. Any conscientious West Pointer who could read knew what an abatis was. But he wasn't about to let Fowler know exactly how much he knew about anything. So he just looked blank.

"You fell some trees," Fowler said. "Every fifth or sixth tree, you chop it down. You drop it facing away from the enemy. The trees around here, they're mostly wild pines, the branches face upward, right? So when they're felled, the branches are facing away from the enemy. Tank runs into the chopped end of the tree, tries to push it along. But the branches snag against the trees you left standing. Pretty soon, that tank is trying to push two or three trees over. Then four or five. Can't be done. Even a big tank like an Abrams can't do it. Fifteen-hundred-horsepower gas turbine on it, sixty-three tons, it's going to stall when it's trying to push all those trees over. Even if they ship the big Russian tanks in against us, it can't be done. That's an abatis, Reacher. Use the power of nature against them. They can't get through those damn trees, that's for sure. Soviets used it against Hitler, Kursk, World War Two. An old Commie trick. Now we're turning it around against them."

"What about infantry?" Reacher said. "Tanks won't come alone. They'll have infantry right there with them. They'll just skip ahead and dynamite the trees."

Fowler grinned.

"They'll try," he said. "Then they'll stop trying. We've got machine gun positions fifty yards north of the abatises. We'll cut them to pieces."

The cautious woman came back out of the kitchen carrying a tray. She put it down on the table in front of Reacher. Eggs, bacon, fried potatoes, beans, all on an enamel plate. A metal pint mug of steaming coffee. Cheap flatware.

"Enjoy," she said.

"Thank you," Reacher said.

"I don't get coffee?" Fowler said.

The cautious woman pointed to the back.

"Help yourself," she said.

Fowler tried a man-to-man look at Reacher and got up. Reacher kept on looking blank. Fowler walked back to the kitchen and ducked in the door. The woman watched him go and laid a hand on Reacher's arm.

"I need to talk to you," she whispered. "Find me after lights-out, tonight. I'll meet you outside the kitchen door, OK?"

"Talk to me now," Reacher whispered back. "I could be gone by then."

"You've got to help us," the woman whispered.

Then Fowler came back out into the hall and the woman's eyes clouded with terror. She straightened up and hurried away.

THERE WERE SIX bolts through each of the long tubes in the bed frame. Two of them secured the mesh panel which held up the mattress. Then there were two at each end, fixing the long tube to the right-angle flanges attached to the legs. She had studied the construction for a long time, and she had spotted an improvement. She could leave one flange bolted to one end. It would stand out like a rigid right-angled hook. Better than separating the flange and then jamming it into the open end. More strength.

But it still left her with six bolts. She would have to take the flange off the leg. An improvement, but not a shortcut. She worked fast. No reason to believe Jackson would fail, but his odds had just worsened. Worsened dramatically.

NEXT TO THE mess hall were the dormitories. There were four large buildings, all of them immaculate and deserted. Two of them were designated as barracks for single men and single women. The other two were subdivided by plywood partitions. Families lived there, the adults in pairs in small cubicles behind the partitions, the children in an open dormitory area. Their beds were three-quarter-size iron cots, lined up in neat rows. There were half-size footlockers at the ends of the cots. No drawings on the walls, no toys. The only decor was a tourist poster from Washington, D.C. It was an aerial photograph taken from the north on a sunny spring day, with the White House in the right foreground, the Mall in the middle and the Capitol end-on to the left. It was framed in plastic and the tourist message had been covered over with paper and a new title had been hand-lettered in its place. The new title read: This Is Your Enemy.

"Where are all the kids right now?" Reacher asked.

"In school," Fowler said. "Winter, they use the mess hall. Summer, they're out in the woods."

"What do they learn?" Reacher asked.

Fowler shrugged.

"Stuff they need to know," he said.

"Who decides what they need to know?" Reacher asked.

"Beau," Fowler said. "He decides everything."

"So what has he decided they need to know?" Reacher asked.

"He studied it pretty carefully," Fowler said. "Comes down to the Bible, the Constitution, history, physical training, woodsmanship, hunting, weapons."

"Who teaches them all that stuff?" Reacher asked.

"The women," Fowler replied.

"The kids happy here?" Reacher asked.

Fowler shrugged again.

"They're not here to be happy," he said. "They're here to survive."

The next hut was empty, apart from another computer terminal, standing alone on a desk in a corner. Reacher could see a big keyboard lock fastened to it.

"I guess this is our Treasury Department," Fowler said. "All our funds are in the Caymans. We need some, we use that computer to send it anywhere we want."

"How much you got?" Reacher asked.

Fowler smiled, like a conspirator.

"Shitloads," he said. "Twenty million in bearer bonds. Less what we've spent already. But we got plenty left. Don't you worry about us getting short."

"Stolen?" Reacher asked.

Fowler shook his head and grinned.

"Captured," he said. "From the enemy. Twenty million."

The final two buildings were storehouses. One stood in line with the last dormitory. The other was set some distance away. Fowler led Reacher into the nearer shed. It was crammed with supplies. One wall was lined with huge plastic drums filled with water.

"Beans, bullets and bandages," Fowler said. "That's Beau's motto. Sooner or later we're going to face a siege. That's for damn sure. And it's pretty obvious the first thing the government is going to do, right? They're going to fire artillery shells armed with plague germs into the lake that feeds our water system. So we've stockpiled drinking water. Twenty-four thousand gallons. That was the first priority. Then we got canned food, enough for two years. Not enough if we get a lot of people coming in to join us, but it's a good start."

The storage shed was crammed. One floor-to-ceiling bay was packed with clothing. Familiar olive fatigues, camouflage jackets, boots. All washed and pressed in some Army laundry, packed up and sold off by the bale.

"You want some?" Fowler asked.

Reacher was about to move on, but then he glanced down at what he was wearing. He had been wearing it continuously since Monday morning. Three days solid. It hadn't been the best gear to start with, and it hadn't improved with age.

"OK," he said.

The biggest sizes were at the bottom of the pile. Fowler heaved and shoved and dragged out a pair of pants, a shirt, a jacket. Reacher ignored the shiny boots. He liked his own shoes better. He stripped and dressed, hopping from foot to foot on the bare wooden floor. He did up the shirt buttons and shrugged into the jacket. The fit felt good enough. He didn't look for a mirror. He knew what he looked like in fatigues. He'd spent enough years wearing them.

Next to the door, there were medical supplies ranged on shelves. Trauma kits, plasma, antibiotics, bandages. All efficiently laid out for easy access. Neat piles, with plenty of space between. Borken had clearly rehearsed his people in rushing around and grabbing equipment and administering emergency treatment.

"Beans and bandages," Reacher said. "What about the bullets?"

Fowler nodded toward the distant shed.

"That's the armory," he said. "I'll show you."

The armory was bigger than the other storage shed. Huge lock on the door. It held more weaponry than Reacher could remember seeing in a long time. Hundreds of rifles and machine guns in neat rows. The stink of fresh gun oil everywhere. Floor-to-ceiling stacks of ammo boxes. Familiar wooden crates of grenades. Shelves full of handguns. Nothing heavier than an infantryman could carry, but it was still a hell of an impressive sight.

THE TWO BOLTS securing the mesh base were the easiest. They were smaller than the others. The big bolts holding the frame together took all the strain. The mesh base just rested in there. The bolts holding it down were not structural. They could have been left out altogether, and the bed would have worked just the same.

She flaked and scraped the paint back to the bare metal. Heated the bolt heads with the towel. Then she pulled the rubber tip off her crutch and bent the end of the aluminum tube into an oval. She used the strength in her fingers to crush the oval tight over the head of the bolt. Used the handle to turn the whole of the crutch like a giant socket wrench. It slipped off the bolt. She cursed quietly and used one hand to crush it tighter. Turned her hand and the crutch together as a unit. The bolt moved.

THERE WAS A beaten earth path leading out north from the ring of wooden buildings. Fowler walked Reacher down it. It led to a shooting range. The range was a long, flat alley painstakingly cleared of trees and brush. It was silent and unoccupied. It was only twenty yards wide, but over a half-mile long. There was matting laid at one end for the shooters to lie on, and far in the distance Reacher could see the targets. He set off on a slow stroll toward them. They looked like standard military-issue plywood cutouts of running, crouching soldiers. The design dated right back to World War II. The crude screen-printing depicted a German infantryman, with a coal-scuttle helmet and a savage snarl. But as he got closer Reacher could see these particular targets had crude painted additions of their own. They had new badges daubed on the chests in yellow paint. Each new badge had three letters. Four targets had: FBI. Four had: ATF. The targets were staggered backward over distances ranging from three hundred yards right back to the full eight hundred. The nearer targets were peppered with bullet holes.

"Everybody has to hit the three-hundred-yard targets," Fowler said. "It's a requirement of citizenship here."

Reacher shrugged. Wasn't impressed. Three hundred yards was no kind of a big deal. He kept on strolling down the half-mile. The four-hundred-yard targets were damaged, the five-hundred-yard boards less so. Reacher counted eighteen hits at six hundred yards, seven at seven hundred, and just two at the full eight hundred.

"How old are these boards?" he asked.

Fowler shrugged.

"A month," he said. "Maybe two. We're working on it."

"You better," Reacher said.

"We don't figure to be shooting at a distance," Fowler replied. "Beau's guess is the UN forces will come at night. When they think we're resting up. He figures they might succeed in penetrating our perimeter to some degree. Maybe by a half-mile or so. I don't think they will, but Beau's a cautious guy. And he's the one with all the responsibility. So our tactics are going to be nighttime outflanking maneuvers. Encircle the UN penetration in the forest and mow it down with cross fire. Up close and personal, right? That training's going pretty well. We can move fast and quiet in the dark, no lights, no sound, no problem at all."

Reacher looked at the forest and thought about the wall of ammunition he'd seen. Thought about Borken's boast: impregnable. Thought about the problems an army faces fighting committed guerrillas in difficult terrain. Nothing is ever really impregnable, but the casualties in taking this place were going to be spectacular.

"This morning," Fowler said. "I hope you weren't upset."

Reacher just looked at him.

"About Loder, I mean," Fowler said.

Reacher shrugged. Thought to himself: it saved me a job of work.

"We need tough discipline," Fowler said. "All new nations go through a phase like this. Harsh rules, tough discipline. Beau's made a study of it. Right now, it's very important. But it can be upsetting, I guess."

"It's you should be upset," Reacher said. "You heard of Joseph Stalin?"

Fowler nodded.

"Soviet dictator," he said.

"Right," Reacher said. "He used to do that."

"Do what?" Fowler asked.

"Eliminate potential rivals," Reacher said. "On trumped-up charges."

Fowler shook his head.

"The charges were fair," he said. "Loder made mistakes."

Reacher shrugged.

"Not really," he said. "He did a reasonable job."

Fowler looked away.

"You'll be next," Reacher said. "You should watch your back. Sooner or later, you'll find you've made some kind of a mistake."

"We go back a long way," Fowler said. "Beau and me."

"So did Beau and Loder, right?" Reacher said. "Stevie will be OK. He's no threat. Too dumb. But you should think about it. You'll be next."

Fowler made no reply. Just looked away again. They walked together back down the grassy half-mile. Took another beaten track north. They stepped off the path to allow a long column of children to file past. They were marching in pairs, boys and girls together, with a woman in fatigues at the head of the line and another at the tail. The children were dressed in cut-down military surplus gear and they were carrying tall staffs in their right hands. Their faces were blank and acquiescent. The girls had untrimmed straight hair, and the boys had rough haircuts done with bowls and blunt shears. Reacher stood and watched them pass. They stared straight ahead as they walked. None of them risked a sideways glance at him.

The new path ran uphill through a thin belt of trees and came out on a flat area fifty yards long and fifty yards wide. It had been leveled by hand. Discarded fieldstone had been painted white and laid at intervals around the edge. It was quiet and deserted.

"Our parade ground," Fowler said, sourly.

Reacher nodded and scanned around. To the north and west, the high mountains. To the east, thick virgin forest. South, he could see over the distant town, across belts of trees, to the fractured ravines beyond. A cold wind lifted his new jacket and grabbed at his shirt, and he shivered.

THE BIGGER BOLTS were much harder. Much more contact area, metal to metal. Much more paint to scrape. Much more force required to turn them. The more force she used, the more the crushed end of the crutch was liable to slip off. She took off her shoe and used it to hammer the end into shape. She bent and folded the soft aluminum around the head of the bolt. Then she clamped it tight with her fingers. Clamped until the slim tendons in her arm stood out like ropes and sweat ran down her face. Then she turned the crutch, holding her breath, waiting to see which would give first, the grip of her fingers or the grip of the bolt.

THE WIND GRABBING at Reacher's shirt also carried some faint sounds to him. He glanced at Fowler and turned to face the western edge of the parade ground. He could hear men moving in the trees. A line of men, bursting out of the forest.

They crashed out of the trees, six men line abreast, automatic rifles at the slope. Camouflage fatigues, beards. The same six guards who had stood in front of the judge's bench that morning. Borken's personal detail. Reacher scanned across the line of faces. The younger guy with the scar was at the left-hand end of the line. Jackson, the FBI plant. They paused and reset their course. Rushed across the leveled ground toward Reacher. As they approached, Fowler stood back, leaving Reacher looking like an isolated target. Five of the men fanned out into a loose arc. Five rifles aimed at Reacher's chest. The sixth man stepped up in front of Fowler. No salute, but there was a deference in his stance which was more or less the same thing.

"Beau wants this guy back," the soldier said. "Something real urgent."

Fowler nodded.

"Take him," he said. "He's beginning to piss me off."

The rifle muzzles jerked Reacher into a rough formation and the six men hustled him south through the thin belt of trees, moving fast. They passed through the shooting range and followed the beaten earth path back to the Bastion. They turned west and walked past the armory and on into the forest toward the command hut. Reacher lengthened his stride and sped up. Pulled ahead. Let his foot hit a root and went down heavily on the stones. First guy to reach him was Jackson. Reacher saw the scarred forehead. He grabbed Reacher's arm.

"Mole in Chicago," Reacher breathed.

"On your feet, asshole," Jackson shouted back.

"Hide out and run for it tonight," Reacher whispered. "Maximum care, OK?"

Jackson glanced at him and replied with a squeeze of his arm. Then he pulled him up and shoved him ahead down the path into the smaller clearing. Beau Borken was framed in his command hut doorway. He was dressed in huge baggy camouflage fatigues, dirty and disheveled. Like he had been working hard. He stared at Reacher as he approached.

"I see we gave you new clothes," he said.

Reacher nodded.

"So let me apologize for my own appearance," Borken said. "Busy day."

"Fowler told me," Reacher said. "You've been building abatises."

"Abatises?" Borken said. "Right."

Then he went quiet. Reacher saw his big white hands, opening and closing.

"Your mission is canceled," Borken said quietly.

"It is?" Reacher said. "Why?"

Borken eased his bulk down out of the doorway and

stepped close. Reacher's gaze was fixed on his blazing eyes and he never saw the blow coming. Borken hit him in the stomach, a big hard fist on the end of four hundred pounds of body weight. Reacher went down like a tree and Borken smashed a foot into his back.

28

"His name is Jackson," Webster said.

"How long has he been in there?" Milosevic asked.

"Nearly a year," Webster said.

Eleven o'clock in the morning, Thursday July third, inside Peterson. The section head at Quantico was faxing material over from Andrews down the Air Force's own secure fax network as fast as the machines could handle it. Milosevic and Brogan were pulling it off the machines and passing it to Webster and McGrath for analysis. On the other side of the table, General Johnson and his aide were scanning a map of the northwest corner of Montana.

"You got people undercover in all these groups?" Johnson asked.

Webster shook his head and smiled.

"Not all of them," he said. "Too many groups, not enough people. I think we just got lucky."

"I didn't know we had people in this one," Brogan said.

Webster was still smiling.

"Lots of things lots of people don't know," he said. "Safer that way, right?"

"So what is this Jackson guy saying?" Brogan asked.

"Does he mention Holly?" Johnson asked.

"Does he mention what the hell this is all about?" Milosevic asked.

Webster blew out his cheeks and waved his hand at the

stack of curling fax paper. McGrath was busy sifting through it. He was separating the papers into two piles. One pile for routine stuff, the other pile for important intelligence. The routine pile was bigger. The important intelligence was sketchy.

"Analysis, Mack?" Webster said.

McGrath shrugged.

"Up to a point, pretty much normal," he said.

Johnson stared at him.

"Normal?" he said.

Webster nodded.

"This is normal," he said. "We got these militia groups all over the country, which is why we can't cover them all. Too damn many. Our last count was way over four hundred groups, all fifty states. Most of them are just amateur wackos, but some of them we consider pretty serious antigovernment terrorists."

"This bunch?" Johnson asked.

McGrath looked at him.

"This bunch is totally serious," he said. "One hundred people, hidden out in the forest. Very well armed, very well organized, very self-contained. Very well funded, too. Jackson has reported mail fraud, phony bank drafts, a little low-grade counterfeiting. Probably armed robbery as well. The feeling is they stole twenty million bucks in bearer bonds, armored car heist up in the north of California. And, of course, they're selling videos and books and manuals to the rest of the wackos, mail order. Big boom industry right now. And naturally they decline to pay income tax or license their vehicles or anything else that might cost them anything."

"Effectively, they control Yorke County," Webster said.

"How is that possible?" Johnson asked.

"Because nobody else does," Webster said. "You ever been up there? I haven't. Jackson says the whole place is abandoned. Everything pulled out, a long time ago. He says there's just a couple dozen citizens still around, spread out over miles of empty territory, bankrupt ranchers, leftover miners, old folk. No effective county government. Borken just eased his way in and took it over."

"He's calling it an experiment," McGrath said. "A prototype for a brand-new nation."

Johnson nodded, blankly.

"But what about Holly?" he said.

Webster stacked the paper and laid his hand on it.

"He doesn't mention her," he said. "His last call was Monday, the day she was grabbed up. They were building a prison. We have to assume it was for her."

"This guy calls in?" Brogan said. "By radio?"

Webster nodded.

"He's got a transmitter concealed in the forest," he said. "He wanders off when he can, calls in. That's why it's all so erratic. He's been averaging one call a week. He's pretty inexperienced and he's been told to be cautious. We assume he's under surveillance. Brave new world up there, that's for damn sure."

"Can we call him?" Milosevic asked.

"You're kidding," Webster said. "We just sit and wait."

"Who does he report to?" Brogan asked.

"Resident Agent at Butte," Webster said.

"So what do we do?" Johnson asked.

Webster shrugged. The room went quiet.

"Right now, nothing," he said. "We need a position."

The room stayed quiet and Webster just looked hard at Johnson. It was a look between one government man and another and it said: you know how it is. Johnson stared back for a long time, expressionless. Then his head moved through a fractional nod. Just enough to say: for the moment, I know how it is.

Johnson's aide coughed into the silence.

"We've got missiles north of Yorke," he said. "They're moving south right now, on their way back here. Twenty grunts, a hundred Stingers, five trucks. They'll be heading straight through Yorke, anytime now. Can we use them?"

Brogan shook his head.

"Against the law," he said. "Military can't participate in law enforcement."

Webster ignored him and glanced at Johnson and waited. They were his men, and Holly was his daughter. The answer was better coming straight from him. There was a silence, and then Johnson shook his head.

"No," he said. "We need time to plan."

The aide spread his hands wide.

"We can plan," he said. "We've got radio contact, ground-to-ground. We should go for it, General."

"Against the law," Brogan said again.

Johnson made no reply. He was thinking hard. McGrath riffled through the pile of papers and pulled the sheet about the dynamite packing Holly's prison walls. He held it face-down on the shiny table. But Johnson shook his head again.

"No," he said again. "Twenty men against a hundred? They're not frontline troops. They're not infantry. And their Stingers won't help us. I assume these terrorists don't have an air force, right? No, we wait. Bring the missile unit right back here, fastest. No engagement."

The aide shrugged and McGrath slipped the dynamite report back into the pile. Webster looked around and slapped both palms lightly on the tabletop.

"I'm going back to D.C.," he said. "Got to get a position."

Johnson shrugged his shoulders. He knew nothing could start without a trip back to D.C. to get a position. Webster turned to McGrath.

"You three move up to Butte," he said. "Get settled in the office there. If this guy Jackson calls, put him on maximum alert."

"We can chopper you up there," the aide said.

"And we need surveillance," Webster said. "Can you get the Air Force to put some camera planes over Yorke?"

Johnson nodded.

"They'll be there," he said. "Twenty-four hours a day. We'll give you a live video feed into Butte. A rat farts, you'll see it."

"No intervention," Webster said. "Not yet."

29

SHE HEARD FOOTSTEPS in the corridor at the exact moment the sixth bolt came free. A light tread. Not Jackson. Not a man treading carefully. A woman, walking normally. The steps halted outside her door. There was a pause. She rested the long tube back on the frame. A key went into the lock. She pulled the mattress back into place. Dragged the blanket over it. Another pause. The door opened.

A woman came into the room. She looked like all of them looked, white, lean, long straight hair, strong plain face, no makeup, no adornment, red hands. She was carrying a tray, with a white cloth mounded up over it. No weapon.

"Lunch," she said.

Holly nodded. Her heart was pounding. The woman was standing there, the tray in her hands, looking around the room, staring hard at the new pine walls.

"Where do you want this?" she asked. "On the bed?"

Holly shook her head.

"On the floor," she said.

The woman bent and placed the tray on the floor.

"Guess you could use a table," she said. "And a chair."

Holly glanced down at the flatware and thought: tools.

"You want me to get them to bring you a chair?" the woman asked.

"No," Holly said.

"Well, I could use one," the woman said. "I've got to

wait and watch you eat. Make sure you don't steal the silverware.''

Holly nodded vaguely and circled around the woman. Glanced at the open door. The woman followed her gaze and grinned.

"Nowhere to run,'' she said. "We're a long way from anywhere, and there's some difficult terrain in the way. North, you'd reach Canada in a couple of weeks, if you found enough roots and berries and bugs to eat. West, you'd have to swim the river. East, you'd get lost in the forest or eaten by a bear, and even if you didn't, you're still a month away from Montana. South, we'd shoot you. The border is crawling with guards. You wouldn't stand a chance.''

"The road is blocked?'' Holly asked.

The woman smiled.

"We blew the bridge,'' she said. "There is no road, not anymore.''

"When?'' Holly asked her. "We drove in.''

"Just now,'' the woman said. "You didn't hear it? I guess you wouldn't, not with these walls.''

"So how does Reacher get sent out?'' Holly asked. "He's supposed to be carrying some sort of a message.''

The woman smiled again.

"That plan has changed,'' she said. "Mission canceled. He's not going.''

"Why not?'' Holly asked.

The woman looked straight at her.

"We found out what happened to Peter Bell,'' she said.

Holly went quiet.

"Reacher killed him,'' the woman said. "Suffocated him. In North Dakota. We were just informed. But I expect you know all about it, right?''

Holly stared at her. She thought: Reacher's in big trouble. She saw him, handcuffed and alone somewhere.

"How did you find out?'' she asked quietly.

The woman shrugged.

"We have a lot of friends,'' she said.

Holly kept on staring at her. She thought: the mole. They know we were in North Dakota. Takes a map and a ruler to figure out where we are now. She saw computer keyboards clicking and Jackson's name scrolling up on a dozen screens.

"What's going to happen to Reacher?" she asked.

"A life for a life," the woman said. "That's the rule here. Same for your friend Reacher as for anybody else."

"But what's going to happen to him?" Holly asked again.

The woman laughed.

"Doesn't take much imagination," she said. "Or maybe it does. I don't expect it's going to be anything real simple."

Holly shook her head.

"It was self-defense," she said. "The guy was trying to rape me."

The woman looked at her, scornfully.

"So how is that self-defense?" she said. "Wasn't trying to rape him, was he? And you were probably asking for it, anyhow."

"What?" Holly said.

"Shaking your tail at him?" the woman said. "We know all about smart little city bitches like you. Poor old Peter never stood a chance."

Holly just stared at her. Then she glanced at the door.

"Where is Reacher now?" she asked.

"No idea," the woman said. "Chained to a tree some-where, I guess."

Then she grinned.

"But I know where he's going," she said. "The parade ground. That's where they usually do that sort of stuff. We're all ordered up there to watch the fun."

Holly stared at her. Then she swallowed. Then she nodded.

"Will you help me with this bed?" she asked. "Something wrong with it."

The woman paused. Then she followed her over.

"What's wrong with it?" she asked.

Holly pulled the blanket back and heaved the mattress onto the floor.

"The bolts seem a little loose," she said.

"Where?" the woman said.

"Here," Holly said.

She used both hands on the long tube. Whipped it upward and spun and smashed it like a blunt spear into the side of the woman's head. The flange hit her like a metal fist. Skin tore and a neat rectangle of bone punched deep into her brain and she bounced off the mattress and was dead before she hit the floor. Holly stepped carefully over the tray of lunch and limped calmly toward the open door.

30

HARLAND WEBSTER GOT back to the Hoover Building from Colorado at three o'clock Thursday afternoon, East Coast time. He went straight to his office suite and checked his messages. Then he buzzed his secretary.

"Car," he said.

He went down in his private elevator to the garage and met his driver. They walked over to the limousine and got in.

"White House," Webster said.

"You seeing the President, sir?" the driver asked, surprised.

Webster scowled forward at the back of the guy's head. He wasn't seeing the President. He didn't see the President very often. He didn't need reminding of that, especially not by a damn driver sounding all surprised that there even was such a possibility.

"Attorney General," he said. "White House is where she is right now."

His driver nodded silently. Cursed himself for opening his big mouth. Drove on smoothly and unobtrusively. The distance between the Hoover Building and the White House was exactly sixteen hundred yards. Less than a mile. Not even far enough to click over the little number in the speedometer on the limousine's dash. It would have been quicker to walk. And cheaper. Firing up the cold V-8 and hauling all that bulletproof plating sixteen hundred yards really ate up the gas. But the Director couldn't walk anywhere. Theory was he'd get assassinated. Fact was, there were probably about eight people in the city who would recognize him. Just another D.C. guy in a gray suit and a quiet tie. Anonymous. Another reason old Webster was never in the best of tempers, his driver thought.

WEBSTER KNEW THE Attorney General pretty well. She was his boss, but his familiarity with her did not come from their face-to-face meetings. It came instead from the background checks the Bureau had run prior to her confirmation. Webster probably knew more about her than anybody else on earth did. Her parents and friends and ex-colleagues all knew their own separate perspectives. Webster had put all of those together and he knew the whole picture. Her Bureau file took up as much disk space as a short novel. Nothing at all in the file made him dislike her. She had been a lawyer, faintly radical at the start of her career, built up a decent practice, grabbed a judgeship, never annoyed the law enforcement community, without ever becoming a rabid foaming-at-the-mouth pain in the ass. An ideal appointment, sailed through her confirmation with no problem at all. Since then, she had proven to be a good boss and a great ally. Her name was Ruth Rosen and the only problem Webster had with her was that she was twelve years younger than him, very good-looking, and a whole lot more famous than he was.

His appointment was for four o'clock. He found Rosen alone in a small room, two floors and eight Secret Service agents away from the Oval Office. She greeted him with a strained smile and an urgent inclination of her elegant head.

"Holly?" she asked.

He nodded. He gave her the spread, top to bottom. She listened hard and ended up pale, with her lips clamped tight.

"We totally sure this is where she is?" she asked.

He nodded again.

"Sure as we can be," he said.

"OK," she said. "Wait there, will you?"

She left the small room. Webster waited. Ten minutes, then twenty, then a half hour. He paced. He gazed out of the

window. He opened the door and glanced out into the corridor. A Secret Serviceman glanced back at him. Took a pace
forward. Webster shook his head in answer to the question
the guy hadn't asked and closed the door again. Just sat down
and waited.

Ruth Rosen was gone an hour. She came back in and
closed the door. Then she just stood there, a yard inside the
small room, pale, breathing hard, some kind of shock on her
face. She said nothing. Just let it dawn on him that there was
some kind of a big problem happening.

"What?" he asked.

"I'm out of the loop on this," she said.

"What?" he asked again.

"They took me out of the loop," she said. "My reactions
were wrong. Dexter is handling it from here."

"Dexter?" he repeated. Dexter was the President's White
House Chief of Staff. A political fixer from the old school.
As hard as a nail, and half as sentimental. But he was the
main reason the President was sitting there in the Oval Office
with a big majority of the popular vote.

"I'm very sorry, Harland," Ruth Rosen said. "He'll be
here in a minute."

He nodded sourly and she went back out the door and left
him to wait again.

THE RELATIONSHIP BETWEEN the rest of the FBI and the Field
Office in Butte, Montana, is similar to the relationship between Moscow and Siberia, proverbially speaking. It's a standard Bureau joke. Screw up, the joke goes, and you'll be
working out of Butte tomorrow. Like some kind of an inter-
nal exile. Like KGB foul-ups were supposedly sent out to
write parking tickets in Siberia.

But on that Thursday July third, the Field Office in Butte
felt like the center of the universe for McGrath and Milosevic
and Brogan. It felt like the most desirable posting in the
world. None of the three had ever been there before. Not on
business, not on vacation. None of them would have ever
considered going there. But now they were peering out of
the Air Force helicopter like kids on their way to the Magic
Kingdom. They were looking at the landscape below and

swiveling their gaze northwest toward where they knew Yorke County was hiding under the distant hazy mist.

The Resident Agent at Butte was a competent Bureau veteran still reeling after a personal call from Harland Webster direct from the Hoover Building. His instructions were to drive the three Chicago agents to his office, brief them on the way, get them installed, rent them a couple of jeeps, and then get the hell out and stay the hell out until further notice. So he was waiting at the Silver Bow County airport when the dirty black Air Force chopper clattered in. He piled the agents into his government Buick and blasted back north to town.

"Distances are big around here," he said to McGrath. "Don't ever forget that. We're still two hundred forty miles shy of Yorke. On our roads, that's four hours, absolute minimum. Me, I'd get some mobile units and move up a lot closer. Basing yourselves down here won't help you much, not if things start to turn bad up there."

McGrath nodded.

"You hear from Jackson again?" he asked.

"Not since Monday," the Resident Agent said. "The dynamite thing."

"Next time he calls, he speaks to me, OK?" McGrath said.

The Butte guy nodded. Fished one-handed in his pocket while he drove. Pulled out a small radio receiver. McGrath took it from him. Put it into his own pocket.

"Be my guest," the Butte guy said. "I'm on vacation. Webster's orders. But don't hold your breath. Jackson doesn't call often. He's very cautious."

The Field Office was just a single room, second floor of a two-floor municipal building. A desk, two chairs, a computer, a big map of Montana on the wall, a lot of filing space, and a ringing telephone. McGrath answered it. He listened and grunted. Hung up and waited for the Resident Agent to take the hint.

"OK, I'm gone," the old guy said. "Silver Bow Jeep will bring you a couple of vehicles over. Anything else you guys need?"

"Privacy," Brogan said.

The old guy nodded and glanced around his office. Then he was gone.

"Air Force has put a couple of spy planes up there," McGrath said. "Satellite gear is coming in by road. The General and his aide are coming here. Looks like they're going to be our guests for the duration. Can't really argue with that, right?"

Milosevic was studying the map on the wall.

"Wouldn't want to argue with that," he said. "We're going to need some favors. You guys ever seen a worse-looking place?"

McGrath and Brogan joined him in front of the map. Milosevic's finger was planted on Yorke. Ferocious green and brown terrain boiled all around it.

"Four thousand square miles," Milosevic said. "One road and one track."

"They chose a good spot," Brogan said.

I SPOKE WITH the President," Dexter said.

He sat back and paused. Webster stared at him. What the hell else would he have been doing? Pruning the Rose Garden? Dexter was staring back. He was a small guy, burned up, dark, twisted, the way a person gets to look after spending every minute of every day figuring every possible angle.

"And?" Webster said.

"There are sixty-six million gun owners in this country," Dexter said.

"So?" Webster asked.

"Our analysts think they all share certain basic sympathies," Dexter said.

"What analysts?" Webster said. "What sympathies?"

"There was a poll," Dexter said. "Did we send you a copy? One adult in five would be willing to take up arms against the government, if strictly necessary."

"So?" Webster asked again.

"There was another poll," Dexter said. "A simple question, to be answered intuitively, from the gut. Who's in the right, the government or the militias?"

"And?" Webster said.

"Twelve million Americans sided with the militias," Dexter said.

Webster stared at him. Waited for the message.

"So," Dexter said. "Somewhere between twelve and sixty-six million voters."

"What about them?" Webster asked.

"And where are they?" Dexter asked back. "You won't find many of them in D.C. or New York or Boston or L.A. It's a skewed sample. Some places they're a tiny minority. They look like weirdos. But other places, they're a majority. Other places, they're absolutely normal, Harland."

"So?" he said.

"Some places they control counties," Dexter said. "Even states."

Webster stared at him.

"God's sake, Dexter, this isn't politics," he said. "This is Holly."

Dexter paused and glanced around the small White House room. It was painted a subtle off-white. It had been painted and repainted that same subtle color every few years, while Presidents came and went. He smiled a connoisseur's smile.

"Unfortunately, everything's politics," he said.

"This is Holly," Webster said again.

Dexter shook his head. Just a slight movement.

"This is emotion," he said. "Think about innocent little emotional words, like patriot, resistance, crush, underground, struggle, oppression, individual, distrust, rebel, revolt, revolution, rights. There's a certain majesty to those words, don't you think? In an American context?"

Webster shook his head doggedly.

"Nothing majestic about kidnapping women," he said. "Nothing majestic about illegal weapons, illegal armies, stolen dynamite. This isn't politics."

Dexter shook his head again. The same slight movement.

"Things have a way of becoming politics," he said. "Think about Ruby Ridge. Think about Waco, Harland. That wasn't politics, right? But it became politics pretty damn soon. We hurt ourselves with maybe sixty-six million voters there. And we were real dumb about it. Big reactions are what these people want. They figure that harsh reprisals will upset people, bring more people into their fold. And we gave them big reactions. We fueled their fire. We made it look like big government was just about itching to crush the little guy."

The room went silent.

"The polls say we need a better approach," Dexter said. "And we're trying to find one. We're trying real hard. So how would it look if the White House stopped trying just because it happens to be Holly who's involved? And right now? The Fourth of July weekend? Don't you understand anything? Think about it, Harland. Think about the reaction. Think about words like vindictive, self-interested, revenge, personal, words like that, Harland. Think about what words like those are going to do to our poll numbers."

Webster stared at him. The off-white walls crushed in on him.

"This is about Holly, for God's sake," he said. "This is not about poll numbers. And what about the General? Has the President said all this to him?"

Dexter shook his head.

"I've said it all to him," he said. "Personally. A dozen times. He's been calling every hour, on the hour."

Webster thought: now the President won't even take Johnson's calls anymore. Dexter has really fixed him.

"And?" he asked.

Dexter shrugged.

"I think he understands the principle," he said. "But naturally, his judgment is kind of colored right now. He's not a happy man."

Webster lapsed into silence. Started thinking hard. He was a smart enough bureaucrat to know if you can't beat them, you join them. You force yourself to think like they think.

"But busting her out could do you good," he said. "A lot of good. It would look tough, decisive, loyal, no-nonsense. Could be advantageous. In the polls."

Dexter nodded.

"I totally agree with you," he said. "But it's a gamble, right? A real big gamble. A quick victory is good, a foul-up is a disaster. A big gamble, with big poll numbers at stake. And right now, I'm doubting if you can get the quick victory.

Right now, you're half-cocked. So right now my money would be on the foul-up."

Webster stared at him.

"Hey, no offense, Harland," Dexter said. "I'm paid to think like this, right?"

"So what the hell are you saying here?" Webster asked him. "I need to move the Hostage Rescue Team into place right now?"

"No," Dexter said.

"No?" Webster repeated incredulously.

Dexter shook his head.

"Permission denied," he said. "For the time being."

Webster just stared at him.

"I need a position," he said.

The room stayed silent. Then Dexter spoke to a spot on the off-white wall, a yard to the left of Webster's chair.

"You remain in personal command of the situation," he said. "Holiday weekend starts tomorrow. Come talk to me Monday. If there's still a problem."

"There's a problem now," Webster said. "And I'm talking to you now."

Dexter shook his head again.

"No, you're not," he said. "We didn't meet today, and I didn't speak with the President today. We didn't know anything about it today. Tell us all about it on Monday, Harland, if there's still a problem."

Webster just sat there. He was a smart enough guy, but right then he couldn't figure if he was being handed the deal of a lifetime, or a suicide pill.

JOHNSON AND HIS aide arrived in Butte an hour later. They came in the same way, Air Force helicopter from Peterson up to the Silver Bow County airport. Milosevic took an air-to-ground call as they were on approach and went out to meet them in a two-year-old Grand Cherokee supplied by the local dealership. Nobody spoke on the short ride back to town. Milosevic just drove and the two military men bent over charts and maps from a large leather case the aide was carrying. They passed them back and forth and nodded, as if further comment was unnecessary.

The upstairs room in the municipal building was suddenly crowded. Five men, two chairs. The only window faced southeast over the street. The wrong direction. The five men were instinctively glancing at the blank wall opposite. Through that wall was Holly, two hundred and forty miles away.

"We're going to have to move up there," General Johnson said.

His aide nodded.

"No good staying here," he said.

McGrath had made a decision. He had promised himself he wouldn't fight turf wars with these guys. His agent was Johnson's daughter. He understood the old guy's feelings. He wasn't going to squander time and energy proving who was boss. And he needed the old guy's help.

"We need to share facilities," he said. "Just for the time being."

There was a short silence. The General nodded slowly. He knew enough about Washington to decode those five words with a fair degree of accuracy.

"I don't have many facilities available," he said in turn. "It's the holiday weekend. Exactly seventy-five percent of the U.S. Army is on leave."

Silence. McGrath's turn to do the decoding and the slow nodding.

"No authorization to cancel leave?" he asked.

The General shook his head.

"I just spoke with Dexter," he said. "And Dexter just spoke with the President. Feeling was this thing is on hold until Monday."

The crowded room went silent. The guy's daughter was in trouble, and the White House fixer was playing politics.

"Webster got the same story," McGrath said. "Can't even bring the Hostage Rescue Team up here yet. Time being, we're on our own, the three of us."

The General nodded to McGrath. It was a personal gesture, individual to individual, and it said: we've leveled with each other, and we both know what humiliation that cost us, and we both know we appreciate it.

"But there's no harm in being prepared," the General said.

"Like the little guy suspects, the military is comfortable with secret maneuvers. I'm calling in a few private favors that Mr. Dexter need never know about."

The silence in the room eased. McGrath looked a question at him.

"There's a mobile command post already on its way," the General said.

He took a large chart from his aide and spread it out on the desk.

"We're going to rendezvous right here," he said.

He had his finger on a spot northwest of the last habitation in Montana short of Yorke. It was a wide curve on the road leading into the county, about six miles shy of the bridge over the ravine.

"The satellite trucks are heading straight there," he said. "I figure we move in, set up the command post, and seal off the road behind us."

McGrath stood still, looking down at the map. He knew that to agree was to hand over total control to the military. He knew that to disagree was to play petty games with his agent and this man's daughter. Then he saw that the General's finger was resting a half-inch south of a much better location. A little farther north, the road narrowed dramatically. It straightened to give a clear view north and south. The terrain tightened. A better site for a roadblock. A better site for a command post. He was amazed that the General hadn't spotted it. Then he was flooded with gratitude. The General had spotted it. But he was leaving room for McGrath to point it out. He was leaving room for give-and-take. He didn't want total control.

"I would prefer this place," McGrath said.

He tapped the northerly location with a pencil. The General pretended to study it. His aide pretended to be impressed.

"Good thinking," the General said. "We'll revise the rendezvous."

McGrath smiled. He knew damn well the trucks were already heading for that exact spot. Probably already there. The General grinned back. The ritual dance was completed.

"What can the spy planes show us?" Brogan asked.

"Everything," the General's aide said. "Wait until you

see the pictures. The cameras on those babies are unbeliev-
able.''

''I don't like it,'' McGrath said. ''It's going to make them
nervous.''

The aide shook his head.

''They won't even know they're there,'' he said. ''We're
using two of them, flying straight lines, east to west and west
to east. They're thirty-seven thousand feet up. Nobody on the
ground is even going to be aware of them.''

''That's seven miles up,'' Brogan said. ''How can they see
anything from that sort of height?''

''Good cameras,'' the aide said. ''Seven miles is nothing.
They'll show you a cigarette pack lying on the sidewalk from
seven miles. The whole thing is automatic. The guys up there
hit a button, and the camera tracks whatever it's supposed to
track. Just keeps pointing at the spot on the ground you
chose, transmitting high-quality video by satellite, then you
turn around and come back, and the camera swivels around
and does it all again.''

''Undetectable?'' McGrath asked.

''They look like airliners,'' the aide said. ''You look up
and you see a tiny little vapor trail and you think it's TWA
on the way somewhere. You don't think it's the Air Force
checking whether you polished your shoes this morning,
right?''

''Seven miles, you'll see the hairs on their heads,'' Johnson said. ''What do you think we spent all those defense
dollars on? Crop dusters?''

McGrath nodded. He felt naked. Time being, he had nothing to offer except a couple of rental jeeps, two years old,
waiting at the sidewalk.

''We're getting a profile on this Borken guy,'' he said.
''Shrinks at Quantico are working it up now.''

''We found Jack Reacher's old CO,'' Johnson said. ''He's
doing desk duty in the Pentagon. He'll join us, give us the
spread.''

McGrath nodded.

''Forewarned is forearmed,'' he said.

The telephone rang. Johnson's aide picked it up. He was
the nearest.

"When are we leaving?" Brogan asked.

McGrath noticed he had asked Johnson direct.

"Right now, I guess," Johnson said. "The Air Force will fly us up there. Saves six hours on the road, right?"

The aide hung up the phone. He looked like he'd been kicked in the gut.

"The missile unit," he said. "We lost radio contact, north of Yorke."

31

HOLLY PAUSED IN the corridor. Smiled. The woman had left her weapon propped against the wall outside the door. That had been the delay. She had used the key, put the tray on the floor, unslung her weapon, propped it against the wall, and picked up the tray again before nudging open the door.

She swapped the iron tube for the gun. Not a weapon she had used before. Not one she wanted to use now. It was a tiny submachine gun. An Ingram MAC 10. Obsolete military issue. Obsolete for a reason. Holly's class at Quantico had laughed about it. They called it the phone booth gun. It was so inaccurate you had to be in a phone booth with your guy to be sure of hitting him. A grim joke. And it fired way too quickly. A thousand rounds per minute. One touch on the trigger and the magazine was empty.

But it was a better weapon than part of an old iron bed frame. She checked the magazine. It was full, thirty shells. The chamber was clean. She clicked the trigger and watched the mechanism move. The gun worked as well as it was ever going to. She smacked the magazine back into position. Straightened the canvas strap and slung it tight over her shoulder. Clicked the cocking handle to the fire position and closed her hand around the grip. Took a firm hold on her crutch and eased to the top of the stairs.

She stood still and waited. Listened hard. No sound. She went down the stairs, slowly, a step at a time, the Ingram out in front of her. At the bottom, she waited and listened again. No sound. She crossed the lobby and arrived at the doors. Eased them open and looked outside.

The street was deserted. But it was wide. It looked like a huge city boulevard to her. To reach safety on the other side was going to take her minutes. Minutes out there in the open, exposed to the mountain slopes above. She estimated the distance. Breathed hard and gripped her crutch. Jabbed the Ingram forward. Breathed hard again and took off at a lurching run, jamming the crutch down, leaping ahead with her good leg, swinging the gun left and right to cover both approaches.

She threw herself at the mound in front of the ruined county office. Scrabbled north around behind it and fought through grabbing undergrowth. Entered the forest parallel to the main track, but thirty yards from it. Leaned on a tree and bent double, gasping with exertion and fear and exhilaration.

This was the real thing. This was what the whole of her life had led her to. She could hear her father's war stories in her head. The jungles of Vietnam. The breathless fear of being hunted in the green undergrowth. The triumph of each safe step, of each yard gained. She saw the faces of the tough quiet men she had known on the bases as a child. The instructors at Quantico. She felt the disappointment of her posting to a safe desk in Chicago. All the training wasted, because of who she was. Now it was different. She straightened up. Took a deep breath. Then another. She felt her genes boiling through her. Before, they'd felt like resented intruders. Now they felt warm and whole and good. Her father's daughter? You bet your ass.

REACHER WAS CUFFED around the trunk of a hundred-foot pine. He had been dragged down the narrow track to the Bastion. Burning with fury. One punch and one kick was more than he had yielded since his early childhood. The rage was burying the pain. And blurring his mind. A life for a life, the fat bastard had said. Reacher had twisted on the floor and the words had meant nothing to him.

But they meant something now. They had come back to him as he stood there. Men and women had strolled up to him and smiled. Their smiles were the sort of smiles he had seen before, long ago. The smiles of bored children living on an isolated base somewhere, after they had been told the circus was coming to town.

SHE THOUGHT HARD. She had to guess where he was. And she had to guess where the parade ground was. She had to get herself halfway between those two unknown locations and set up an ambush. She knew the ground sloped steeply up to the clearing with the huts. She remembered being brought downhill to the courthouse. She guessed the parade ground had to be a large flat area. Therefore it had to be farther uphill, to the northwest, where the ground leveled out in the mountain bowl. Some distance beyond the huts. She set off uphill through the trees.

She tried to figure out where the main path was running. Every few yards, she stopped and peered south, turning left and right to catch a glimpse of the gaps in the forest canopy where the trees had been cleared. That way, she could deduce the direction of the track. She kept herself parallel to it, thirty or forty yards away to the north, and fought through the tough whippy stems growing sideways from the trunks. It was all uphill, and steep, and it was hard work. She used her crutch like a boatman uses a pole, planting it securely in the soil and thrusting herself upward against it.

In a way, her knee helped her. It made her climb slowly and carefully. It made her quiet. And she knew how to do this. From old Vietnam stories, not from Quantico. The Academy had concentrated on urban situations. The Bureau had taught her how to stalk through a city street or a darkened building. How to stalk through a forest came from an earlier layer of memory.

SOME PEOPLE STROLLED up and strolled away, but some of them stayed. After a quarter hour, there was a small crowd of maybe fifteen or sixteen people, mostly men, standing aimlessly in a wide semicircle around him. They kept their distance, like rubberneckers at a car wreck, behind an invisible police line. They stared at him, silently, not much in their faces. He stared back. He let his gaze rest on each one in turn, several seconds at a time. He kept his arms hitched as high behind him as he could manage. He wanted to keep his feet free for action, in case any of them felt like starting the show a little early.

SHE SMELLED THE first sentry before she saw him. He was moving upwind toward her, smoking. The odor of the cigarette and the unwashed uniform drifted down to her and she pulled silently to her right. She looped a wide circle around him and waited. He walked on down the hill and was gone.

The second sentry heard her. She sensed it. Sensed him stopping and listening. She stood still. Thought hard. She didn't want to use the Ingram. It was too inaccurate. She was certain to miss with it. And the noise would be fatal. So she bent down and scratched up two small stones. An old jungle trick she had been told about as a child. She tossed the first stone twenty feet to her left. Waited. Tossed the second thirty feet. She heard the sentry figure something was moving slowly away to the left. Heard him drift in that direction. She drifted right. A wide circle, and onward, up the endless hill.

FOWLER SHOULDERED THROUGH the small semicircle of onlookers. Stepped up face-to-face with him. Stared hard at him. Then six guards were coming through the crowd. Five of them had rifles leveled and the sixth had a length of chain in his hand. Fowler stood aside and the five rifles jammed hard into Reacher's gut. He glanced down at them. The safety catches were off and they were all set to automatic fire.

"Time to go," Fowler said.

He vanished behind the sturdy trunk and Reacher felt the cuffs come off. He leaned forward off the tree and the muzzles tracked back, following the motion. Then the cuffs went back on, with the chain looped into them. Fowler gripped the chain and Reacher was dragged through the Bastion, facing the five guards. They were all walking backward, their rifles leveled a foot from his head. People were lined into a tight cordon. He was dragged between them. The people hissed and muttered at him as he passed. Then they broke ranks and ran ahead of him, up toward the parade ground.

• • •

THE THIRD SENTRY caught her. Her knee let her down. She had to scale a high rocky crag, and because of her leg, she had to do it backward. She sat on the rock like it was a chair and used her good leg and the crutch to push herself upward, a foot at a time. She reached the top and rolled over on her back on the ground, gasping from the effort, and then she squirmed upright and stood, face-to-face with the sentry.

For a split second, she was blank with surprise and shock. He wasn't. He had stood at the top of the bluff and watched every inch of her agonizing progress. So he wasn't surprised. But he was slow. An opponent like Holly, he should have been quick. He should have been ready. Her reaction clicked in before he could get started. Basic training took over. It came without thinking. She balled her fist and threw a fast low uppercut. Caught him square in the groin. He folded forward and down and she wrapped her left arm around his throat and crunched him in the back of his neck with her right forearm. She felt his vertebrae smash and his body go slack. Then she clamped her palms over his ears and twisted his head around, savagely, one way and then the other. His spinal cord severed and she turned him and dropped him over the crag. He thumped and crashed his way down over the rocks, dead limbs flailing. Then she cursed and swore, bitterly. Because she should have taken his rifle. It was worth a dozen Ingrams. But there was no way she was going to climb all the way down to get it. Climbing back up again would delay her too long.

THE PARADE GROUND was full of people. All standing in neat ranks. Reacher guessed there were maybe a hundred people there. Men and women. All in uniform. All armed. Their weapons formed a formidable array of firepower. Each person had either a fully automatic rifle or a machine gun slung over their left shoulder. Each person had an automatic pistol on their belt. They all had ammunition pouches and grenades hung regulation-style from loops on their webbing. Many of them had smeared night camouflage on their faces.

Their uniforms were adapted from U.S. Army surplus. Camouflage jackets, camouflage pants, jungle boots, forage caps. Same stuff as Reacher had seen piled up in the storehouse. But each uniform had additions. Each jacket had an immaculate shoulder flash, woven in maroon silk, spelling out Montana Militia in an elegant curve. Each jacket had the wearer's name stenciled onto olive tape and sewn above the breast pocket. Some of the men had single chromium stars punched through the fabric on the breast pocket. Some kind of rank.

Beau Borken was standing on an upturned wooden crate, west edge of the leveled area, his back to the forest, his massive bulk looming over his troops. He saw Fowler and Reacher and the guards arriving through the trees.

"Attention!" he called.

There was a shuffling as the hundred militia members snapped into position. Reacher caught a smell of canvas on the breeze. The smell of a hundred Army-surplus uniforms. Borken waved a bloated arm and Fowler used the chain to drag Reacher up toward the front of the gathering. The guards seized his arms and shoulders and he was turned and maneuvered so he was left standing next to the box, suddenly isolated, facing the crowd.

"We all know why we're here," Borken called out to them.

SHE HAD NO idea how far she had come. It felt like miles. Hundreds of feet uphill. But she was still deep in the woods. The main track was still forty yards south on her left. She felt the minutes ticking away and her panic rising. She gripped the crutch and moved on northwest again, as fast as she dared.

Then she saw a building ahead of her. A wooden hut, visible through the trees. The undergrowth petered out into stony shale. She crept to the edge of the wood and stopped. Listened hard over the roar of her breathing. Heard nothing. She gripped the crutch and raised the Ingram tight against the strap. Limped across the shale to the corner of the hut. Looked out and around.

It was the clearing where they had arrived the night before. A wide circular space. Stony. Ringed with huts. Deserted. Quiet. The absolute silence of a recently abandoned place. She came out from behind the hut and limped to the center of the clearing, pirouetting on her crutch, jabbing the Ingram in a wide circle, covering the trees on the perimeter. Nothing. Nobody there.

She saw two paths, one running west, a wider track running north. She swung north and headed back into the cover of the trees. She forgot all about trying to stay quiet and raced north as fast as she could move.

W̲E̲ ̲A̲L̲L̲ ̲K̲N̲O̲W̲ why we're here,'' Borken called out again.

The orderly crowd shuffled, and a wave of whispering rose to the trees. Reacher scanned the faces. He saw Stevie in the front rank. A chromium star through his breast pocket. Little Stevie was an officer. Next to Stevie he saw Joseph Ray. Then he realized Jackson was not there. No scarred forehead. He double-checked. Scanned everywhere. No sign of him anywhere on the parade ground. He clamped his teeth to stop a smile. Jackson was hiding out. Holly might still make it.

S̲H̲E̲ ̲S̲A̲W̲ ̲H̲I̲M̲. She stared out of the forest over a hundred heads and saw him standing next to Borken. His arms were cuffed behind him. He was scanning the crowd. Nothing in his face. She heard Borken say: we all know why we're here. She thought: yes, I know why I'm here. I know exactly why I'm here. She looked left and right. A hundred people, rifles, machine guns, pistols, grenades. Borken on the box with his arms raised. Reacher, helpless beside him. She stood in the trees, heart thumping, staring. Then she took a deep breath. Set the Ingram to the single-shot position and fired into the air. Burst out of the trees. Fired again. And again. Three shots into the air. Three bullets gone, twenty-seven left in the magazine. She clicked the Ingram back to full auto and moved into the crowd, parting it in front of her with slow menacing sweeps of her gun hand.

She was one woman moving slowly through a crowd of a hundred people. They parted warily around her, and then as she passed them by, they unslung their weapons and cocked them and leveled them at her back. A wave of loud mechanical noises trailed behind her like a slow tide. By the time she reached the front rank, she had a hundred loaded weapons trained on her from behind.

"Don't shoot her!" Borken screamed. "That's an order! Nobody fire!"

He jumped down off the box. Panic in his face. He raised his arms out wide and danced desperately around her, shielding her body with his huge bulk. Nobody fired. She limped away from him and turned to face the crowd.

"Hell are you doing?" Borken screamed at her. "You think you can shoot a hundred people with that little popgun?"

Holly shook her head.

"No," she said quietly.

Then she reversed the Ingram and held it to her chest.

"But I can shoot myself," she said.

32

THE CROWD WAS silent. Their breathing was swallowed up by the awesome mountain silence. Everybody was staring at Holly. She was holding the Ingram reversed, the muzzle jammed into a spot above her heart. Thumb backward on the trigger, tensed. Borken's bloated face was greased with panic. His huge frame was shaking and trembling. He was hopping around next to his upturned box, staring wide-eyed at her. She was looking back at him, calmly.

"I'm a hostage, right?" she said to him. "Important to them, important to you, because of who I am. All kinds of importance to all kinds of people. You expect them to do stuff to keep me alive. So now it's your turn. Let's talk about what stuff you're prepared to do to keep me alive."

Borken saw her glance at Reacher.

"You don't understand," he screamed at her. Wild urgency in his voice. "I'm not going to kill this guy. This guy stays alive. The situation has changed."

"Changed how?" she asked, calmly.

"I'm commuting his sentence," Borken said. Still panic in his voice. "That's why we're here. I was just going to announce it. We know who he is. We just found out. We were just informed. He was in the Army. Major Jack Reacher. He's a hero. He won the Silver Star."

"So?" Holly asked.

"He saved a bunch of Marines," Borken said urgently.

"In Beirut. Ordinary fighting men. He pulled them out of a burning bunker. Marines will never attack us while he's here. Never. So I'm going to use him as another hostage. He's good insurance, against the damn Marines. I need him."

She stared at him. Reacher stared at him.

"His sentence is commuted," Borken said again. "Five years on punishment detail. That's all. Nothing else. No question about it. I need him alive."

He stared at her with a salesman's beam like the problem was solved. She stared back and forth between him and Reacher. Reacher was watching the crowd. The crowd was angry. The circus had left town before the performance. Reacher felt like they had all taken a step toward him. They were testing Borken's power over them. Holly glanced at him, fear in her eyes. Nodded to him. An imperceptible movement of her head. She would be safe, she was saying, whatever happened. Her identity protected her like an invisible magic cloak. Reacher nodded back. Without turning around, he judged the distance to the trees behind him. Maybe twenty feet. Shove Fowler at the front rank, drag the chain, sprint like hell, he might be in the trees before anybody could aim a weapon. Twenty feet, standing start, using the momentum of shouldering Fowler away to help him, maybe four or five strides, maybe three seconds, maybe four. In the trees, he would stand a chance against the bullets. He imagined them smacking into the trunks either side of him as he ran and dodged. A forest is a fugitive's best friend. It takes a lot of luck to hit a guy running through trees. He shifted his weight and felt his hamstrings tighten. Felt the flood of adrenaline. Fight or flight. But then Borken flung his arms wide again. Held them out like an angel's wings and used the awesome power of his eyes on his people.

"I have made my decision," he called. "Do you understand?"

There was a long pause. It went on for seconds. Then a hundred heads snapped back.

"Yes sir!" a hundred voices yelled.

"Do you understand?" he called again.

A hundred heads snapped back again.

"Yes sir!" a hundred voices yelled.

"Five years on punishment detail," Borken called. "But only if he can prove who he is. We are informed this man is the only non-Marine in history to win the Marine Sniper competition. We are told this man can put six bullets through a silver dollar a thousand yards away. So I'm going to shoot against him. Eight hundred yards. If he wins, he lives. If he loses, he dies. Do you understand?"

A hundred heads snapped back.

"Yes sir!" a hundred voices yelled.

The rumble from the crowd started up again. This time, they sounded interested. Reacher smiled inwardly. Smart move, he thought. They wanted a spectacle, Borken was giving them one. Fowler breathed out and pulled a key from his pocket. Ducked around and unlocked the handcuffs. The chain fell to the floor. Reacher breathed out and rubbed his wrists.

Then Fowler stepped over to Holly in the press of people. Stepped right in front of her. She paused for a long moment and glanced at Borken. He nodded.

"You have my word," he said, with as much dignity as he could recover.

She glanced at Reacher. He shrugged and nodded. She nodded back and looked down at the Ingram. Clicked the safety on and looped the strap off her shoulder. Grinned and dropped the gun to the floor. Fowler bent at her feet and scooped it up. Borken raised his arms for quiet.

"To the rifle range," he called out. "Orderly fashion. Dismiss."

Holly limped over and walked next to Reacher.

"You won the Wimbledon?" she asked, quietly.

He nodded.

"So can you win this?" she asked.

He nodded again.

"With my head in a bag," he said.

"Is that such a good idea?" she asked quietly. "Guy like this, he's not going to be happy to get beat."

Reacher shrugged.

"He wants a big performance, he's going to get one," he said. "He's all shaken up. You started it. I want to keep it going. Long run, it'll do us good."

"Well, take care," she said.
"Watch me," Reacher said.

Two brand-new targets were placed side by side at the extreme end of the range. Borken's was on the left, with ATF daubed across its chest. Reacher's was on the right, with FBI over its heart. The rough matting was pulled back to give maximum distance. Reacher figured he was looking at about eight hundred and thirty yards. Fifty yards shy of a full half-mile. A hell of a long way.

The swarm of people had settled into a rough semicircle, behind and beside the matting. The nearer targets were flung into the undergrowth to clear their view. Several people had field glasses. They peered up the range and then their noise faded as one after the other they settled into quiet anticipation.

Fowler made the trip to the armory in the clearing below. He walked back with a rifle in each hand. One for Borken, one for Reacher. Identical guns. The price of a small family car in each hand. They were .50-inch Barrett Model 90s. Nearly four feet long, over twenty-two pounds in weight. Bolt-action repeaters, fired a bullet a full half-inch across. More like an artillery shell than a rifle bullet.

"One magazine each," Borken said. "Six shots."

Reacher took his weapon and laid it on the ground at his feet. Little Stevie marshaled the crowd backward to clear the matting. Borken checked his rifle and flicked the bipod legs out. Smacked the magazine into place. He set the weapon down gently on the matting.

"I shoot first," he said.

He dropped to his knees and forced his bulk down behind the rifle. Pulled the stock to him and snuggled it in close. Dragged the bipod legs an inch to the left and swung the butt a fraction to the right. He smacked the bolt in and out and pressed himself close to the ground. Eased his cheek against the stock and put his eye to the scope. Joseph Ray stepped from the edge of the crowd and offered Reacher his field glasses. Reacher nodded silently and took them. Held them ready. Borken's finger tightened against the trigger. He fired the first shot.

The Barrett's huge muzzle brake blasted gas sideways and downward. Dust blasted back up off the matting. The rifle kicked and boomed. The sound crashed through the trees and came back off the mountains, seconds later. A hundred pairs of eyes flicked from Borken to the target. Reacher raised the field glasses and focused eight hundred and thirty yards up the range.

It was a miss. The target was undamaged. Borken peered through the scope and grimaced. He hunkered down again and waited for the dust to clear. Reacher watched him. Borken was just waiting. Steady breathing. Relaxed. Then his finger tightened again. He fired the second shot. The rifle kicked and crashed and the dust blasted upward. Reacher raised the field glasses again. A hit. There was a splintered hole on the target's right shoulder.

There was a murmur from the crowd. Field glasses were passed from hand to hand. The whispers rose and fell. The dust settled. Borken fired again. Too quickly. He was still wriggling. Reacher watched him making the mistake. He didn't bother with the field glasses. He knew that half-inch shell would end up in Idaho.

The crowd whispered. Borken glared through the scope. Reacher watched him do it all wrong. His relaxation was disappearing. His shoulders were tensed. He fired the fourth. Reacher handed the field glasses back to Joseph Ray on the edge of the crowd. He didn't need to look. He knew Borken was going to miss with the rest. In that state, he'd have missed at four hundred yards. He'd have missed at two hundred. He'd have missed across a crowded room.

Borken fired the fifth and then the sixth and stood up slowly. He lifted the big rifle and used the scope to check what everybody already knew.

"One hit," he said.

He lowered the rifle and looked across at Reacher.

"Your shot," he said. "Life or death."

Reacher nodded. Fowler handed him his magazine. Reacher used his thumb to test the spring. He pressed down on the first bullet and felt the smooth return. The bullets were shiny. Polished by hand. Sniper's bullets. He bent and lifted the heavy rifle. Held it vertical and clicked the magazine into place. He didn't smack at it, like Borken had done. He pressed it home gently with his palm.

He opened the bipod legs, one at a time. Clicked them against their detents. Glanced up the range and laid the rifle on the matting. Squatted next to it and lay down, all in one fluid motion. He lay like a dead man, arms flung upward around the gun. He wanted to lie like that for a long time. He was tired. Deathly tired. But he stirred and laid his cheek gently against the stock. Snuggled his right shoulder close to the butt. Clamped his left hand over the barrel, fingers under the scope. Eased his right hand toward the trigger. Moved his right eye to the scope. Breathed out.

Firing a sniper rifle over a long distance is a confluence of many things. It starts with chemistry. It depends on mechanical engineering. It involves optics and geophysics and meteorology. Governing everything is human biology.

The chemistry is about explosions. The powder behind the bullet in the shell case has to explode perfectly, predictably, powerfully, instantly. It has to smash the projectile down the barrel at maximum speed. The half-inch bullet in the Barrett chamber weighs a hair over two ounces. One minute it's stationary. A thousandth of a second later, it's doing nearly nineteen hundred miles an hour, leaving the barrel behind on its way to the target. That powder has to explode fast, explode completely, and explode hard. Difficult chemistry. Weight for weight, that explosion has got to be the best explosion on the planet.

Then mechanical engineering takes over for a spell. The bullet itself has to be a perfect little artifact. It's got to be as good as any manufactured article has ever been. It has got to be cast better than any jewelry. It must be totally uniform in size and weight. Perfectly round, perfectly streamlined. It has to accept ferocious rotation from the rifling grooves inside the barrel. It has to spin and hiss through the air with absolutely no wobble, no bias.

The barrel has to be tight and straight. No good at all if a previous shot has heated and altered the barrel shape. The barrel has to be a mass of perfect metal, heavy enough to remain inert. Heavy enough to kill the tiny vibrations of the bolt and the trigger and the firing pin. That's why the Barrett

Reacher was holding cost as much as a cheap sedan. That's why Reacher's left hand was loosely clamped over the top of the gun. He was damping any residual shock with it.

Optics play a big part. Reacher's right eye was an inch behind a Leupold & Stevens scope. A fine instrument. The target was showing small, behind the fine data lines etched into the glass. Reacher stared hard at it. Then he eased the stock down and saw the target disappear and the sky swim into view. He breathed out again and stared at the air.

Because geophysics are crucial. Light travels in a straight line. But it's the only thing that does. Bullets don't. Bullets are physical things which obey the laws of nature, like any other physical things. They follow the curvature of the earth. Eight hundred and thirty yards is a significant piece of curvature. The bullet comes out of the barrel and rises above the line of sight, then it passes through it, then it falls below it. In a perfect curve, like the earth.

Except it's not a perfect curve, because the very first millisecond the bullet is gone, gravity is plucking at it like a small insistent hand. The bullet can't ignore it. It's a two-ounce copper-jacketed lead projectile traveling at nearly nineteen hundred miles an hour, but gravity has its way. Not very successfully, at first, but its best ally soon chips in. Friction. From the very first millisecond of its travel, air friction is slowing the bullet down and handing gravity a larger and larger say in its destiny. Friction and gravity work together to haul that bullet down.

So you aim way high. You aim maybe ten feet directly above the target and eight hundred and thirty yards later the curvature of the earth and the pull of its gravity bring that bullet home to where you want it.

Except you don't aim directly above the target. Because that would be to ignore meteorology. Bullets travel through air, and air moves. It's a rare day when the air is still. The air moves one way or another. Left or right, up or down, or any combination. Reacher was watching the leaves on the trees, and he could see a slow steady breeze coming out of the north. Dry air, moving slowly right to left across his line of sight. So he was aiming about eight feet to the right and ten feet above where he wanted to put the bullet. He was going to launch that projectile and let nature curve it left and down.

Human biology was all that stood in the way. Snipers are people. People are quivering, shuddering masses of flesh and muscle. The heart is beating away like a giant pump, and the lungs are squeezing huge volumes of air in and out. Every nerve and every muscle is trembling with microscopic energy. Nobody is ever still. Even the calmest person is vibrating like crazy. Say there's a yard between the rifle's firing pin and the muzzle. If the muzzle moves a tiny fraction, then eight hundred and thirty yards later, the bullet is going to miss by eight hundred and thirty tiny fractions. A multiplying effect. If the shooter's vibration disturbs the muzzle by even a hundredth of an inch, the bullet will be eight-point-three inches off target. About the width of a man's head.

So Reacher's technique was to wait. Just to gaze through the sight until his breathing was regular and his heartbeat was slow. Then to tighten the trigger finger slowly and wait some more. Then to count the heartbeats. One-and-two-and-three-and-four. Keep on waiting until the rhythm was slow. Then to fire between beats. Right when the vibration was as small as a human being could get it.

He waited. He breathed out, long and slow. His heart beat once. It beat again. He fired. The stock jumped against his shoulder and his view was obliterated by the blast of dust from the matting under the muzzle. The heavy thump of the shot crashed off the mountainsides and came back to him with a wave of whispering from the crowd. He had missed. The running, crouching screen-print with FBI daubed on its chest was undamaged.

He let the dust settle and checked the trees. The wind was steady. He breathed out and let his heart rate drop. He fired again. The big rifle kicked and crashed. The dust flew. The crowd stared and whispered. Another miss.

Two misses. He breathed steadily and fired again. A miss. And again. Another miss. He paused for a long time. Picked up his rhythm again and fired the fifth. He missed the fifth. The crowd was restless. Borken lumbered nearer.

"All on the last shot," he said, grinning.

Reacher made no reply. No way could he afford the physical disturbance involved in speaking. The disruption to his breathing, the muscular contraction of his lungs and throat would be fatal. He waited. His heart beat. And again. He fired the sixth. He missed. He dropped the sight and stared at the plywood target. Undamaged.

Borken was staring at him. Questions in his eyes. Reacher got to his knees and lifted the rifle. Snapped the empty magazine out. Pushed the bolt home. Traced a finger along the neat engraving on the side of the stock. Folded the bipod legs. Laid the warm gun neatly on the matting. He stood up and shrugged. Borken stared at him. Glanced at Fowler. Fowler glanced back, puzzled. They had watched a man shooting for his life, and they had watched him miss every shot.

"You knew the rules," Borken said quietly.

Reacher stood still. Ignored him. Gazed up at the blue sky. A pair of vapor trails were crawling across it, like tiny chalk lines far overhead in the stratosphere.

"Wait, sir," Joseph Ray called loudly.

He came forward out of the crowd. Bristling with urgency. Self-important. Things to say. He was one of the few men in the Bastion with any actual military service behind him, and he prided himself on seeing things that other people missed. He thought it gave him an edge. Made him useful in special ways.

He looked hard at the matting and lay himself down exactly where Reacher had lain. Glanced down the range to the targets. Closed one eye and stared through half his field glasses like a telescope. Focused on the screen-print of the running man. Moved his line of sight a fraction and focused just beyond the hunch of the target's shoulder. Stared into the distance and nodded to himself.

"Come on," he said.

He got to his feet and started jogging down the range. Fowler went with him. Eight hundred and thirty yards later, Ray passed the target without a second glance. Kept on jogging. Fowler followed. Fifty yards. A hundred. Ray dropped to his knees and stared backward. Aligned himself with the target and the matting, way back in the far distance. Turned and pointed forward, using his whole arm and finger like a rifle barrel. Stood up again and walked fifty more yards to a particular tree.

It was an orphan silver birch. A straggly wild survivor, forcing its way up alongside the tall pines. Its trunk was contorted as it fought for light and air, one way and then the next. It was narrow, not more than seven or eight inches across. Six feet from the ground, it had six bullet holes in it. Big fresh half-inch holes. Three of them were in a perfect straight vertical line maybe seven inches high. The other three were curled in a loose curve to the right, running from the top hole out and back to the middle hole and out and back again to the bottom hole. Joseph Ray stared hard at them. Then he realized what they were. He grinned. The six holes made a perfect capital B, right there on the white bark. The letter covered an area of maybe seven inches by five. About the dimensions of a fat man's face.

Fowler shouldered past Ray and turned and leaned on the trunk. Stood and pressed the back of his head against the ragged holes. Raised his field glasses and looked back down the range toward the matting. He figured he was more than a hundred and fifty yards behind the target. The target had been more than eight hundred yards from the matting. He did the math in his head.

"A thousand yards," he breathed.

Fowler and Joseph Ray paced it out together on the way back to Borken. Ray kept his stride long, just about exactly a yard. Fowler counted. Nine hundred and ninety strides, nine hundred and ninety yards. Borken knelt on the matting and used Ray's field glasses. He closed one eye and stared across the distance. He could barely even see the white tree. Reacher watched him try to keep the surprise out of his face. Thought to himself: you wanted a big performance, you got one. You like it, fat boy?

"OK," Borken said. "So let's see how damn smart you're going to act now."

THE FIVE GUARDS that had been six when Jackson was with them formed up in a line. They moved forward and took up position around Reacher and Holly. The crowd started filing away, quietly. Their feet crunched and slid on the stony ground. Then that sound was gone and the rifle range was quiet.

Fowler stooped and picked up the guns. He hefted one in each hand and walked away through the trees. The five guards unslung their weapons with the loud sound of palms slapping on wood and metal.

"OK," Borken said again. "Punishment detail."

He turned to Holly.

"You too," he said. "You're not too damn valuable for that. You can help him. He's got a task to perform for me."

The guards stepped forward and marched Reacher and Holly behind Borken, slowly down through the trees to the Bastion and on along the beaten earth track to the command hut clearing. They halted there. Two of the guards peeled off and walked to the stores. They were back within five minutes with their weapons shouldered. The first guard was carrying a long-handled shovel in his left hand and a crowbar in his right. The second was carrying two olive fatigue shirts. Borken took them from him and turned to face Reacher and Holly.

"Take your shirts off," he said. "Put these on."

Holly stared at him.

"Why?" she said.

Borken smiled.

"All part of the game," he said. "You're not back by nightfall, we turn the dogs loose. They need your old shirts for the scent."

Holly shook her head.

"I'm not undressing," she said.

Borken looked at her and nodded.

"We'll turn our backs," he said. "But you only get one chance. You don't do it, these boys will do it for you, OK?"

He gave the command and the five guards fanned out in a loose arc, facing the trees. Borken waited for Reacher to turn away and then swiveled on his heels and stared up in the air.

"OK," he said. "Get on with it."

The men heard unbuttoning sounds and the rasp of cotton. They heard the old shirt fall to the ground and the new one slipping on. They heard fingernails clicking against buttons.

"Done," Holly muttered.

Reacher took off his jacket and his shirt and shivered in the mountain breeze. He took the new shirt from Borken and shrugged it on. Slung the jacket over his shoulder. Borken nodded and the guard handed Reacher the shovel and the crowbar. Borken pointed into the forest.

"Walk due west a hundred yards," he said. "Then north another hundred. You'll know what to do when you get there."

Holly looked at Reacher. He looked back and nodded. They strolled together into the trees, heading west.

THIRTY YARDS INTO the woods, as soon as they were out of sight, Holly stopped. She planted her crutch and waited for Reacher to turn and rejoin her.

"Borken," she said. "I know who he is. I've seen his name in our files. They tagged him for a robbery, northern California somewhere. Twenty million dollars in bearer bonds. Armored car driver was killed. Sacramento office investigated, but they couldn't make it stick."

Reacher nodded.

"He did it," he said. "That's for damn sure. Fowler admitted it. Says they've got twenty million in the Caymans. Captured from the enemy."

Holly grimaced.

"It explains the mole in Chicago," she said. "Borken can afford a pretty handsome bribe with twenty million bucks in the bank, right?"

Reacher nodded again, slowly.

"Anybody you know would take a bribe?" he asked.

She shrugged.

"They all bitch about the salary," she said.

He shook his head.

"No," he said. "Think of somebody who doesn't bitch about it. Whoever's got Borken's bearer bonds behind him isn't worried about money anymore."

"Some of them don't grumble," she said. "Some of them just put up with it. Like me, for instance. But I guess I'm different."

He looked at her. Walked on.

"You're different," he repeated. "That's for damn sure."

He said it vaguely, thinking about it. They walked on for ten yards. He was walking slower than his normal pace and she was limping at his side. He was lost in thought. He was hearing Borken's high voice claiming: she's more than his daughter. He was hearing her own exasperated voice asking: why the hell does everybody assume everything that ever happens to me is because of who my damn father is? Then he stopped walking again and looked straight at her.

"Who are you, Holly?" he asked.

"You know who I am," she said.

He shook his head again.

"No, I don't," he said. "At first I thought you were just some woman. Then you were some woman called Holly Johnson. Then you were an FBI agent. Then you were General Johnson's daughter. Then Borken told me you're even more than that. She's more than his daughter, he said. That stunt you pulled, he was shitting himself. You're some kind of a triple-A gold-plated hostage, Holly. So who the hell else are you?"

She looked at him. Sighed.

"Long story," she said. "Started twenty-eight years ago. My father was made a White House Fellow. Seconded to Washington. They used to do that, with the fast-track guys. He got friendly with another guy. Political analyst, aiming to be a congressman. My mother was pregnant with me, his wife was pregnant, he asked my parents to be godparents, my father asked them to be godparents. So this other guy stood up at my christening."

"And?" Reacher said.

"The guy got into a career," Holly said. "He's still in Washington. You probably voted for him. He's the President."

REACHER WALKED ON in a daze. Kept glancing at Holly, gamely matching him stride for stride. A hundred yards west of the punishment hut, there was an outcrop of rock, bare of trees. Reacher and Holly turned there and walked north, into the breeze.

"Where are we going?" Holly said. Her voice had an edge of worry.

Reacher stopped suddenly. He knew where they were going. The answer was on the breeze. He went cold. His skin
crawled. He stared down at the implements in his hands like
he'd never seen such things before.

"You stay here," he said.

She shook her head.

"No," she said. "I'm coming with you, wherever it is."

"Please, Holly," he said. "Stay here, will you?"

She looked surprised by his voice, but she kept on shaking
her head.

"I'm coming with you," she said again.

He gave her a bleak look and they walked on north. He
forced himself onward, toward it. Fifty yards. Each step required a conscious effort of will. Sixty yards. He wanted to
turn and run. Just run and never stop. Hurl himself across the
wild river and get the hell out. Seventy yards. He stopped.

"Stay here, Holly," he said again. "Please."

"Why?" she asked.

"You don't need to see this," he said, miserably.

She shook her head again and walked on. He caught her
up. They smelled it long before they saw it. Faint, sweet,
unforgettable. One of the most common and one of the most
terrible smells in mankind's long and awful history. The
smell of fresh human blood. Twenty paces after they smelled
it, they heard it. The buzzing of a million flies.

Jackson was crucified between two young pines. His hands
had been dragged apart and nailed to the trees through the
palms and wrists. He had been forced up onto his toes and
his feet had been nailed flat against the base of the trunks.
He was naked and he had been mutilated. He had taken several minutes to die. Reacher was clear on that.

He stood immobile, staring at the crawling mass of blue
shiny flies. Holly had dropped her crutch and her face was
white. Ghastly staring white. She fell to her knees and
retched. Spun herself away from the dreadful sight and fell
forward on her face. Her hands clawed blindly in the forest
dirt. She bucked and screamed into the buzzing forest silence.
Screamed and cried.

Reacher watched the flies. His eyes were expressionless.
His face was impassive. Just a tiny muscle jumping at the

corner of his jaw gave anything away. He stood still for several minutes. Holly went silent, on the forest floor beside him. He dropped the crowbar. Slung his jacket over a low branch. Stepped over directly in front of the body and started digging.

He dug with a quiet fury. He smashed the shovel into the earth as hard as he could. He chopped through tree roots with single savage blows. When he hit rocks, he heaved them out and hurled them into a pile. Holly sat up and watched him. She watched the blazing eyes in his impassive face and the bulging muscles in his arms. She followed the relentless rhythm of the shovel. She said nothing.

The work was making him hot. The flies were checking him out. They left Jackson's body and buzzed around his head. He ignored them. Just strained and gasped his way six feet down into the earth. Then he propped the shovel against a tree. Wiped his face on his sleeve. Didn't speak. Took the crowbar and stepped close to the corpse. Batted away the flies. Levered the nails out of the left hand. Jackson's body flopped sideways. The left arm pointed grotesquely down into the pit. The flies rose in an angry cloud. Reacher walked around to the right hand. Pried the nails out. The body flopped forward into the hole. Reacher extracted the nails from the feet. The body tumbled free into the grave. The air was dark with flies and loud with their sound. Reacher slid down into the hole and straightened the corpse out. Crossed the arms over the chest.

He climbed back out. Without pausing he picked up the shovel and started filling the hole. He worked relentlessly. The flies disappeared. He worked on. There was too much dirt. It mounded up high when he had finished, like graves always do. He pounded the mound into a neat shape and dropped the shovel. Bent and picked up the rocks he'd cleared. Used them to shore up the sides of the mound. Placed the biggest one on top, like some kind of a headstone.

Then he stood there, panting like a wild man, streaked with dirt and sweat. Holly watched him. Then she spoke for the first time in an hour.

"Should we say a prayer?" she asked.

Reacher shook his head.

"Way too late for that," he said quietly.

"You OK?" she asked.

"Who's the mole?" he asked in turn.

"I don't know," she said.

"Well, think about it, will you?" he said, angrily.

She glared up at him.

"Don't you think I have been?" she said. "What the hell else do you think I was doing for the last hour?"

"So who the hell is it?" he asked. Still angry.

She paused. Went quiet again.

"Could be anybody," she said. "There are a hundred agents in Chicago."

She was sitting on the forest floor, small, miserable, defeated. She had trusted her people. She had told him that. She had been full of naive confidence. I trust my people, she had said. He felt a wave of tenderness for her. It crashed over him. Not pity, not concern, just an agonizing tenderness for a good person whose bright new world was suddenly dirty and falling apart. He stared at her, hoping she would see it. She stared back, eyes full of tears. He held out his hands. She took them. He lifted her to her feet and held her. He lifted her off the ground and crushed her close. Her breasts were against his pounding chest. Her tears were against his neck.

Then her hands were behind his head, pulling him close. She squirmed her face up and kissed him. She kissed him angrily and hungrily on the mouth. Her arms were locking around his neck. He felt her wild breathing. He knelt and laid her gently on the soft earth. Her hands burrowed at his shirt buttons. His at hers.

They made love naked on the forest floor, urgently, passionately, greedily, as if they were defying death itself. Then they lay panting and spent in each other's arms, gazing up at the sunlight spearing down through the leaves.

HE STROKED HER hair and felt her breathing slow down. He held her silently for a long time, watching the dust motes dancing in the sunbeams over her head.

"Who knew your movements on Monday?" he asked softly.

She thought about it. Made no reply.

"And which of them didn't know about Jackson then?" he asked.

No reply.

"And which of them isn't short of money?" he asked.

No reply.

"And which of them is recent?" he asked. "Which of them could have come close enough to Beau Borken somewhere to get bought off? Sometime in the past? Maybe investigating the robbery thing in California?"

She shuddered in his arms.

"Four questions, Holly," he said. "Who fits?"

She ran through all the possibilities. Like a process of elimination. An algorithm. She boiled the hundred names down. The first question eliminated most of them. The second question eliminated a few more. The third question eliminated a handful. It was the fourth question which proved decisive. She shuddered again.

"Only two possibilities," she said.

33

MILOSEVIC AND BROGAN were strapped side by side in the rear of the Air Force chopper. McGrath and Johnson and the General's aide were crushed into the middle row of seats. The aircrew were shoulder to shoulder in the front. They lifted off from Silver Bow and clattered away northwest over the town of Butte, nose down, low altitude, looking for maximum airspeed. The helicopter was an old Bell, rebuilt with a new engine, and it was pushing a hundred and twenty miles an hour, which made for a lot of noise inside. Consequently McGrath and Johnson were screaming into their radio mikes to make themselves understood.

McGrath was patched through to the Hoover Building. He was trying to talk to Harland Webster. He had one hand cupped over the mike and the other was clamping the earphone to his head. He was talking about the missile unit. He didn't know if Webster was hearing him. He just repeated his message over and over, as loud as he could. Then he flicked the switch and tore off the headset. Tossed it forward to the copilot.

Johnson was talking to Peterson. Radio contact had not been restored. He limited himself to requesting an update by secure landline direct to the mobile command post in two hours' time. He failed to decipher the reply. He pulled off his headset and looked a question at McGrath. McGrath shrugged back at him. The helicopter clattered onward.

• • •

Harland Webster heard the shrieking din cut off. He hung up his phone in the sudden silence of his office. Leaned forward and buzzed his secretary.

"Car," he said.

He walked through to the elevator and rode down to the garage. Walked over to his limousine. His driver was holding the door for him.

"White House," he said.

This time, the driver said nothing. Just fired it up and eased out of the garage. Bumped up and out into the afternoon rush. Crawled the sixteen hundred yards west in silence. Webster was directed to the same off-white room. He waited there a quarter hour. Dexter came in. Clearly not pleased to see him back so soon.

"They've stolen some missiles," Webster said.

"What missiles?" Dexter asked.

He described everything as well as he could. Dexter listened. Didn't nod. Didn't ask any questions. Didn't react. Just told him to wait in the room.

The air force Bell put down on a gravel turnout two hundred yards south of where the road into Yorke narrowed and straightened into the hills. The pilot kept the engine turning and the five passengers ducked out and ran bent over until they were out of the fierce downdraft. There were vehicles on the road ahead. A random pattern of military vehicles slewed across the blacktop. One of them was turning slowly in the road. It turned in the narrow space between the rocky walls and straightened as it approached. It slowed and halted fifty yards away. General Johnson stepped out into view. The car moved forward and stopped in front of him. It was a new Chevrolet, sprayed a dull olive green. There were white stenciled letters and figures on the hood and along the sides. An officer slid out. He saluted the General and skipped around to open all the doors. The five men squeezed in and the car turned again and rolled the two hundred yards north to the mess of vehicles.

"The command post is on its way, sir," the officer said.

"Should be here inside forty minutes. The satellite trucks are an hour behind it. I suggest you wait in the car. It's getting cold outside."

"Word from the missile unit?" Johnson asked.

The officer shook his head in the gloom.

"No word, sir," he said.

W̲EBSTER WAITED MOST of an hour. Then the door of the small off-white room cracked open. A Secret Service agent stood there. Blue suit, curly wire running up out of his collar to his earpiece.

"Please come with me, sir," the agent said.

Webster stood up and the guy raised his hand and spoke into his cuff. Webster followed him along a quiet corridor and into an elevator. The elevator was small and slow. It took them down to the first floor. They walked along another quiet corridor and paused in front of a white door. The agent knocked once and opened it.

The President was sitting in his chair behind his desk. The chair was rotated away and he had his back to the room. He was staring out through the bulletproof windows at the darkness settling over the garden. Dexter was in an armchair. Neither asked him to sit down. The President didn't turn around. As soon as he heard the door click shut, he started speaking.

"Suppose I was a judge," he said. "And suppose you were some cop and you came to me for a warrant?"

Webster could see the President's face reflected in the thick glass. It was just a pink smudge.

"OK, sir, suppose I was?" he said.

"What have you got?" the President asked him. "And what haven't you got? You don't even know for sure Holly's there at all. You've got an undercover asset in place and he hasn't confirmed it to you. You're guessing, is all. And these missiles? The Army has lost radio contact. Could be temporary. Could be any number of reasons for that. Your undercover guy hasn't mentioned them."

"He could be experiencing difficulties, sir," Webster said. "And he's been told to be cautious. He doesn't call in with a running commentary. He's undercover, right? He can't just disappear into the forest any old time he wants to.''

The President nodded. The pink smudge in the glass moved up and down. There was a measure of sympathy there.

"We understand that, Harland," he said. "We really do. But we have to assume that with matters of this magnitude, he's going to make a big effort, right? But you've heard nothing. So you're giving us nothing but speculation.''

Webster spread his hands. Spoke directly to the back of the guy's head.

"Sir, this is a big deal," he said. "They're arming themselves, they've taken a hostage, they're talking about secession from the Union.''

The President nodded.

"Don't you understand, that's the problem?" he said. "If this were about three weirdos in a hut in the woods with a bomb, we'd send you in there right away. But it isn't. This could lead to the biggest constitutional crisis since 1860.''

"So you agree with me," Webster said. "You're taking them seriously.''

The President shook his head. Sadly, like he was upset but not surprised Webster didn't get the point.

"No," he said. "We're not taking them seriously. That's what makes this whole thing so damn difficult. They're a bunch of deluded idiots, seeing plots everywhere, conspiracies, muttering about independence for their scrubby little patch of worthless real estate. But the question is: how should a mature democratic nation react to that? Should it massacre them all, Harland? Is that how a mature nation reacts? Should it unleash deadly force against a few deluded idiot citizens? We spent a generation condemning the Soviets for doing that. Are we going to do the same thing?''

"They're criminals, sir," Webster said.

"Yes, they are," the President agreed, patiently. "They're counterfeiters, they own illegal weapons, they don't pay federal taxes, they foment racial hatred, maybe they even robbed an armored car. But those are details, Harland. The broad picture is they're disgruntled citizens. And how do we respond to that? We encourage disgruntled citizens in Eastern Europe to stand up and declare their nationhood, right? So how do we deal with our own disgruntled citizens, Harland? Declare war on them?''

Webster clamped his jaw. He felt adrift. Like the thick carpets and the quiet paint and the unfamiliar scented air inside the Oval Office were choking him.

"They're criminals," he said again. It was all he could think of to say.

The President nodded. Still a measure of sympathy.

"Yes, they are," he agreed again. "But look at the broad picture, Harland. Look at their main offense. Their main offense is they hate their government. If we deal with them harshly for that, we could face a crisis. Like we said, there are maybe sixty million Americans ready to be tipped over the edge. This Administration is very aware of that, Harland. This Administration is going to tread very carefully.''

"But what about Holly?" he asked. "You can't just sacrifice her.''

There was a long silence. The President kept his chair turned away.

"I can't react because of her, either," he said quietly. "I can't allow myself to make this personal. Don't you see that? A personal, emotional, angry response would be wrong. It would be a bad mistake. I have to wait and think. I've talked it over with the General. We've talked for hours. Frankly, Harland, he's pissed at me, and again frankly, I don't blame him. He's just about my oldest friend, and he's pissed at me. So don't talk to me about sacrifice, Harland. Because sacrifice is what this office is all about. You put the greater good in front of friendship, in front of all your own interests. You do it all the time. It's what being President means.''

There was another long silence.

"So what are you saying to me, Mr. President?" Webster asked.

Another long silence.

"I'm not saying anything to you," the President said. "I'm saying you're in personal command of the situation. I'm saying come see Mr. Dexter Monday morning, if there's still a problem.''

•   •   •

Nobody waited in the car. Too restless for that. They got out into the chill mountain air and milled aimlessly around. Johnson and his aide strolled north with the driver and looked at the proposed location for the command post. McGrath and Brogan and Milosevic kept themselves apart as a threesome. McGrath smoked, lost in thought. Time to time, he would duck back into the Army Chevrolet and use the car phone. He called the Montana State Police, the power company, the phone company, the Forest Service.

Brogan and Milosevic strolled north. They found an armored vehicle. Not a tank, some kind of a personnel carrier. There was the officer who had met them with the car and maybe eight soldiers standing near it. Big, silent men, pitching tents on the shoulder in the lee of the rocks. Brogan and Milosevic nodded a greeting to them and strolled back south. They rejoined McGrath and waited.

Within forty minutes they all heard the faint roar of heavy diesels far to the south. The noise built and then burst around the curve. There was a small convoy of trucks. Big, boxy vehicles, mounted high on exaggerated drivetrains, big wheels, huge tires, axles grinding around. They roared nearer, moving slow in low gear. The officer from the car ran to meet them. Pointed them up to where he wanted them. They roared slowly past and stopped two abreast in the road where it straightened into the rock cutting.

There were four vehicles. Black and green camouflage, rolls of netting on the flanks, stenciled numbers and big single stars in white. The front two trucks bristled with antennas and small dishes. The rear two were accommodations. Each vehicle had hydraulic jacks at each corner. The drivers lowered the jacks and the weight came up off the tires. The jacks pushed against the camber of the road and leveled the floors. Then the engines cut off and the loud diesel roaring died into the mountain silence.

The four drivers vaulted down. They ran to the rear of their trucks and opened the doors. Reached in and folded down short aluminum ladders. Went up inside and flicked switches. The four interiors lit up with green light. The drivers came back out. Regrouped and saluted the officer.

"All yours, sir," the point man said.

The officer nodded. Pointed to the Chevy.

"Drive back in that," he said. "And forget you were ever here."

The point man saluted again.

"Understood, sir," he said.

The four drivers walked to the Chevy. Their boots were loud in the silence. They got in the car and fired it up. Turned in the road and disappeared south.

Back in his office, Webster found the Borken profile on his desk and a visitor waiting for him. Green uniform under a khaki trench coat, maybe sixty, sixty-two, iron-gray stubble on part of his head, battered brown leather briefcase under his arm, battered canvas suit carrier on the floor at his feet.

"I understand you need to talk to me," the guy said. "I'm General Garber. I was Jack Reacher's CO for a number of years."

Webster nodded.

"I'm going to Montana," he said. "You can talk to me there."

"We anticipated that," Garber said. "If the Bureau can fly us out to Kalispell, the Air Force will take us on the rest of the way by helicopter."

Webster nodded again. Buzzed through to his secretary. She was off duty.

"Shit," Webster said.

"My driver is waiting," Garber said. "He'll take us out to Andrews."

Webster called ahead from the car and the Bureau Lear was waiting ready. Twenty minutes after leaving the White House, Webster was in the air heading west over the center of the city. He wondered if the President could hear the scream of his engines through his thick bulletproof glass.

The air force technicians arrived with the satellite trucks an hour after the command post had been installed. There were two vehicles in their convoy. The first was similar to the command post itself, big, high, boxy, hydraulic jacks at each corner, a short aluminum ladder for access. The second was a long flatbed truck with a big satellite dish mounted high on an articulated mechanism. As soon as it was parked and level, the mechanism kicked in and swung the dish up to find the planes, seven miles up in the darkening sky. It locked on and the delicate electronics settled down to tracking the moving signals. There was a continuous motor sound as the dish moved through a subtle arc, too slowly for the eye to detect. The techs hauled out a cable the thickness of a sapling's trunk from the flatbed and locked it into a port on the side of the closed truck. Then they swarmed up inside and fired up the monitors and the recorders.

McGrath hitched a ride with the soldiers in the armored carrier. They rumbled a mile south and met a waiting Montana State Police cruiser on the road. The state guy conferred with McGrath and opened his trunk. Pulled out a box of red danger flares and an array of temporary road signs. The soldiers jogged south and put a pair of flares either side of a sign reading: Danger, Road Out. They came back north and set up a trio of flares in the center of the blacktop with a sign reading: Bridge Out Ahead. Fifty yards farther north, they blocked the whole width of the road with more flares. They strung Road Closed signs across behind them. When the state guy had slalomed his way back south and disappeared, the soldiers took axes from their vehicle and started felling trees. The armored carrier nudged them over and pushed them across the road, engine roaring, tires squealing. It lined them up in a rough zigzag. A vehicle could get through, but only if it slowed to a dead crawl and threaded its way past. Two soldiers were posted as sentries on the shoulders. The other six rode back north with McGrath.

Johnson was in the command vehicle. He was in radio contact with Peterson. The news was bad. The missile unit had been out of radio contact for more than eight hours. Johnson had a rule of thumb. He had learned it by bitter experience in the jungles of Vietnam. The rule of thumb said: when you've lost radio contact with a unit for more than eight hours, you mark that unit down as a total loss.

WEBSTER AND GARBER did not talk during the plane ride. That was Webster's choice. He was experienced enough as a bureaucrat to know that whatever he heard from Garber, he'd only have to hear all over again when the full team was finally assembled. So he sat quietly in the noisy jet whine and read the Borken profile from Quantico. Garber was looking questions at him, but he ignored them. Explain it to Garber now, and he'd only have to do it all over again for McGrath and Johnson.

The evening air at Kalispell was cold and gray for the short noisy walk across the apron to the Air Force Bell. Garber identified himself to the copilot who dropped a short ladder to the tarmac. Garber and Webster scrambled up inside and sat where they were told. The copilot signaled with both hands that they should fasten their harnesses and that the ride would take about twenty-five minutes. Webster nodded and listened to the beat of the rotor as it lifted them all into the air.

GENERAL JOHNSON HAD just finished another long call to the White House when he heard the Bell clattering in. He stood framed in the command post doorway and watched it put down on the same gravel turnout, two hundred yards south. He saw two figures spill out and crouch away. He saw the chopper lift and yaw and turn south.

He walked down and met them halfway. Nodded to Garber and pulled Webster to one side.

"Anything?" he asked.

Webster shook his head.

"No change," he said. "White House is playing safe. You?"

"Nothing," Johnson said.

Webster nodded. Nothing more to say.

"What we got here?" he asked.

"Far as the White House knows, nothing," Johnson said. "We've got two camera planes in the air. Officially, they're on exercises. We've got eight Marines and an armored car. They're on exercises, too. Their COs know where they are, but they don't know exactly why, and they're not asking."

"You sealed the road?" Webster asked.

Johnson nodded.

"We're all on our own up here," he said.

34

REACHER AND HOLLY sat alone in the forest, backs to two adjacent pines, staring at the mound above Jackson's grave. They sat like that until the afternoon light faded and died. They didn't speak. The forest grew cold. The time for the decision arrived.

"We're going back," Holly said.

It was a statement, not a question. A lot of resignation in her voice. He made no reply. He was breathing low, staring into space, lost in thought. Reliving in his mind her taste and smell. Her hair and her eyes. Her lips. The feel of her, strong and lithe and urgent underneath him.

"Nightfall," she said.

"Not just yet," he said.

"We have to," she said. "They'll send the dogs after us."

He didn't speak again. Just sat there, eyes locked into the distance.

"There's nowhere else to go," she said.

He nodded slowly and stood up. Stretched and caught his breath as his tired muscles cramped. Helped Holly up and took his jacket down off the tree and shrugged it on. Left the crowbar lying in the dirt next to the shovel.

"We leave tonight," he said. "Shit's going to hit the fan tomorrow. Independence Day."

"Sure, but how?" she asked.

"I don't know yet," he said.

"Don't take risks on my account," she said.

"You'd be worth it," he said.

"Because of who I am?" she asked.

He nodded.

"Because of who you are," he said. "Not because of who your father is. Or your damn godfather. And no, I didn't vote for him."

She stretched up and kissed him on the mouth.

"Take care, Reacher," she said.

"Just be ready," he said. "Maybe midnight."

She nodded. They walked the hundred yards south to the rocky outcrop. Turned and walked the hundred yards east to the clearing. Came out of the woods straight into a semicircle of five guards waiting for them. Four rifles. Center man was Joseph Ray. He was in charge of the detail, with a Glock 17 in his hand.

"She goes back to her room," Ray said. "You go in the punishment hut."

The guards formed up. Two of them stepped either side of Holly. Her eyes were blazing and they didn't try to take her elbows. Just walked slowly beside her. She turned and glanced back at Reacher.

"See you later, Holly," Reacher called.

"Don't you bet on that, Ms. Johnson," Joseph Ray said, and laughed.

He escorted Reacher to the door of the punishment hut. Took out a key and unlocked the door. Swung it open. Pushed Reacher through, gun out and ready. Then he pulled the door closed again and relocked it.

The punishment hut was the same size and shape as Borken's command hut. But it was completely empty. Bare walls, no windows, lights meshed with heavy wire. On the floor near one end was a perfect square of yellow paint, maybe twelve inches by twelve. Apart from that, the hut was featureless.

"You stand on that square," Ray said.

Reacher nodded. He was familiar with that procedure. Being forced to stand at attention, hour after hour, never moving, was an effective punishment. He had heard about it, time to time. Once, he'd seen the results. After the first few hours, the pain starts. The back goes, then the agony spreads upward from the shins. By the second or third day, the ankles swell and burst and the thighbones strike upward and the neck collapses.

"So stand on it," Ray said.

Reacher stepped to the corner of the hut and bent to the floor. Made a big show of brushing the dust away with his hand. Turned and lowered himself gently so he was sitting comfortably in the angle of the walls. Stretched his legs out and folded his hands behind his head. Crossed his ankles and smiled.

"You got to stand on the square," Ray said.

Reacher looked at him. He had said: believe me, I know tanks. So he had been a soldier. A grunt, in a motorized unit. Probably a loader, maybe a driver.

"Stand up," Ray said.

Give a grunt a task, and what's the thing he's most afraid of? Getting chewed out by an officer for failing to do it, that's what.

"Stand up, damn it," Ray said.

So either he doesn't fail, or if he does, he conceals it. No grunt in the history of the world has ever just gone to his officer and said: I couldn't do it, sir.

"I'm telling you to stand up, Reacher," Ray said quietly.

If he fails, he keeps it a big secret. Much better that way.

"You want me to stand up?" Reacher asked.

"Yeah, stand up," Ray said.

Reacher shook his head.

"You're going to have to make me, Joe," he said.

Ray was thinking about it. It was a reasonably slow thought process. Its progress was visible in his body language. First, the Glock came up. Then it went back down. Shooting at the prisoner was its own admission of failure. It was the same thing as saying: I couldn't make him do it, sir. Then he glanced at his hands. Glanced across at Reacher. Glanced away. Unarmed combat was rejected. He stood there, in a fog of indecision.

"Where did you serve?" Reacher asked him.

Ray shrugged.

"Here and there," he said.

"Like where and where?" Reacher asked.

"I was in Germany twice," Ray said. "And I was in Desert Storm."

"Driver?" Reacher asked.

"Loader," Ray answered.

Reacher nodded.

"You boys did a good job," he said. "I was in Desert Storm. I saw what you boys did."

Ray nodded. He took the opening, like Reacher knew he would. If you can't let them beat you, you let them join you. Ray moved casually to his left and sat down on the floor, back against the door, Glock resting against his thigh. He nodded again.

"We whupped them," he said.

"You sure did," Reacher said. "You whupped them real good. So, Germany and the desert. You liked it there?"

"Not much," Ray said.

"You liked their systems?" Reacher asked.

"What systems?" Ray asked back.

"Their governments," Reacher said. "Their laws, their liberties, all that stuff."

Ray looked mystified.

"Never noticed," he said. "Never paid any attention."

"So how do you know they're better than ours?" Reacher asked.

"Who says they're better?" Ray said.

"You do," Reacher said. "Last night you were telling me how bad it is here in America. Got to be better everywhere else, right?"

Ray shook his head.

"I never told you that," he said.

"So is it or isn't it?" Reacher asked.

"I don't know," Ray said. "Probably. Lot of things wrong with America."

Reacher nodded.

"Lot of things," he said. "I agree with you. But I'll tell you something. It's better in America than everyplace else. I know, because I've been everyplace else. Everyplace else is worse. A lot worse. Lot of things wrong in America, but plenty more things wrong everyplace else. You guys should think about that."

Ray looked across through the gloom.

"You think we're wrong?" he asked.

Reacher nodded.

"I know you're wrong," he said. "For certain. All that stuff you were telling me is bullshit. All of it. It's not happening."

"It is happening," Ray said. "Beau says so."

"Think about it, Joe," Reacher said. "You were in the service. You saw how it all operated. You think those guys could organize all that stuff and keep it a secret? They ever even give you a pair of boots the right size?"

Ray laughed.

"Not hardly," he said.

"Right," Reacher said. "So if they can't organize your damn boots, how can they organize all this other stuff Beau is talking about? What about these transmitters hidden in all the new cars? You think Detroit can do all that stuff? They'd be recalling them all because they didn't work right. You a gambling man, Joe?"

"Why?" he asked.

"What are the odds?" Reacher said. "Against they could organize a huge massive conspiracy like that and keep it all a secret for years and years?"

A slow smile spread across Ray's face and Reacher saw that he was losing. Like talking to the wall. Like teaching a chimpanzee to read.

"But they haven't kept it a secret," Ray said triumphantly. "We found out about it. I told you, Beau's got the proof. He's got the documents. It's not a secret at all. That's why we're here. Beau's right, no doubt about it. He's a smart guy."

Reacher closed his eyes and sighed.

"You better hope so," he said. "He's going to need to be."

"He's a smart guy," Ray said again. "And he's got staying power. He's putting us all together. There were a dozen groups up here. Their leaders quit and left. All their people came and joined Beau, because they trust him. He's a smart guy, Reacher, and he's our only hope left. You won't change anybody's mind about him. You can forget about that. Far as we're concerned, we love him, and we trust him to do right.''

"What about Jackson?'' Reacher asked. "You think he did right about that?''

Ray shrugged.

"Jackson was a spy,'' he said. "Shit like that happens. Beau's studied the history. It happened in 1776, right? Redcoats had spies all over. We hanged them then, just the same. Plenty of old ladies back east got old oak trees in their front yards, famous for being where they strung up the redcoat spies. Some of them charge you a buck and a half just to take a look at them. I know, I went there once.''

"What time is lights-out here?'' Reacher asked.

"Ten o'clock,'' Ray said. "Why?''

Reacher paused. Stared at him. Thought back over their conversation. Gazed at his lean, mobile face. Looked into his crazy eyes, burning deep under his brow.

"I got to be someplace else after lights-out,'' Reacher said.

Ray laughed again.

"And you think I'm going to let you?'' he said.

Reacher nodded.

"If you want to live,'' he said.

Ray lifted the pistol off his thigh and pointed it one-handed at Reacher's head.

"I'm the one got the gun here,'' he said.

"You wouldn't live to pull the trigger,'' Reacher said.

"Trigger's right here,'' Ray said. "You're all the way over there.''

Reacher waved him a listen-up gesture. Leaned forward and spoke quietly.

"I'm not really supposed to tell you this,'' he said. "But we were warned we'd meet a few guys smarter than the average, and we're authorized to explain a couple of things to them, if the operational circumstances make it advisable.''

"What circumstances?'' Ray asked. "What things?''

"You were right,'' Reacher said. "Most of the things you've said are correct. A couple of inaccuracies, but we spread a little disinformation here and there.''

"What are you talking about?" Ray asked.

Reacher lowered his voice to a whisper.

"I'm World Army," he said. "Commander of the advance party. I've got five thousand UN troops in the forest. Russians, mostly, a few Chinese. We've been watching you on the satellite surveillance. Right now, we've got an X-ray camera on this hut. There's a laser beam pointed at your head. Part of the SDI technology."

"You're kidding," Ray said.

Reacher shook his head. Deadly serious.

"You were right about the microchips," he said. "Look at this."

He stood up slowly and pulled his shirt up to his chest. Turned slightly so Ray could see the huge scar on his stomach.

"Bigger than the modern ones," he said. "The latest ones go in with no mess at all. The ones we put in the babies? But these old ones work just the same. The satellites know where I am at all times, like you said. You start to pull that trigger, the laser blows your head off."

Ray's eyes were burning. He looked away from Reacher's scar and glanced nervously up at the roof.

"*Suis pas américain,*" Reacher said. "*Suis soldat français, agent du gouvernement mondial depuis plusieurs années, parti en mission clandestine il y a deux mois. Il faut évaluer l'élément de risque que votre bande représente par ici.*"

He spoke as fast as he could and ended up sounding exactly like an educated Parisian woman. Exactly like he recalled his dead mother sounding. Ray nodded slowly.

"You foreign?" he asked.

"French," Reacher said. "We operate international brigades. I said I'm here to check out the degree of risk you people represent to us."

"I saw you shooting," Reacher said. "I spotted it. A thousand yards."

"Guided by satellite," Reacher said. "I told you, SDI technology, through the microchip. We can all shoot two miles, perfect score every time."

"Christ," Ray said.

"I need to be out in the open at ten o'clock," Reacher said. "It's a safety procedure. You got a wife here?"

Ray nodded.

"What about kids?" Reacher asked. "Any of these kids yours?"

Ray nodded again.

"Sure," he said. "Two boys."

"If I'm not out by ten, they all die," Reacher said. "If I get taken prisoner, the whole place gets incinerated. Can't afford for my microchip to get captured. I told them you guys wouldn't understand how it works, but my chief said some of you could be smarter than I thought. Looks like my chief was right."

Ray nodded proudly and Reacher checked his watch.

"It's seven-thirty, right?" he said. "I'm going to sleep two and a half hours. The satellite will wake me at ten exactly. You wait and see."

He lay back down on the floor and curled his arm under his head. Set the alarm in his head for two minutes to ten. Said to himself: don't let it fail me tonight.

35

I REFUSE TO believe it," General Garber said.

"He's involved," Webster said in reply. "That's for damn sure. We got the pictures, clear as day."

Garber shook his head.

"I was promoted lieutenant forty years ago," he said. "Now I'm a three-star general. I've commanded thousands of men. Tens of thousands. Got to know most of them well. And out of all of them, Jack Reacher is the single least likely man to be involved in a thing like this."

Garber was sitting ramrod-straight at the table in the mobile command post. He had shed his khaki raincoat to reveal an old creased uniform jacket. It was a jacket which bore the accumulated prizes of a lifetime of service. It was studded with badges and ribbons. It was the jacket of a man who had served forty years without ever making a single mistake.

Johnson was watching him carefully. Garber's grizzled old head was still. His eyes were calm. His hands were laid comfortably on the table. His voice was firm, but quiet. Definite, like he was being asked to defend the proposition that the sky was blue and the grass was green.

"Show the General the pictures, Mack," Webster said.

McGrath nodded and opened his envelope. Slid the four stills over the table to Garber. Garber held each one up in turn, tilted to catch the green light from the overhead. Johnson was watching his eyes. He was waiting for the flicker of doubt, then the flicker of resignation. He saw neither.

"These are open to interpretation," Garber said.

His voice was still calm. Johnson heard an officer loyally defending a favored subordinate. Webster and McGrath heard a policeman of sorts expressing a doubt. They figured forty years' service had bought the guy the right to be heard.

"Interpretation how?" Webster asked.

"Four isolated moments out of a sequence," Garber said. "They could be telling us the wrong story."

Webster leaned over and pointed at the first still.

"He's grabbing her stuff," he said. "Plain as day, General."

Garber shook his head. There was silence. Just electronic hum throughout the vehicle. Johnson saw a flicker of doubt. But it was in McGrath's eyes, not Garber's. Then Brogan rattled his way up the ladder. Ducked his head into the truck.

"Surveillance tapes, chief," he said. "We've been reviewing the stuff the planes got earlier. You should come see it."

He ducked out again and the four men glanced at each other and got up. Walked the short distance through the cold evening to the satellite truck and up the ladder. Milosevic was in shirtsleeves, bathed in the blue light from a bank of video screens. He shuttled a tape back and pressed play. Four screens lit up with a perfect clear overhead view of a tiny town. The quality of the picture was magnificent. Like a perfect movie picture, except filmed vertically downward, not horizontal.

"Yorke," Milosevic said. "The old courthouse, bottom right. Now watch."

He hit fast wind and watched the counter. Slowed the tape and hit play again.

"This is a mile and a quarter away," he said. "The camera tracked northwest. There's a parade ground, and this rifle range."

The camera had zoomed out for a wide view of the area. There were two clearings with huts to the south, and a flat parade ground to the north. In between was a long narrow scar in the undergrowth, maybe a half-mile long and twenty yards wide. The camera zoomed right out for a moment, to establish the scale, then it tightened in on a crowd at the eastern end of the range. Then it tightened further to a small knot of people standing on some brown matting. There were four men clearly visible. And one woman. General Johnson gasped and stared at his daughter.

"When was this?" he asked.

"Few hours ago," Milosevic said. "She's alive and well."

He froze the picture and tapped his fingernail four times on the glass.

"Reacher," he said. "Stevie Stewart. We figure this one is Odell Fowle. And the fat guy is Beau Borken. Matches his file photo from California."

Then he hit play again. The camera held steady on the matting, from seven miles up in the sky. Borken pressed his bulk to the floor and lay motionless. Then a silent puff of dust was seen under the muzzle of his rifle.

"They're shooting a little over eight hundred yards," Milosevic said. "Some kind of a competition, I guess."

They watched Borken's five final shots, and then Reacher picked up his rifle.

"That's a Barrett," Garber said.

Reacher lay motionless and then fired six silent shots, well spaced. The crowd milled around, and eventually Reacher was lost to sight in the trees to the south.

"OK," Webster said. "How do you want to interpret that, General Garber?"

Garber shrugged. A dogged expression on his face.

"He's one of them, no doubt about it," Webster said. "Did you see his clothes? He was in uniform. Showing off on the range? Would they give him a uniform and a rifle to play with if he wasn't one of their own?"

Johnson spooled the tape back and froze it. Looked at Holly for a long moment. Then he walked out of the trailer. Called over his shoulder to Webster.

"Director, we need to go to work," he said. "I want to make a contingency plan well ahead of time. No reason for us not to be ready for this."

Webster followed him out. Brogan and Milosevic stayed at the video console. McGrath was watching Garber. Garber was staring at the blank screen.

"I still don't believe it," he said.

He turned and saw McGrath looking at him. Nodded him out of the trailer. The two men walked together into the silence of the night.

"I can't prove it to you," Garber said. "But Reacher is on our side. I'll absolutely guarantee that, personally."

"Doesn't look that way," McGrath said. "He's the classic type. Fits our standard profile perfectly. Unemployed ex-military, malcontent, dislocated childhood, probably full of all kinds of grievances."

Garber shook his head.

"He's none of those things," he said. "Except unemployed ex-military. He was a fine officer. Best I ever had. You're making a big mistake."

McGrath saw the look on Garber's face.

"So you'd trust him?" he asked. "Personally?"

Garber nodded grimly.

"With my life," he said. "I don't know why he's there, but I promise you he's clean, and he's going to do what needs doing, or he's going to die trying."

EXACTLY SIX MILES north, Holly was trusting to the same instinct. They had taken her disassembled bed away, and she was lying on the thin mattress on the floorboards. They had taken the soap and the shampoo and the towel from the bathroom as a punishment. They had left the small pool of blood from the dead woman's head untouched. It was there on the floor, a yard from her makeshift bed. She guessed they thought it would upset her. They were wrong. It made her happy. She was happy to watch it dry and blacken. She was thinking about Jackson and staring at the stain like it was a Rorschach blot telling her: you're coming out of the shadow now, Holly.

WEBSTER AND JOHNSON came up with a fairly simple contingency plan. It depended on geography. The exact same geography they assumed had tempted Borken to choose Yorke as the location for his bastion. Like all plans based on geography, it was put together using a map. Like all plans put together using a map, it was only as good as the map was accurate. And like most maps, theirs was way out of date.

They were using a large-scale map of Montana. Most of its information was reliable. The main features were correct. The western obstacle was plain to see.

"We assume the river is impassable, right?" Webster said.

"Right," Johnson agreed. "The spring melts are going to be in full flow. Nothing we can do there before Monday. When we get some equipment."

The roads were shown in red like a man had placed his right hand palm-down on the paper. The small towns of Kalispell and Whitefish nestled under the palm. Roads fanned out like the four fingers and the thumb. The index finger ran up through a place called Eureka to the Canadian border. The thumb ran out northwest through Yorke and stopped at the old mines. That thumb was now amputated at the first knuckle.

"They assume you'll come up the road," Johnson said. "So you won't. You'll loop east to Eureka and come in through the forest."

He ran his pencil down the thumb and across the back of the hand. Back up the index finger and stopped it at Eureka. Fifty miles of forest lay between Eureka and Yorke. The forest was represented on the map by a large green stain. Deep and wide. They knew what that green stain meant. They could see what it meant by looking around them. The area was covered in virgin forest. It ran rampant up and down the mountainsides. Most places, the vegetation was so dense a man could barely squeeze between the tree trunks. But the green stain to the east of Yorke was a national forest. Owned and operated by the Forest Service. The green stain showed a web of threads running through it. Those threads were Forest Service tracks.

"I can get my people here in four hours," Webster said. "The Hostage Rescue Team. On my own initiative, if it comes to it."

Johnson nodded.

"They can walk right through the woods," he said. "Probably drive right through."

Webster nodded.

"We called the Forest guys," he said. "They're bringing us a detailed plan."

"Perfect," Johnson said. "If things turn bad, you call your team in, send them direct to Eureka, we'll all make a little noise on the southern flank, and they muscle in straight through from the east."

Webster nodded again. The contingency plan was made. Until the National Forests guy came up the short aluminum ladder into the command post. McGrath brought him inside with Milosevic and Brogan. Webster made the introductions and Johnson asked the questions. Straightaway the Forest guy started shaking his head.

"Those tracks don't exist," he said. "At least, most of them don't."

Johnson pointed to the map.

"They're right here," he said.

The Forest guy shrugged. He had a thick book of topographical plans under his arm. He opened it up to the correct page. Laid it over the map. The scale was much larger, but it was obvious the web of threads was a different shape.

"Mapmakers know there are tracks," the guy said. "So they just show them any old place."

"OK," Johnson said. "We'll use your maps."

The Forest guy shook his head.

"These are wrong, too," he said. "They might have been right at some stage, but they're wrong now. We spent years closing off most of these tracks. Had to stop the bear hunters getting in. Environmentalists made us do it. We bulldozed tons of dirt into the openings of most of the through tracks. Ripped up a lot of the others. They'll be totally overgrown by now."

"OK, so which tracks are closed?" Webster asked. He had turned the plan and was studying it.

"We don't know," the guy said. "We didn't keep very accurate records. Just sent the bulldozers out. We caught a lot of guys closing the wrong tracks, because they were nearer, or not closing them at all, because that was easier. The whole thing was a mess."

"So is there any way through?" Johnson asked.

The Forest guy shrugged.

"Maybe," he said. "Maybe not. No way of knowing, except to try it. Could take a couple of months. If you do get through, keep a record and let us know, OK?"

Johnson stared at him.

"Let me get this straight," he said. "You're the damn Forest Service, and you want us to tell you where your own tracks are?"

The guy nodded.

"That's about the size of it," he said. "Like I told you, our records are lousy. The way we figured it, who the hell would ever care?"

The General's aide walked him back to the roadblock. There was silence in the command vehicle. McGrath and Brogan and Milosevic studied the map.

"We can't get through, they can't get through," McGrath said. "We've got them bottled up. We need to start exploiting that."

"How?" Webster said.

"Control them," McGrath said. "We already control their road. We can control their power and their telephone line, too. The lines more or less follow the road. Separate spurs up out of Kalispell. We should cut the phone line so it terminates right here, in this vehicle. Then they can't communicate with anybody except us. Then we tell them we control their power. Threaten to cut it off if they don't negotiate."

"You want a negotiation?" Johnson asked.

"I want a stalling tactic," McGrath said. "Until the White House loosens up."

Webster nodded.

"OK, do it," he said. "Call the phone company and get the line run in here."

"I already did," McGrath said. "They'll do it first thing in the morning."

Webster yawned. Checked his watch. Gestured to Milosevic and Brogan.

"We should get a sleeping rota going," he said. "You two turn in first. We'll sleep two shifts, call it four hours at a time."

Milosevic and Brogan nodded. Looked happy enough about it.

"See you later," McGrath said. "Sleep tight."

They left the trailer and closed the door quietly. Johnson was still fiddling with the map. Twisting it and turning it on the table.

"Can't they do the phone thing faster?" he asked. "Like tonight?"

Webster thought about it and nodded. He knew fifty percent of any battle is keeping the command structure harmonious.

"Call them again, Mack," he said. "Tell them we need it now."

McGrath called them again. He used the phone at his elbow. Had a short conversation which ended with a chuckle.

"They're sending the emergency linemen," he said. "Should be done in a couple of hours. But we'll get an invoice for it. I told them to send it to the Hoover Building. The guy asked me where that was."

He got up and waited in the doorway. Johnson and Webster stayed at the table. They huddled together over their map. They looked at the southern ravine. It had been formed a million years ago when the earth shattered under the weight of a billion tons of ice. They assumed it was accurately represented on paper.

36

Reacher woke up exactly two minutes before ten o'clock. He did it in his normal way, which was to come round quickly, motionless, no change in his breathing. He felt his arm curled under his head and opened his eyes the smallest fraction possible. The other side of the punishment hut, Joseph Ray was still sitting against the door. The Glock was on the floor beside him. He was checking his watch.

Reacher counted off ninety seconds in his head. Ray was glancing between the roof of the hut and his watch. Then he looked across at Reacher. Reacher snapped upright in one fluid movement. Pressed his palm against his ear like he was listening to a secret communication. Ray's eyes were wide. Reacher nodded and stood up.

"OK," he said. "Open the door, Joe."

Ray took out the key from his pocket. Unlocked the door. It swung open.

"You want to take the Glock?" Ray asked.

He held the gun out, butt first. Anxiety in his eyes. Reacher smiled. He had expected nothing less. Ray was dumb, but not that dumb. He had been given two and a half hours to scope it out. This was a final test. If he took the gun, he was bullshitting. He was certain it was unloaded and the clip was in Ray's pocket.

"Don't need it," Reacher said. "We've got the whole

place covered. I got weapons at my disposal more powerful than a nine-millimeter, believe me, Joe.''

Ray nodded and straightened up.

"Don't forget the laser beams," Reacher said. "You step out of this hut, you're a dead man. Nothing I can do about that right now. *Vous comprenez, mon ami?*''

Ray nodded again. Reacher slipped out into the night. Ray swung the door closed. Reacher backtracked silently and waited around the corner of the hut. Knelt down and found a small rock. Hefted it in his hand and waited for Ray to follow him.

He didn't come. Reacher waited eight minutes. Long experience had taught him: if they don't come after six minutes, they aren't coming at all. People think in five-minute segments, because of the way clocks are laid out. They say: I'll wait five minutes. Then, because they're cautious, they add another minute. They think it's smart. Reacher waited the first five, then the extra one, then added two more for the sake of safety. But Ray didn't come. He wasn't going to.

Reacher avoided the clearing. He kept to the trees. He skirted the area in the forest. Ignored the beaten earth paths. He wasn't worried about the dogs. They weren't out. Fowler had talked about mountain lions roaming. Nobody leaves dogs out at night where there are mountain lions on the prowl. That's a sure way of having no dogs left in the morning.

He made a complete circuit of the Bastion, hidden in the trees. The lights were all out and the whole place was still and silent. He waited in the trees behind the mess hall. The kitchen was a square hut, awkwardly connected to the back of the main structure. There were no lights on, but the door was open, and the woman who had served him breakfast was waiting in the shadows. He watched her from the trees. He waited five minutes. Then six. No other movement anywhere. He tossed his small rock onto the path to her left. She jumped at the sound. He called softly. She came out of the shadows. Alone. She walked over to the trees. He took her elbow and pulled her back into the darkness.

"How did you get out of there?" she whispered to him.

It was impossible to tell how old she was. Maybe twenty-five, maybe forty-five. She was a handsome woman, lean, long straight hair, but careworn and worried. A flicker of spirit and resilience underneath. She would have been comfortable a hundred years ago, stumbling down the Oregon Trail.

"How did you get out?" she whispered again.

"I walked out the door," Reacher whispered back.

The woman just looked at him blankly.

"You've got to help us," she whispered.

Then she stopped and wrung her hands and twisted her head left and right, peering into the dark, terrified.

"Help how?" he asked. "Why?"

"They're all crazy," the woman said. "You've got to help us."

"How?" he asked again.

She just grimaced, arms held wide, like it was obvious, or like she didn't know where to start, or how.

"From the beginning," he said.

She nodded, twice, swallowing, collecting herself.

"People have disappeared," she said.

"What people?" he asked. "How did they disappear?"

"They just disappeared," she said. "It's Borken. He's taken over everything. It's a long story. Most of us were up here with other groups, just surviving on our own, with our families, you know? I was with the Northwestern Freemen. Then Borken started coming around, talking about unity? He fought and argued. The other leaders disagreed with his views. Then they just started disappearing. They just left. Borken said they couldn't stand the pace. They just disappeared. So he said we had to join with him. Said we had no choice. Some of us are more or less prisoners here."

Reacher nodded.

"And now things are happening up at the mines," she said.

"What things?" he asked her.

"I don't know," she said. "Bad things, I guess. We're not allowed to go up there. They're only a mile up the road, but they're off limits. Something was going on there today. They said they were all working in the south, on the border, but when they came back for lunch, they came from the north. I saw them from the kitchen window. They were smiling and laughing.''

''Who?'' Reacher asked.

''Borken and the ones he trusts,'' she said. ''He's crazy. He says they'll attack us when we declare independence and we have to fight back. Starting tomorrow. We're all scared. We got families, you know? But there's nothing we can do. You oppose him, and you either get banished, or he raves at you until you agree with him. Nobody can stand up to him. He controls us, totally.''

Reacher nodded again. The woman sagged against him. Tears were on her cheeks.

''And we can't win, can we?'' she said. ''Not if they attack us. There's only a hundred of us, trained up. We can't beat an army with a hundred people, can we? We're all going to die.''

Her eyes were wide and white and desperate. Reacher shrugged. Shook his head and tried to make his voice sound calm and reassuring.

''It'll be a siege,'' he said. ''That's all. A standoff. They'll negotiate. It's happened before. And it'll be the FBI, not the Army. The FBI know how to do this kind of a thing. You'll all be OK. They won't kill you. They won't come here looking to kill anybody. That's just Borken's propaganda.''

''Live free or die,'' she said. ''That's what he keeps saying.''

''The FBI will handle it,'' he said again. ''Nobody's looking to kill you.''

The woman clamped her lips and screwed her wet eyes shut and shook her head wildly.

''No, Borken will kill us,'' she said. ''He'll do it, not them. Live free or die, don't you understand? If they come, he'll kill us all. Or else he'll make us all kill ourselves. Like a mass suicide thing? He'll make us do it, I know he will.''

Reacher just stared at her.

''I heard them talking,'' she said. ''Whispering about it all the time, making secret plans. They said women and children would die. They said it was justifiable. They said it was historic and important. They said the circumstances demanded it.''

"You heard them?" Reacher asked. "When?"

"All the time," she whispered again. "They're always making plans. Borken and the ones he trusts. Women and children have to die, they said. They're going to make us kill ourselves. Mass suicide. Our families. Our children. At the mines. I think they're going to make us go in the mines and kill ourselves."

HE STAYED IN the woods until he was well north of the parade ground. Then he tracked east until he saw the road, running up out of Yorke. It was potholed and rough, gleaming gray in the moonlight. He stayed in the shadow of the trees and followed it north.

The road wound up a mountainside in tight hairpin bends. A sure sign it led to something worthwhile, otherwise the labor consumed in its construction would have been meaningless. After a mile of winding and a thousand feet of elevation, the final curve gave out onto a bowl the size of a deserted stadium. It was part natural, part blasted, hanging there in the belly of the giant peaks. The back walls of the bowl were sheer rock faces. There were semicircular holes blasted into them at intervals. They looked like giant mouse holes. Some of them had been built out with waste rock, to provide sheltered entrances. Two of the entrances had been enlarged into giant stone sheds, roofed with timber.

The bowl was floored with loose shale. There were piles of earth and spoil everywhere. Ragged weeds and saplings were forcing their way through. Reacher could see the rusted remains of rail tracks, starting nowhere and running a few yards. He squatted against a tree, well back in the woods, and watched.

There was nothing happening. The whole place was deserted and silent. Quieter than silent. It had that total absence of sound that gets left behind when a busy place is abandoned. The natural sounds were long gone. The swaying trees cleared, the rushing streams diverted, the rustling vegetation burned off, replaced by clattering machines and shouting men. Then when the men and the machines leave, there is nothing left behind to replace their noise. Reacher strained his ears, but heard nothing at all. Silent as the moon.

He stayed in the woods. To approach from the south meant to approach uphill. He skirted around to the west and gained an extra hundred feet of height. Paused and looked down into the bowl from a new perspective.

Still nothing. But there had been something. Some recent activity. The moonlight was showing vehicle tracks in the shale. There was a mess of ruts in and out of one of the stone sheds. A couple of years' worth. The motor pool. There were newer ruts into the other stone shed. The bigger shed. Bigger ruts. Somebody had driven some large vehicles into that shed. Recently.

He scrambled down out of the woods and onto the shale. His shoes on the small flat stones sounded like rifle shots in the silent night. The crunch of his steps came back off the sheer walls like thunder. He felt tiny and exposed, like a man in a bad dream walking naked across a football field. He felt like the surrounding mountains were a huge crowd in the bleachers, staring silently at him. He stopped behind a pile of rock and squatted and listened. The echo of his footsteps crashed and died into silence. He heard nothing. Just a total absence of sound.

He crept noisily to the doors of the smaller shed. Up close, it was a big structure. Probably built to shelter giant machines and pumping engines. The doors were twelve feet high. They were built out of peeled logs, strapped together with iron. They were like the sides of a log house, hinged into a mountainside.

There was no lock. It was hard to imagine how there could have been. No lock Reacher had ever seen could have matched the scale of those doors. He put his back against the right-hand door and levered the left-hand one open a foot. The iron hinge moved easily on a thick film of grease. He slid sideways through the gap and stepped inside.

It was pitch-dark. He could see nothing. He stood and waited for his night vision to build. But it never came. Your eyes can open wider and wider, wide as they can get, but if there's no light at all, you won't see anything. He could smell a strong smell of damp and decay. He could hear the silence vanishing backward into the mountain, like there was a long chamber or tunnel in front of him. He moved inward, hands held out in front of him like a blind man.

He found a vehicle. His shin hit the front fender before his hands hit the hood. It was high. A truck or a pickup. Civilian. Smooth-gloss automotive spray. Not matte military paint. He trailed his fingers round the edge of the hood. Down the side. A pickup. He felt his way around the back and up the other side. Felt for the driver's door. Unlocked. He opened it. The courtesy light blazed like a million-candlepower searchlight. Bizarre shadows were thrown all around. He was in a giant cavern. It had no back. It opened right into the hillside. The rock roof sloped down and became a narrow excavated seam, running far out of sight.

He reached into the pickup cab and switched the headlights on. The beams were reflected off the rock. There were a dozen vehicles parked in neat lines. Old sedans and pickups. Surplus jeeps with crude camouflage. And the white Ford Econoline with the holes in the roof. It looked sad and abandoned after its epic journey from Chicago. Worn out and low on its springs. There were workbenches with old tools hanging above them. Cans of paint and drums of oil. Bald tires in piles and rusted tanks of welding gas.

He searched the nearest vehicles. Keys in all of them. A flashlight in the glove box of the third sedan he checked. He took it. Stepped back to the pickup and killed its headlights. Walked back to the big wooden doors and out into the night.

He waited and listened. Nothing. He swung the motor pool door closed and set off for the larger shed. A hundred yards across the noisy shale. The larger shed had the same type of log doors. Even bigger. And they were locked. The lock was the crudest thing he had ever seen. It was an old warped log laid across two iron brackets and chained into place. The chains were fastened with two big padlocks. Reacher ignored them. No need to fiddle with the padlocks. He could see that the warp in the old log would let him in.

He forced the doors apart where they met at the bottom. The curve in the log in the brackets let them gap by about a foot. He put his arms inside, then his head, then his shoulders. He scrabbled with his feet and pushed his way through. Stood up inside and flicked the flashlight on.

It was another giant cavern. Same darkness. Same strong smell of damp and decay. Same sloping roof running backward to a low seam. The same hush, like all the sound was sucking back deep into the mountain. The same purpose. A vehicle store. But these vehicles were all identical. Five of them. Five current-issue U.S. Army trucks. Marked with the white stencils of the Army Air Artillery. Not new trucks, but well maintained. Neat canvas siding at the rear.

Reacher walked around to the back of the first truck. Stepped up onto the tow-hitch and looked over the tailgate. Empty. It had slatted wooden benches running forward along each side. A troop carrier. Reacher couldn't begin to count the miles he'd traveled on benches like those, swaying, staring at the steel floor, waiting to get where he was going.

The steel floor was stained. At odds with the clean exterior. There were black stains on the floor. Some kind of a thick liquid, dried into pools. Reacher stared at them. Couldn't begin to count the number of stains like that he'd seen. He jumped down and ran to the second vehicle. Stepped up and leaned in with the flashlight.

There were no benches in the rear of the second vehicle. Instead, there were racks bolted to both sides. Precisely constructed racks, welded up out of angle iron and fitted with steel clips and thick rubber pads to hold their delicate cargo. The left-hand rack held five missile launchers. Slim steel tubes, six feet long, dull black metal, with a large box of electronics and an open sight and a pistol grip bolted to the forward end. Five of them, precisely parallel, neatly aligned.

The right-hand rack held twenty-five Stinger missiles. Inches apart, side by side in their rubber mountings, control surfaces folded back, ready to load. Dull alloy, with batch numbers stenciled on, and a broad band of garish orange paint wrapping the fuel section.

Reacher ran to the other three trucks. Each was the same. Five launchers, twenty-five missiles. A total of twenty launchers and one hundred missiles. The entire ordnance requirement of a whole Air Artillery mobile unit. A unit which deployed twenty men. He walked back to the first truck and stared in at the blood on the floor. Then he heard the rats. At first he thought it was footsteps outside on the shale. He snapped the flashlight off. Then he realized the sounds were nearer, and behind him. There were rats scuffling at the rear of the cavern. He lit the flashlight up again and jogged into the cave and found the twenty men.

They were heaped into a large pile of corpses just before the roof got too low for a man to stand. Twenty dead soldiers. A hell of a mess. They had all been shot in the back. Reacher could see that. They had been standing together in a group somewhere, and they had been mown down with heavy machine gun fire from the rear. He bent and grunted and turned a couple of them over. Not the toughest guys he'd ever seen. Docile, reservist types, deployed to a lonely base deep inside friendly territory. Ambushed and murdered for their weapons.

But how? He knew how. An old ground-to-air unit, nearing obsolescence, stationed in the far north of Montana. A leftover from Cold War paranoia. Certainly due for decommissioning. Probably already in the process of decommissioning. Probably on its way south to Peterson in Colorado. Final orders probably transmitted in clear by radio. He recalled the radio scanner back in the communications hut. The operator beside it, patiently turning the dial. He imagined the recall order being accidentally intercepted, the operator running to Borken, Borken's bloated face lighting up with an opportunistic smile. Then some hasty planning and a brutal ambush somewhere in the hills. Twenty men shot down, thrown into their own truck, piled into this cavern. He stood and gazed at the appalling sight. Then he snapped the flashlight off again.

Because he had been right about the noise. It was the noise of footsteps on the shale outside. He heard them again. They were getting closer. They were building to a deafening crunching sound in the night. They were heading straight for the shed. On the shale, no way of telling how many people there were.

He heard them stop outside the massive doors. Heard the jingle of keys. Heard the padlocks rattle. The chains were pulled off and the log lifted aside. The doors sagged open. He dropped to the ground. Lay facedown and pressed himself up against the pile of cold and oozing bodies.

Four feet. Two voices. Voices he knew well. Fowler and

Borken. Talking quietly, walking confidently. Reacher let his body sag against the pile. A rat ran over his hand.

"Did he say when?" Fowler was asking.

His voice was suddenly loud against the rock.

"First thing tomorrow morning," Borken was saying. "Phone company starts its linemen when? About eight o'clock? Maybe seven-thirty?"

"Let's be cautious," Fowler said. "Let's call it seven-thirty. First thing they do is cut the line."

They had flashlights. The beams flicked and swung as they walked.

"No problem," Borken said. "Seven o'clock here is nine o'clock on the East Coast. Perfect timing. We'll do it at seven. D.C. first, then New York, then Atlanta. Should be all done by ten past. Ten minutes that shook the world, right? Twenty minutes to spare."

They stopped at the second truck. Unbolted the tailgate. It came down with a loud metallic clang.

"Then what?" Fowler asked.

"Then we wait and see," Borken replied. "Right now, they've only got eight Marines up here. They don't know what to do. They're not sure about the forest. White House is pussyfooting, like we thought. Give them twelve hours for a decision, they can't try anything before dark tomorrow, earliest. And by then this place will be way down their list of priorities."

They were leaning into the truck. Their voices were muffled by the thick canvas siding.

"Does he need the missile as well?" Fowler asked.

"Just the launcher," Borken answered. "It's in the electronic part."

Reacher lay among the scuffling rats and heard the sound of the clips being undone. Then the squeak of the rubber as a launcher came out of its mountings. Then the rattle of the tailgate bolts ramming home. The footsteps receded. The flashlight beams flicked back toward the doors.

The hinges creaked and the bulky timber doors thumped shut. Reacher heard the launcher being laid gently on the shale and the gasps as the two men lifted the old log back into the brackets. The rattle of the chain and the click of the padlocks. The crunch of the footsteps crossing the shale.

He rolled away from the corpses and hit out at a rat. Caught it with an angry backhand and sent it squealing off into the dark. He sat up and waited. Walked slowly to the door. Listened hard. Waited six minutes. Put his hands into the gap at the bottom of the doors and pulled them apart.

They wouldn't move more than an inch. He laid his palms flat on the smooth timbers and bunched up his shoulders and heaved. They were rock-solid. Like trying to push over a tree. He tried for a minute. He was straining like a weight lifter. The doors were jammed. Then he suddenly realized why. They had put the warped old log back in the brackets the other way around. The curve pointing in toward him, not out away from him. Clamping the doors with extra efficiency, instead of allowing the foot of loose movement it had allowed before.

He pictured the log as he had seen it. More than a foot thick, warped, but dried like iron. Curving away, it was no problem. Curving in, it would be immovable. He glanced at the Army trucks. Gave it up. There was no space to hit the doors with any kind of momentum. The truck would be pressing on them with all the torque of a big diesel engine, but it wouldn't be enough. He couldn't imagine how much force it would take to shatter that old log.

He thought about using a missile. Gave it up. Too noisy, and it wouldn't work anyway. They didn't arm themselves until they were thirty feet into the air. And they only carried six and a half pounds of explosive. Enough to smash a jet engine in flight, but six and a half pounds of explosive against those old timbers would be like scratching at them with a nail file. He was trapped inside, and Holly was waiting.

It was not in his nature to panic. Never had been. He was a calm man, and his long training had made him calmer. He had been taught to assess and evaluate, and to use pure force of will to succeed. You're Jack Reacher, he had been told. You can do anything. First his mother had told him, then his father, then the quiet deadly men in the training schools. And he had believed them.

But at the same time, he hadn't believed them. Part of his mind always said: you've just been lucky. Always lucky. And in the quiet times, he would sit and wait for his luck to run out. He sat on the stony ground with his back against the timbers of the door and asked himself: has it run out now?

He flicked the flashlight beam around the cavern. The rats were staying away from him. They were interested in the darkness in back. They're deserting me, he thought. Deserting the sinking ship. Then his mind clicked in again. No, they're interested in the tunnels, he thought. Because tunnels lead places. He remembered the giant mouse holes blasted into the rock face, north wall of the bowl. Maybe all interconnected by these narrow seams in back.

He ran back into the depth of the cavern, past the trucks, past the grotesque heap of corpses. Back to where he could no longer stand. A rat disappeared into the seam to his left. He dropped to his stomach and flicked the flashlight on. Crawled after it.

He crawled into a skeleton. He scrabbled with his feet and came face-to-face with a grinning skull. And another. There were four or five skeletons jammed into the excavated seam. Jumbled bones in a pile. He gasped in shock and backed off a foot. Looked carefully. Used the flashlight close up.

All males. He could see that from the five pelvises. The skulls showed gunshot wounds. All in the temples. Neat entry wounds, neat exit holes. Jacketed high-velocity handgun bullets. Fairly recent, certainly within a year. The flesh hadn't decayed. It had been eaten off. He could see the parallel scrape marks on the bones from rodent teeth.

The bones were all disturbed. The rats had hauled them away to eat. There were scraps of clothing material here and there. Some of the rib cages were still covered. Rats don't disturb clothing much. Not on the torso. Why should they? They eat their way in through the inside. The soft parts first. They come to the ribs from the back.

The clothing material was khaki and olive green. Some black and gray camouflage. Reacher saw a colored thread. Traced it back to a shoulder flash hidden under a gnawed shoulder blade. It was a curved felt badge embroidered in silk. It said: Northwestern Freemen. He pulled at the skeleton's jacket. The rib cage collapsed. The breast pocket had three chromium stars punched through.

Reacher made a thorough search, lying on his stomach, up

to his armpits in bones. He pieced together five separate uniforms. He found two more badges. One said: White Christian Identity. The other said: Montana Constitutional Militia. He lined up the five splintered skulls. Checked the teeth. He was looking at five men, middle-aged, maybe between forty and fifty. Five leaders. The leaders who had disappeared. The leaders who could not stand the pace. The leaders who had abandoned their members to Beau Borken.

The roof was too low for Reacher to climb over the bones. He had to push them aside and crawl through them. The rats showed no interest. These bones were picked clean. Their new feast lay back inside the cavern. They swarmed back in that direction. He held the flashlight out in front of him and pushed on into the mountain against the squealing tide.

He lost his sense of direction. He hoped he was going roughly west, but he couldn't tell. The roof came down to a couple of feet. He was crawling through an old geological seam, excavated long ago for its ore. The roof came down even more. Down to a foot and a half. It was cold. The seam narrowed. His arms were out in front of him. The seam became too narrow to pull them back. He was crawling down a slim rock tube, a billion tons of mountain above him, no idea where he was going. And the flashlight was failing. The battery was spent. Its light was fading to a dull orange glow.

He was breathing hard. And shaking. Not from exertion. From dread. From terror. This was not what he had expected. He had visualized a stroll down a spacious abandoned gallery. Not this narrow crack in the rock. He was pushing himself headfirst into his worst childhood nightmare. He was a guy who had survived most things, and he was a guy who was rarely afraid. But he had known since his early boyhood that he was terrified of being trapped in the dark in a space too small to turn his giant frame. All his damp childhood nightmares had been about being closed into tight spaces. He lay on his stomach and screwed his eyes shut. Lay and panted and gagged. Forced the air in and out through his clamping throat. Then he inched himself slowly onward into the nightmare.

The glow from the flashlight finally died a hundred yards into the tunnel. The darkness was total. The seam was narrowing. It was pushing his shoulders down. He was forcing himself into a space that was way too small for him. His face was forced sideways. He fought to stay calm. He remembered what he had said to Borken: people were smaller then. Scrappy little guys, migrating west, seeking their fortune in the bowels of the mountain. People half the size of Reacher, squirming along, maybe on their backs, chipping the bright veins out of the rock roof.

He was using the dead flashlight like a blind man uses a white cane. It smashed on solid rock two feet ahead of his face. He heard the tinkle of glass over the rasping of his breath. He struggled ahead and felt with his hands. A solid wall. The tunnel went no farther. He tried to move backward. He couldn't move at all. To push himself backward with his hands, he had to raise his chest to get leverage. But the roof was too low to let him do that. His shoulders were jammed up hard against it. He could get no leverage. His feet could push him forward, but they couldn't pull him backward. He went rigid with panic. His throat clamped solid. His head hit the roof and his cheek hit the grit floor. He fought a scream by breathing fast.

He had to go back. He hooked his toes into the grit. Turned his hands inward and planted his thumbs on the floor. Pulled with his toes and pushed with his thumbs. He moved backward a fraction and then the rock clamped hard against his sides. To slide his weight backward, his shoulder muscles were bunching and jamming against the rock. He breathed out and let his arms go limp. Pulled with his toes. They scrabbled uselessly in the grit. He helped them with his thumbs. His shoulders bunched and jammed again. He jerked his hips from side to side. He had a couple of inches to spare. He smashed his hands into the shale and heaved backward. His body jammed solid, like a wedge in a door. He tilted sideways and banged his cheek on the roof. Jerked back down and caught his other cheek on the floor. The rock was crushing in on his ribs. This time, he couldn't fight the scream. He had to let it go. He opened his mouth and wailed in terror. The air in his lungs crushed his chest against the floor and his back against the roof.

He couldn't tell if his eyes were open or shut. He pushed

forward with his feet and regained the inch he'd moved back.
He stretched with his arms. Felt up ahead again. His shoulders were jammed so tight he couldn't move his hands
through much of an angle. He spread his fingers and scrabbled them left and right, up and down. Solid rock ahead. No
way to go forward. No way to move backward.

He was going to die trapped inside the mountain. He knew
it. The rats knew it. They were sniffing up behind him. Coming closer. He felt them at his feet. He kicked out and sent
them squealing away. But they came back. He felt their
weight on his legs. They were swarming over him. They
burrowed up around his shoulders. Slid under his armpits. He
felt cold oily fur on his face as they forced their way past.
The flick of their tails as they ran ahead.

To where? He let them run over his arm, to estimate their
direction. They were moving ahead of him, into the blind
darkness. He felt with his hands. Felt them flowing left. Their
passage was stirring the air. The air was cool. He felt it move,
a faint breeze, on the sweat on the left side of his face. He
jammed himself hard against the right-hand wall and moved
his left arm sideways, ahead of him. Felt for the left-hand
wall. It wasn't there. He was stuck at a junction in the tunnels. A new seam ran at a right angle away from the end of
the seam he was in. A tight, narrow right angle. Ninety degrees. He forced himself backward as far as his thumbs would
push him. He scraped his face on the end wall and jammed
his side into the rock. Folded himself arms first around the
corner and dragged his legs behind him.

The new seam was no better. It was no wider. The roof
was no higher. He hauled himself along, gasping and sweating and shaking. He propelled himself with his toes, an inch
at a time. The rats forced their way past him. The rock tore
at his sides and his back. But there was still a slight breeze
on his face. The tunnel was heading somewhere. He was
gasping and panting. He crawled on. Then the new seam
widened. Still very low. A flat, low crack in the rock. He
crawled on through it, exhausted. Fifty yards. A hundred.
Then he felt the roof soar away above him. He pushed on
with his toes and suddenly he felt the air change and he was
lying halfway into the motor pool cavern. He realized his

eyes were wide open and the white Econoline was right there in front of him in the dark.

He rolled onto his back and lay gasping on the grit. Gasping and shaking. Staggered to his feet and looked back. The seam was invisible. Hidden in the shadow. He made it as far as the white truck and collapsed against its side. The luminous figures on his watch showed he'd been in the tunnels nearly three hours. Most of the time jammed there sweating in panic. A three-hour screaming nightmare come to life. His pants and his jacket were shredded. Every muscle in his body was on fire. His face and hands and elbows and knees were bleeding. But it was the fear that had done it to him. The fear of not getting through. He could still feel the rock pressing down on his back and pressing up on his chest. He could feel it clamping inward on his ribs. He got up again and limped to the doors. Pushed them open and stood in the moonlight, arms out, eyes crazy, mouth open, breathing in lungfuls of the sweet night air.

He WAS HALFWAY across the bowl before he started thinking straight. So he ran back and ducked into the motor pool once more. Found what he wanted. He found it on one of the jeep's tow-hook assemblies. Some heavy stiff wire, ready to feed a trailer's electric circuits. He wrenched it out and stripped the insulation with his teeth. Ran back to the moonlight.

He kept close to the road, all the way back to Yorke. Two miles, twenty minutes at a slow agonizing jog through the trees. He looped around behind the ruined northeastern block and approached the courthouse from the rear. Circled it silently in the shadows. Waited and listened.

He tried to think like Borken. Complacent. Happy with his perimeter. Constant information from inside the FBI. Reacher locked into the punishment hut, Holly locked into her prison room. Would he post a sentry? Not tonight. Not when he was expecting heavy action tomorrow and beyond. He would want his people fresh. Reacher nodded to himself and gambled he was right.

He arrived at the courthouse steps. Deserted. He tried the door. Locked. He smiled. Nobody posts a sentry behind a locked door. He bent the wire into a shallow hook and felt for the mechanism. An old two-lever. Eight seconds. He stepped inside. Waited and listened. Nothing. He went up the stairs.

The lock on Holly's door was new. But cheap. He worked quietly, which delayed him. Took him more than thirty seconds before the last tumbler clicked back. He pulled the door open slowly and stepped onto the built-up floor. Glanced apprehensively at the walls. She was on a mattress on the floor. Fully dressed and ready. Awake and watching him. Huge eyes bright in the gloom. He gestured her outside. Turned and climbed down and waited in the corridor for her. She picked up her crutch and limped to the door. Climbed carefully down the step and stood next to him.

"Hello, Reacher," she whispered. "How are you doing?"

"I've felt better," he whispered back. "Time to time."

She turned and glanced back into her room. He followed her gaze and saw the dark stain on the floor.

"Woman who brought me lunch," she whispered.

He nodded.

"What with?" he whispered back.

"Part of the bed frame," she said.

He saw the satisfaction on her face and smiled.

"That should do it," he said, quietly. "Bed frames are good for that."

She took a last look at the room and gently closed the door. Followed him through the dark and slowly down the stairs. Across the lobby and through the double doors and out into the bright silent moonlight.

"Christ," she said, urgently. "What happened to you?"

He glanced down and checked himself over in the light of the moon. He was gray from head to foot with dust and grit. His clothing was shredded. He was streaked with sweat and blood. Still shaky.

"Long story," he said. "You got somebody in Chicago you can trust?"

"McGrath," she said immediately. "He's my Agent-in-Charge. Why?"

They crossed the wide street arm in arm, looking left and right. Skirted the mound in front of the ruined office building. Found the path running northwest.

"You need to send him a fax," he said. "They've got missiles. You need to warn him. Tonight, because their line is going to be cut first thing in the morning."

"The mole tell them that?" she asked.

He nodded.

"How?" she asked. "How is he communicating?"

"Shortwave radio," Reacher said. "Has to be. Anything else is traceable."

He swayed and leaned on a tree. Gave her the spread, everything, beginning to end.

"Shit," she said. "Ground-to-air missiles? Mass suicide? A nightmare."

"Not our nightmare," he said. "We're out of here."

"We should stay and help them," she said. "The families."

He shook his head.

"Best help is for us to get out," he said. "Maybe losing you will change their plan. And we can tell them about the layout around here."

"I don't know," she said.

"I do," he said. "First rule is stick to priorities. That's you. We're out of here."

She shrugged and nodded.

"Now?" she asked.

"Right now," he said.

"How?" she asked.

"Jeep through the forest," he said. "I found their motor pool. We get up there, steal a jeep, by then it should be light enough to find our way through. I saw a map in Borken's office. There are plenty of tracks running east through the forest."

She nodded and he pushed off the tree. They hustled up the winding path to the Bastion. A mile, in the dark. They stumbled on the stones and saved their breath for walking. The clearing was dark and silent. They worked their way around beyond the mess hall to the back of the communications hut. They came out of the trees and Reacher stepped close and pressed his ear to the plywood siding. There was no sound inside.

He used the wire again and they were inside within ten

seconds. Holly found paper and pen. Wrote her message. Dialed the Chicago fax number and fed the sheet into the machine. It whirred obediently and pulled the paper through. Fed it back out into her waiting hand. She hit the button for the confirmation. Didn't want to leave any trace behind. Another sheet fed out. It showed the destination number correct. Timed the message at ten minutes to five, Friday morning, the fourth of July. She shredded both papers small and buried the pieces in the bottom of a trashcan.

Reacher rooted around on the long counter and found a paper clip. Followed Holly back out into the moonlight and relocked the door. Dodged around and found the cable leading down from the shortwave whip into the side of the hut. Took the paper clip and worried at it until it broke. Forced the broken end through the cable like a pin. Pushed it through until it was even, a fraction showing at each side. The metal would short-circuit the antenna by connecting the wire inside to the foil screen. The signal would come down out of the ether, down the wire, leak into the foil and run away to ground without ever reaching the shortwave unit itself. The best way to disable a radio. Smash one up, it gets repaired. This way, the fault is untraceable, until an exhausted technician finally thinks to check.

"We need weapons," Holly whispered to him.

He nodded. They crept together to the armory door. He looked at the lock. Gave it up. It was a huge thing. Unpickable.

"I'll take the Glock from the guy guarding me," he whispered.

She nodded. They ducked back into the trees and walked through to the next clearing. Reacher tried to think of a story to explain his appearance to Joseph Ray. Figured he might say something about being beamed over to the UN. Talk about how high-speed beaming can rip you up a little. They crept around behind the punishment hut and listened. All quiet. They skirted the corner and Reacher pulled the door. Walked straight into a nine-millimeter. This time, it wasn't a Glock. It was a Sig-Sauer. Not Joseph Ray's. It was Beau Borken's. He was standing just inside the door with Little Stevie at his side, grinning.

37

FOUR-THIRTY IN THE morning, Webster was more than ready for the watch change. Johnson and Garber and the General's aide were dozing in their chairs. McGrath was outside with the telephone linemen. They were just finishing up. The job had taken much longer than they had anticipated. Some kind of interface problem. They had physically cut the phone line coming out of Yorke, and bent the stiff copper down to a temporary terminal box they had placed at the base of a pole. Then they had spooled cable from the terminal box down the road to the mobile command vehicle. Connected it into one of the communications ports.

But it didn't work. Not right away. The linemen had fussed with multimeters and muttered about impedances and capacitances. They had worked for three solid hours. They were ready to blame the Army truck for the incompatibility when they thought to go back and check their own temporary terminal box. The fault lay there. A failed component. They wired in a spare and the whole circuit worked perfectly. Four thirty-five in the morning, McGrath was shaking their hands and swearing them to silence when Webster came out of the trailer. The two men stood and watched them drive away. The noise of their truck died around the curve. Webster and McGrath stayed standing in the bright moonlight. They stood there for five minutes while McGrath smoked. They didn't speak. Just gazed north into the distance and wondered.

"Go wake your boys up," Webster said. "We'll stand down for a spell."

McGrath nodded and walked down to the accommodation trailers. Roused Milosevic and Brogan. They were fully dressed on their bunks. They got up and yawned. Came down the ladder and found Webster standing there with Johnson and his aide. Garber standing behind them.

"The telephone line is done," Webster said.

"Already?" Brogan said. "I thought it was being done in the morning."

"We figured sooner was better than later," Webster said. He inclined his head toward General Johnson. It was a gesture which said: he's worried, right?

"OK," Milosevic said. "We'll look after it."

"Wake us at eight," Webster said. "Or earlier if necessary, OK?"

Brogan nodded and walked north to the command vehicle. Milosevic followed. They paused together for a look at the mountains in the moonlight. As they paused, the fax machine inside the empty command trailer started whirring. It fed its first communication face upward into the message tray. It was ten to five in the morning, Friday the fourth of July.

BROGAN WOKE GENERAL Johnson an hour and ten minutes later, six o'clock exactly. He knocked loudly on the accommodation trailer door and got no response, so he went in and shook the old guy by the shoulder.

"Peterson Air Force Base, sir," Brogan said. "They need to talk to you."

Johnson staggered up to the command vehicle in his shirt and pants. Milosevic joined Brogan outside in the predawn glow to give him some privacy. Johnson was back out in five minutes.

"We need a conference," he called.

He ducked back into the trailer. Milosevic walked down and roused the others. They came forward, Webster and the General's aide yawning and stretching, Garber ramrod-straight. McGrath was dressed and smoking. Maybe hadn't tried to sleep at all. They filed up the ladder and took their places around the table, bleak red eyes, hair fuzzed on the back from the pillows.

"Peterson called," Johnson told them. "They're sending a helicopter search-and-rescue out, first light, looking for the missile unit."

His aide nodded.

"That would be standard procedure," he said.

"Based on an assumption," Johnson said. "They think the unit has suffered some kind of mechanical and electrical malfunction."

"Which is not uncommon," his aide said. "If their radio fails, their procedure would be to repair it. If a truck also broke down at the same time, their procedure would be to wait as a group for assistance."

"Circle the wagons?" McGrath asked.

The aide nodded again.

"Exactly so," he said. "They would pull off the road and wait for a chopper."

"So do we tell them?" McGrath asked.

The aide sat forward.

"That's the question," he said. "Tell them what exactly? We don't even know for sure that these maniacs have got them at all. It's still possible it's just a radio problem and a truck problem together."

"Dream on," Johnson said.

Webster shrugged. He knew how to deal with such issues.

"What's the upside?" he said.

"There is no upside," Johnson said. "We tell Peterson the missiles have been captured, the cat's out of the bag, we lose control of the situation, we're seen to have disobeyed Washington by making an issue out of it before Monday."

"OK, so what's the downside?" Webster asked.

"Theoretical," Johnson said. "We have to assume they've been captured, so we also have to assume they've been well hidden. In which case the Air Force will never find them. They'll just fly around for a while and then go home and wait."

Webster nodded.

"OK," he said. "No upside, no downside, no problem."

There was a short silence.

"So we sit tight," Johnson said. "We let the chopper fly."

McGrath shook his head. Incredulous.

"Suppose they use them to shoot the chopper down?" he asked.

The General's aide smiled an indulgent smile.

"Can't be done," he said. "The IFF wouldn't allow it."

"IFF?" McGrath repeated.

"Identify Friend or Foe," the aide said. "It's an electronic system. The chopper will be beaming a signal. The missile reads it as friendly, refuses to launch."

"Guaranteed?" McGrath asked.

The aide nodded.

"Foolproof," he said.

Garber glowered at him. But he said nothing. Not his field of expertise.

"OK," Webster said. "Back to bed. Wake us again at eight, Brogan."

ON THE TARMAC at Peterson, a Boeing CH-47D Chinook was warming its engines and sipping the first of its eight hundred and fifty-eight gallons of fuel. A Chinook is a giant aircraft, whose twin rotors thump through an oval of air a hundred feet long and sixty wide. It weighs more than ten tons empty, and it can lift another eleven. It's a giant flying box, the engines and the fuel tanks strapped to the top and the sides, the crew perched high at the front. Any helicopter can search, but when heavy equipment is at stake, only a Chinook can rescue.

Because of the holiday weekend, the Peterson dispatcher assigned a skeleton crew of two. No separate spotter. He figured he didn't need one. How difficult could it be to find five Army trucks on some shoulder in Montana?

YOU SHOULD HAVE stayed here," Borken said. "Right, Joe?"

Reacher glanced into the gloom inside the punishment hut. Joseph Ray was standing to attention on the yellow square. He was staring straight ahead. He was naked. Bleeding from the mouth and nose.

"Right, Joe?" Borken said again.

Ray made no reply. Borken walked over and crashed his fist into his face. Ray stumbled and fell backward. Staggered against the back wall and scrambled to regain his position on the square.

"I asked you a question," Borken said.

Ray nodded. The blood poured off his chin.

"Reacher should have stayed here," he said.

Borken hit him again. A hard straight right to the face. Ray's head snapped back. Blood spurted. Borken smiled.

"No talking when you're on the square, Joe," he said. "You know the rules."

Borken stepped back and placed the muzzle of the Sig-Sauer in Reacher's ear. Used it to propel him out into the clearing. Gestured Stevie to follow.

"You stay on the square, Joe," he called over his shoulder.

Stevie slammed the door shut. Borken reversed his direction and used the Sig-Sauer to shove Reacher toward him.

"Tell Fowler to get rid of this guy," he told him. "He's outlived his usefulness, such as it ever was. Put the bitch back in her room. Put a ring of sentries right around the building. We got things to do, right? No time for this shit. Parade ground at six-thirty. Everybody there. I'm going to read them the proclamation, before we fax it."

MCGRATH COULDN'T SLEEP. He walked back to the accommodations trailer with the others and got back on his bunk, but he gave it up after ten minutes. Quarter to seven in the morning, he was back in the command vehicle with Brogan and Milosevic.

"You guys take a break if you want," he said. "I'll look after things here."

"We could go organize some breakfast," Brogan said. "Diners in Kalispell should be open by now."

McGrath nodded vaguely. Started into his jacket for his wallet.

"Don't worry about it," Brogan said. "I'll pay. My treat."

"OK, thanks," McGrath said. "Get coffee. Lots of it."

Brogan and Milosevic stood up and left. McGrath stood in the doorway and watched them drive an Army sedan south. The sound of the car faded and he was left with the silent humming of the equipment behind him. He turned to sit down. The clock ticked around to seven. The fax machine started whirring.

Holly smoothed her hands over the old mattress like Reacher was there on it. Like it was really his body under her, scarred and battered, hot and hard and muscular, not a worn striped cotton cover stuffed with ancient horsehair. She blinked the tears out of her eyes. Blew a deep sigh and focused on the next decision. No Reacher, no Jackson, no weapon, no tools, six sentries in the street outside. She glanced around the room for the thousandth time and started scoping it out all over again.

McGrath woke the others by thumping on the sides of the accommodations trailer with both fists. Then he ran back to the command post and found a third copy of the message spooling out of the machine. He already had two. Now he had three.

Webster was the first into the trailer. Then Johnson, a minute behind. Then Garber, and finally the General's aide. They rattled up the ladder one by one and hurried over to the table. McGrath was absorbed in reading.

"What, Mack?" Webster asked him.

"They're declaring independence," McGrath said. "Listen to this."

He glanced around the four faces. Started reading out loud.

"Governments are instituted among men," he read. "Deriving their just powers from the consent of the governed. It is the right of the people to alter or abolish them after a long train of abuses and usurpations."

"They're quoting from the original," Webster said.

"Paraphrasing," Garber said.

McGrath nodded.

"Listen to this," he said again. "The history of the present government of the United States is a history of repeated injuries and usurpations all designed to establish an absolute tyranny over the people."

"What the hell is this?" Webster said. "1776 all over again?"

"It gets worse," McGrath said. "We therefore are the representatives of the Free States of America, located initially in what was formerly Yorke County in what was formerly Montana, and we solemnly publish and declare that this territory is now a free and independent State, which is absolved of allegiance to the United States, with all political connection totally dissolved, and that as a free and independent State has full power to levy war, conclude peace, defend its land borders and its airspace, contract alliances, establish commerce, and to do all other things as all independent States may do."

He looked up. Shuffled the three copies into a neat stack and laid them on the table in silence.

"Why three copies?" Garber asked.

"Three destinations," McGrath said. "If we hadn't intercepted them, they'd be all over the place by now."

"Where?" Webster asked.

"First one is a D.C. number," McGrath said. "I'm guessing it's the White House."

Johnson's aide scooted his chair to the computer terminal. McGrath read him the number. He tapped it in, and the screen scrolled down. He nodded.

"The White House," he said. "Next?"

"New York somewhere," McGrath said. Read out the number from the second sheet.

"United Nations," the aide said. "They want witnesses."

"Third one, I don't know," McGrath said. "Area code is 404."

"Atlanta, Georgia," Garber said.

"What's in Atlanta, Georgia?" Webster asked.

The aide was busy at the keyboard.

"CNN," he said. "They want publicity."

Johnson nodded.

"Smart moves," he said. "They want it all on live TV. Christ, can you imagine? The United Nations as umpires and round-the-clock coverage on the cable news? The whole world watching?"

"So what do we do?" Webster asked.

There was a long silence.

"Why did they say airspace?" Garber asked out loud.

"They were paraphrasing," Webster said. "1776, there wasn't any airspace."

"The missiles," Garber said. "Is it possible they've disabled the IFF?"

There was another long silence. They heard a car pull up. Doors slammed. Brogan and Milosevic rattled up the ladder and stepped into the hush. They carried brown bags and Styrofoam cups with plastic lids.

THE GIANT SEARCH-AND-RESCUE Chinook made it north from Peterson in Colorado to Malmstrom Air Force Base outside of Great Falls in Montana without incident. It touched down there and fuel bowsers came out to meet it. The crew walked to the mess for coffee. Walked back twenty minutes later. Took off again and swung gently in the morning air before lumbering away northwest.

38

W<small>E'RE GETTING NO</small> reaction,'' Fowler said. "Makes us wonder why.''

Reacher shrugged at him. They were in the command hut. Stevie had dragged him through the trees to the Bastion, and then Fowler had dragged him back again with two armed guards. The punishment hut was unavailable. Still occupied by Joseph Ray. They used the command hut instead. They sat Reacher down and Fowler locked his left wrist to the arm of the chair with a handcuff. The guards took up position on either side, rifles sloped, watchful. Then Fowler walked up to join Borken and Stevie for the ceremony on the parade ground. Reacher heard faint shouting and cheering in the distance as the proclamation was read out. Then he heard nothing. Ninety minutes later, Fowler came back to the hut alone. He sat down behind Borken's desk and lit a cigarette, and the armed guards remained standing.

"We faxed it an hour ago,'' Fowler said. "No reaction.''

Reacher smelled his smoke and gazed at the banners on the walls. Dark reds and dull whites, vivid crooked symbols in black.

"Do you know why we're getting no reaction?'' Fowler asked.

Reacher just shook his head.

"You know what I think?'' Fowler said. "They cut the line. Phone company is colluding with the federal agents. We were told it would happen at seven-thirty. It obviously happened earlier.''

Reacher shrugged again. Made no reply.

''We would expect to be informed about a thing like that,'' Fowler said.

He picked up his Glock, and propped it in front of him, butt on the desktop, swiveling it like naval artillery left and right.

''And we haven't been,'' he said.

''Maybe your pal from Chicago has given you up,'' Reacher said.

Fowler shook his head. His Glock came to rest, aimed at Reacher's chest.

''We've been getting a stream of intelligence,'' he said. ''We know where they are, how many of them there are, what their intentions are. But now, when we still need information, we aren't getting it. Communication has been interrupted.''

Reacher said nothing.

''We're investigating,'' Fowler said. ''We're checking the radio right now.''

Reacher said nothing.

''Anything you want to tell us about the radio?'' Fowler asked.

''What radio?'' Reacher said.

''It worked OK yesterday,'' Fowler said. ''Now it doesn't work at all, and you were wandering around all night.''

He ducked down and rolled open the drawer where Borken kept the Colt Marshal. But he didn't come out with a revolver. He came out with a small black radio transmitter.

''This was Jackson's,'' he said. ''He was most anxious to show us where it was hidden. In fact he was begging to show us. He screamed and cried and begged. Just about tore his fingernails off digging it up, he was so anxious.''

He smiled and put the unit carefully in his pocket.

''We figure we just switch it on,'' he said. ''That should put us straight through to the federal scum, person to person. This stage of the process, we need to talk direct. See if we can persuade them to restore our fax line.''

''Terrific plan,'' Reacher said.

"The fax line is important, you see," Fowler said. "Vital. The world must be allowed to know what we're doing here. The world must be allowed to watch and witness. History is being made here. You understand that, right?"

Reacher stared at the wall.

"They've got cameras, you know," Fowler said. "Surveillance planes are up there right now. Now it's daylight again, they can see what we're doing. So how can we exploit that fact?"

Reacher shook his head.

"You can leave me out of it," he said.

Fowler smiled.

"Of course we'll leave you out of it," he said. "Why would they care about seeing you nailed to a tree? You're nothing but a piece of shit, to us and to them. But Holly Johnson, there's a different story. Maybe we'll call them up on their own little transmitter and tell them to watch us do it with their own spy cameras. That might make them think about it. They might trade a fax line for her left breast."

He ground out his cigarette. Leaned forward. Spoke quietly.

"We're serious here, Reacher," he said. "You saw what we did to Jackson. We could do that to her. We could do that to you. We need to be able to communicate with the world. We need that fax line. So we need the shortwave to confirm what the hell they've done with it. We need those things very badly. You understand that, right? So if you want to avoid a lot of unnecessary pain, for you and for her, you better tell me what you did to the radio."

Reacher was twisted around, looking at the bookcase. Trying to recall the details of the inexpert translations of the Japanese Pearl Harbor texts he'd read.

"Tell me now," Fowler said softly. "I can keep them away from you and from her. No pain for either of you. Otherwise, nothing I can do about it."

He laid his Glock on the desk.

"You want a cigarette?" he asked.

He held out the pack. Smiled. The good cop. The friend. The ally. The protector. The oldest routine in the book. Requiring the oldest response. Reacher glanced around. Two guards, one on each side of him, the right-hand guard nearer, the left-hand guard back almost against the side wall. Rifles held easy in the crook of their arms. Fowler behind the desk, holding out the pack. Reacher shrugged and nodded. Took a cigarette with his free right hand. He hadn't smoked in ten years, but when somebody offers you a lethal weapon, you take it.

"So tell me," Fowler said. "And be quick."

He thumbed his lighter and held it out. Reacher bent forward and lit his cigarette from the flame. Took a deep draw and leaned back. The smoke felt good. Ten years, and he still enjoyed it. He inhaled deeply and took another lungful.

"How did you disable our radio?" Fowler asked.

Reacher took a third pull. Trickled the smoke out of his nose and held the cigarette like a sentry does, between the thumb and forefinger, palm hooded around it. Take quick deep pulls, and the coal on the end of a cigarette heats up to a couple of thousand degrees. Lengthens to a point. He rotated his palm, like he was studying the glowing tip while he thought about something, until the cigarette was pointing straight forward like an arrow.

"How did you disable our radio?" Fowler asked again.

"You'll hurt Holly if I don't tell you?" Reacher asked back.

Fowler nodded. Smiled his lipless smile.

"That's a promise," he said. "I'll hurt her so bad, she'll be begging to die."

Reacher shrugged unhappily. Sketched a listen-up gesture. Fowler nodded and shuffled on his chair and leaned close. Reacher snapped forward and jammed the cigarette into his eye. Fowler screamed and Reacher was on his feet, the chair cuffed to his wrist clattering after him. He windmilled right and the chair swung through a wide arc and smashed against the nearer guard's head. It splintered and jerked away as Reacher danced to his left. He caught the farther guard with a forearm smash to the throat as his rifle came up. Snapped back and hit Fowler with the wreckage of the chair. Used the follow-through momentum to swing back to the first guard. Finished him with an elbow to the head. The guy went down. Reacher grabbed his rifle by the barrel and swung straight back at the other guard. Felt skull bones explode under the butt. He dropped the rifle and spun and smashed the chair to pieces against Fowler's shoulders. Grabbed him by the ears and smashed his face into the desktop, once, twice, three times. Took a leg from the broken chair and jammed it crossways under his throat. Folded his elbows around each exposed end and locked his hands together. Tested his grip and bunched his shoulders. Jerked hard, once, and broke Fowler's neck against the chair leg with a single loud crunch.

He took both rifles and the Glock and the handcuff key. Out the door and around to the back of the hut. Straight into the trees. He put the Glock in his pocket. Took the handcuff off his wrist. Put a rifle in each hand. Breathing hard. He was in pain. Swinging the heavy wooden chair had opened the red weal on his wrist into a wound. He raised it to his mouth and sucked at it and buttoned the cuff of his shirt over it.

Then he heard a helicopter. The faint bass thumping of a heavy twin-rotor machine, a Boeing, a Sea Knight or a Chinook, far to the southeast. He thought: last night Borken talked about eight Marines. They've only got eight Marines, he said. The Marines use Sea Knights. He thought: they're going for a frontal assault. Holly's paneled walls flashed into his mind and he set off racing through the trees.

He got as far as the Bastion. The thumping from the air built louder. He risked stepping out onto the stony path. It was a Chinook. Not a Sea Knight. Search-and-rescue markings, not Marine Corps. It was following the road up from the southeast, a mile away, a hundred feet up, using its vicious downdraft to part the surrounding foliage and aid its search. It looked slow and ponderous, hanging nose down in the air, yawing slightly from side to side as it approached. Reacher guessed it must be pretty close to the town of Yorke itself.

Then he glanced into the clearing and saw a guy, fifty yards away. A grunt, camouflage fatigues. A Stinger on his shoulder. Turning and aiming through the crude open sight. He saw him acquire the target. The guy steadied himself and stood with his feet apart. His hand fumbled for the activator. The missile's infrared sensor turned on. Reacher waited for the IFF to shut it down. It didn't happen. The missile started squealing its high-pitched tone. It was locked on the heat from the Chinook's engines. The guy's finger tightened on the trigger.

Reacher dropped the rifle in his left hand. Swung the other one up and clicked the safety off with his thumb as he did so. Stepped to his left and leaned his shoulder on a tree. Aimed at the guy's head and fired.

But the guy fired first. A fraction of a second before Reacher's bullet killed him, he pulled the Stinger's trigger. Two things happened. The Stinger's rocket motor lit up. It exploded along its launch tube. Then the guy was hit in the head. The impact knocked him sideways. The launcher caught the rear of the missile and flipped it. It came out and stalled tail down in the air like a javelin, cushioned on the thrust of its launch, virtually motionless.

Then it corrected itself. Reacher watched in horror as it did exactly what it was designed to do. Its eight little wings popped out. It hung almost vertical until it acquired the helicopter again. Then its second-stage rocket lit up and it blasted into the sky. Before the guy's body hit the ground, it was homing in on the Chinook at a thousand miles an hour.

The Chinook was lumbering steadily northwest. A mile away. Following the road. The road ran straight up through the town. Between the abandoned buildings. On the southeast corner the first building it passed was the courthouse. The Chinook was closing on it at eighty miles an hour. The Stinger was heading in to meet it at a thousand miles an hour.

One mile at a thousand miles an hour. One thousandth of an hour. A fraction over three and a half seconds. It felt like a lifetime to Reacher. He watched the missile all the way. A wonderful, brutal weapon. A simple, unshakable purpose. Designed to recognize the exact heat signature of aircraft exhaust, designed to follow it until it either got there or ran out of fuel. A simple three-and-a-half-second mission.

The Chinook pilot saw it early. He wasted the first second of its flight, frozen. Not in horror, not in fear, just in simple disbelief that a heat-seeking missile had been fired at him from a small wooded clearing in Montana. Then his instinct and training took over. Evade and avoid. Evade the missile, avoid crashing on settlements below. Reacher saw him throw the nose down and the tail up. The big Chinook wheeled away and spewed a wide fan of exhaust into the atmosphere. Then the tail flipped the other way, engines screaming, superheated fumes spraying another random arc. The missile patiently followed the first curve. Tightened its radius. The Chinook dropped slowly and then rose violently in the air. Spiraled upward and away from the town. The missile turned and followed the second arc. Arrived at where the heat had been a split second before. Couldn't find it. It turned a full lazy circle right underneath the helicopter. Caught an echo of the new maneuver and set about climbing a relentless new spiral.

The pilot won an extra second, but that was all. The Stinger caught him right at the top of his desperate climb. It followed the trail of heat all the way into the starboard engine itself. Exploded hard against the exhaust nacelle.

Six and a half pounds of high explosive against ten tons of aircraft, but the explosive always wins. Reacher saw the starboard engine disintegrate, then the rear rotor housing blow off. Shattered fragments of the drivetrain exploded outward like shrapnel and the rotor detached and spun away in terrible slow motion. The Chinook stalled in the air and fell, tail down, checked only by the screaming forward rotor, and slowly spun to the earth, like a holed ship slips slowly below the sea.

HOLLY HEARD THE helicopter. She heard the low-frequency beat pulsing faintly through her walls. She heard it grow louder. Then she heard the explosion and the shriek of the forward rotor grabbing the air. Then she heard nothing.

She jammed her elbow into her crutch and limped across to the diagonal partition. The prison room was completely empty except for the mattress. So her search was going to have to start again in the bathroom.

ONLY ONE QUESTION," Webster said. "How long can we keep the lid on this?"

General Johnson said nothing in reply. Neither did his aide. Webster moved his gaze across to Garber. Garber was looking grim.

"Not too damn long," he said.

"But how long?" Webster asked. "A day? An hour?"

"Six hours," Garber said.

"Why?" McGrath asked.

"Standard procedure," Garber said. "They'll investigate the crash, obviously. Normally they'd send another chopper out. But not if there's a suspicion of ground fire. So they'll come by road from Malmstrom. Six hours."

Webster nodded. Turned to Johnson.

"Can you delay them, General?" he asked.

Johnson shook his head.

"Not really," he said. His voice was low and resigned. "They just lost a Chinook. Crew of two. I can't call them and say, do me a favor, don't investigate that. I could try, I guess, and they might agree at first, but it would leak, and then we'd be back where we started. Might gain us an hour."

Webster nodded.

"Seven hours, six hours, what's the difference?" he said.

Nobody replied.

"We've got to move now," McGrath said. "Forget the White House. We can't wait any longer. We need to do something right now, people. Six hours from now, the whole situation blows right out of control. We'll lose her."

Six hours is three hundred and sixty minutes. They wasted the first two sitting in silence. Johnson stared into space. Webster drummed his fingers on the table. Garber stared at McGrath, a wry expression on his face. McGrath was staring at the map. Milosevic and Brogan were standing in the silence, holding the brown bags of breakfast and the Styrofoam cups.

"Coffee here, anybody wants it," Brogan said.

Garber waved him over.

"Eat and plan," he said.

"Map," Johnson said.

McGrath slid the map across the table. They all sat forward. Back in motion. Three hundred and fifty-eight minutes to go.

"Ravine's about four miles north of us," the aide said. "All we got is eight Marines in a LAV-25."

"That tank thing?" McGrath asked.

The aide shook his head.

"Light armored vehicle," he said. "LAV. Eight wheels, no tracks."

"Bulletproof?" Webster asked.

"For sure," the aide said. "They can drive it all the way to Yorke."

"If it gets through the ravine," Garber said.

Johnson nodded.

"That's the big question," he said. "We need to go take a look."

THE LIGHT ARMORED vehicle looked just like a tank to McGrath's hasty civilian glance, except there were eight wheels on it instead of tracks. The hull was welded up out of brutal sloping armor plates and there was a turret with a gun. The driver sat forward, and the commander sat in the turret. In the rear, two rows of three Marines sat back to back, facing weapon ports. Each port had its own periscope. McGrath could visualize the vehicle rumbling into battle, invulnerable, weapons bristling out of those ports. Down into the ravine, up the other side, along the road to Yorke to the courthouse. He pulled Webster to one side and spoke urgently.

"We never told them," he said. "About the dynamite in the walls."

"And we're not going to," Webster said quietly. "The old guy would freak out. He's close to falling apart right now. I'm going to tell the Marines direct. They're going in there. They'll have to deal with it. Makes no difference if Johnson knows in advance or not."

McGrath intercepted Johnson and Webster ran over to the armored vehicle. McGrath saw the Marine commander leaning down from the turret. Saw him nodding and grimacing as Webster spoke. Then the General's aide fired up the Army Chevrolet. Johnson and Garber crammed into the front with him. McGrath jumped in back. Brogan and Milosevic crushed in alongside him.

Webster finished up and raced back to the Chevy. Squeezed in next to Milosevic. The LAV fired up its big diesel with a blast of black smoke. Then it crunched into gear and lumbered off north. The Chevy accelerated in its wake.

FOUR MILES NORTH, they crested a slight rise and entered a curve. Slowed and jammed to a stop in the lee of a craggy outcrop. The Marine commander vaulted down from the turret and ran north on the road. Webster and Johnson and McGrath got out and hurried after him. They paused together in the lee of the rock face and crept around the curve. Stared out and down into the ravine. It was an intimidating sight.

It ran left to right in front of them, more or less straight. And it was not just a trench. It was a trench and a step. The whole crust of the earth had fractured, and the southern plate had fallen below the level of the northern plate. Like adjacent sections of an old concrete highway, where a car thumps up an inch at the seam. Expanded to geological size, that inch was a fifty-foot disparity.

Where the earth had fractured and fallen, the edges had broken up into giant boulders. The scouring of the glaciers had tumbled those boulders south. The ice and the heave and the weather over a million years had raked out the fracture and turned it into a trench. It had cut back the rock plates to where they became solid again. Some places, it had carved a hundred-yard width. Other places, tougher seams of rock had kept the gap down to twenty yards.

Then the roots of a thousand generations of trees and the frozen water of the winters had eroded the edges until there was a steep ragged descent to the bottom and a steep ragged rise back up the northern side to the top, fifty feet higher than the starting point. There were stunted trees and tangled undergrowth and rock slides. The road itself was lifted progressively on concrete trestles and rose gently across a bridge. Then more concrete trestles set it down on the level ground to the north and it snaked away through the forest into the mountains.

But the bridge was blown. Charges had been exploded against the two center trestles. A twenty-foot section of the center span had fallen a hundred feet into the trench. The four men in the lee of the outcrop could see fragments of the road lying shattered in the bottom of the ravine.

"What do you think?" Johnson asked urgently.

The Marine commander was giving it a fast sweep through his field glasses. Left and right, up and down, examining the exact terrain.

"I think it's shit, sir," he said.

"Can you get through?" Johnson asked him.

The guy lowered his field glasses and shook his head.

"Not a hope in hell," he said.

He stepped across shoulder to shoulder with the General, so Johnson could share the same line of sight. Started talking rapidly and pointing as he did so.

"We could get down to the bottom," he said. "We could go in right there, where the rock slide gives us a reasonable descent. But getting up the other side is the problem, sir. The LAV can't climb much more than forty-five degrees. Most of the north face looks a lot steeper than that. Some places, it's near enough vertical. Any gentle slopes are overgrown. And they've felled trees. See there, sir?"

He pointed to a wooded area on the slope opposite. Trees had been felled and left lying with their chopped ends facing south.

"Abatises," the Marine said. "The vehicle is going to stall against them. No doubt about that. Coming uphill, slowly, those things would stop a tank. We go in there, we'll be trapped in the ditch, no doubt at all."

"So what the hell do we do?" Johnson said.

The Marine officer shrugged.

"Bring me some engineers," he said. "The gap they blew is only about twenty feet wide. We can bridge that."

"How long will that take?" Webster asked.

The Marine shrugged again.

"All the way up here?" he said. "Six hours? Maybe eight?"

"Way too long," Webster said.

Then the radio receiver in McGrath's pocket started crackling.

39

REACHER WAS HIDING out in the woods. Worried about the dogs. They were the only thing he wasn't certain about. People, he could handle. Dogs, he had very little experience.

He was in the trees, north of the Bastion, south of the rifle range. He had heard the Chinook hit the ground from a mile away. It hit tail first, smashing and tearing into the wooded slope. It looked to have slipped sideways in the air and missed the courthouse by two hundred yards. No explosions. Not from the courthouse or from the chopper itself. No sound of fuel tanks going up. Reacher was reasonably optimistic for the crew. He figured the trees and the collapse of the big boxy body might have cushioned the impact for them. He had known chopper crews survive worse.

He had an M-16 rifle in his hand and a Glock in his pocket. The Glock was fully loaded. Seventeen shells. The M-16 had the short clip. Twenty shells, less the one that had killed the guy with the missile. The second M-16 had the long clip. A full load of thirty. But it was hidden in the trees. Because Reacher had a rule: choose the weapon you know for certain is in working order.

He felt instinctively that the focus of attention would be in the southeast direction. That was where Holly was being held, and that was where the Chinook had come down. That was where the opposition forces would be massing. He felt people would be turning to face southeast, apprehensively, staring down into the rest of the United States, waiting. So he turned his back and headed northwest.

He moved cautiously. The bulk of the enemy was elsewhere, but he knew there were squads out looking for him. He knew they had already discovered Fowler's body. He had seen two separate patrols, searching the woods. Six men in each, heavily armed, crashing through the undergrowth, searching. Not difficult to avoid. But the dogs would be difficult to avoid. That was why he was worried. That was why he was moving cautiously.

He stayed in the trees and skirted the western end of the rifle range. Tracked back east around the parade ground. Fifty yards north, he turned again and paralleled the road up to the mines. He stayed in the trees and moved at a fast jog. Used the time to start laying out some priorities. And a timescale. He figured he had maybe three hours. Bringing down the Chinook was going to provoke some kind of a violent reaction. No doubt about that. But in all his years in the service, he had never known anything to happen faster than three hours. So he had three hours, and a lot of ground to cover.

He slowed to a fast walk when the rocky ground started rising under his feet. Followed a wide uphill circle west and cut straight in to the edge of the bowl where the mine entrances were. He heard diesel engines idling. He bent double and crept across to the cover of a rock. Looked out and down.

He was just above halfway up the slope surrounding the bowl. Looking more or less due east across its diameter. The log doors of the farther shed were standing open. Four of the missile unit's trucks were standing on the shale. The four with the weapon racks in back. The troop carrier was still inside.

There was a handful of men in the bowl. They were set in an approximate circle around the cluster of trucks. Reacher counted eight guys. Fatigues, rifles, tense limbs. What had the kitchen woman said? The mines were off limits. Except to the people Borken trusted. Reacher watched them. Eight trusted lieutenants, acting out a reasonable imitation of sentry duty.

He watched them for a couple of minutes. Slid his rifle to his shoulder. He was less than a hundred yards away. He could hear the rattle of the shale as the sentries moved around. He clicked the selector to the single-shot position. He had nineteen shells in the box, and he needed to fire a minimum of eight. He needed to be cautious with ammunition.

The M-16 is a good rifle. Easy to use, easy to maintain. Easy to aim. The carrying handle has a grooved top which lines up with an identical groove in the front sight. At a hundred yards, you squint down the handle groove and let it merge with the front groove, and what you see is what you hit. Reacher rested his weight on the rock and lined up the first target. Practiced the slight sweep that would take him onto the second. And the third. He rehearsed the full sequence of eight shots. He didn't want his elbow snagging somewhere in the middle.

He returned to the first target. Waited a beat and fired. The sound of the shot crashed through the mountains. The right front tire of the first truck exploded. He swept the sights onto the left front. Fired again. The truck dropped to its rims like a stunned ox falling to its knees.

He kept firing steadily. He had fired five shots and hit five tires before anybody reacted. As he fired the sixth he saw in the corner of his eye the sentries diving for cover. Some were just dropping to the ground. Others were running for the shed. He fired the seventh. Paused before the eighth. The farthest tire was the hardest shot. The angle was oblique. The sidewall was unavailable to him. He was going to have to fire at the treads. Possible that the shell might glance off. He fired. He hit. The tire burst. The front of the last truck dropped.

The nearest sentry was still on his feet. Not heading for the shed. Just standing and staring toward the rock Reacher was behind. Raising his rifle. It was an M-16, same as Reacher's. Long magazine, thirty shells. The guy was standing there, sighting it in on the rock. A brave man, or an idiot. Reacher crouched and waited. The guy fired. His weapon was set on automatic. He loosed off a burst of three. Three shots in a fifth of a second. They smashed into the trees fifteen feet above Reacher's head. Twigs and leaves drifted down and landed near him. The guy ran ten yards closer. Fired again. Three more shells. Way off to Reacher's left. He heard the whine of the bullets and the thunking as they hit the trees before he heard the muzzle blast. Bullets which travel faster than sound do that. You hear it all in reverse order. The bullet gets there before the sound of the shot.

Reacher had decisions to make. How close was he going to let this guy get? And was he going to fire a warning shot? The next burst of three was nearer. Low, but nearer. Not more than six feet way. Reacher decided: not much damn closer, and no warning shot. The guy was all pumped up. No percentage in trying a warning shot. This guy was not going to get calmed down in any kind of a hurry.

He lay on his side. Straightened his legs and came out at the base of the rock. Fired once and hit the guy in the chest. He went down in a heap on the shale. The rifle flew off to his right. Reacher stayed where he was. Watched carefully. The guy was still alive. So Reacher fired again. Hit him through the top of the head. Kinder not to leave him with a sucking chest wound for the last ten minutes of his life.

The echoes of the brief firefight died into the mountain silence and then the air was still. The other seven guys were nowhere. The trucks were all resting nose down on their front rims. Disabled. Maybe they could be driven out of the bowl, but the first of the mountain hairpins was going to strip the blown tires right off. The trucks were neutralized. No doubt about that.

Reacher crawled backward ten yards and stood up in the trees. Jogged down the slope and headed back toward the Bastion. Seventeen shells in the Glock, nine in the rifle. Progress, at a price.

THE DOGS FOUND him halfway back. Two big rangy animals. German shepherds. He saw them at the same time as they saw him. They were loping along with that kind of infinite energy big dogs display. Long bounding strides, eager expressions, wet mouths gaping. They stopped short on stiff front legs and switched direction in a single fluid stride. Thirty yards away. Then twenty. Then ten. Acceleration. New energy in their movement. Snarls rising in their throats.

People, Reacher was certain about. Dogs were different. People had freedom of choice. If a man or a woman ran snarling toward him, they did so because they chose to. They were asking for whatever they got. His response was their problem. But dogs were different. No free will. Easily misled. It raised an ethical problem. Shooting a dog because it had been induced to do something unwise was not the sort of thing Reacher wanted to do.

He left the Glock in his pocket. The rifle was better. It was about two and a half feet longer than the handgun. An extra two and a half feet of separation seemed like a good idea. The dogs stopped short of him. The fur on their shoulders was raised. The fur down their backs was raised, following their spines. They crouched, front feet splayed, heads down, snarling loudly. They had yellow teeth. Lots of them. Their eyes were brown. Reacher could see fine dark eyelashes, like a girl's.

One of them was forward of the other. The leader of the pack. He knew dogs had to have a pecking order. Two dogs, one of them had to be superior to the other. Like people. He didn't know how dogs worked it out for themselves. Posturing, maybe. Maybe smell. Maybe fighting. He stared at the forward dog. Stared into its eyes. Time to time, he had heard people talking about dogs. They said: never show fear. Stare the dog down. Don't let it know you're afraid. Reacher wasn't afraid. He was standing there with an M-16 in his hands. The only thing he was worried about was having to use it.

He stared silently at the dog like he used to stare at some service guy gone bad. A hard, silent stare like a physical force, like a cold, crushing pressure. Bleak, cold eyes, unblinking. It had worked a hundred times with people. Now it was working with the lead dog.

The dog was only partially trained. Reacher could see that. It could go through the motions. But it couldn't deliver. It hadn't been trained to ignore its victim's input. It was eye to eye with him, backing off fractionally like his glare was a painful weight on its narrow forehead. Reacher turned up the temperature. Narrowed his eyes and bared his own teeth. Sneered like a tough guy in a bad movie. The dog's head dropped. Its eyes swiveled upward to maintain contact. Its tail dropped down between its legs.

"Sit," Reacher said. He said it calmly but firmly. Plenty of emphasis on the plosive consonant at the end of the word. The dog moved automatically. Shuffled its hind legs inward and sat. The other dog followed suit, like a shadow. They sat side by side and stared up at him.

"Lie down," Reacher said.

The dogs didn't move. Just stayed sitting, looking at him, puzzled. Maybe the wrong word. Not the command they were accustomed to.

"Down," Reacher said.

They slid their front paws forward and dropped their bellies to the forest floor. Looking up at him.

"Stay," Reacher said.

He gave them a look like he meant it and moved off south. Forced himself to walk slow. Five yards into the trees, he turned. The dogs were still on the ground. Their necks were twisted around, watching him walk away.

"Stay," he called again.

They stayed. He walked.

HE COULD HEAR people in the Bastion. The sound of a fair-sized crowd trying to keep quiet. He heard it when he was still north of the parade ground. He skirted the area in the trees and walked around the far end of the rifle range. Came through the trees behind the mess hall. Opposite the kitchen door. He walked a circle deep in the woods behind the buildings until he got an angle. Crept forward to take a look.

There were maybe thirty people in the Bastion. They were standing in a tight group. Edging forward into a cluster. All men, all in camouflage fatigues, all heavily armed. Rifles, machine guns, grenade launchers, pockets bulging with spare magazines. The crowd ebbed and flowed. Shoulders touched and parted. Reacher glimpsed Beau Borken in the center of the mass of people. He was holding a small black radio transmitter. Reacher recognized it. It was Jackson's. Borken had retrieved it from Fowler's pocket. He was holding it up to his ear. Staring into space like he'd just switched it on and was waiting for a reply.

40

MCGRATH SNATCHED THE radio from his pocket. Flipped it open and stared at it. It was crackling loudly in his hand. Webster stepped forward and took it from him. Ducked back to the cover of the rock face and clicked the button.

"Jackson?" he said. "This is Harland Webster."

McGrath and Johnson crowded in on him. The three men crouched against the rock wall. Webster moved the unit an inch from his ear so the other two could listen in. In the cover of the rock, in the silence of the mountains, they could hear it crackling and hissing and the fast breathing of a person on the other end. Then they heard a voice.

"Harland Webster?" the voice said. "Well, well, the head man himself."

"Jackson?" Webster said again.

"No," the voice said. "This is not Jackson."

Webster glanced at McGrath.

"So who is it?" he asked.

"Beau Borken," the voice said. "And as of today, I guess that's President Borken. President of the Free States of America. But feel free to speak informally."

"Where's Jackson?" Webster asked.

There was a pause. Nothing to hear except the faint electronic sound of FBI telecommunications technology. Satellites and microwaves.

"Where's Jackson?" Webster asked again.

"He died," the voice said.

Webster glanced at McGrath again.

"How?" he asked.

"Just died," Borken said. "Relatively quickly, really."

"Was he sick?" Webster asked.

There was another pause. Then there was the sound of laughter. A high, tinny sound. A loud, shrieking laugh which overloaded Webster's earpiece and spilled into distortion and bounced off the rock wall.

"No, he wasn't sick, Webster," Borken said. "He was pretty healthy, up until the last ten minutes."

"What did you do to him?" Webster asked.

"Same as I'm going to do to the General's little girl," Borken said. "Listen up, and I'll tell you the exact details. You need to pay attention, because you need to know what you're dealing with here. We're serious here. We mean business, you understand? You listening?"

Johnson pushed in close. White and sweating.

"You crazy bastards," he yelled.

"Who's that?" Borken asked. "That the General himself?"

"General Johnson," Webster said.

There was a chuckle on the radio. Just a short, satisfied sound.

"A full house," Borken said. "The Director of the FBI and the Joint Chairman. We're flattered, believe me. But I guess the birth of a new nation deserves nothing less."

"What do you want?" Webster asked.

"We crucified him," Borken said. "We found a couple of trees a yard apart, and we nailed him up. We're going to do that to your daughter, General, if you step out of line. Then we cut his balls off. He was pleading and screaming for us not to, but we did it anyway. We can't do that to your kid, her being a woman and all, but we'll find some equivalent, you know what I mean? Do you think she'll be screaming and pleading, General? You know her better than me. Personally, I'm betting she will be. She likes to think she's a tough cookie, but when she sees those blades coming close, she's going to change her damn tune pretty quick, I'm just about sure of that."

Johnson turned whiter. All his blood just drained away. He fell back and sat heavily against the rock. His mouth was working soundlessly.

"What the hell do you bastards want?" Webster yelled.

There was another silence. Then the voice came back, quiet and firm.

"I want you to stop yelling," it said. "I want you to apologize for yelling at me. I want you to apologize for calling me a rude name. I'm the President of the Free States, and I'm owed some courtesy and deference, wouldn't you say?"

His voice was quiet, but McGrath heard it clearly enough. He looked across at Webster in panic. They were close to losing, before they had even started. First rule was to negotiate. To keep them talking, and gradually gain the upper hand. Establish dominance. Classic siege theory. But to start out by apologizing for yelling was to kiss goodbye any hope of dominance. That was to lie down and roll over. From that point on, you were their plaything. McGrath shook his head urgently. Webster nodded back. Said nothing. Just held the radio without speaking. He knew how to do this. He had been in this situation before. Several times. He knew the protocol. Now, the first one to speak was the weaker one. And it wasn't going to be him. He and McGrath gazed at the ground and waited.

"You still there?" Borken asked.

Webster kept on staring down. Saying nothing.

"You there?" Borken said again.

"What's on your mind, Beau?" Webster asked, calmly.

There was angry breathing over the air.

"You cut my phone line," Borken said. "I want it restored."

"No, we didn't," Webster said. "Doesn't your phone work?"

"My faxes," Borken said. "I got no response."

"What faxes?" Webster said.

"Don't bullshit me," Borken said. "I know you cut the line. I want it fixed."

Webster winked at McGrath.

"OK," he said. "We can do that. But you've got to do something for us first."

"What?" Borken asked.

"Holly," Webster said. "Bring her down to the bridge and leave her there."

There was another silence. Then the laughter started up again. High and loud.

"No dice," Borken said. "And no deals."

Webster nodded to himself. Lowered his voice. Sounded like the most reasonable man on earth.

"Listen, Mr. Borken," he said. "If we can't deal, how can we help each other?"

Another silence. McGrath stared at Webster. The next reply was crucial. Win or lose.

"You listen to me, Webster," the voice said. "No deals. You don't do exactly what I say, Holly dies. In a lot of pain. I hold all the cards, and I'm not doing deals. You understand that?"

Webster's shoulders slumped. McGrath looked away.

"Restore the fax line," the voice said. "I need communications. The world must know what we're doing here. This is a big moment in history, Webster. I won't be denied by your stupid games. The world must witness the first blows being struck against your tyranny."

Webster stared at the ground.

"This decision is too big for you alone," Borken said. "You need to consult with the White House. There's an interest there too, wouldn't you say?"

Even over the tinny hand-held radio, the force of Borken's voice was obvious. Webster was flinching like a physical weight was against his ear. Flinching and gasping, as his heart and lungs fought each other for space inside his chest.

"Make your decision," Borken said. "I'll call back in two minutes."

Then the radio went dead. Webster stared at it like he had never seen such a piece of equipment before. McGrath leaned over and clicked the button off.

"OK," he said. "We stall, right? Tell him we're fixing the line. Tell him it will take an hour, maybe two. Tell him we're in contact with the White House, the UN, CNN, whoever. Tell him whatever the hell he wants to hear."

"Why is he doing this?" Webster asked, vaguely. "Escalating everything? He's making it so we have to attack him. So we have to, right? Like he wants us to. He's giving us no choice. He's provoking us.''

"He's doing it because he's crazy," McGrath said.

"He must be," Webster said. "He's a maniac. Otherwise I just can't understand why he's trying to attract so much attention. Because like he says, he holds all the cards already.''

"We'll worry about that later, chief," McGrath said. "Right now, we just need to stall him."

Webster nodded. Forced himself back to the problem in hand.

"But we need longer than two hours," he said. "Hostage Rescue will take at least four to get over here. Maybe five, maybe six.''

"OK, it's the Fourth of July," McGrath said. "Tell him the linemen are all off duty. Tell him it could take us all day to get them back.''

They stared at each other. Glanced at Johnson. He was right out of it. Just slumped against the rock face, white and inert, barely breathing. Ninety hours of mortal stress and emotion had finally broken him. Then the radio in Webster's hand crackled again.

"Well?" Borken asked, when the static cleared.

"OK, we agree," Webster said. "We'll fix the line. But it's going to take some time. Linemen are off duty for the holidays.''

There was a pause. Then a chuckle.

"Independence Day," Borken said. "Maybe I should have chosen another date.''

Webster made no reply.

"I want your Marines where I can see them," Borken said.

"What Marines?" Webster said.

There was another short laugh. Short and complacent.

"You got eight Marines," Borken said. "And an armored car. We got lookouts all over the place. We've been watching you. Like you're watching us with those damn planes. You're lucky Stingers don't shoot that high, or you'd have more than a damn helicopter on the ground by now.''

Webster made no reply. Just scanned the horizon. McGrath

was doing the same thing, automatically, looking for the glint of the sun on field glasses.

"I figure you're close to the bridge right now," Borken said. "Am I right?"

Webster shrugged. McGrath prompted him with a nod.

"We're close to the bridge," Webster said.

"I want the Marines on the bridge," Borken said. "Sitting on the edge in a neat little row. Their vehicle behind them. I want that to happen now, you understand? Or we go to work on Holly. Your choice, Webster. Or maybe it's the General's choice. His daughter, and his Marines, right?"

Johnson roused himself and glanced up. Five minutes later the Marines were sitting on the fractured edge of the roadway, feet dangling down into the abyss. Their LAV was parked up behind them. Webster was still in the lee of the rock face with McGrath and Johnson. The radio still pressed to his ear. He could hear muffled sounds. Like Borken had pressed his hand over the microphone and was using a walkie-talkie. He could hear his muffled voice alternating with crackly replies. Then he heard the hand come away and the voice come back again, loud and clear in the earpiece.

"OK, Webster, good work," Borken said to him. "Our scouts can see all eight of them. So can our riflemen. If they move, they die. Who else have you got there with you?"

Webster paused. McGrath shook his head urgently.

"Can't you see?" Webster asked. "I thought you were watching us."

"Not right now," Borken said. "I pulled my people back a little. Into our defensive positions."

"There's nobody else here," Webster said. "Just me and the General."

There was another pause.

"OK, you two can join the Marines," Borken said. "On the bridge. On the end of the line."

Webster waited for a long moment. A blank expression on his face. Then he got up and nodded to Johnson. Johnson got up unsteadily and the two of them walked forward together around the curve. Left McGrath on his own, crouched in the lee of the rock.

• • •

Mᴄɢʀᴀᴛʜ ᴡᴀɪᴛᴇᴅ ᴛʜᴇʀᴇ two minutes and crawled back south to the Chevrolet. Garber and Johnson's aide were in front and Milosevic and Brogan were in back. They were all staring at him.

"What the hell happened?" Brogan asked.

"We're in deep, deep shit," McGrath said.

Two minutes of hurried explanation, and the others agreed with him.

"So what now?" Garber asked.

"We go get Holly," McGrath said. "Before he realizes we're bullshitting him."

"But how?" Brogan asked.

McGrath glanced at him. Glanced at Milosevic.

"The three of us," he said. "End of the day, this is a Bureau affair. Call it whatever you want, terrorism, sedition, kidnapping, it's all FBI territory."

"We're going to do it?" Milosevic said. "Just the three of us? Right now?"

"You got a better way?" McGrath said. "You want something done properly, you do it yourself, right?"

Garber was twisted around, scanning along the three faces on the rear seat.

"So go do it," he said.

McGrath nodded and held up his right hand, the thumb and the first two fingers sticking out.

"I'm the thumb," he said. "I go in east of the road. Brogan, you're the first finger. You walk a mile west of the road and go in from there. Milo, you're the second finger. You walk two miles west and go north from there. We infiltrate separately, spaced out a mile between each of us. We meet up back on the road a half-mile shy of the town. Clear?"

Brogan made a face. Then he nodded. Milosevic shrugged. Garber glanced at McGrath and the General's aide started the Chevy and rolled it gently south. He stopped it again after four hundred yards, where the road came back out of the rock cover and there was clear access left and right into the countryside. The three FBI men checked their weapons. They each had a government-issue .38 in a shiny brown leather shoulder holster. Full load of six, plus another six in a speed-loader in their pockets.

"Try to capture a couple of rifles," McGrath said. "Don't worry about taking prisoners. You see somebody, you shoot the bastard down, OK?"

Milosevic had the longest walk, so he was first to go. He ducked across the road and struck out due west across the mountain scrub. He made it to a small stand of trees and disappeared. McGrath lit a cigarette and sent Brogan after him. Garber waited until Brogan was in the trees, then he turned back to McGrath.

"Don't forget what I told you about Reacher," he said. "I'm not wrong about that guy. He's on your side, believe me."

McGrath shrugged and said nothing. Smoked in silence. Opened the Chevy's door and slid out. Ground out the cigarette under his shoe and walked away east, across the grassy shoulder and onto the scrub.

MCGRATH WAS NOT far off fifty, and a heavy smoker, but he was a fit man. He had that type of mongrel constitution that age and smoke could not hurt. He was short at five seven, but sturdy. About one-sixty, made up of that hard slabby muscle which needs no maintenance and never fades into fat. He felt the same as he had as a kid. No better, no worse. His Bureau training had been a long time ago, and fairly rudimentary compared to what people were getting now. But he'd aced it. Physically, he'd been indestructible. Not the fastest guy in his class, but easily the best stamina. The training runs in the early days of Quantico had been crude. Around and around in the Virginia woods, using natural obstacles. McGrath would come in maybe third or fourth every time. But if they were sent around again, he could do the same exact time, just about to the second. The faster guys would be struggling at his side as he pounded relentlessly onward. Then they would fall back. Second time around, McGrath would come in first. Third time around, he would be the only guy to finish.

So he was jogging comfortably as he approached the southern edge of the ravine. He had worked about three hundred yards east to a point where the slopes were reasonable and not directly overlooked. He went straight down without pausing. Short, stiff strides against the incline. The footing was loose. He skidded on small avalanches of gravel and used the stunted trees to check his speed. He dodged around the litter of rocks in the bottom of the trench and started up the northern slope.

Going up was harder. He kicked his toes into the gravel for grip and hauled himself upward with handfuls of grass. He zigzagged between the small trees and bushes, looking for leverage. The extra fifty feet on the northern rim was a punishment. He tracked right to where a small landslide had created a straight path at a kinder angle. Slipped and slid upward through the crushed rock to the top.

He waited in the overhang, where the earth had fallen away beneath the crust of roots. Listened hard. Heard nothing except silence. He lifted himself onto the rim. Stood there with his chest against the earth, head and shoulders exposed, looking north into enemy territory. He saw nothing. Just the gentle initial slopes, then the hills, then the giant mountains glowering in the far distance. Blue sky, a million trees, clean air, total silence. He thought: you're a long way from Chicago, Mack.

Ahead of him was a belt of scrub where the ancient rock was too close to the surface for much to grow. Then a ragged belt of trees, interrupted at first by rocky outcrops, then growing denser into the distance. He could see the curved gap in the treetops where the road must run. Three hundred yards to his left. He rolled up onto the grass and ran for the trees. Worked left toward the road and shadowed it north in the forest.

He jogged along, dodging trees like a slow-motion parody of a wide receiver heading for the end zone. The map was printed in his mind. He figured he had maybe three miles to go. Three miles at a slow jog, not much better than a fast walk, maybe forty-five, fifty minutes. The ground was rising gently under his feet. Every fourth or fifth stride, his feet hit the floor a fraction sooner than they should have as the gradient lifted him into the hills. He tripped a couple of times on roots. Once, he slammed into a pine trunk. But he pounded on, relentlessly.

After forty minutes, he stopped. He figured Brogan and

Milosevic were having a similar journey, but they were dealing with extra distance because they had tracked west at the outset. So he expected a delay. With luck, they would be about twenty minutes behind him. He walked deeper into the woods and sat down against a trunk. Lit a cigarette. He figured he was maybe a half-mile shy of the rendezvous. The map in his head said the road was about due to arrow up into the town.

He waited fifteen minutes. Two cigarettes. Then he stood up and walked on. He went cautiously. He was getting close. He made two diversions to his left and found the road. Just crept through the trees until he caught the gleam of sun on the gray cement. Then he dodged back and continued north. He walked until he saw the forest thinning ahead. He saw sunlight on open spaces beyond the last trees. He stopped and stepped left and right to find a view. He saw the road running up to the town. He saw buildings. A gray ruin on a knoll on the left. The courthouse on the right. Better preserved. Gleaming white in the sunshine. He stared through the trees at it for a long moment. Then he turned back. Paced five hundred yards back into the woods. Drifted over toward the road until he could just make out the gray gleam through the trees. Leaned on a trunk and waited for Brogan and Milosevic.

THIS TIME, HE resisted the attraction of another cigarette. He had learned a long time ago that to smoke while in hiding was not a smart thing to do. The smell drifts, and a keen nose can detect it. So he leaned on the tree and stared down in frustration. Stared at his shoes. They were ruined from the scramble up the north face of the ravine. He had jabbed them hard into the rocky slope and they were scratched to pieces. He stared at the ruined toe caps and instantly knew he had been betrayed. Panic rose in his throat. His chest seized hard. It hit him like a prison door swinging gently shut. It swung soundlessly inward on greased hinges and clanged shut right in his face.

What had Borken said on the radio? He had said: like you're watching us with those damn planes. But what had the General's aide told him back in the Butte office? You look up and you see a tiny vapor trail and you think it's TWA. You don't think it's the Air Force checking if you've shined your shoes this morning. So how did Borken know there were surveillance planes in the sky? Because he had been told. But by who? Who the hell knew?

He glanced around wildly and the first thing he saw was a dog coming at him from dead ahead. Then another. They bounded through the trees at him. He heard a sound from behind him. The crunch of feet and the flick of branches. Then the same sound from his right. The snicking and slapping of a weapon from his left. The dogs were at his feet. He spun in a panic-stricken circle. All around him men were coming at him through the trees. Lean, bearded men, in camouflage gear, carrying rifles and machine guns. Grenades slung from their webbing. Maybe fifteen or twenty men. They stepped forward calmly and purposefully. They were in a complete ring, right around him. He turned one way, then the other. He was surrounded. They were raising their weapons. He had fifteen or twenty automatic weapons pointing straight at him like spokes in a wheel.

They stood silent, weapons ready. McGrath glanced from one to the next, in a complete wide circle. Then one of them stepped forward. Some kind of an officer. His hand went straight in under McGrath's jacket. Jerked the .38 out of his holster. Then the guy's hand went into McGrath's pocket. Closed over the speedloader and pulled it out. The guy slipped both items into his own pocket and smiled. Swung his fist and hit McGrath in the face. McGrath staggered and was prodded back forward with the muzzle of a rifle. Then he heard tires on the road. The grumble of a motor. He glanced left and caught a flash of olive green in the sun. A jeep. Two men in it. The soldiers pressed in and forced him out of the forest. They jostled him through the trees and onto the shoulder. He blinked in the sun. He could feel his nose was bleeding. The jeep rolled forward and stopped alongside him. The driver stared at him with curiosity. Another lean, bearded man in uniform. In the passenger seat was a huge man wearing black. Beau Borken. McGrath recognized him from his Bureau file photograph. He stared at him. Then Borken leaned over and grinned.

"Hello, Mr. McGrath," he said. "You made good time."

41

REACHER WATCHED THE whole thing happen. He was a hundred and fifty yards away in the trees. Northwest of the ambush, high up the slope on the other side of the road. There was a dead sentry at his feet. The guy was lying in the dirt with his head at right angles to his neck. Reacher had his field glasses raised to his eyes. Watching. Watching what, he wasn't exactly sure.

He had caught the gist of the radio conversation in the Bastion. He had heard Borken's side. He had guessed the replies. He had heard the southern lookouts calling in on the walkie-talkies. He knew about the Marines on the bridge. He knew about Webster and Johnson sitting there alongside them, on the end of the line.

He had wondered who else was down there. Maybe more military, maybe more FBI. The military wouldn't come. Johnson would have ordered them to sit tight. If anybody came, it would be the FBI. He figured they might have substantial numbers standing by. He figured they would be coming in, sooner or later. He needed to exploit them. Needed to use them as a diversion while he got Holly out. So he had moved southeast to wait for their arrival. Now, an hour later, he was gazing down at the short stocky guy getting loaded into the jeep. Dark suit, white shirt, town shoes. FBI, for sure.

But not the Hostage Rescue Team. This guy had no equipment. The HRT came in all loaded down with paramilitary gear. Reacher was familiar with their procedures. He had read some of their manuals. Heard about some of their training. He knew guys who had been in and out of Quantico. He knew how the HRT worked. They were a high-technology operation. They looked like regular soldiers, in blue. They had vehicles. This guy he was watching was on foot in the forest. Dressed like he had just stepped out of a meeting.

It was a puzzle. Eight Marines. No Hostage Rescue Team. An unarmed search-and-rescue Chinook. Then Reacher suddenly thought maybe he understood. Maybe this was a very clandestine operation. Low-profile. Invisible. They had tracked Holly all the way west from Chicago, but for some reason they maybe weren't gathering any kind of a big force. They were dealing with it alone. Some tactical reason. Maybe a political reason. Maybe something to do with Holly and the White House. Maybe the policy was to deal with this secretly, deal with it hard, tackle it with a tight little team. So tight the right hand didn't know what the left was doing. Hence the unarmed search-and-rescue chopper. It had come in blind. Hadn't known what it was getting into.

In which case this ambushed guy he was watching was direct from Chicago. Part of the original operation that must have started up back on Monday. He looked like a senior guy. Maybe approaching fifty. Could be Brogan, Holly's section head. Could even be McGrath, the top boy. In either case that made Milosevic the mole. Question was, was he up here as well, or was he still back in Chicago?

The jeep turned slowly in the road. The Bureau guy in the suit was in back, jammed between two armed men. His nose was bleeding and Reacher could see a swelling starting on his face. Borken had twisted his bulk around and was talking at him. The rest of the ambush squad was forming up in the road. The jeep drove past them, north toward town. Passed by thirty yards from where Reacher was standing in the trees. He watched it go. Turned and picked up his rifle. Strolled through the woods, deep in thought.

His problem was priority order. He had a rule: stick to the job in hand. The job in hand was getting Holly away safe. Nothing else. But this Bureau guy was in trouble. He thought about Jackson. The last Bureau guy they'd gotten hold of.

Maybe this new guy was heading for the same fate. In which case, he ought to intervene. And he liked the look of the guy. He looked tough. Small, but strong. A lot of energy. Some kind of charisma there. Maybe an ally would be a smart thing to have. Two heads, better than one. Two pairs of hands. Four trigger fingers. Useful. But his rule was: stick to the job in hand. It had worked for him many times over the years. It was a rule which had served him well. Should he bend that rule? Or not? He stopped and stood concealed in the forest while the ambush squad marched by on the road. Listened to the sound of their footsteps die away. Stood there and thought about the guy some more and forced himself toward a tough decision.

GENERAL GARBER WATCHED the whole thing happen, too. He was a hundred and fifty yards south of the ambush. West side of the road, behind a rocky outcrop, exactly three hundred yards south of where Reacher had been. He had waited three minutes and then followed McGrath in through the ravine. Garber was also a reasonably fit man, but a lot older, and it had cost him a lot to keep pace with McGrath. He had arrived at the rocky outcrop and collapsed, out of breath. He figured he had maybe fifteen or twenty minutes to recover before the rendezvous took place. Then his plan was to follow behind the three agents and see what was going to happen. He didn't want anybody making mistakes about Jack Reacher.

But the rendezvous had never happened. He had watched the ambush and realized a lot of mistakes had been made about a lot of things.

YOU'RE GOING TO die," Borken said.

McGrath was jammed between two soldiers on the back seat of the jeep. He was bouncing around because the road was rough. But he couldn't move his arms, because the seat was not really wide enough for three people. So he put the shrug into his injured face instead.

"We're all going to die," he said. "Sooner or later."

"Sooner or later, right," Borken said. "But for you, it's going to be sooner, not later."

Borken was twisted around in the front seat, staring. McGrath looked past him at the vast blue sky. He looked at the small white clouds and thought: who was it? Who knew? Air Force operational personnel, he guessed, but that link was ludicrous. Had to be somebody nearer and closer. Somebody more involved. The only possibilities were Johnson or his aide, or Webster himself, or Brogan, or Milosevic. Garber, conceivably. He seemed pretty hot on excusing this Reacher guy. Was this some military police conspiracy to overthrow the Joint Chiefs?

"Who was it, Borken?" he asked.

"Who was what, dead man?" Borken asked back.

"Who's been talking to you?" McGrath said.

Borken smiled and tapped his finger on his temple.

"Common cause," he said. "This sort of issue, there are a lot more people than you think on our side."

McGrath glanced back to the sky and thought about Dexter, safe in the White House. What had Webster said he'd said? Twelve million people? Or was it sixty-six million?

"You're going to die," Borken said again.

McGrath shifted his focus back.

"So tell me who it was, before I do," he said.

Borken grinned at him.

"You'll find out," he said. "It's going to be a big surprise."

The jeep pulled up in front of the courthouse. McGrath twisted and looked up at it. There were six soldiers standing guard outside the building. They were fanned into a rough arc, facing south and east.

"She in there?" he asked.

Borken nodded and smiled.

"Right now she is," he said. "I may have to get her out later."

The walkie-talkie on his belt burst into life. A loud burst of static and a quick distorted message. He pressed the key and bent his head down. Acknowledged the information without unclipping the unit. Then he pulled the radio transmitter from his pocket. Flipped it open and pulled up the short antenna. Pressed the send button.

"Webster?" he said. "You lied to me. Twice. First, there

were three of your agents down there with you. We just rounded them all up.''

He listened to the response. Kept the radio tight against his ear. McGrath could not hear what Webster was saying.

''Doesn't matter anyway,'' Borken said. ''They weren't all on your side. Some people in this world will do anything for money.''

He paused for a response. Apparently there was none.

''And you bullshitted me,'' Borken said. ''You weren't going to fix the line at all, were you? You were just stringing me along.''

Webster was starting a reply, but Borken cut him off.

''You and Johnson,'' he said. ''You can get off the bridge now. The Marines stay there. We're watching. You and Johnson walk back to your trucks. Get yourselves in front of those TVs. Should be some interesting action pretty soon.''

He clicked off the radio and folded it back into his pocket. A big wide smile on his face.

''You're going to die,'' he said to McGrath for the third time.

''Which one?'' McGrath asked. ''Brogan or Milosevic?''

Borken grinned again.

''Guess,'' he said. ''Figure it out for yourself. You're supposed to be the big smart federal investigator. Agent-in-Charge, right?''

The driver jumped down and pulled a pistol from his holster. Aimed it two-handed at McGrath's head. The left-hand guard squeezed out and unslung his rifle. Held it ready. The right-hand guy did the same. Then Borken eased his bulk down.

''Out,'' he said. ''We walk from here.''

McGrath shrugged and eased himself down into the circle of weapons. Borken stepped behind him and caught his arms. Cuffed his wrists together behind his back. Then he shoved him forward. Pointed beyond the ruined county office.

''Up there, dead man,'' he said.

They left the jeep behind them next to the courthouse. The two guards formed up. McGrath stumbled across the street and up onto the lumpy knoll. He was pushed past the dead tree. He was pushed left until he found the path. He followed it around behind the old building. The rough ground bit up through the thin soles of his ruined city shoes. He might as well have been walking barefoot.

"Faster, asshole," Borken grunted at him.

The guards were behind him, prodding him forward with the muzzles of their rifles. He picked up the pace and stumbled on through the woods. He felt the blood clotting on his lip and nose. After a mile, he came out into the clearing he recognized from the surveillance pictures. It looked bigger. From seven miles overhead, it had looked like a neat hole in the trees, with a tidy circle of buildings. From ground level, it looked as big as a stadium. Rough shale on the floor of the clearing, big wooden huts propped expertly on solid concrete piles.

"Wait here," Borken said.

He walked away and the two guards took up station either side of McGrath as he gazed around. He saw the communications hut, with the phone wire and the whip antenna. He saw the other buildings. Smelled stale institutional food coming out of the largest. Saw the farthest hut, standing on its own. Must be their armory, he thought.

He glanced up and saw the vapor trails in the sky. The urgency of the situation was written up there, white on blue. The planes had abandoned their innocent east-west trawling. Their trails had tightened into continuous circles, one just inside the other. They were flying around and around, centered seven miles above his head. He stared up at them and mouthed: help! He wondered if their lenses were good enough to pick that out. Wondered if maybe Webster or Johnson or Garber or Johnson's gofer could lip-read. His best guess was: yes, and no.

REACHER'S PROBLEM WAS a hell of an irony. For the first time in his life, he wished his opponents were better shots. He was concealed in the trees a hundred yards northwest of the courthouse. Looking down at six sentries. They were ranged in a loose arc, to the south and east beyond the big white building. Reacher's rifle was trained on the nearest man. But he wasn't shooting. Because if he did, the six men were going to shoot back. And they were going to miss.

Reacher was happy with an M-16 and a range of a hundred yards. He could pretty much absolutely guarantee to hit what he wanted with that weapon at that range. He would bet his life on it. Many times, he had. And normally, the worse shots his opponents were, the happier he'd be about it. But not in this situation.

He would be shooting from a northwest direction. His opponents would be shooting back from the southeast. They would hear his shots, maybe see some muzzle flash, they would take aim, and they would fire. And they would miss. They would shoot high and wide. The targets on the rifle range were mute evidence for that conclusion. There had been some competent shooting at three and four hundred yards. The damaged targets bore witness to that fact. But Reacher's experience was that guys who could shoot just about competently at three or four hundred yards on a range would be useless in a firefight. Lying still on a mat and sighting in on a target in your own time was one thing. Shooting into a noisy confused hailstorm of bullets was a very different thing. A different thing entirely. The guy defending the missile trucks had proved that. His salvos had been all over the place. And that was the problem. Shooting back from the southeast, these guys' stray rounds were going to be all over the place, too. Up and down, left and right. The down rounds and the left rounds were no problem. They were just going to damage the scrubby vegetation. But the up rounds and the right rounds were going to hit the courthouse.

The M-16 uses bullets designated M855. Common NATO rounds, 5.56 millimeters in caliber, just a fraction under a quarter-inch wide. Fairly heavy for their size, because they are a sandwich of lead and steel, inside a copper jacket. Designed for penetration. Those stray rounds which hit the courthouse were going to impact the siding at two thousand miles an hour. They were going to punch through the old wood like it wasn't there at all. They were going to smash through the unstable dynamite like a train wreck. The energy of their impact was going to act like a better blasting cap than anything any mining company had ever possessed. That was what those bullets were designed to do. Some committee had asked for a bullet capable of shooting through the sides of ammunition trucks. And that's what had been delivered.

So Reacher wasn't shooting. Three sentries, he might have risked it. He figured he could get off three aimed shots in maybe three seconds. Too fast for any reaction. But six was too many. They were too spaced out. Too much physical movement was required between rounds. The later targets would have time to react. Not much time. Certainly not enough to be accurate. That was the problem.

Reversing the geometry would be no help, either. He could work himself right around to the south. It would take him maybe twenty minutes to skirt around in the trees and come back at them from the opposite direction. But then what? He would be looking at his targets, uphill. The courthouse would be right behind them. He could hit each of them in the head, no problem at all. But he couldn't ask the bullets just to stop there in midair. He couldn't prevent those high-energy copper-jackets bursting on out of the back of those skulls and heading on their uphill trajectories straight toward the courthouse's second-story walls. He shook his head and lowered his rifle.

MCGRATH SAW BORKEN conferring with somebody on the edge of the clearing. It was the guy who had led the ambush squad. The guy who had taken his gun and his bullets and punched him in the face. The two of them were glancing at their watches and glancing up at the sky. They were nodding. Borken slapped the guy on the shoulder and turned away. Ducked into the trees and disappeared back toward the town. The ambush leader started in toward McGrath. He was smiling. He was unslinging his rifle.

"Showtime," he called.

He stepped near and reversed the rifle in his hands as he did so. Smashed the butt into McGrath's stomach. McGrath went down on the shale. One guard jammed the muzzle of his rifle into McGrath's throat. The other jammed his into McGrath's stomach, right where the blow had landed.

"Lie still, asshole," the unit leader said. "I'll be back in a minute."

McGrath could not move his head because of the rifle in his throat, but he followed the guy with his eyes. He was going into the next-to-last hut in line. Not the armory, which stood on its own. Some kind of an equipment store. He came out with a mallet and ropes and four metal objects. Dull-green, Army issue. As he got nearer, McGrath recognized what they were. They were tent pegs. Maybe eighteen inches long, designed for some kind of big mess tent.

The guy dropped his load on the shale. The metal pegs clinked on the stones. The guy nodded to the soldier with the gun in McGrath's belly, who straightened up and stepped away. The unit leader took his place. Used his own weapon to keep McGrath pinned down.

The soldier got busy. He seemed to know what he was supposed to do. He used the mallet to drive the first peg into the ground. The ground was stony and the guy had to work hard. He was swinging the mallet in a big arc and using a lot of force. He drove the peg down until it was two-thirds buried. Then he paced off maybe eight feet and started driving the second. McGrath followed him with his eyes. When the second peg was in, the guy paced another eight feet at a right angle and hammered the third peg in. The fourth peg completed an exact square, eight feet on a side. McGrath had a pretty good idea what that square was for.

"We normally do this in the woods," the unit leader said. "We normally do it vertically, with trees."

Then the guy pointed upward at the sky.

"But we need to let them see," he said. "They can't see properly in the woods. This time of year, too many leaves in the way, right?"

The guard who had driven the tent pegs into the ground was panting from the exertion. He changed places with his leader again. Jammed his rifle into McGrath's gut and leaned on it, recovering. McGrath gasped and squirmed under the pressure. The leader squatted down and sorted through the ropes. Untangled one and caught McGrath by the ankle. Looped the rope around and tied it off, hard. Used the rope to drag McGrath by the leg into the approximate center of the square. Then he tied the loose end to the fourth peg. Tied it tight and tested it.

The second length of rope went around McGrath's other ankle. It was tied off to the third peg. McGrath's legs were forced apart at a right angle. His hands were still cuffed behind his back, crushed against the rocky ground. The leader used the sole of his boot to roll McGrath's upper body sideways. Ducked down and unlocked the cuff. Caught a wrist and looped a rope around. Tied it tight and hauled the wrist up to the second peg. He pulled on it until McGrath's arm was stretched tight, in a perfect straight line with the opposite leg. Then he tied it tight to the peg and reached down for the other wrist. The soldiers jammed their muzzles in tighter. McGrath stared up at the vapor trails and gasped in pain as his arm was stretched tight and he was tied into a perfect cross.

The two soldiers jerked their rifles away and stepped back. They stood with their leader. Gazing down. McGrath lifted his head and looked wildly around. Pulled on the ropes, and then realized he was only pulling the knots tighter. The three men stepped farther back and glanced up at the sky. McGrath realized they were making sure the cameras got an uninterrupted view.

THE CAMERAS WERE getting an uninterrupted view. Seven miles in the sky, the pilots were flying circles, one on a tight radius of a few miles, the other outside him on a wider path. Their cameras were trained downward, under the relentless control of their computers. The inside plane was focusing tight on the clearing where McGrath was spread-eagled. The outer camera was zoomed wider, taking in the whole of the area from the courthouse in the south to the abandoned mines in the north. Their real-time video signals were bouncing down more or less vertically to the dish vehicle parked behind the mobile command post. The dish was focusing the datastream and feeding it through the thick armored cable into the observation truck. Then the decoding computers were feeding the large color monitors. Their phosphor screens were displaying the appalling truth. General Johnson and his aide and Webster were motionless in front of them. Motionless, silent, staring. Video recorders were whirring away, dispassionately recording every second's activity taking place six miles to the north. The whole vehicle was humming with faint electronic energy. But it was as silent as a tomb.

"Can you zoom in?" Webster asked quietly. "On Mc-Grath?"

The General's aide twisted a black rubber knob. Stared at the screen. He zoomed in until the individual pixels in the picture began to clump together and distort. Then he backed off a fraction.

"Close as we can get," he said.

It was close enough. McGrath's spread-eagled figure just about filled the screens. The unit leader could be seen from directly above, stepping over the lengths of rope as he circled. He had a knife in his hand. A black handle, a shiny blade, maybe ten inches long. It looked like a big kitchen knife. The sort of thing a gourmet cook might buy. Useful for slicing a tough cut of steak into strips. The sort of tool that would get set out on the kitchen counter by someone making a stew or a stroganoff.

They saw the guy lay the knife flat on McGrath's chest. Then he used both hands to fold back the flaps on McGrath's jacket. He loosened McGrath's tie and pulled it sideways, almost up under his ear. Then he grasped the shirt and tore it open. The cotton pulled apart under the knife, leaving the knife where it was, now next to the skin. The guy pulled the tails out of the waistband and tucked the shirt right back to the sides. Carefully, well out of the way, like he was a surgeon faced with a difficult emergency procedure.

They saw the guy pick up the knife again. He was squatted down to McGrath's right, leaning over slightly, holding the knife. He was holding it point down, close to McGrath's belly. The electronic pink of McGrath's skin was reflected in the faces of the watchers inside the observation vehicle.

They saw the guy raise the knife an inch. They saw his index finger slide along the back of the blade, like he was adjusting his grip for extra precision. They saw the blade move down. The pale sun glinted on the steel. Then their view was disrupted. A silent puff of pink mist obscured the picture. When it cleared, the knife was still in the guy's hand. But the guy had no head. His whole head was a shattered pink wound, and he was toppling slowly sideways.

42

THE LEFT-HAND GUARD went down easily enough, too. Reacher put a bullet through the side of his head, just above the ear, and he fell heavily, right on top of the spread-eagled Bureau guy. But the right-hand guard reacted. He spun away and hurdled the taut ropes, racing for the trees. Reacher paused a beat and dropped him ten feet away. The guy sprawled and slid noisily through the shale and put up a slick of dust. Twitched once and died.

Then Reacher waited. The last staccato echo of the three shots came back off the farthest mountains and faded into quiet. Reacher watched the trees, all around the Bastion. Watched for movement. The sunlight was bright. Too bright to be sure. There was a lot of contrast between the brightness of the clearing and the dark of the forest. So he waited.

Then he came out from behind the radio hut at a desperate run. He sprinted straight across the clearing to the mess in the middle. Hauled the bodies out of the way. The guard was sprawled right on top of the Bureau guy. The unit leader was across his legs. He dumped them out of the way and found the knife. Sawed through the four coarse ropes. Dragged the Bureau guy upright and pushed him off back the way he'd come. Then he grabbed the two nearest rifles and sprinted after him. Caught him up halfway. The guy was just tottering along. So Reacher caught him under the arms and bundled him to safety. Threw him well into the trees behind the huts and stood bent over, panting. Then he took the magazines off the new rifles and put one in his pocket and one on his own gun. They were both the elongated thirty-shot versions. He'd been down to six rounds. Now he had sixty. A tenfold increase. And he had another pair of hands.

"Are you Brogan?" he asked. "Or McGrath?"

The guy answered stiffly and neutrally. There was fear and panic and confusion in his face.

"McGrath," he said. "FBI."

Reacher nodded. The guy was shaken up, but he was an ally. He took Fowler's Glock out of his pocket and held it out to him, butt first. McGrath was panting quietly and glancing wildly toward the deep cover of the trees. There was aggression in his stance. His hands were balled into fists.

"What?" Reacher asked him, concerned.

McGrath darted forward and snatched the Glock and stepped back. Raised it and went into a shooting stance and pointed it two-handed. At Reacher's head. The cut ends of the ropes trailed down from his wrists. Reacher just stared blankly at him.

"Hell are you doing?" he asked.

"You're one of them," McGrath said back. "Drop the rifle, OK?"

"What?" Reacher said again.

"Just do it, OK?" McGrath said.

Reacher stared at him, incredulous. Pointed through the trees at the sprawled bodies in the Bastion.

"What about that?" he asked. "Doesn't that mean anything to you?"

The Glock did not waver. It was rock-steady, pointed straight at his head, at the apex of a perfect braced position. McGrath looked like a picture in a training manual, except for the ropes hanging like streamers from his wrists and ankles.

"Doesn't that count for something?" Reacher asked again, pointing.

"Not necessarily," McGrath growled back. "You killed Peter Bell, too. We know that. Just because you don't allow your troops to rape and torture your hostages doesn't necessarily put you on the side of the angels."

Reacher looked at him for a long moment, astonished. Thought hard. Then he nodded cautiously and dropped the rifle exactly halfway between the two of them. Drop it right at his own feet, McGrath would just tell him to kick it over toward him. Drop it too near McGrath's feet, and it wouldn't work. This guy was an experienced agent. From the look of his shooting stance, Reacher was expecting at least a basic level of competence from him.

McGrath glanced down. Hesitated. He clearly didn't want Reacher near him. He didn't want him stepping nearer to nudge the rifle on toward him. So he slid his own foot forward to drag the weapon back close. He was maybe ten inches shorter than Reacher, all told. Aiming the Glock at Reacher's head from six feet away, he was aiming it upward at a fairly steep angle. As he slid his foot forward, he decreased his effective height by maybe an inch, which automatically increased the upward slope of his arms by a proportionate degree. And as he slid his foot forward, it brought him slightly closer to Reacher, which increased the upward angle yet more. By the time his toe was scrabbling for the weapon, his upper arms were near his face, interfering with his vision. Reacher waited for him to glance down again.

He glanced down. Reacher let his knees go and fell vertically. Lashed back upward with his forearm and batted the Glock away. Swiped a wide arc with his other arm behind McGrath's knees and dumped him flat on his back in the dirt. Closed his hand over McGrath's wrist and squeezed gently until the Glock shook free. He picked it up by the barrel and held it the wrong way around.

"Look at this," he said.

He shook his cuff back and exposed the crusted weal on his left wrist.

"I'm not one of them," he said. "They had me handcuffed most of the time."

Then he held the Glock out, butt first, offering it again. McGrath stared at it, and then stared back into the clearing. He ducked his head left and right to take in the bodies. Glanced back at Reacher, still confused.

"We had you down as a bad guy," he said.

Reacher nodded.

"Evidently," he said. "But why?"

"Video in the dry cleaner's," McGrath said. "Looked just like you were snatching her up."

Reacher shook his head.

"Innocent passerby," he said.

McGrath kept on looking hard at him. Quizzically, thinking. Reacher saw him arrive at a decision. He nodded in turn and accepted the Glock and laid it on the forest floor, exactly between them, like its positioning was a symbol, a treaty. He started fumbling at his shirt buttons. Cut ends of rope flailed at his wrists and ankles.

"OK, can we start over?" he said, embarrassed.

Reacher nodded and stuck out his hand.

"Sure," he said. "I'm Reacher, you're McGrath. Holly's Agent-in-Charge. Pleased to meet you."

McGrath smiled ruefully and shook hands limply. Then he started fumbling at the knots on his wrist, one-handed.

"You know a guy called Garber?" McGrath asked.

Reacher nodded.

"Used to work for him," he said.

"Garber told us you were clean," McGrath said. "We didn't believe him."

"Naturally," Reacher said. "Garber always tells the truth. So nobody ever believes him."

"So I apologize," McGrath said. "I'm sorry, OK? But just try and see it my way. You've been public enemy number one for five days."

Reacher waved the apology away and stood up and helped McGrath to his feet. Bent back down to the dirt and picked up the Glock and handed it to him.

"Your nose OK?" he asked.

McGrath slipped the gun into his jacket pocket. Touched his nose gently and grimaced.

"Bastard hit me," he said. "I think it's broken. Just turned and hit me, like they couldn't wait."

There was a noise in the woods, off to the left. Reacher caught McGrath's arm and pulled him deeper into the forest. Pushed through the brush and got facing east. He stood silently and listened for movement. McGrath was taking the ropes off his ankles and winding himself up to ask a question.

"So is Holly OK?" he said.

Reacher nodded. But grimly.

"So far," he said. "But it's going to be a hell of a problem getting her out."

"I know about the dynamite," McGrath said. "That was the last thing Jackson called in. Monday night."

"It's a problem," Reacher said again. "One stray round, and she's had it. And there are a hundred trigger-happy people up here. Whatever we do, we need to do it carefully. Have you got reinforcements coming in? Hostage Rescue?"

McGrath shook his head.

"Not yet," he said. "Politics."

"Maybe that's good," Reacher said. "They're talking about mass suicide if they look like getting beat. Live free or die, you know?"

"Whichever," McGrath said. "Their choice. I don't care what happens to them. I just care about Holly."

They fell silent and crept together through the trees. Stopped deep in the woods, about level with the back of the mess hall. Now Reacher was winding himself up to ask a question. But he waited, frozen, a finger to his lips. There was noise to his left. A patrol, sweeping the fringe of the forest. McGrath made to move, but Reacher caught his arm and stopped him. Better to stand stock-still than to risk making noise of their own. The patrol came nearer. Reacher raised his rifle and switched it to rapid fire. Smothered the sound of the click with his palm. McGrath held his breath. The patrol was visible, ten feet away through the trees. Six men, six rifles. They were glancing rhythmically as they walked, left and right, left and right, between the edge of the sunny clearing and the dark green depths of the woods. Reacher breathed out, silently. Amateurs, with poor training and bad tactics. The bright sun in their eyes on every second glance was ruining their chances of seeing into the gloom of the forest. They were blind. They passed by without stopping. Reacher followed the sound of their progress and turned back to McGrath.

"Where are Brogan and Milosevic?" he whispered.

McGrath nodded, morosely.

"I know," he said, quietly. "One of them is bent. I finally

figured that out about half a second before they grabbed me up.''

"Where are they?" Reacher asked again.

"Up here somewhere," McGrath said. "We came in through the ravine together, a mile apart."

"Which one is it?" Reacher asked.

McGrath shrugged.

"I don't know," he said. "Can't figure it out. I've been going over and over it. They both did good work. Milosevic found the dry cleaner. He brought the video in. Brogan did a lot of work tracing it all back here to Montana. He traced the truck. He liaised with Quantico. My gut says neither one is bent."

"When was I ID'd?" Reacher asked.

"Thursday morning," McGrath said. "We had your complete history."

Reacher nodded.

"He called it in right away," he said. "These people suddenly knew who I was, Thursday morning."

McGrath shrugged again.

"They were both there at the time," he said. "We were all down at Peterson."

"Did you get Holly's fax?" Reacher asked.

"What fax?" McGrath said. "When?"

"This morning," Reacher said. "Early, maybe ten to five? She faxed you a warning."

"We're intercepting their line," McGrath said. "In a truck, down the road here. But ten to five, I was in bed."

"So who was minding the store?" Reacher asked.

McGrath nodded.

"Milosevic and Brogan," he said, sourly. "The two of them. Ten to five this morning, they'd just gone on duty. Whichever one of them it is must have gotten the fax and concealed it. But which one, I just don't know."

Reacher nodded back.

"We could figure it out," he said. "Or we could just wait and see. One of them will be walking around best of friends and the other will be in handcuffs, or dead. We'll be able to tell the difference."

McGrath nodded, sourly.

"I can't wait," he said.

Then Reacher stiffened and pulled him ten yards farther into the woods. He had heard the patrol coming back through the trees.

INSIDE THE COURTROOM, Borken had heard the three shots. He was sitting in the judge's chair, and he heard them clearly. They went: crack crack . . . crack and repeated a dozen times as each of the distant slopes cannoned the echo back toward him. He sent a runner back to the Bastion. A mile there, a mile back on the winding path through the woods. Twenty minutes wasted, and then the runner got back panting with the news. Three corpses, four cut ropes.

"Reacher," Borken said. "I should have wasted him at the beginning."

Milosevic nodded in agreement.

"I want him kept away from me," Milosevic said. "I heard the autopsy report on your friend Peter Bell. I just want my money and safe passage out of here, OK?"

Borken nodded. Then he laughed. A sharp, nervous laugh that was part excitement, part tension. He stood up and walked out from behind the bench. Laughed and grinned and slapped Milosevic on the shoulder.

HOLLY JOHNSON KNEW no more than most people do about dynamite. She couldn't remember its exact chemical composition. She knew ammonium nitrate and nitrocellulose were in there somewhere. She wondered about nitroglycerin. Was that mixed in too? Or was that some other kind of explosive? Either way, she figured dynamite was some kind of a sticky fluid, soaked into a porous material and molded into sticks. Heavy sticks, quite dense. If her walls were packed with heavy dense sticks, they would absorb a lot of sound. Like a soundproofing layer in a city apartment. Which meant the shots she'd heard had been reasonably close.

She'd heard: crack crack . . . crack. But she didn't know who was shooting at who, or why. They weren't handgun shots. She knew the flat bark of a handgun from her time at Quantico. These were shots from a long gun. Not the heavy thump of the big Barretts from the rifle range. A lighter weapon than that. Somebody firing a medium-caliber rifle three times. Or three people firing once, in a ragged volley. But whichever it was, something was happening. And she had to be ready.

GARBER HEARD THE shots, too. Crack crack . . . crack, maybe a thousand yards northwest of him, maybe twelve hundred. Then a dozen spaced echoes coming back from the mountainsides. He was in no doubt about what they represented. An M-16, firing singles, the first pair in a tight group of two which the military called a double tap. The sound of a competent shooter. The idea was to get the second round off before the first shell case hit the ground. Then a third target, or maybe an insurance shot into the second. An unmistakable rhythm. Like a signature. The audible signature of somebody with hundreds of hours of weapons training behind him. Garber nodded to himself and moved forward through the trees.

IT MUST BE Brogan,'' Reacher whispered.

McGrath looked surprised.

"Why Brogan?" he asked.

They were squatted down, backs to adjacent trunks, thirty yards into the woods, invisible. The search patrol had tracked back and missed them again. McGrath had given Reacher the whole story. He had rattled through the important parts of the investigation, one professional to another, in a sort of insider's shorthand. Reacher had asked sharp questions and McGrath had given short answers.

"Time and distance," Reacher said. "That was crucial. Think about it from their point of view. They put us in the truck, and they raced off straight to Montana. What's that? Maybe seventeen hundred miles? Eighteen hundred?"

"Probably," McGrath allowed.

"And Brogan's a smart guy," Reacher said. "And he knows you're a smart guy. He knows you're smart enough to know that he's smart enough. So he can't dead-end the whole thing. But what he can do is keep you all far enough behind the action to stop you being a problem. And that's what he did. He managed the flow of information. The communication had to be two-way, right? So Monday, he knew they'd rented a truck. But right through Wednesday, he was still focusing you on stolen trucks, right? He wasted a lot of time with that Arizona thing. Then he finally makes the big breakthrough with the rental firm and the stuff with the mud, and he looks like the big hero, but in reality what he's done is keep you way behind the chase. He's given them all the time they need to get us here."

"But he still got us here, right?" McGrath said. "A ways behind them, OK, but he brought us right here all the same."

"No loss to him," Reacher said. "Borken was just itching to tell you where she was, soon as she was safely here, right? The destination was never going to be a secret, was it? That was the whole point. She was a deterrent to stop you attacking. No point in that, without telling you exactly where she was."

McGrath grunted. Thinking about it. Unconvinced.

"They bribed him," Reacher said. "You better believe it. They've got a big war chest, McGrath. Twenty million dollars, stolen bearer bonds."

"The armored car robbery?" McGrath asked. "Northern California somewhere? They did that?"

"They're boasting about it," Reacher said.

McGrath ran it through his head. Went pale. Reacher saw it and nodded.

"Right," he said. "Let me make a guess: Brogan was never short of money, was he? Never groused about the salary, did he?"

"Shit," McGrath said. "Two alimony checks every month, girlfriend, silk jackets, and I never even thought twice about it. I was just so grateful he wasn't one of the moaners."

"He's collecting his next payment right now," Reacher said. "And Milosevic is dead or locked up somewhere."

McGrath nodded slowly.

"And Brogan worked out of California," he said. "Before he came to me. Shit, I never thought twice. A buck gets ten he was the exact agent who went after Borken. He said Sacramento couldn't make it stick. Said the files were unclear as to why not. Why not is because Borken was handing him bucketfuls of dollars to make sure it didn't stick. And the bastard was taking them.''

Reacher nodded. Said nothing.

"Shit," McGrath said again. "Shit, shit, shit. My fault."

Still Reacher said nothing. More tactful just to keep quiet. He understood McGrath's feelings. Understood his position. He had been in the same position himself, time to time in the past. He had felt the knife slip in, right between the shoulder blades.

"I'll deal with Brogan later," McGrath said finally. "After we go get Holly. She mention me at all? She realize I'd come get her? She mention that?"

Reacher nodded.

"She told me she trusted her people," he said.

43

For the first time in twenty years, General Garber had killed a man. He hadn't meant to. He had meant to lay the man out and take his weapon. That was all. The man was part of an inner screen of sentries. They were posted at haphazard intervals in a line a hundred yards south of the courthouse. Garber had trawled back and forth in the woods and scoped them out. A ragged line of sentries, maybe forty or fifty yards between each one, two on the shoulders of the road and the rest in the forest.

Garber had selected the one nearest to a straight line between himself and the big white building. The man was going to have to move. Garber needed direct access. And he needed a weapon. So he had selected the man and worked nearer to him. He had scraped up a fist-sized rock from the damp forest floor. He had worked around behind him.

Their lack of training made the whole thing easy. A sentry screen should be mobile. They should be moving side to side along the length of the perimeter they are told to defend. That way, they cover every inch of the territory, and they find out if the next man in line has been ambushed and dumped on the floor. But these men were static. Just standing there. Watching and listening. Bad tactic.

The selected man was wearing a forage cap. It was camouflaged with the wrong camouflage. It was a black and gray interrupted pattern. Carefully designed to be very effective in an urban environment. Useless in a sun-dappled forest. Garber had come up behind the man and swung the rock. Hit him neatly on the back of the head.

Hit him too hard. Problem was, people are different. There's no set amount of impact that will do it. Not like playing pool. You want to roll the ball into the corner pocket, you know just about exactly how hard you need to cue. But skulls are different. Some are hard. This man's wasn't. It cracked like an eggshell and the spinal cord severed right up at the top and the man was dead before he hit the ground.

"Shit," Garber breathed.

He wasn't worried about the ethics of the situation. Not worried about that at all. Thirty years of dealing with hard men gone bad had defined a whole lot of points for him, ethically. He was worried about buzzards. Unconscious men don't attract them. Dead men do. Buzzards circling overhead spread information. They tell the other sentries: one of your number is dead.

So Garber changed his plan slightly. He took the dead man's M-16 and moved forward farther than he really wanted to. He moved up to within twenty yards of where the trees petered out. He worked left and right until he saw a rock outcrop, ten yards beyond the edge of the woods. That would be the site of his next cautious penetration. He slipped behind a tree and squatted down. Stripped the rifle and checked its condition. Reassembled it, and waited.

HARLAND WEBSTER ROLLED back the videotape for the fourth time and watched the action again. The puff of pink mist, the guard going down, the second guard taking off, the camera's sudden jerked zoom out to cover the whole of the clearing, the second guard silently sprawling. Then a long pause. Then Reacher's crazy sprint. Reacher tossing bodies out of the way, slashing at the ropes, bundling McGrath to safety.

"We made a mistake about that guy," Webster said.

General Johnson nodded.

"I wish Garber was still here," he said. "I owe him an apology."

"Planes are low on fuel," the aide said into the silence.

Johnson nodded again.

"Send one back," he said. "We don't need both of them up there anymore. Let them spell each other."

The aide called Peterson and within half a minute three of the six screens in the vehicle went blank as the outer plane peeled off and headed south. The inner plane relaxed its radius and zoomed its camera out to cover the whole area. The close-up of the clearing fell away to the size of a quarter and the big white courthouse swam into view, bottom right-hand corner of the screens. Three identical views on three glowing screens, one for each of them. They hunched forward in their chairs and stared. The radio in Webster's pocket started crackling.

"Webster?" Borken's voice said. "You there?"

"I'm here," Webster replied.

"What's with the plane?" Borken said. "You losing interest or something?"

For a second, Webster wondered how he knew. Then he remembered the vapor trails. They were like a diagram, up there in the sky.

"Who was it?" he asked. "Brogan or Milosevic?"

"What's with the plane?" Borken asked again.

"Low fuel," Webster said. "It'll be back."

There was a pause. Then Borken's voice came back.

"OK," he said.

"So who was it?" Webster asked again. "Brogan or Milosevic?"

But the radio just went dead on him. He clicked the button off and caught Johnson looking at him. Johnson's face was saying: the military man turned out good and the Bureau guy turned out bad. Webster shrugged. Tried to make it rueful. Tried to make it mean: we both made mistakes. But Johnson's face said: you should have known.

"Could be a problem, right?" the aide said. "Brogan and Milosevic? Whichever one is the good guy, he still thinks Reacher's his enemy. And whichever one is the bad guy, he knows Reacher's his enemy."

Webster looked away. Turned back to the bank of screens.

BORKEN PUT THE radio back in the pocket of his black uniform. Drummed his fingers on the judge's desk. Looked at the people looking back at him.

"One camera is enough," he said.

"Sure," Milosevic said. "One is as good as two."

"We don't need interference right now," Borken said. "So we should nail Reacher before we do anything else."

Milosevic glanced around, nervously.

"Don't look at me," he said. "I'm staying in here. I just want my money."

Borken looked at him. Still thinking.

"You know how to catch a tiger?" he asked. "Or a leopard or something? Out in the jungle?"

"What?" Milosevic asked.

"You tether a goat to a stake," Borken said. "And lie in wait."

"What?" Milosevic asked again.

"Reacher was willing to rescue McGrath, right?" Borken said. "So maybe he's willing to rescue your pal Brogan, too."

GENERAL GARBER HEARD the commotion and risked moving up a few yards. He made it to where the trees thinned out and he crouched. Shuffled sideways to his left to get a better view. The courthouse was dead ahead up the rise. The south wall was face-on to him, but he had a narrow angle down the front. He could see the main entrance. He could see the steps up to the door. He saw a gaggle of men come out. Six men. There were two flanking point men, alert, scanning around, rifles poised. The other four were carrying somebody, spread-eagled, facedown. The person had been seized by the wrists and the ankles. It was a man. Garber could tell by the voice. He was bucking and thrashing and screaming. It was Brogan.

Garber went cold. He knew what had happened to Jackson. McGrath had told him. He raised his rifle. Sighted in on the nearer point man. Tracked him smoothly as he moved right to left. Then his peripheral vision swept the other five. Then he thought about the sentry screen behind him. He grimaced and lowered the rifle. Impossible odds. He had a rule: stick to the job in hand. He'd preached it like a gospel for forty years. And the job in hand was to get Holly Johnson out alive. He crept backward into the forest and shrugged at the two men beside him.

The Chinook crew had clambered out of their wrecked craft and stumbled away into the forest. They had thought they were heading south, but in their disorientation they had moved due north. They had passed straight through the sentry screen without knowing anything about it and come upon a three-star general sitting at the base of a pine. The general had hauled them down and told them to hide. They thought they were in a dream, and they were hoping to wake up. They said nothing and listened as the screaming faded behind the ruined county offices.

REACHER AND MCGRATH heard it minutes later. Faintly, at first, deep in the forest to their left. Then it built louder. They moved together level with a gap between huts where they could see across the Bastion to the mouth of the track. They were ten feet into the forest, far enough back to be well concealed, far enough forward to observe.

They saw the two point men burst out into the sunlight. Then four more men, walking in step, rifles slung, leaning outward, arms counterbalancing something heavy they were carrying. Something that was bucking and thrashing and screaming.

"Christ," McGrath whispered. "That's Brogan."

Reacher stared for a long time. Silent. Then he nodded.

"I was wrong," he said. "Milosevic is the bad guy."

McGrath clicked the Glock's trigger to release the safety device.

"Wait," Reacher whispered.

He moved right and signaled McGrath to follow. They stayed deep in the trees and paralleled the six men and Brogan across the clearing. The men were moving slow across the shale, and Brogan's screaming was getting louder. They looped past the bodies and the tent pegs and the cut ropes and walked on.

"They're going to the punishment hut," Reacher whispered.

They lost sight of them as the trees closed around the path to the next clearing. But they could still hear the screaming.

Sounded like Brogan knew exactly what was going to happen to him. McGrath remembered recounting Borken's end of the conversation on the radio. Reacher remembered burying Jackson's mangled body.

They risked getting a little closer to the next clearing. Saw the six men head for the windowless hut and stop at the door. The point men turned and covered the area with their rifles. The guy gripping Brogan's right wrist fumbled the key out of his pocket with his spare hand. Brogan yelled for help. He yelled for mercy. The guy unlocked the door. Swung it open. Stopped in surprise on the threshold and shouted.

Joseph Ray came out. Still naked, his clothes balled in his arms. Dried blood all over the bottom of his face like a mask. He danced and stumbled over the shale in his bare feet. The six men watched him go.

"Who the hell's that?" McGrath whispered.

"Just some asshole," Reacher whispered back.

Brogan was dropped onto the ground. Then he was hauled upright by the collar. He was staring wildly around and screaming. Reacher saw his face, white and terrified, mouth open. The six men threw him into the hut. They stepped in after him. The door slammed. McGrath and Reacher moved closer. They heard screams and the thump of a body hitting the walls. Those sounds went on for several minutes. Then it went quiet. The door opened. The six men filed out, smiling and dusting their hands. The last man darted back for a final kick. Reacher heard the blow land and Brogan scream. Then the guy locked the door and hustled after the others. They crunched over the stones and were gone. The clearing fell silent.

HOLLY LIMPED ACROSS the raised floor to the door. Pressed her ear onto it and listened. All quiet. No sound. She limped back to her mattress and picked up the spare pair of fatigue trousers. Used her teeth to pick the seams. Tore the material apart until she had separated the front panel of one of the legs. It gave her a piece of canvas cloth maybe thirty inches long and six wide. She took it into the bathroom and ran the sink full of hot water. Soaked the strip of cloth in it. Then she took off her trousers. Squeezed the soaking canvas out and bound it as tight as she could around her knee. Tied it off and put her trousers back on. Her idea was the hot wet cloth might shrink slightly as it dried. It might tighten more. It was near as she was going to get to solving her problem. Keeping the joint rigid was the only way to kill the pain.

Then she did what she'd been rehearsing. She pulled the rubber foot off the bottom of her crutch. Smashed the metal end into the tile in the shower. The tile shattered. She reversed the crutch and used the end of the curved elbow clip to pry the shards off the wall. She selected two. Each was a rough triangle, narrow at the base and pointed. She used the edge of the elbow clip to scrape away the clay at the leading point. Left the vitrified white surface layer intact, like the blade of a knife.

She put her weapons in two separate pockets. Pulled the shower curtain to conceal the damage. Put the rubber foot back on the crutch. Limped back to her mattress, and sat down to wait.

THE PROBLEM WITH using just one camera was that it had to be set to a fairly wide shot. That was the only way to cover the whole area. So any particular thing was small on the screen. The group of men carrying something had shown up like a large insect crawling across the glass.

"Was that Brogan?" Webster asked out loud.

The aide ran the video back and watched again.

"He's facedown," he said. "Hard to tell."

He froze the action and used the digital manipulator to enlarge the picture. Adjusted the joystick to put the spread-eagled man in the center of the screen. Zoomed right in until the image blurred.

"Hard to tell," he said again. "It's one of them, that's for sure."

"I think it was Brogan," Webster said.

Johnson looked hard. Used his finger and thumb against the screen to estimate the guy's height, head to toes.

"How tall is he?" he asked.

HOW TALL IS he?" Reacher asked suddenly.

"What?" McGrath said.

Reacher was behind McGrath in the trees, staring out at the punishment hut. He was staring at the front wall. The wall was maybe twelve feet long, eight feet high. Right to left, there was a two-foot panel, then the door, thirty inches wide, hinged on the right, handle on the left. Then a panel probably seven and a half feet wide running down to the end of the building.

"How tall is he?" Reacher asked again.

"Christ, does it matter?" McGrath said.

"I think it does," Reacher said.

McGrath turned and stared at him.

"Five nine, maybe five ten," he said. "Not an especially big guy."

The cladding was made up of horizontal eight-by-fours nailed over the frame. There was a seam halfway up. The floor was probably three-quarters board laid over two-by-fours. Therefore the floor started nearly five inches above the bottom of the outside cladding. About an inch and a half below the bottom of the doorway.

"Skinny, right?" Reacher said.

McGrath was still staring at him.

"Thirty-eight regular, best guess," he said.

Reacher nodded. The walls would be two-by-fours clad inside and out with the plywood. Total thickness five and a half inches, maybe less if the inside cladding was thinner. Call it the inside face of the end wall was five inches in from the corner, and the floor was five inches up from the bottom.

"Right-handed or left-handed?" Reacher asked.

"Speak to me," McGrath hissed.

"Which?" Reacher said.

"Right-handed," McGrath said. "I'm pretty sure."

The two-by-fours would be on sixteen-inch centers. That was the standard dimension. But from the corner of the hut to the right-hand edge of the door, the distance was only two feet. Two feet less five inches for the thickness of the end wall was nineteen inches. There was probably a two-by-four set right in the middle of that span. Unless they skimped it, which was no problem. The wall would be stuffed with Fiberglas wadding, for insulation.

"Stand back," Reacher whispered.

"Why?" McGrath said.

"Just do it," Reacher replied.

McGrath moved out of the way. Reacher put his eyes on a spot ten inches in from the end of the hut and just shy of five feet up from the bottom. Swayed left and rested his shoulder on a tree. Raised his M-16 and sighted it in.

"Hell are you doing?" McGrath hissed.

Reacher made no reply. Just waited for his heart to beat and fired. The rifle cracked and the bullet punched through the siding a hundred yards away. Ten inches from the corner, five feet from the ground.

"Hell are you doing?" McGrath hissed again.

Reacher just grabbed his arm and pulled him into the woods. Dragged him north and waited. Two things happened. The six men burst back into the clearing. And the door of the punishment hut opened. Brogan was framed in the doorway. His right arm was hanging limp. His right shoulder was shattered and pumping blood. In his right hand, he was holding his Bureau .38. The hammer was back. His finger was tight on the trigger.

Reacher snicked the M-16 to burst fire. Stitched five bursts of three shells into the ground, halfway across the clearing. The six men skidded away, like they were suddenly facing an invisible barrier or a drop off a tall cliff. They ran for the woods. Brogan stepped out of the hut. Stood in a bar of sunshine and tried to lift his revolver. His arm wouldn't work. It hung uselessly.

"Decoy," Reacher said. "They thought I'd go in after him. He was waiting behind the door with his gun. I knew he was the bad guy. But they had me fooled for a moment."

McGrath nodded slowly. Stared at the government-issue .38 in Brogan's hand. Remembered his own being confiscated. He raised the Glock and wedged his wrist against a tree. Sighted down the barrel.

"Forget it," Reacher said.

McGrath kept his eyes on Brogan and shook his head.

"I'm not going to forget it," he said quietly. "Bastard sold Holly out."

"I meant forget the Glock," Reacher said. "That's a hundred yards. Glock won't get near. You'd be lucky to hit the damn hut from here.''

McGrath lowered the Glock and Reacher handed him the M-16. Watched with interest as McGrath sighted it in.

''Where?'' Reacher asked.

''Chest,'' McGrath said.

Reacher nodded.

''Chest is good,'' he said.

McGrath steadied himself and fired. He was good, but not really good. The rifle was still set to burst fire, and it loosed three rounds. The first hit Brogan in the upper left of his forehead, and the other two stitched upward and blasted fragments off the doorframe. Good, but not very. But good enough to do the job. Brogan went down like a marionette with the strings cut. He just telescoped into the ground, right in front of the doorway. Reacher took the M-16 back and sprayed the trees on the edge of the clearing until the magazine clicked empty. Reloaded and handed the Glock back to McGrath. Nodded him east through the forest. They turned together and walked straight into Joseph Ray. He was unarmed and half dressed. Blood dried on his face like brown paint. He was fumbling with his shirt buttons. They were done up into the wrong holes.

''Women and children are going to die,'' he said.

''You all got an hour, Joe,'' Reacher said back to him. ''Spread the word. Anybody wants to stay alive, better head for the hills.''

The guy just shook his head.

''No,'' he said. ''We've got to assemble on the parade ground. Those are our instructions. We've got to wait for Beau there.''

''Beau won't be coming,'' Reacher said.

Ray shook his head again.

''He will be,'' he said. ''You won't beat Beau, whoever you are. Can't be done. We got to wait for him. He's going to tell us what to do.''

''Run for it, Joe,'' Reacher said. ''For Christ's sake, get your kids out of here.''

''Beau says that they have to stay here,'' Ray said. ''Either to enjoy the fruits of victory, or to suffer the consequences of defeat.''

Reacher just stared at him. Ray's bright eyes shone out. His teeth flashed in a brief defiant smile. He ducked his head and ran away.

"Women and children are going to die?'' McGrath repeated.

"Borken's propaganda," Reacher said. "He's got them all convinced compulsory suicide is the penalty for getting beat around here."

"And they're standing still for it?'' McGrath asked.

"He controls them," Reacher said. "Worse than you can imagine."

"I'm not interested in beating them," McGrath said. "Right now, I just want to get Holly out."

"Same thing," Reacher said.

They walked on in silence, through the trees in the direction of the Bastion.

"How did you know?'' McGrath asked. "About Brogan?''

Reacher shrugged.

"I just felt it," he said. "His face, I guess. They like hitting people in the face. They did it to you. But Brogan was unmarked. I saw his face, no damage, no blood. I figured that was wrong. The excitement of an ambush, the tension, they'd have worked it off by roughing him up a little. Like they did with you. But he was theirs, so he just walked in, handshakes all around."

McGrath nodded. Put his hand up and felt his nose.

"But what if you were wrong?'' he said.

"Wouldn't have mattered," Reacher said. "If I was wrong, he wouldn't have been standing behind the door. He'd have been down on the floor with a bunch of broken ribs, because all that thumping around would have been for real."

McGrath nodded again.

"And all that shouting," Reacher said. "They paraded along, real slow, with the guy shouting his head off. They were trying to attract my attention."

"They're good at that," McGrath said. "Webster's worried about it. He doesn't understand why Borken seems so set on getting attention, escalating this whole thing way bigger than he needs to.''

They were in the woods. Halfway between the small clearing and the Bastion. Reacher stopped. Like the breath had been knocked out of him. His hands went up to his mouth. He stood breathless, like all the air had been sucked off the planet.

"Christ, I know why," he said. "It's a decoy."

"What?" McGrath asked.

"I'm getting a bad feeling," Reacher said.

"About what?" McGrath asked him, urgently.

"Borken," Reacher said. "Something doesn't add up. His intentions. Strike the first blow. But where's Stevie? You know what? I think there are two first blows, McGrath. This stuff up here and something else, somewhere else. A surprise attack. Like Pearl Harbor, like his damn war books. That's why he's set on escalating everything. Holly, the suicide thing. He wants all the attention up here.''

44

HOLLY WAS STANDING upright and facing her door when
they came for her. The tight wrap on her knee was drying
stiff. So she had to stand, because her leg would no longer
bend. And she wanted to stand, because that was the best
way to do it.

She heard the footsteps in the lobby. Heard them clatter
up the stairs. Two men, she estimated. She heard them halt
outside her door. Heard the key slide in and the lock click
back. She blinked once and took a breath. The door opened.
Two men crowded in. Two rifles. She stood upright and faced
them. One stepped forward.

"Outside, bitch," he said.

She gripped her crutch. Leaned on it heavily and limped
across the floor. Slowly. She wanted to be outside before
anybody realized she could move better than they thought.
Before anybody realized she was armed and dangerous.

STRIKE THE FIRST blow," Reacher said. "I interpreted that
all wrong."

"Why?" McGrath asked urgently.

"Because I haven't seen Stevie," Reacher said. "Not
since early this morning. Stevie's not here anymore. Stevie's
gone somewhere else."

"Reacher, you're not making any sense," McGrath said.

Reacher shook his head like he was clearing it and snapped

back into focus. Set off racing east through the trees. Talking quiet, but urgently.

"I was wrong," he said. "Borken said they were going to strike the first blow. Against the system. I thought he meant the declaration of independence. I thought that was the first blow. The declaration, and the battle to secure this territory. I thought that was it. On its own. But they're doing something else as well. Somewhere else. They're doing two things at once. Simultaneous."

"What are you saying?" McGrath asked.

"Attention," Reacher said. "The declaration of independence is focusing attention up here in Montana, right?"

"Sure," McGrath said. "They planned to have CNN and the United Nations up here watching it happen. That's a lot of attention."

"But they'd have been in the wrong place," Reacher said. "Borken had a bookcase full of theory telling him not to do what they expect. A whole shelf all about Pearl Harbor. And I overheard him talking in the mine. When he was fetching the missile launcher. Fowler was with him. Borken told Fowler by tonight this place will be way down the list of priorities. So they're doing something else someplace else as well. Something different, maybe something bigger. Twin blows against the system."

"But what?" McGrath asked. "And where? Near here?"

"No," Reacher said. "Probably far away. Like Pearl Harbor was. They're reaching out, trying to land a killer blow somewhere. Because there's a time factor here. It's all co-ordinated."

McGrath stared at him.

"They planned it well," Reacher said. "Getting everybody's attention fixed up here. Independence. That stuff they were going to do with you. They were going to kill you slowly, with the cameras watching. Then the threats of mass suicide, women and children dying. A high-stakes siege. So nobody would be looking anywhere else. Borken's cleverer than I thought. Twin blows, each one covering for the other. Everybody's looking up here, then something big happens someplace else, everybody's looking down there, and he consolidates his new nation back up here."

"But where is it happening, for God's sake?'' McGrath asked. "And what the hell is it?''

Reacher stopped and shook his head.

"I just don't know,'' he said.

Then he froze. There was a crashing noise up ahead and a patrol of six men burst around a tight thicket of pines and stopped dead in front of them. They had M-16s in their hands, grenades on their belts, and surprise and delight on their faces.

BORKEN HAD DEPLOYED every man he had to the search for Reacher, except for the two he had retained to deal with Holly. He heard them start down the courthouse stairs. He pulled the radio from his pocket and flipped it open. Extended the stubby antenna and pressed the button.

"Webster?'' he said. "Get focused in, OK? We'll talk again in a minute.''

He didn't wait for any reply. Just snapped the radio off and turned his head as he tracked the sound of the footsteps on their way outside.

FROM SEVENTY-FIVE YARDS south, Garber saw them come out the door and down the steps. He had moved out of the woods. He had moved forward and crouched behind the outcrop of rock. He figured that was safe enough, now he had backup of a sort. The Chinook crewmen were thirty yards behind him, well separated, well hidden, instructed to yell if anybody approached from the rear. So Garber was resting easy, staring up the slope at the big white building.

He saw two armed men, bearded, starting down the steps. They were dragging a smaller figure with a crutch. A halo of dark hair, neat green fatigues. Holly Johnson. He had never seen her before. Only in the photographs the Bureau men had shown him. The photographs had not done her justice. Even from seventy-five yards, he could feel the glow of her character. Some kind of radiant energy. He felt it, and pulled his rifle closer.

THE M-16 IN Reacher's hands was a 1987 product manufactured by the Colt Firearms Company in Hartford, Connecticut. It was the A2 version. Its principal new feature was the replacement of automatic fire with burst fire. For the sake of economy, the trigger relocked after each burst of three shells. The idea was to waste less ammunition.

Six targets, three shells each from the fresh magazine, a total of eighteen shells and six trigger pulls. Each burst of three shells took a fifth of a second, so the firing sequence itself amounted to just one and a fifth seconds. It was pulling the trigger over and over again which wasted the time. It wasted so much time for Reacher that he ran into trouble after the fourth guy was down. He wasn't aiming. He was just tracking a casual left-to-right arc, close range into the bodies in front of him. The opposing rifles were coming up as a unit. The first four never got there. But the fifth and the sixth were already raised horizontal by the time the fourth went back down, two and a quarter seconds into the sequence.

So Reacher gambled. It was the sort of instinctive gamble you take so fast that to call it a split-second decision is to understate the speed by an absurd factor. He skipped his M-16 straight to the sixth guy, totally sure that McGrath would take the fifth guy with the Glock. The sort of instinctive gamble you take based on absolutely nothing at all except a feeling, which is itself based on absolutely nothing at all except the look of the guy, and how he compares with the look of other people worth trusting in the past.

The flat crack of the Glock was lost under the rattle of the M-16, but the fifth guy went down simultaneous with the sixth. Reacher and McGrath crashed sideways together into the brush and flattened into the ground. Stared through the sudden dead silence at the cordite smoke rising gently through the shafts of sunlight. No movement. No survivors. McGrath blew a big sigh and stuck out his hand, from flat on the ground. Reacher twisted around and shook it.

"You're pretty quick for an old guy," he said.

"That's how I got to be an old guy," McGrath said back.

They stood up slowly and ducked back farther into the trees. Then they could hear more people moving toward them in the forest. A stream of people was moving northwest out of the Bastion. McGrath raised the Glock again and Reacher snicked the M-16 back to singles. He had twelve shells left. Too few to waste, even with the A2's economy measure. Then they saw women through the trees. Women and children. Some men with them. Family groups. They were marching in columns of two. Reacher saw Joseph Ray, a woman at his side, two boys marching blankly in front of him. He saw the woman from the mess kitchen, marching side by side with a man. Three children walking stolidly in front of them.

"Where are they going?" McGrath whispered.

"The parade ground," Reacher said. "Borken ordered it, right?"

"Why don't they just run for it?" McGrath said.

Reacher shrugged and said nothing. He had no explanation. He stood concealed and watched the blank faces pass through the dappled woods. Then he touched McGrath's arm and they sprinted on through the trees and came out behind the mess hall. Reacher glanced cautiously around. Stretched up and grabbed at the roof overhang. Put a foot on the window ledge and hauled himself up onto the shingles. Crawled up the slope of the roof and steadied himself against the bright metal chimney. Raised the stolen field glasses and trained them southeast, down toward the town, thinking: OK, but what the hell else is happening? And where?

GENERAL JOHNSON'S AIDE had the most aptitude with the computer controls, either from familiarity with such things, or from being younger. He used the rubber knobs and the joystick to focus on the area in front of the courthouse steps. Then he zoomed out a touch to frame the view. He had the western face of the courthouse on the right of the screen and the eastern face of the ruined county office on the left. In between were the two lawns, one abandoned and scrubby, the other still reasonably flat. The road ran vertically up the center of the picture, like a map. The jeep which had brought McGrath in was still there where they had dumped it. The aide used it to check his focus. It came in crisp and clear. It was a military-surplus vehicle. Smudged white stencils. They could see the windshield folded down, and a canvas map case, and a jerrican for fuel and a short-handled shovel clipped on the rear.

They all saw the two men bring Holly out. From above, they were in a perfect straight diagonal line, with Holly alone in the middle, like the shape you see when a die rolls a three. They brought her out and waited. Then they saw a huge figure lumbering down the courthouse steps behind them. Borken. He stepped into the road and looked up. Right into the camera, invisible seven miles above him. He stared and waved. Raised his right hand high. There was a black gun in it. Then he looked down and fiddled with something in his left hand. Raised it to his ear. The radio on the desk in front of Webster crackled. Webster picked it up and flipped it open.

"Yes?" he said.

They saw Borken waving up at the camera again.

"See me?" he said.

"We see you," Webster said quietly.

"See this?" Borken said.

He raised the gun again. The General's aide zoomed in tight. Borken's huge bulk filled the screen. Upturned pink face, black pistol held high.

"We see it," Webster said.

The aide zoomed back out. Borken resumed his proper perspective.

"Sig-Sauer P226," Borken said. "You familiar with that weapon?"

Webster paused. Glanced around.

"Yes," he said.

"Nine-millimeter," Borken said. "Fifteen shots to a clip."

"So?" Webster asked.

Borken laughed. A loud sound in Webster's ear.

"Time for some target practice," Borken said. "And guess what the target is?"

They saw the two men move toward Holly. Then they saw Holly's crutch come up. She held it level with both hands. She smashed it hard into the first man's gut. She whipped it back and swung it. Spun and hit the second man in the head. But it was light aluminum. No weight behind it. She dropped it and her hands went to her pockets. Came out with something in each palm. Things that glinted and caught the sun.

She skipped forward and slashed desperately at the face in front of her. Danced and whirled and swung the glinting weapons.

The aide jerked the zoom control. The first man was down, clutching at his throat and face. Blood on his hands. Holly was spinning fast circles, slashing at the air like a panther in a cage, turning on a stiff leg, the other foot dancing in and out as she darted left and right. Webster could hear distorted breathing and gasping through the earpiece. He could hear shouting and screaming. He stared at the screen and pleaded silently: go left, Holly, go for the jeep.

She went right. Swung her left hand high and held her right hand low, like a boxer. Darted for the second man. He raised his rifle, but crossways, in a sheer panic move to ward off the slashing blow. He punched the rifle up to meet her arm, and her wrist cracked against the barrel. Her weapon flew off into the air. She kicked hard under the rifle and caught him in the groin. He wheeled away and collapsed. She darted for Borken. Her glittering hand swung a vicious arc. Webster heard a shriek in his ear. The camera showed Borken ducking away, Holly swarming after him.

But the first man was up again, behind her. Hesitating. Then he was swinging his rifle like a bat. He caught her with the stock flat on the back of her head. She went limp. Her leg stayed stiff. She collapsed over it like she was falling over a gate and sprawled on the road at Borken's feet.

TWO DOWN. ONE of them was Holly. Reacher adjusted the field glasses and stared at her. Two still standing. A grunt with a rifle, and Borken with a handgun and the radio. All in a tight knot, visible through the trees twelve hundred yards southeast and three hundred feet below. Reacher stared at Holly, inert on the ground. He wanted her. He loved her for her courage. Two armed men and Borken, and she'd gone for it. Hopeless, but she'd gone for it. He lowered the field glasses and hitched his legs around the chimney. Like he was riding a metal horse. The chimney was warm. His upper body was flat on the slope of the roof. His head and shoulders were barely above the ridge. He raised the field glasses again, and held his breath, and waited.

• • •

THEY SAW BORKEN'S agitated gestures and then the injured man was getting up and moving in with the other who had hit her. They saw them pinning her arms behind her and dragging her to her feet. Her head was hanging down. One leg was bent, and the other was stiff. They propped her on it and paused. Borken signaled them to move. They dragged her away across the road. Then Borken's voice came back in Webster's ear, loud and breathy.

"OK, fun's over," he said. "Put her old man on."

Webster handed the radio to Johnson. He stared at it. Raised it to his ear.

"Anything you want," he said. "Anything at all. Just don't hurt her."

Borken laughed. A loud, relieved chuckle.

"That's the kind of attitude I like," he said. "Now watch this."

The two men dragged Holly up the knoll in front of the ruined office building. Dragged her over to the stump of the dead tree. They turned her and walked her until her back thumped against the wood. They wrapped her arms around the stump behind her. Her head came up. She shook it, in a daze. One man held both wrists while the other fumbled with something. Handcuffs. He locked her wrists behind the tree. The two men stepped away, back toward Borken. Holly fell and slid down the stump. Then she pushed back and stood up. Shook her head again and gazed around.

"Target practice," Borken said into the radio.

Johnson's aide fiddled with the zoom and made the picture bigger. Borken was walking away. He walked twenty yards south and turned, the Sig-Sauer pointing at the ground, the radio up at his face.

"Here goes," he said.

He turned side-on and raised his arm. Held it out absolutely straight, shoulders turned like a duelist in an old movie. Squinted down the barrel and fired. The pistol kicked silently and there was a puff of dust in the ground, three feet from where Holly was standing still.

Borken laughed again.

"Bad shot," he said. "I need the practice. Might take me

a while to get close. But I've got fourteen more shells, right?''

He fired again. A puff of dust from the earth. Three feet the other side of the stump.

"Thirteen left," Borken said. "I guess CNN is your best bet, right? Call them and tell them the whole story. Make it an official statement. Get Webster to back you up. Then patch them through on this radio. You won't give me my fax line, I'm going to have to communicate direct.''

"You're crazy," Johnson said.

"You're the one who's crazy," Borken said. "I'm a force of history. I can't be stopped. I'm shooting at your daughter. The President's godchild. You don't understand, Johnson. The world is changing. I'm changing it. The world must be my witness.''

Johnson was silent. Stunned.

"OK," Borken said. "I'm going to hang up now. You make that call. Thirteen bullets left. I don't hear from CNN, the last one kills her.''

Johnson heard the line go dead and looked up at the screens and saw Borken drop the radio on the ground. Saw him raise the Sig-Sauer two-handed. Saw him sight it in. Saw him put a round right between his daughter's feet.

REACHER RESTED AGAINST the warm chimney and lowered the glasses. Ran a desperate calculation through his head. A calculation involving time and distance. He was twelve hundred yards away to the northwest. He couldn't get there in time. And he couldn't get there silently. He lay chest down on the roof of the mess hall and called down to McGrath. His voice was already quiet and relaxed. Like he was ordering in a restaurant.

"McGrath?" he said. "Go break into the armory. It's the hut on the end, apart from the others.''

"OK," McGrath called. "What do you want?"

"You know what a Barrett looks like?" Reacher called. "Big black thing, scope, big muzzle brake on it. Find a full magazine. Probably next to them.''

"OK," McGrath said again.

"And hurry," Reacher said.

• • •

GARBER'S VIEW UP from the south cleared when the two soldiers came back around and stood behind Beau Borken. They hung back, like they didn't want to put him off his aim. Borken was maybe sixty feet from Holly, shooting up the rise of the knoll. Garber was seventy yards away down the steep slope. Holly was just left of straight ahead. Borken was just to the right. His black bulk was perfectly outlined against the whiteness of the south wall of the courthouse. Garber saw that somebody had blanked the upper-story windows with new white wood. Borken's head was framed dead center against one of the new rectangles. Garber smiled. It would be like shooting for a small pink bull's-eye on a sheet of white paper. He snicked the M-16 to burst fire and checked it visually. Then he raised it to his shoulder.

MCGRATH STRETCHED UP on his toes and passed the Barrett up toward Reacher. Reacher stretched his hand down and pulled it up. Glanced at it and passed it back down.

"Not this one," he said. "Find one with the serial number ending in five-zero-two-four, OK?"

"Why?" McGrath called.

"Because I know for sure it shoots straight," Reacher said. "I used it before."

"Christ," McGrath said. He set off again at a dead run. Reacher lay back on the roof, trying to keep his heartbeat under control.

BORKEN'S TENTH SHOT was still wide, but not by much. Holly jumped as far as her cuffs would allow. Borken took to pacing back and forth in delight. He was pacing and laughing and stopping to shoot. Garber was tracking his huge bulk left and right against the whiteness of the building. Just waiting for him to stop moving. Because Garber had a rule: make the first shot count.

MCGRATH FOUND THE rifle Reacher had used before and passed it up to the roof. Reacher took it and checked the number. Nodded. McGrath ran like crazy for the mouth of the stony track. Disappeared down it at a sprint. Reacher watched him go. Thumbed the big bullets in the magazine and checked the spring. Pressed the magazine home gently with his palm. Raised the Barrett to his shoulder and balanced it carefully on the ridgeline. Pulled the stock in and ducked his eye to the scope. Used his left thumb to ease the focus out to twelve hundred yards. It racked the lens right out to the stop. He laid his left palm over the barrel. Operated the silky mechanism and put a round in the breech. Stared down at the scene below.

The telescope on the rifle bunched it all up, but the geometry was fine. Holly was up on the knoll, slightly to the right of dead ahead. Handcuffed to the dead tree. He stared at her face for a long moment. Then he nudged the scope. Borken was below her, maybe sixty feet farther on, firing up the rise at her, slightly to the left. He was walking short arcs, back and forth. But anywhere he chose to stop, there was a hundred miles of empty country behind his head. The courthouse walls were well away from Reacher's trajectory. Safe enough. Safe, but not easy. Twelve hundred yards was a hell of a distance. He breathed out and waited for Borken to stop pacing.

Then he froze. In the corner of his eye, he caught the gleam of sun on dull metal. Maybe seventy yards farther on down the slope. A rock. A man behind the rock. A rifle. A familiar head, grizzled hair on some of it. General Garber. Garber, with an M-16, behind a rock, moving the muzzle side to side as he tracked his target, who was walking short arcs seventy yards directly in front of him.

Reacher breathed out and smiled. He felt a warm flood of gratitude. Garber. He had backup. Garber, shooting from just seventy yards. In that split second, he knew Holly was safe. The warm flood of gratitude coursed through him.

Then it changed to an icy blast of panic. His brain kicked in. The compressed geometry below him exploded into a dreadful diagram. Like something on a page, like a textbook explanation of a disaster. From Garber's angle, the courthouse was directly behind Borken. When Borken stopped moving, Garber was going to fire at him. He might hit, or he might miss. Either way, his bullet was going to hit the courthouse wall. Probably right up there in the southeastern corner, second floor. The ton of old dynamite would go up in a percussive fireball a quarter-mile wide. It would vaporize Holly and shred Garber himself. The shock wave would probably knock Reacher right off the mess hall roof, twelve hundred yards away. How the hell could Garber not know?

Borken stopped pacing. Stood sideways on and steadied himself. Reacher blew out a lungful of air. He moved the Barrett. He put the crosshairs dead center on Holly Johnson's temple, right where the soft dark hair billowed down toward her eyes. He kept his lungs empty and waited for the next thump of his heart. Then he squeezed the trigger.

GARBER WATCHED BORKEN'S arm come up. Waited until he had steadied. Squinted down the M-16's sighting grooves and put the pink and white head dead center. It sat there, big and obvious against the blur of sunny white wall behind it. He waited like he'd been taught to a lifetime ago. Waited until his breath was out and his heart was between beats. Then he pulled the trigger.

GENERAL JOHNSON HAD closed his eyes. His aide was staring at the screen. Webster was watching through a lattice of fingers, mouth open, like a child with a new baby-sitter watching a horror movie on television, way after his bedtime.

FIRST THING OUT of the barrel of Reacher's Barrett was a blast of hot gas. The powder in the cartridge exploded in a fraction of a millionth of a second and expanded to a super-heated bubble. That bubble of gas hurled the bullet down the barrel and forced ahead of it and around it to explode out into the atmosphere. Most of it was smashed sideways by the muzzle brake in a perfectly balanced radial pattern, like a doughnut, so that the recoil moved the barrel straight back against Reacher's shoulder without deflecting it either sideways or up or down. Meanwhile, behind it, the bullet was starting to spin inside the barrel as the rifling grooves grabbed at it.

Then the gas ahead of the bullet was heating the oxygen in the air to the point where the air caught fire. There was a brief flash of flame and the bullet burst out through the exact center of it, spearing through the burned air at nineteen hundred miles an hour. A thousandth of a second later, it was a yard away, followed by a cone of gunpowder particles and a puff of soot. Another thousandth of a second later, it was six feet away, and its sound was bravely chasing after it, three times slower.

The bullet took five hundredths of a second to cross the Bastion, by which time the sound of its shot had just passed Reacher's ears and cleared the ridge of the roof. The bullet had a hand-polished copper jacket, and it was flying straight and true, but by the time it passed soundlessly over McGrath's head it had slowed a little. The friction of the air had heated it and slowed it. And the air was moving it. It was moving it right to left as the gentle mountain breeze tugged imperceptibly at it. Half a second into its travel, the bullet had covered thirteen hundred feet and it had moved seven inches to the left.

And it had dropped seven inches. Gravity had pulled it in. The more gravity pulled, the more the bullet slowed. The more it slowed, the more gravity deflected it. It speared onward in a perfect graceful curve. A whole second after leaving the barrel, it was nine hundred yards into its journey. Way past McGrath's running figure, but still over the trees. Still three hundred yards short of its target. Another sixth of a second later, it was clear of the trees and alongside the ruined office building. Now it was a slow bullet. It had pulled four feet left, and five feet down. It passed well clear of Holly and was twenty feet beyond her before she heard the hiss in the air. The sound of its shot was still to come. It had just about caught up with McGrath, running through the trees.

Then there was a second bullet in the air. And a third, and a fourth. Garber fired a full second and a quarter later than Reacher. His rifle was set to auto. It fired a burst of three. Three shells in a fifth of a second. His bullets were smaller and lighter. Because they were lighter, they were faster. They came in at well over two thousand miles an hour. He was nearer the target. Because his bullets were faster and lighter and he was nearer, friction and gravity never really chipped in. His three bullets stayed pretty straight.

Reacher's bullet hit Borken in the head a full second and a third after he fired it. It entered the front of his forehead and was out of the back of his skull three ten-thousandths of a second later. In and out without really slowing much more at all, because Borken's skull and brains were nothing to a two-ounce lead projectile with a needle point and a polished copper jacket. The bullet was well on over the endless forest beyond before the pressure wave built up in Borken's skull and exploded it.

The effect is mathematical and concerns kinetic energy. The way it had been explained to Reacher, long ago, was all about equivalents. The bullet weighed only two ounces, but it was fast. Equivalent to something heavy, but slow. Two ounces moving at a thousand miles an hour was maybe similar to something weighing ten pounds moving at three miles an hour. Maybe something like a sledgehammer swinging hard in a man's hand. That was pretty much the effect. Reacher was watching it through the scope. Heart in his mouth. A full second and a third is a long time to wait. He watched Borken's skull explode like it had been burst from the inside with a sledgehammer. It came apart like a diagram. Reacher saw curved shards of bone bursting outward and red mist blooming.

But what he couldn't see were Garber's three bullets, hurtling through the mess unimpeded, and flying straight on toward the courthouse wall.

45

THE CLASSIC MISTAKE in firing an automatic weapon is to let the recoil from the first bullet jerk the barrel upward, so that the second bullet goes high, and the third higher still. But Garber did not make that mistake. He had enough hours on the range to be reliable from seventy yards. He had been through enough edgy situations to know how to stay cool and concentrated. He put all three bullets right through the exact center of the pink cloud that had been Borken's head.

They spent two ten-thousandths of a second traveling through it and flew on uninterrupted. They smashed through the new plywood sheeting in the window frame. The leading bullet was distorted slightly by the impact and jerked left, tearing through the inner pine siding twenty-two inches later. It crossed Holly's room and reentered the wall to the left of the doorway. Smashed right through and buried itself in the far wall of the corridor.

The second bullet came in through the first bullet's hole and therefore traversed the twenty-two inch gap in a straight line. It came out through the inner siding and was thrown to the right. Crossed the room and smashed on through the bathroom partition and shattered the cheap white ceramic toilet.

The third shell was rising just a fraction. It hit a nail in the outer wall and turned a right angle. Drilled itself sideways and down through eight of the new two-by-fours like a demented termite before its energy was expended. It ended up looking like a random blob of lead pressed into the back of the new pine boarding.

REACHER SAW GARBER'S muzzle flash through his scope. Knew he must be firing triples. Knew he must have hit the courthouse wall. He stared down from twelve hundred yards away and gripped the ridge of the roof and shut his eyes. Waited for the explosion.

GARBER KNEW HIS shots hadn't killed Borken. There hadn't been time. Even dealing with tiny fractions of a second, there's a rhythm. Fire . . . hit. Borken had been hit before his bullets could possibly have gotten there. So somebody else was up and shooting. There was a team in action. Garber smiled. Fired again. Pumped his trigger finger nine more times and stitched Borken's two soldiers all over the court-house wall with his remaining twenty-seven shells.

MILOSEVIC CAME OUT of the courthouse lobby and down the steps at a run. He had his Bureau .38 held high in his right hand and his gold shield in his left.

"FBI agent!" he screamed. "Everybody freeze!"

He glanced to his right at Holly and then at Garber on his way up to meet him and at McGrath racing around from behind the office building. McGrath went straight for Holly. He hugged her tight against the dead tree. She was laughing. She couldn't hug back, because her arms were still cuffed behind the post. McGrath let her go and ran down the slope. Smacked a high five with Milosevic.

"Who's got the keys?" McGrath yelled.

Garber pointed over toward the two dead soldiers. Mc-Grath ran to them and searched through the oozing pockets. Came out with a key and ran back up to the knoll. Ducked around to the back of the stump and unlocked Holly's wrists. She staggered away and McGrath darted forward and grabbed her arm. Milosevic found her crutch on the road and tossed it over. McGrath caught it and handed it to her. She got steady and came down the rise, arm in arm with McGrath. They made it to level ground and stood there together, gazing around in the sudden deafening quiet.

"Who do I thank?" Holly asked.

She was holding McGrath's arm, staring at the remains of Borken, lying sixty feet away. The corpse was flat on its back, high and wide. It had no head.

"This is General Garber," McGrath said. "Top boy in the military police."

Garber shook his head.

"Wasn't me," he said. "Somebody beat me to it."

"Wasn't me," Milosevic said.

Then Garber nodded behind them.

"Probably this guy," he said.

Reacher was on his way down the knoll. Out of breath. A frame six five high and two hundred and twenty pounds in weight is good for a lot of things, but not for sprinting a mile.

"Reacher," Holly said.

He ignored her. Ignored everybody. Just ran on south and turned to stare up at the white wall. He saw bullet holes. A lot of bullet holes. Probably thirty holes, most of them scattered over the second floor in the southeastern corner. He stared at them for a second and ran for the jeep parked at the curb. Snatched the shovel from its clips under the spare fuel can. Sprinted for the steps. Crashed through the door and up the stairs to Holly's room. Ran for the front wall.

He could see at least a dozen exit holes punched through the wood. Ragged splintered holes. He smashed the blade of the shovel into one of them. Split the pine board lengthways and used the shovel to wrench it off. Smashed the shovel behind the next and tore it away from the nails securing it. By the time McGrath was in the room, he had exposed four feet of studding. By the time Holly joined them, they were staring into an empty cavity.

"No dynamite," she said, quietly.

Reacher ducked away to the adjacent wall. Tore enough boards off to be sure.

"There never was any," Holly said. "Shit, I can't believe it."

"There was some," McGrath said. "Jackson called it in. Described the whole thing. I saw his report. He unloaded the truck with seven other guys. He carried it up here. He saw it going into the walls, for God's sake. A ton of dynamite. Kind of a hard thing to be confused about.''

"So they put it in," Reacher said. "And then they took it out. They let people see it going in, then they took it out again secretly. They used it somewhere else.''

"Took it out again?" Holly repeated.

"Women and children have to die," Reacher said, slowly.

"What?" Holly asked. "What are you saying?"

"But not here," he said. "Not these women and children.''

"What?" Holly said again.

"Not mass suicide," Reacher said. "Mass murder.''

Then he just went blank. He was silent. But in his head, he was hearing something. He was hearing the same terrible blast he had heard thirteen years before. The sound of Beirut. The sound of the Marine compound, out near the airport. He was hearing it all over again, and it was deafening him.

"Now we know what it is," he muttered through the shattering roar.

"What is it?" McGrath asked.

"Low on its springs," Reacher said. "But we don't know where it's gone.''

"What?" Holly said again.

"Women and children have to die," Reacher repeated. "Borken said so. He said the historical circumstances justified it. But he didn't mean these women and these children up here.''

"What the hell are you talking about?" McGrath said.

Reacher glanced at him, and then at Holly, surprised, like he was seeing them both for the first time.

"I was in the motor pool," he said. "I saw the truck. Our truck? It was parked up, low on its springs, like it had a heavy weight inside.''

"What?" Holly said again.

"They've made themselves a truck bomb," Reacher said. "Stevie's delivering it somewhere, some public place. That's the other attack. They're going to explode it in a crowd. There's a whole ton of dynamite in it. And he's six hours ahead of us.''

McGrath was first down the stairs.

"Into the jeep," he yelled.

Garber ran for the jeep. But Milosevic was much nearer. He vaulted in and fired it up. Then McGrath was helping Holly into the front seat. Reacher was on the sidewalk, staring south, lost in thought. Milosevic was drawing his revolver. He was thumbing the hammer back. Garber stopped. Raised his rifle and aimed. Milosevic leaned across in front of Holly. McGrath jumped away. Milosevic stamped on the gas and roared away one-handed with the muzzle jammed into Holly's side. One-handed over the rough road, the jeep was all over the place. No chance of hitting Milosevic. Garber could see that. He lowered his rifle and watched them go.

BOTH OF THEM?" Webster said to himself. "Please, God, no."

"We could use another chopper right now," the aide said. "I don't think we have to worry about the missiles anymore."

He panned the camera north and west and zoomed in on the mountain bowl in front of the mine entrances. The four missile trucks were sitting inert. The sprawled body of the dead sentry was nearby.

"OK, call in a chopper," Johnson said.

"Better coming direct from you, sir," the aide said.

Johnson turned sideways to use the phone. Then he spun back to watch as the jeep drove into shot. It bounced up out of the last hairpin into the bowl and raced across the shale. Swerved around the dead trucks and slewed to a stop in front of the left-hand shed. Milosevic jumped out and danced around the hood. Revolver steady on Holly as he approached. He pulled her out by the arm and dragged her to the big wooden doors. Levered one open with his foot and pushed her inside. He followed her in and the huge door swung shut. Webster glanced away from the screen.

"Call the chopper, sir," the aide said.

"Make it a fast one," Webster added.

QUICKEST WAY TO the mines was a shortcut through the Bastion. It was deserted and quiet. They ran through it and headed north across the rifle range toward the parade ground.

Stopped short in the woods. The whole remaining militia population was standing silently in neat ranks, quiet fearful faces turned to the front, where Borken's upturned box still awaited his arrival.

Reacher ignored them and led the others around in the trees. Then in a straight line to the road. Straight north along it. Reacher was carrying the big Barrett. He had retrieved it from the mess hall roof, because he liked it. Garber was hurrying at his side. McGrath was pushing ahead as fast as he could, desperate to get to Holly.

They ducked back into the woods before the last hairpin and Reacher scouted ahead. He holed up behind the rock he'd used before and covered every inch of the bowl with the Barrett's scope. Then he waved the other two up to join him.

"They're in the motor pool," he said. "Left-hand shed."

He pointed with the fat barrel of the sniper rifle and the others saw the abandoned jeep and nodded. He ran over the shale and crouched behind the hood of the first missile truck. Garber sent McGrath next. Then he ran over. They crouched together behind the truck and stared at the log doors.

"What now?" Garber asked. "Frontal assault?"

"He's got a gun to her head," McGrath said. "I don't want her hurt, Reacher. She's precious to me, OK?"

"Any other way in?" Garber asked.

Reacher stared at the doors and the roaring of the Beirut bomb receded and was replaced by the quiet whimpering of an earlier nightmare. He spent a minute trawling desperately for an alternative. He thought about the rifles and the missiles and the trucks. Then he gave it up.

"Keep him occupied," he said. "Talk to him, anything."

He left the Barrett and took the Glock back from McGrath. Dodged to the next truck, and the next, all the way level with the entrance to the other cavern. The charnel house, full of bodies and skeletons and rats. He heard McGrath calling to Milosevic in a faint faraway voice and he ran to the big log doors. Ducked in through the gap and moved back into the dark.

He had no flashlight. He felt his way around the troop carrier and eased on into the mountain. He held his hand above his head and felt the roof come down. Felt for the bodies in the pile and skirted them. Crouched and headed left for the skeletons. The rats were hearing him and smelling him and squealing angry warnings all the way back to their nests. He dropped to his knees and then lay down and swam through the pile of damp bones. Felt the roof of the tunnel lower and the sides press in. Took a deep breath and felt the fear come back.

THE FASTEST HELICOPTER available on that day was a Marine Corps Night Hawk stationed at Malmstrom. It was a long, fat, humped machine, but it was quick. Within minutes of Johnson's call, it was spinning up and receiving orders to head west and north to a gravel turnout on the last road in Montana. Then it was in the air. The Marine pilot found the road and followed it north, fast and low, until he spotted a cluster of Army command vehicles parked tight into a rock cutting. He swung back and put down on the turnout and waited. Saw three men racing south toward him. One was a civilian, and two were Army. One was a Colonel and the other was the Chairman of the Joint Chiefs of Staff. The pilot shrugged at his crewman who pointed upward through the Plexiglas canopy. There was a lone vapor trail maybe thirty-six thousand feet up. Some big jet was unwinding a tight spiral and streaking south. The pilot shrugged again and figured whatever was happening, it was happening to the south. So he made a provisional course calculation and was surprised when the brass clambered aboard and ordered him to head north into the mountains.

REACHER WAS LAUGHING. He was hauling himself along through the tunnel and laughing out loud. Shaking and crying with laughter. He was no longer afraid. The tight clamp of the rock on his body was like a caress. He had done this once, and survived it. It was possible. He was going to get through.

The fear had disappeared as suddenly as it had come. He had pushed through the pile of bones in the dark and stretched out and felt the rock clamp down against his back. His chest had seized and his throat had gagged tight. He had felt the hot damp flush of panic and pressed himself into the ground. He had felt his strength drain away. Then he had focused. The job in hand. Holly. Milosevic's revolver pushed against the dark billow of her hair, her fabulous eyes dull with despair. He had seen her in his mind at the end of the tunnel. Holly. Then the tunnel seemed to straighten and become a warm smooth tube. An exact fit for his bulky shoulders. Like it was tailored for him, and him alone. A simple horizontal journey. He had learned a long time ago that some things were worth being afraid of. And some things were not. Things that he had done before and survived did not justify fear. To be afraid of a survivable thing was irrational. And whatever else he was, Reacher knew he was a rational man. In that split second the fear disappeared and he felt himself relax. He was a fighter. An avenger. And Holly was waiting for him. He thrust his arms forward like a swimmer diving for the water and swarmed through the mountain toward her.

He charged along with a tidy rhythm. Like marching out on the open road, but doing it lying down in the dark. Small deft movements of hands and feet. Head lowered. Laughing with relief. He felt the tunnel get smaller and hug him. He slid on through. He felt the blank wall ahead and folded himself neatly around the corner. Breathed easily and stopped laughing. Told himself it was time for quiet. He crawled on as fast as he could. Slowed up when he sensed the roof soaring away above him. Crept forward until the smell of the air told him he was nearly through.

Then he heard the helicopter. He heard the faint thumping of the rotors in the distance. He heard feet scuffling forty yards in front of him. The inarticulate sound of surprise and panic. He heard Milosevic's voice. High-pitched West Coast accent.

"Keep that chopper away from here," Milosevic screamed through the door.

The noise was getting nearer. Growing louder.

"Keep it away, you hear?" Milosevic screamed. "I'll kill her, McGrath. That's a promise, you hear?"

It was totally dark. There were vehicles between Reacher and the cracks of light around the door. But not the white truck. That was gone. He rolled up into the space where it had been and pulled the Glock from his pocket. The thumping of the rotor blades was very close. It was battering the doors and filling the cavern.

"I'll trade her with you," Milosevic screamed through the door. "I get out of here unharmed, you get her back, OK? McGrath? You hear me?"

If there was a reply, Reacher didn't hear it.

"I'm not with these guys," Milosevic screamed. "This whole thing is nothing to do with me. Brogan got me into it. He made me do it."

The noise was shattering. The heavy doors were shaking.

"I did it for the money, that's all," Milosevic screamed. "Brogan was giving me money. Hundreds of thousands of dollars, McGrath. You'd have done the exact same thing. Brogan was making me rich. He bought me a Ford Explorer. The Limited Edition. Thirty-five grand. How the hell else was I ever going to get one?"

Reacher listened to the screaming voice in the darkness. He didn't want to shoot him. For one crazy moment, he felt absurdly grateful to him, because he had banished his child-hood nightmare. He had forced him to confront it and defeat it. He had made him a better man. He wanted to run up to him and shake him by the hand. He could picture himself doing it. But then the picture changed. He needed to run up to him and shake him by the throat and ask him if he knew where Stevie had taken the white truck. That was what he needed to do. That was why he didn't want to shoot him. He crept forward in the deafening noise and skirted around the vehicles.

He was operating in a one-dimensional world. He could see nothing, because of the darkness. He could hear nothing, because of the helicopter. He sensed movement near the doors. Came out from behind a pickup and saw a shape framed against the cracks of light. A shape that should have been two shapes. Wide at the top, four legs, Milosevic with his arm around Holly's throat, his gun at her head. He waited for his vision to build. Their faces faded in from black to gray. Holly in front of Milosevic. Reacher raised the Glock. Circled left to get an angle. His shin caught a fender. He staggered and backed into a pile of paint cans. They crashed silently to the rock floor, inaudible in the crushing noise from outside. He sprinted closer to the light.

Milosevic sensed it and turned. Reacher saw his mouth open in a silent shout. Saw him twist and push Holly out in front of him like a shield. Saw him stall with indecision, his revolver up in the air. Reacher dodged right, then danced back left. He saw Milosevic track him both ways. Saw Holly use the sway to tear herself out of his grip. The rotor noise was shattering. He saw Milosevic glancing left and right. Saw him making his decision. Reacher was armed, Holly was not. Milosevic lunged forward. The .38 flashed silently in the noise. The brief white flame was blinding in the dark. Reacher lost his sense of where Holly was. He cursed and held his fire. He saw Milosevic aim again. Beyond him, he saw Holly's arm come up and stretch around his head from behind. He saw her hand touch his face with gentle precision. He saw him stumble. Then the door heaved open and Holly staggered away from the shattering flood of noise and sunlight and crashed straight into his arms.

The sunlight fell in a bright bar across Milosevic. He was lying on his back. His .38 was in his hand. The hammer was back. There was a shard of bathroom tile sticking out of his head where his left eye should have been. It was maybe three inches in and three inches out. A small worm of blood was running away from the point of entry.

Then the open door was crowded with people. Reacher saw McGrath and Garber standing in a blast of dust. A Night Hawk was landing behind them. Three men were spilling out and running over. A civilian and a Colonel. And General Johnson. Holly twisted and saw them and buried her face back in Reacher's chest.

Garber was the first to them. He pulled them out into the light and the noise. They stumbled awkwardly, four-legged. The downdraft tore at them. Dust blasted off the shale. McGrath stepped near and Holly pulled herself from Reacher's grip and threw herself at him and hugged him hard. Then General Johnson was moving in on her through the crowd.

"Holly," he mouthed through the din.

She straightened in the light. Grinned at him. Hooked her

hair back behind her ears. Pulled away from McGrath and hugged her father close.

"Still stuff for me to do, Dad," she screamed over the engines. "I'll tell you everything later, OK?"

46

REACHER MADE A twirling signal with his hand to tell the helicopter pilot to keep the engines spinning and ran through the noise and the eddying dust to take the Barrett back from Garber. He waved the others toward the machine. Hustled them up the ladder and followed them in through the sliding door. Laid the Barrett on the metal floor and dumped himself into a canvas chair. Pulled his headset on. Thumbed the button and called through to the pilot.

"Stand by, OK?" he said. "I'll give you a course as soon as I've got one."

The pilot nodded and ran the engines up out of idle. The rotor thumped faster and the noise built louder. The weight of the aircraft came up off the tires.

"Where the hell are we going?" Webster shouted.

"We're chasing Stevie, chief," McGrath shouted back. "He's driving the truck. The truck is full of dynamite. He's going to explode it somewhere. Remember what the Kendall sheriff said? Stevie always got sent out to do the dirty work? You want me to draw you a damn picture?"

"But he can't have gotten out of here," Webster yelled. "The bridge is blown. And there are no tracks through the forest. They closed them all."

"Forest Service guy didn't say that," McGrath yelled back. "They closed some of them. He wasn't sure which ones, was all. What he said was maybe there's a way through, maybe there isn't.''

"They had two years to spy it out,'' Reacher shouted. "You said the pickup had spent time on Forest Service tracks, right? Crushed sandstone all over the underside? They had two whole years to find a way through the maze.''

Webster glanced to his left, east, over to where the forest lay beyond the giant mountain. He nodded urgently, eyes wide.

"OK, so we got to stop him,'' he yelled. "But where has he gone?''

"He's six hours ahead of us,'' Reacher shouted. "We can assume the forest was pretty slow. Call it two hours? Then four hours on the open road. Maybe two hundred miles? Diesel Econoline, hauling a ton, can't be averaging more than about fifty.''

"But which damn direction?'' Webster yelled through the noise.

Holly glanced at Reacher. That was a question they had asked each other a number of times, in relation to that exact same truck. Reacher opened up the map in his head and trawled around it all over again, clockwise.

"Could have gone east,'' he shouted. "He'd still be in Montana, past Great Falls. Could be down in Idaho. Could be in Oregon. Could be halfway to Seattle.''

"No,'' Garber yelled. "Think about it the other way around. That's the key to this thing. Where has he been ordered to go? What would the target be?''

Reacher nodded slowly. Garber was making sense. The target.

"What does Borken want to attack?'' Johnson yelled.

Borken had said: you study the system and you learn to hate it. Reacher thought hard and nodded again and thumbed his mike and called through to the pilot.

"OK, let's go,'' he said. "Straight on south of here should do it.''

The noise increased louder and the Night Hawk lifted heavily off the ground. It swung in the air and rose clear of the cliffs. Slipped south and banked around. Dropped its nose and accelerated hard. The noise moved up out of the cabin and settled to a deep roar inside the engines. The ground tilted and flashed past below. Reacher saw the mountain hairpins unwinding and the parade ground sliding past. The knot of tiny people was breaking up. They were drifting away into the trees and being swallowed up under the green canopy. Then the narrow slash of the rifle range was under them, then the broad stony circle of the Bastion. Then the aircraft rose sharply as the ground fell away so that the big white courthouse slipped by underneath as small as a dollhouse. Then they were over the ravine, over the broken bridge, and away into the vast forested spaces to the south.

Reacher tapped the pilot on the shoulder and spoke through the intercom.

"What speed are we doing?" he asked.

"Hundred and sixty," the pilot said.

"Course?" Reacher asked.

"Dead on south," the pilot said.

Reacher nodded. Closed his eyes and started to calculate. It was like being back in grade school. He's two hundred miles ahead, doing fifty miles an hour. You're chasing him at a hundred and sixty. How long before you catch him? Grade school math had been OK for Reacher. So had fighting in the yard. The fighting part had stayed with him better than the math. He was sure there must be some kind of a formula for it. Something with x and y all over the damn page. Something equaling something else. But if there was a formula, he had long ago forgotten it. So he had to do it by trial and error. Another hour, Stevie would be two hundred and fifty miles from home. The Night Hawk would have done one hundred and sixty. Way behind. An hour after that, Stevie would be three hundred miles out, and the Night Hawk would be three hundred and twenty. Overshot. Therefore they were going to catch him somewhere near the top of the second hour. If they were headed in the right direction.

Flathead Lake came into view, far ahead and far below. Reacher could see the roads snaking across the rugged terrain. He thumbed the button on his mike.

"Still south?" he asked.

"Dead on," the pilot said.

"Still one-sixty?" Reacher asked.

"Dead on," the pilot said again.

"OK, stick with it," Reacher said. "Hour and fifty minutes, maybe."

"So where is he going?" Webster asked.

"San Francisco," Reacher said.

"Why?" McGrath asked.

"Or Minneapolis," Reacher said. "But I'm gambling on San Francisco."

"Why?" McGrath asked again.

"San Francisco or Minneapolis," Reacher said. "Think about it. Other possibilities would be Boston, New York, Philly, Cleveland, Richmond in Virginia, Atlanta, Chicago, St. Louis, and Kansas City in Missouri, or Dallas in Texas."

McGrath just shrugged blankly. Webster looked puzzled. Johnson glanced at his aide. Garber was motionless. But Holly was smiling. She smiled and winked at Reacher. He winked back and the Night Hawk thumped on south over Missoula at a hundred and sixty miles an hour.

CHRIST, IT'S THE Fourth of July," Webster said suddenly.

"Tell me about it," Reacher said. "Lots of people gathered in public places. Families, kids and all."

Webster nodded grimly.

"OK, where exactly in San Francisco?" he asked.

"I'm not sure," Reacher said.

"North end of Market," Holly said. "Right near Embarcadero Plaza. That's where, chief. I've been there on the Fourth. Big parade in the afternoon, fireworks over the water at night. Huge crowds all day long."

"Huge crowds everywhere on the Fourth," Webster said. "You better be guessing right, people."

McGrath looked up. A slow smile was spreading over his bruised face.

"We are guessing right," he said. "It's San Francisco for sure. Not Minneapolis or anyplace else."

Reacher smiled back and winked. McGrath had gotten it.

"You want to tell me why?" Webster asked him.

McGrath was still smiling.

"Go figure," he said. "You're the damn Director."

"Because it's the nearest?" Webster asked.

McGrath nodded.

"In both senses," he said, and smiled again.

"What both senses?" Webster asked. "What are we talking about?"

Nobody answered him. The military men were quiet. Holly and McGrath were staring out through the windows at the ground, two thousand feet below. Reacher was craning up, looking ahead through the pilot's Plexiglas canopy.

"Where are we?" he asked him.

The pilot pointed down at a concrete ribbon below.

"That's U.S. 93," he said. "Just about to leave Montana and enter Idaho. Still heading due south."

Reacher nodded.

"Great," he said. "Follow 93. It's the only road goes south, right? We'll catch him somewhere between here and Nevada."

HE STARTED WORRYING near the top of the second hour. Started worrying badly. Started desperate revisions to his grade school calculations. Maybe Stevie was driving faster than fifty. He was a fast driver. Faster than Bell had been. Maybe he was doing nearer sixty. Where did that put him? Three hundred and sixty miles out. In which case they wouldn't catch him until two hours fifteen minutes had elapsed. What if he was doing seventy? Could that Econoline sustain seventy, hour after hour, with a ton in back? Maybe. Probably. In which case he was four hundred and twenty miles out. A total of two hours forty minutes before they overhauled him. That was the envelope. Somewhere between one hour fifty minutes and two hours forty minutes, somewhere between Montana and Nevada. A whole fifty minutes of rising panic. More than a hundred miles of concrete ribbon to watch before he could know for sure he was wrong and they had to peel off hopelessly northeast toward Minnesota.

The helicopter was flying nose down, top speed, straight along U.S. 93. The seven passengers were craned forward, staring down at the road. They were over a town called Salmon. The pilot was calling out information like a tour guide. The giant peak of Mount McGuire, ten thousand feet, way off to the right. Twin Peaks, ten and a half thousand feet, up ahead to the right. Borah Peak, highest of all, twelve and a half thousand feet, way ahead to the left. The aircraft rose and fell a thousand feet above the terrain. Hurtled along lower than the surrounding peaks, nose down to the highway like a bloodhound.

Time ticked away. Twenty minutes. Thirty. The road was pretty much empty. It connected Missoula in the north to Twin Falls in Idaho, three hundred miles to the south. Neither was a booming metropolis and this was a holiday. Everybody had already gotten where they were going. There was an occasional automobile and an occasional trucker working overtime. No white Econoline. There had been two white vehicles, but they were both pickups. There had been one panel truck, but it was dark green. That was all. Nothing else. No white truck. Sometimes the road was empty all the way to the horizon in front of them. The time was ticking away. Like a bomb. Forty minutes. Fifty.

"I'm going to call Minneapolis," Webster said. "We blew it."

McGrath waited, hoping. He shook his head.

"Not yet," he said. "That's a desperation move. Mass panic. Can you imagine the crowds? The evacuation? People are going to get trampled."

Webster peered out and down. Stared at the road for a full minute. Fifty-four minutes into the fifty-minute envelope.

"Get worse than trampled if that damn truck's already up there," he said. "You want to imagine that?"

Time ticked away. Fifty-eight minutes. An hour. The road stayed empty.

"There's still time," Garber said. "San Francisco or Minneapolis, either one, he's still got to be a long way short."

He glanced at Reacher. Doubt and trust visible in his eyes, in approximately equal measures. More time ticked away. An hour and five minutes. The road still stayed empty, all the way to the distant horizon. The speeding helicopter reeled it in, only to reveal a new horizon, still empty.

"He could be anywhere," Webster said. "San Francisco's wrong, maybe Minneapolis is wrong, too. He could be in Seattle already. Or anywhere."

"Not Seattle," Reacher said.

He stared forward. Stared on and on. Fear and panic had him by the throat. He checked his watch again and again. An hour and ten minutes. Eleven. Twelve. Thirteen. Fourteen. An hour and fifteen minutes. He stared at the watch and the empty ribbon below. Then he sat back and went quiet. Chilled with terror. He had hung on as long as he could, but they had reached the point where the math went absurd. To be this far south without passing him, Stevie would need to be driving at a hundred miles an hour. Or a hundred and twenty. Or a hundred and fifty. He glanced at the others and spoke in a voice which didn't sound like his own.

"I blew it," he said. "It must have been Minneapolis."

Then the thump of the engines faded and for the second time that day the huge bass roar of the bomb came back. He kept his eyes wide open so he wouldn't have to see it, but he saw it anyway. Not Marines this time, not hard men camped out in the heat to do a job, but soft people, women and children, small and smaller, camped out in a city park to watch fireworks, vaporizing and bursting into a hazy pink dew like his friends had done thirteen years before. The bone fragments coming out of children and hissing away through the burning air and hitting other children a hundred yards farther on. Hitting them and tearing through their soft guts like shrapnel and putting the luckiest ones in the hospital for a whole agonizing year.

They were all staring at him. He realized tears were rolling down his cheeks and splashing onto his shirt.

"I'm sorry," he said.

They looked away.

"I got calls to make," Webster said. "Why is it Minneapolis now? Why was it ever San Francisco?"

"Federal Reserve branches," Reacher said quietly. "There are twelve of them. The nearest two to Montana are San Francisco and Minneapolis. Borken hated the Fed. He thought it was the main instrument of the world government. He thought it was a big conspiracy to eliminate the middle classes. It was his special theory. He said it put him ahead in his understanding. And he believed the Fed ordered his father's bank to finagle the old guy into taking a loan so they could deliberately default him later."

"So Borken's attacking the Fed?" Johnson asked urgently. Reacher nodded.

"Twin blows," he said. "In the war against the world government. Attack the old system with a surprise move, like Pearl Harbor. At the same time as setting up a brand-new system for converts to flock to. One bird with two stones."

He stopped talking. Too tired to continue. Too dispirited. Garber was staring at him. Real pain in his face. The beating of the engines was so loud it sounded like total silence.

"The declaration of independence was only half of it," McGrath said. "Double decoy. We were supposed to be focused up there, worried about Holly, worried about a suicide pact, going crazy, while they bombed the Fed behind our backs. I figured San Francisco because of Kendall, remember? I figured Borken would target the nearest branch to where his old man's farm was."

Webster nodded.

"Hell of a plan," he said. "Holiday weekend, agents on leave, big strategic decisions to make, everybody looking in the wrong place. Then the whole world looking at the bombing while Borken secures his territory back up there."

"Where is the Fed in Minneapolis?" Johnson asked urgently.

Webster shrugged vaguely.

"No idea," he said. "I've never been to Minneapolis. I imagine it's a big public building, probably in a nice spot, parks all around, maybe on the river or something. There's a river in Minneapolis, right?"

Holly nodded.

"It's called the Mississippi," she said.

"No," Reacher said.

"It damn well is," Holly said. "Everybody knows that."

"No," Reacher said again. "It's not Minneapolis. It's San Francisco."

"Mississippi goes nowhere near San Francisco," Holly said.

Then she saw a giant smile spreading across Reacher's face. A final gleam of triumph in his tired eyes.

"What?" she said.

"San Francisco was right," he said.

Webster grunted in irritation.

"We'd have passed him already," he said. "Miles back."

Reacher thumbed his mike. Shouted up to the pilot.

"Turn back," he said. "A big wide loop."

Then he smiled again. Smiled and closed his eyes.

"We did pass him," he said. "Miles back. Right over his damn head. They painted the truck green."

The Night Hawk swung away into a high banked loop. The passengers swung their gaze from window to window as the landscape rotated below.

"There was paint in the motor pool," Reacher said. "I tripped over the cans. Probably camouflage base coat. They slapped it on this morning. Damn stuff is probably still wet."

They saw a Kenworth they had passed minutes ago. It was snuffling along a thousand feet below. Then a long stretch of empty pavement. Then a white pickup. More empty road. Then a dark green panel truck, speeding south.

"Down, down," Reacher was calling through.

"Is that it?" McGrath asked.

The gap between the panel truck and the pickup in front was lengthening. The truck was falling back. There was nothing behind it, all the way to the horizon. The Night Hawk was losing height. It was dropping toward the truck the way an eagle heads for a baby rabbit.

"Is that it?" McGrath asked again.

"That's it," Reacher said.

"It sure is," Holly whooped.

"You positive?" McGrath asked.

"Look at the roof," Holly told him.

McGrath looked. The roof was streaked with dark green paint, but he could see it was peppered with tiny holes. Like somebody had fired a shotgun right through it.

"We stared at those damn holes for two whole days," Holly said. "I'll remember them the rest of my life."

"There are a hundred and thirteen of them," Reacher said. "I counted. It's a prime number."

Holly laughed and leaned over. Smacked a joyous high five with him.

"That's our truck," she said. "No doubt about it."

"Can you see the driver?" McGrath asked.

The pilot tilted down and rocked sideways for a close look.

"It's Stevie," Holly shouted back. "For sure. We've got him."

"This thing got weapons?" Webster asked.

"Two big machine guns," the pilot called through. "But I'm not going to use them. That I can't do. Military can't get involved in law enforcement."

"Can you fly this thing straight and level?" Reacher asked him. "Fifty miles an hour? Maybe sixty? Without asking too many questions?"

The pilot laughed. It came through the headsets tinny and distorted.

"I can fly this thing any old way you want me to," he said. "With the General's permission, of course."

Johnson nodded cautiously. Reacher leaned down and picked the Barrett up off the floor. Unfastened his harness and stood up into a crouch. Waved to Holly to change seats with him. She crawled across in front of McGrath and Reacher eased into her place. He could feel the Night Hawk slowing and dropping in the air. He put some length into Holly's harness and fastened it loosely around his waist. Stretched back for the door release. Tugged at the handle and the door slid back on its runners.

Then there was a gale of air coming in as the slipstream howled through the opening and the aircraft was turning half sideways, sliding through the air like a car skids through snow. The green truck was below and behind, maybe two hundred feet down. The pilot was stabilizing his speed until he matched the truck's progress and tilting the aircraft so that Reacher's eyeline was pointing straight down at the road.

"How's this?" the pilot asked.

Reacher thumbed his mike button.

"Dead on," he said. "Anything up ahead?"

"One vehicle coming north," the copilot said. "When that's through, you got nothing at all for ten miles."

"Anything behind?" Reacher asked. He saw the northbound vehicle streak by below.

McGrath stuck his head out into the gale. Ducked back in and nodded.

"Clear behind," he said.

Reacher raised the Barrett to his shoulder. Put a round in the breech. Shooting at a moving vehicle from another moving vehicle is not a great recipe for accuracy, but he was looking at a distance of less than seventy yards and a target about twenty feet long and seven feet wide, so he wasn't worrying about it. He put the crosshairs on a point two-thirds of the way down the length of the roof. He figured the forward movement of the truck and the backward movement of the air might put the bullet dead center through the load compartment. He wondered vaguely whether the three-foot mattress was still in there.

"Wait," Webster shouted. "What if you're wrong? What if it's empty? You're only guessing, right? This whole thing is guesswork. We need proof, Reacher. We need some kind of corroboration here."

Reacher didn't glance back. Kept his eye on the scope.

"Bullshit," he said, quietly, concentrating. "This is going to be all the corroboration we need."

Webster grabbed his arm.

"You can't do this," he said. "You could be killing an innocent man."

"Bullshit," Reacher said again. "If he's an innocent man, I won't be killing him, will I?"

He shook Webster's hand off his arm. Turned to face him.

"Think about it, Webster," he said. "Relax. Be logical. The proof comes after I shoot, right? If he's hauling a bomb, we'll know all about it. If he's hauling fresh air, nothing bad will happen to him. He'll just get another hole in his damn truck. Number one hundred and fourteen."

He turned back to the door. Raised the rifle again. Acquired the target. Out of sheer habit, he waited for his breath to be out and his heart to be between beats. Then he pulled the trigger. It took a thousandth of a second for the sound of the shot to hit his ear, and seventy times as long as that for the big heavy bullet to hit the truck. Nothing happened for a second. Then the truck ceased to exist. It was suddenly a blinding fireball rolling down the highway like a hot white tumbleweed. A gigantic concussion ring blasted outward. The helicopter was hit by a violent shock wave and tossed sideways and five hundred feet higher in the air. The pilot caught it at the top and slewed back. Steadied it in the air and swung around. Dropped the nose. There was nothing to see on the highway except a roiling cloud of thin smoke slowing into a teardrop shape three hundred yards long. No debris, no metal, no hurtling wheels, no clattering wreckage. Nothing at all except microscopic invisible particles of vapor accelerating into the atmosphere way faster than the speed of sound.

THE PILOT STUCK around at a hover for a long moment and then drifted east. Put his craft gently down on the scrub, a hundred yards from the shoulder. Shut the engines down. Reacher sat in the deafening silence and unclipped his belt. Laid the Barrett on the floor and vaulted out through the open door. Walked slowly toward the highway.

A ton of dynamite. A whole ton. A hell of a bang. There was nothing left at all. He guessed there were flattened grasses for a half-mile all around, but that was it. The terrible energy of the explosion had blasted outward and met absolutely nothing at all in its path. Nothing soft, nothing vulnerable. It had blasted outward and then weakened and slowed and died to a puff of breeze miles away and it had hurt nothing. Nothing at all. He stood in the silence and closed his eyes.

Then he heard footsteps behind him. It was Holly. He heard her good leg alternating with her bad leg. A long stride, then a shuffle. He opened his eyes and looked at the road. She walked around in front of him and stopped. Laid her head on his chest and put her arms around him. Squeezed him tight and held on. He raised his hand to her head and smoothed her hair behind her ear, like he had seen her do.

"All done," she said.

"Get a problem, solve a problem," he said. "That's my rule."

She was quiet for a long time.

"I wish it was always that easy," she said.

The way she said it, after the delay, it was like a long speech. Like a closely reasoned argument. He pretended not to know which problem she was talking about.

"Your father?" he said. "You're way, way out of his shadow now."

She shook her head against his chest.

"I don't know," she said.

"Believe it," he said. "That thing you did for me on the parade ground was the smartest, coolest, bravest thing I ever saw anybody do, man or woman, young or old. Better than anything I ever did. Better than anything your old man ever did. He'd give his front teeth for guts like that. So would I. You're way out of anybody's shadow now, Holly. Believe it."

"I thought I was," she said. "I felt like it. I really did. For a while. But then when I saw him again, I felt just the same as I always did. I called him Dad."

"He is your dad," Reacher said.

"I know," she replied. "That's the problem."

He was quiet for a long moment.

"So change your name," he said. "That might do it."

He could feel her holding her breath.

"Is that a proposal?" she asked.

"It's a suggestion," he said.

"You think Holly Reacher sounds good?" she asked.

His turn to stay quiet for a long time. His turn to catch his breath. And finally, his turn to talk about the real problem.

"It sounds wonderful," he said. "But I guess Holly McGrath sounds better."

She made no reply.

"He's the lucky guy, right?" he said.

She nodded. A small motion of her head against his chest.

"So tell him," he said.

She shrugged in his arms.

"I can't," she said. "I'm nervous."

"Don't be," he said. "He might have something similar to tell you."

She looked up. He squinted down at her.

"You think so?" she asked.

"You're nervous, he's nervous," Reacher said. "Somebody should say something. I'm not about to do it for either of you."

She squeezed him harder. Then she stretched up and kissed him. Hard and long on the mouth.

"Thank you," she said.

"For what?" he asked.

"For understanding," she said.

He shrugged. It wasn't the end of the world. Just felt like it.

"Coming?" she asked.

He shook his head.

"No," he said.

She left him on the shoulder of U.S. 93, right there in Idaho. He watched her all the way back to the Night Hawk. Watched her climb the short ladder. She paused and turned. Looked back at him. Then she ducked up and in. The door closed. The rotor thumped. He knew he would never see her again. His clothes tore at him and the dust swirled all around him as the helicopter took off. He waved it away. Watched it until it was lost to sight. Then he took a deep breath and looked left and right along the empty highway. Friday, the Fourth of July. Independence Day.

SATURDAY THE FIFTH and Sunday the sixth, Yorke County was sealed off and secret Army units were moving in and out around the clock. Air Artillery squads recovered the missile unit. They took it south in four Chinooks. Quartermasters went in and recovered all the ordnance they could find. They collected enough for a small war.

Medical corpsmen removed the bodies. They found the twenty men from the missile unit in the cave. They found the skeletons Reacher had crawled through. They found five mutilated bodies in another cave. Dressed like workmen. Like builders or carpenters. They took Fowler out of the command hut and Borken from the road in front of the courthouse. They brought Milosevic down from the mountain bowl and Brogan out of the small clearing west of the Bastion. They found Jackson's rough grave in the forest and dug him up. They laid eighteen dead militiamen and one dead woman side by side on the rifle range and helicoptered them away.

One of Garber's military investigators flew in alone and took the hard disk out of the financial computer and put it on a chopper for transport to Chicago. Engineers moved in and dynamited the mine entrances. Sappers moved into the Bastion and disabled the water supply and tore down the power lines. They set fire to the huts and watched as they burned. Late Sunday night, when the last of the smoke was rising, they marched back to their choppers and lifted away south.

Early Monday morning, Harland Webster was back in the off-white parlor inside the White House. Ruth Rosen was smiling at him and asking how his holiday weekend had been. He was smiling back at her and saying nothing. An hour later, the morning sun was rolling west to Chicago and three agents were arresting Brogan's girlfriend. They grilled her for thirty minutes and advised her to get out of town, leaving behind anything he had ever bought her. Then the same agents took Milosevic's brand-new Ford Explorer out of the Federal Building's parking lot and drove it five miles south. They left it on a quiet street, doors unlocked, keys in. By the time it had been stolen, Holly Johnson was arriving at the knee clinic for an early appointment. An hour after that, she was back at her desk. Before lunch, the missing money from the bearer bond robbery was following a route of her own choosing out of the Caymans. Six o'clock Monday evening she was home and packing. She threw her bags into her car and drove north. Moved into McGrath's house up in Evanston.

Tuesday morning, there were three separate stories on the National Militia Internet. Refugees from an isolated valley in Montana had drifted south and west to new settlements with reports of a recent world government maneuver. Foreign troops had wiped out a band of militia heroes. The foreign battalion had been led by a French mercenary. He had succeeded only because he had used classified SDI technology, including satellites and lasers and microchips. Journalists picked up on the story and called the Hoover Building. Late Tuesday evening, in a prepared statement, an FBI spokesperson denied all knowledge of any such events.

Early Wednesday morning, after five hitched rides and four buses through seven states, Reacher was finally in Wisconsin. It was where he had aimed to be exactly a week before. He liked it there. It struck him as a fine place to be in July. He stayed until Friday afternoon.